LETTERS

FROM HOME

Kristina McMorris is an award-winning author and graduate of Pepperdine University in America. A host of weekly television shows since age nine, she began her foray into fiction writing after discovering a collection of her grandparents' WWII love letters, which inspired this first novel, LETTERS FROM HOME.

For further information about Kristina visit www.Kristina McMorris.com or watch a brief video at www.tinyurl.com/McMorris

LETTERS FROM HOME

KRISTINA McMORRIS

AVON

AVON
A division of HarperCollins*Publishers*
77–85 Fulham Palace Road,
London W6 8JB

www.harpercollins.co.uk

This paperback edition 2011
1

First published in the U.S.A by Kensington Publishing Corp
New York, NY, 2011

A catalogue record for this book is
available from the British Library

ISBN-13: 978-1-84756-241-8

Set in Simoncini Garamond

Printed and bound in Great Britain by
Clays Ltd, St Ives plc

Mixed Sources
Product group from well-managed
forests and other controlled sources
www.fsc.org Cert no. SW-COC-001806
© 1996 Forest Stewardship Council
FSC

RESPECTFULLY DEDICATED

to the veterans of World War II,
a generation of heroes who, like my grandfather,
fought valiantly and courageously
to secure freedom for us all.

And to the unsung heroes
th nary a medal nor ribbon to show for their sacrifices—
!was the women who waited for their loved ones to return
who truly gave purpose to their soldiers' victory.

ACKNOWLEDGMENTS

Some books sprout and flourish solely from the genius and fortitude of the author. In my case, it took an extremely large village to raise a novel. To these dedicated natives, I owe my immense gratitude:

First and foremost, to my beloved Grandma Jean and Merle "Papa" McPherren, without whom this story would not exist—nor this storyteller, for that matter. Your courtship letters are imprinted forever in my heart. I hope I did you proud.

To my mother, Linda Yoshida, for her faith and editorial input as I slaved over every syllable on these pages, but mostly for not calling me crazy the day I, the non-reader / non-writer, phoned to say, "Hey, I think I'll write a book." And to my father, Junki, for teaching me by example that with determination anything is possible in this great country.

For igniting the spark of my journey, I thank Scott Taylor, who once so aptly stated: "It all starts with Kinko's." Truer words were never spoken. I am especially grateful to those readers who survived my early drafts and still managed to keep a straight face while providing feedback and encouragement, among them: my sister Amanda Yoshida, Sue McMorris, Mike Pettinger, Bryan Mueller, my ever-loyal "divas"—Stephanie Stricklen, Sunny Klever, Michele Blaine, and Lynne House—as well as Tracy Callan, who never fails to make me feel "brilliant." Every person should have a Tracy.

I am indebted to Julia Whitby for her keen editing eyes, and to Delilah Marvelle and Elisabeth Naughton for believing wholly in my story even when I wavered. To Steve Powers for his Midwestern limericks (I'm still frightened by just how many are crammed in his brain), and to all the experts who kindly assisted me with foreign languages, 1940s speak, and accents reaching from South Carolina to Australia, thereby making me sound more worldly than I am.

My sincere appreciation goes to Michelle Guthrie, whose incomparable support carried me through, as did that of Jennifer Sidis, who knew when I should type *The End*. To those who inspired me with their contagious passion for learning while making me earn my "stripes": Joel Malone, Scott "Carp" Carpenter, Pat Crouser, and Joe Palese. Also, of course, to the supremely talented Mike Rich, the effervescent Pixie Chicks, and Lt. Lynn "Buck" Compton, whose humility and devotion to serving others exemplifies what it truly means to be a hero.

While I relied upon a myriad of wonderful readers and historical sources, any errors that slipped through are mine alone. For generously sharing their knowledge, I thank: Dr. Gordon Canzler for his medical savvy, history/military buffs LTC Robert A. Lynn and Alan Cagle, author-historian Mark Bando, research buddy Pete Blaine, Chicago transportation–whiz Henry Morris, archivist extraordinaire Robynne Dexter of the U.S. Army Women's Museum, the U.S. Army Military History Institute, Northwestern University Archives, and World War II veteran/historian Ken Brody, who assured me that I "got it right." There is no greater compliment.

Thank you to my insightful and trusting editor, John Scognamiglio, and the rest of the Kensington team for turning my dream into reality; to my film-rights agent, Jon Cassir, at CAA, for raising that dream to a galactic level; and to Jennifer Schober—my literary agent, dear friend, and partner in crime—for whom there are no words strong enough to express my gratitude. Up next: world domination.

And finally, a most heartfelt thanks to my three favorite boys— my husband, Danny, and sons Tristan and Kiernan—for your overflowing love and patience, and for not complaining about six consecutive months of mac-and-cheese dinners while Mommy typed. You, alone, make life worth living. I love you to Jupiter, over a million cars, around a zillion trees—and back.

*Each separate page was like a fluttering flower-petal,
loosed from your own soul, and wafted thus to mine.*

—Edmond Rostand, *Cyrano de Bergerac,* act iv, scene viii

$$\approx 1 \approx$$

July 4, 1944
Chicago, Illinois

Silence in the idling Cadillac grew as suffocating as the city's humidity. Hands clenched on her lap, Liz Stephens averted her narrowed eyes toward the open passenger window. Chattering ladies and servicemen flocked by in the shadows; up and down they traveled over the concrete accordion of entrance steps. The sting of laughter and music drifted through the swinging glass doors, bounced off the colorless sky. Another holiday without gunpowder for celebration. No boom of metallic streamers, no sunbursts awakening the night. Only the fading memory of a simpler time.

A time when Liz knew whom she could trust.

"You know the Rotary doesn't invite just anyone to speak," Dalton Harris said finally. The same argument, same lack of apology in his voice. "What was I supposed to do? Tell my father I couldn't be there because of some *dance?*"

At his condescension, her gaze snapped to his slate gray eyes. "That," she said, "is exactly what you should've done."

"Honey. You're being unreasonable."

"So it's unreasonable, wanting us to spend time together?"

"That's not what I meant." A scratch to the back of his neck punctuated his frustration, a habit that had lost the amusing charm it held when they were kids. Long before the expensive suits, the perfect ties, the tonic-slickening of his dark brown hair.

"Listen." His square jaw slackened as he angled toward her, a debater shifting his approach. "When I was asked to run my dad's campaign, we talked about this. I warned you my schedule would be crazy until the election. And you were the one who said I should do it, that between classes and work, you'd be—"

"As busy as ever," she finished sharply. "Yes. I know what I said." With Dalton in law school and her a sophomore at North-western, leading independent but complementary lives was nothing new; in fact, that had always been among the strengths of their relationship. Which was why he should know their separate activities weren't the issue tonight.

"Then what's the problem?"

"The problem is, anything else pops up, campaign or otherwise, and you don't think twice about canceling on me."

"I am *not* canceling. I'm asking you to come with me."

Liz had attended enough political fund-raisers with him to know that whispers behind plastered smiles and greedy glad-handing would be highlights of the night. A night she could do without, even if not for her prior commitment.

"I already told you," she said, "I promised the girls weeks ago I'd be here." The main reason she'd agreed, given her condensed workload from summer school, was to repay Betty for accompanying her to that droning version of *Henry V* last week—just so Dalton's ticket hadn't gone to waste. "Why can't you make an exception? Just this once?"

He dropped back in his seat, drew out a sigh. "Lizzy, it's just a dance."

No, it's not. It's more than that. I have to know I can depend on you! Her throat fastened around her retort. Explosions of words, she knew all too well, could bring irreversible consequences.

She grabbed the door handle. "I have to go." Before he could exit and circle around to open her side, she let herself out.

"Wait," he called as she shut the door. "Sweetheart, hold on."

The sudden plea in his voice tugged at her like strings, halting her. Could it be that he had changed his mind? That he was still the same guy she could count on?

She slid her hand into the pocket of her ivory wraparound dress, a shred of hope cupped in her palm, before pivoting to face him.

Dalton leaned across the seat toward her. "We'll talk about this later, all right?"

Disappointment throbbed inside, a recurrent bruise. Bridling her reaction, she replied with a nod, fully aware her agreement would translate into a truce.

"Have a good time," he said, then gripped the steering wheel and drove away.

As she turned for the stairs, she pulled her hand from her pocket, and discovered she'd been holding but a stray thread. The first sign of a seam unraveling.

In the entry of the dance hall, Liz stretched up on the balls of her feet to see over hats and heads. Her gaze penetrated the light haze of smoke to reach the stage. There, uniformed musicians played from behind star-patterned barricades of red, white, and blue. Flags and an oversized United Service Organization banner created a vibrant backdrop, Americana at its finest. In front of the band, her roommate Betty Cordell and two other women shared a standing microphone, harmonizing the final notes of "Don't Sit Under the Apple Tree."

The audience broke into applause.

"Swell," Liz groaned. She'd missed Betty's entire debut.

Correcting her presumption, the trio jumped into another jingle.

"Thank God." Though not a particularly religious person, Liz figured it never hurt to offer a small token of appreciation to the Almighty.

Now to find her other roommate, Julia Renard. Despite the teeming room, it took only a moment to spy the girl's fiery, collar-length curls, her ever-chic attire.

Liz wove through the sea of military uniforms and thick wafts of Aqua Velva. Ignoring a duet of catcalls, she slid into the empty chair next to her friend. "I'm so sorry I'm late."

"Let me guess," Julia ventured in her honey-sweet voice. "Mr. Donovan lost his dentures, or Thelma refused to take her pills, convinced you're trying to poison her."

Liz edged out a smile.

"You know, it wouldn't kill you to get off work at a decent hour. You're making the rest of us look bad." She used her thumb to wipe something off Liz's cheek. "So, is Dalton parking the car?"

Liz tried for a casual shrug. "A political thing came up at the last minute." *Again* trailed her statement as the unspoken word.

"Oh," Julia replied. Not even her glowing smile could hide the sympathy invading her copper eyes.

"It's fine," Liz insisted. "I can't stay long anyway. I've got an essay on Hawthorne due Friday."

Julia nodded, then detoured from the awkward pause. "Hey, I think I still have notes on Hawthorne from last semester. Want to borrow them?"

"Sure, thanks," Liz said, before considering the source. "Unless you've got doodle designs covering the actual notes."

Julia scrunched her mouth, pondering. "Well, there might be a few. . . ."

Liz couldn't help but giggle. If past lives existed, Julia had to have been an elite fashion designer with a permanently attached sketchpad. A keen knack for sewing served as further proof, as showcased by their roommate's new dress.

"Speaking of which." Liz motioned toward Betty. "You've really outdone yourself, Jules." In the center of the crooning trio, the blonde sparkled in the form-fitted garment matching her ocean blue eyes. The fabric and buttons were so dazzling, Julia had obviously purchased the materials herself. No doubt the dress was already Betty's favorite. From the exquisite sweetheart neckline to the elegant flow around her hips, every stitch perfectly flattered her hourglass curves. "Rita Hayworth?" Liz guessed at the inspiration.

"Yep," Julia said proudly. "From the gown in *Blood and Sand*. Except I shortened it to the knee, and improved on the sleeves."

"You're amazing." *Too amazing to waste your talent solely as a homemaker,* she wanted to say. But there was no need traversing that well-covered territory.

"It was nothing." Julia blushed, waved her off. "You want something to drink?"

Liz only intended to stay for three songs, four tops. But some coffee to ripen her brain for a long night of reading wasn't a bad idea. "A cup of joe would be great."

"Coming right up."

As Julia headed toward the snack table by the stage, Liz settled in her seat. She massaged the tension out of her palms and returned her attention to Betty. In a seasoned motion, the girl tossed her finger-waved mane off her shoulders. The bounce of her hips succeeded as a diversion from her moderate singing ability, evidenced by the front line of awestruck troops, her ideal audience.

Leave it to Betty. Up there, living carefree, without regrets. No academic pressures, no parents' expectations looming overhead—

Jealous souls will not be answered. The passage interrupted Liz's thoughts, one of many Shakespearean quotes she had memorized from her father's personal tutorials.

"One quote for every sun kiss," he would say during the lessons that ended far too soon.

Now, glancing down at the constellation of freckles on her arms, Liz recalled those long-gone days. She considered the morals her father had passed along, and wondered how different their lives would be if only she'd abided by them.

"What the hell are you up to now?" Morgan McClain demanded as his brother ducked behind his back.

"Don't move. Need you to cover me." Charlie raised his shoulders to his sandy blond crew cut.

When Morgan glimpsed the silver flask in his brother's hand, he shook his head. Charlie wasn't the only enlisted man at the dance calling for "liquid reinforcement," just the only one daring enough to dip into his supply ten feet from the volunteers' snack station. Luckily, the herd of GIs standing around them at the foot of the stage offered plenty of khaki camouflage. Or at least Morgan clung to that hope as his brother choked on the drink. Whiskey, from the smell of it.

"Hurry up, will ya?" Morgan told him. Typically, he would have voiced his disproval, but with Charlie's tension over tomorrow's departure vibrating the air, he decided to let it go. So long as the kid didn't get carried away.

"Ahh, much better," Charlie rasped, emerging from the protective shadow. He stepped up behind a couple of GIs from another outfit, both of them wolf whistling at the platinum blond singer on stage. "Sorry, fellas"—Charlie clapped them on the back—"but she's already agreed to mother my fourteen children."

"Don't fool yourself, shorty," the tall guy spat out. "You wouldn't know how to use it even if you could find it."

Charlie straightened, adding a few inches to his compact stature. "Hey, at least I *have* one, spaghetti bender."

"What'd you say?" The Italian GI angled his head over his wide shoulder.

"You heard me." Charlie took a step back. He rocked from side to side, dukes raised like Jack Dempsey.

As usual, Morgan would have to shut him up before a bigger guy's right hook beat him to it. "Zip it, Charlie," he ordered, then regarded the Italian. "Don't pay him any mind. It's his first day out of the loony bin." Not a stretch to believe, considering the mismatched challenge.

The GI's mouth twitched, from either amusement or agitation. To be safe, Morgan gestured to the stage and said, "Don't look now, but I think that red-hot tomato's got her eye on you, pal." The sentence launched the soldier's attention back to the bombshell, where it stuck like glue.

Problem handled.

Except for the instigator.

"So help me, Charlie," Morgan muttered, "if you weren't . . . my . . . if . . ." The lecture dissolved at a vision beyond his brother's shoulder. Across the room a petite beauty sat alone, swaying to the music. Strands of chestnut brown hair slipped from the knot at the nape of her neck, a frame for her heart-shaped face. Creamy skin, feminine curves, full, rounded lips. Each feature was no less than eye catching, but it was the way she moved—like wheat in a summer breeze—that mesmerized him.

"Hey, you okay?"

Morgan heard the question but didn't realize it was directed at him until a fluttering object broke the trance: a wave of Charlie's fingers.

"Huh? Uh, yeah. Yeah, I'm fine."

Charlie swept a glance over the room, tracing the distraction. Soon a gleam appeared in his hazel eyes. "Aha, I see . . ." He twisted around and declared, "Gentlemen, we've located our primary target. We're goin' in."

Before Morgan could object, his brother began pressing him through the crowd like a restive racehorse into the starting gate. GIs whooped, whistled, and hollered "attaboys" in his direction. If he retreated now, the razzing would only worsen.

He pulled a deep breath. Adjusting his tucked necktie, he imagined introducing himself; he got as far as his name when a red-haired woman joined the brunette's table. A growing audience. His shoes turned to cinder blocks. He raised an arm to stop his brother, who swooped under and pounced into place, blocking the women's view of the stage.

"Pardon me, ladies," Charlie said. "We're in dire need of your assistance."

"Why? You lost, soldier?" the redhead teased.

"Not anymore." He grinned, sporting his dimples. "Now that I've found my way to your heart."

When the gals exchanged incredulous looks, Morgan considered sneaking away, preserving his dignity while the possibility remained. But the mere sight of the brunette's profile locked his knees. Unbelievably, she was even prettier up close.

"Wait a minute," Charlie went on. "I think we've met you girls before. You're Gor and Geous, ain't ya?" Their lack of response didn't faze him. "All right, what are your lovely names, then?"

Nothing. Just blank stares.

"Afraid I'm not going anywhere till I know." Charlie crossed his arms and waited, a rare showing of following through.

The brunette released a sharp sigh. "Fine. I'm Liz, this is Julia, and *you're* leaving."

Morgan pressed down a grin.

"Leaving?" Charlie repeated. "How could I, after finding the two prettiest gals in the city?"

Julia shook her head. "Has any of this actually worked on a girl before?"

"She means a *human* girl," Liz added.

"Ouch!" Charlie stumbled backward as though her insult had struck more than his ego. "You sure know how to hurt a guy." For the pathetic come-on alone, Morgan could think of a worse punishment.

"Goodness me," Liz exclaimed, hand on her chest. "Where are my manners?"

"Not to worry, apology accepted." Charlie's assurance drove straight through her sarcasm, arching her brow. "Besides. I owe *you* an apology as well, for not introducing myself properly."

The situation was deteriorating. But it wasn't too late. If Morgan moved now, blended into the crowd, he just might escape the quicksand of humiliation. His brother could find his way back on his own.

"My name's Charlie," he said as Morgan edged away, "but good friends and peachy gals like you call me Chap. And this dashing gentleman over here is my brother, Staff Sergeant Morgan McClain."

Staff sergeant? Morgan bristled at the lie, and found himself trapped by their gazes. He held his breath, arms at his sides, as if preparing for Saturday inspection.

Liz stretched her neck over her shoulder, curiosity forcing a peek. With Morgan's charcoal black hair and olive complexion, she questioned if he and the fair-skinned knucklehead were actually brothers.

"Evening," Morgan said, the word barely audible. A fitted service shirt outlined his broad build. His facial features were of the average sort, but he had an allure about him, an unnamable quality Liz couldn't dismiss.

"Hi," she replied as Charlie continued.

"Honestly, ladies, here's our situation." His serious tone implied a change in strategy. "You see, me and Morgan, we're leaving for war soon. As two of the U.S. Army's finest, we'll be fighting on the front lines. So without much time left to live, I've got just one thing I'm wishin' for." He knelt, presenting Julia his palm. "To dance with this red-haired knockout before I go."

"Sorry, Casanova, but I'm already spoken for." She held up her left hand to display her engagement ring. Daily polishing, since her fiancé's fleet shipped out a month ago, kept the gold shiny as new.

"Well, then . . ." The gears clearly cranked away in Charlie's mind. "How 'bout a dance to celebrate your engagement?"

Liz replied for her. "How 'bout we celebrate when your squad tosses you overboard?" She heard Morgan quietly laugh, a second before his brother directed his plea to Liz.

"C'mon," he said. "Is this how you thank a man who'll be risking his life for *your* freedom?"

She felt a smile threatening to surface. "If you got these lines out of a book from the drugstore, you should really get your nickel back."

"Hey, I'm just trying to save your friend Julie, here, from years of guilt. Imagine the headlines: 'Soldier denied a final dance . . . dies for his country . . .'"

Julia giggled, hand covering her mouth. "Okay, okay." She rolled her eyes. "One song." Together they headed toward the dance floor, where skirts flared and couples dipped to the band's emboldening tune.

After a moment, Morgan stepped closer and pointed to Julia's chair. "May I?"

"Why not," Liz said, a verbal shrug. Her night was tumbling downhill at avalanche speed. Rather than curling up at home, losing herself in classical literary works, she was stuck in a dance hall packed with slick soldiers on the prowl.

Morgan sat beside her, their shoulders only inches apart. If this guy was hunting for a khaki-whacky girl, he was barking up the wrong table. She leaned away, just as Charlie began spinning Julia round and round like a top. Liz grew hopeful that her friend would rush back, ready to head out. But then both dancers broke into a fit of laughter, confirming Liz was on her own.

"So—" Morgan cleared his throat. "You're Liz?"

"You're not going to use your brother's goofy lines, are you?"

"No, miss. I was—just asking about your name."

The sincerity in his voice underscored her own brusqueness. He hadn't done anything to deserve such treatment. At least not yet. "I'm sorry," she said, softening. "Yes, it's Liz." As she extended her hand, his mouth curved into a smile.

"It's real nice to meet you," he said.

Something about his touch caused her pulse to sprint. She released her grasp and sipped her coffee, despite it being a few degrees too hot. "So tell me, why do they call your brother Chap?"

"It's short for Charlie Chaplin. Got the name 'cause he loves making people laugh."

As if on cue, Charlie hopped around Julia like an island native performing a tribal mating ritual. His partner appeared as entertained as spectators on the sideline.

Liz tightened her lips, but a giggle snuck through. "And you really claim that guy as your brother?"

Morgan hesitated before nodding slowly. "Yep. But only by blood." A caring glimmer shone in his eyes, emerald gems speckled with gold. A miner's prized find.

Her leg started to quiver. Surely a side effect of the coffee and a tiring day of work. She tamed her knee. "I assume you've got a nickname too?"

"Just Mac, short for McClain. Nothing fancy."

"Well," she said, "at least it's nothing to blush over. My roommate's told me about plenty I wouldn't dare repeat."

"I can imagine." He grinned. "Suppose I should be grateful Farm Boy didn't stick."

The mention of a life so different from her own intrigued her. "Then you're a farmer?"

He half shrugged, a movement suggesting embarrassment. "My uncle owns a good chunk of land in southern Illinois. I've been managing it the past few years."

"What kind of farm is it?"

"You mean the crops?"

She nodded.

"Feed corn mostly. And we alternate with soybeans. Rotated the lower half last season and—" He bit off the ending, rubbed the faint cleft in his chin. "Probably more than you wanted to know."

"Not at all. Really. I'm interested." More than she should have been.

"Guess you can tell, us plow jockeys don't get out a whole lot."

"Except for USO dances and taking out your girlfriends, right?" It was a forward question, but if only he'd confess he had a sweetheart, Liz could stop her nerves from jittering.

"Charlie does do more wooing than working," he admitted. "But me, afraid I don't do much else but tend the fields."

She caught herself in a smile, a betrayal in its fervor.

"And what do *you* do," he asked, "when you're not at USO dances?"

Propriety prompted her to enlighten him about her courtship with Dalton and their path to matrimony, an eventual yet inevitable step in her practical plan—a checklist to a respectable future. Instead, she replied, "Guess I spend most of my time studying. That and taking care of elderly folks, a job I love for some reason." She wrinkled her nose. "Sounds odd, I know."

The polite, humoring head shake she expected didn't come. Rather, he seemed to examine the words, taking them in. "Not a thing wrong with helping out people who need it." He peered at her with those polished green gems, their deep shade nearly hypnotic. "So what are you studying, Liz?"

"Well—I'm . . ." She had to sift her mind for the answer. When had this become a hard question? "English," she remembered. "I want to be a literature professor."

"Wow, that's wonderful." He sounded genuinely impressed. A nice contrast to those who viewed her desire to work as an assault on the family structure. "What made you decide on that?"

"It's what my father does."

Morgan nodded, then asked, "But, what made *you* want to be a teacher?"

She stumbled over the inquiry—direct, thoughtful, unexpected. Her father's legacy had always sufficed as a natural explanation; no one had ever bothered to probe further.

"Sorry." He shifted in his chair. "Didn't mean to put you on the spot."

At a loss for an answer, she merely gave a nod, then opted for deflection. Or perhaps she yearned to know more about him. "And what about you? Any plans after the service?"

"Oh, we'll likely buy up some acreage. Charlie's pushing for cattle ranching, but we'll see."

"Ahh," she said, head tilted. "But what is it that *you* want?"

He grinned broadly, a nonverbal *touché,* and replied, "To put down roots, I suppose. Raise a family. Can't imagine anything more important."

The warmth in his words reached for her heart like invisible hands. Fortunately, she spied the single-striped chevron at the top of his sleeve—private first class—grounds for challenging his integrity. "By the way," she said, "when did you get promoted to staff sergeant?"

He half glanced at his shoulder and his expression dropped. "Um, well, you see. I'm not exactly . . . a staff sergeant. Yet."

With Betty as a roommate, Liz had learned a great deal about military insignias. The fact that his rank was three grades lower than the one boasted by his brother didn't mean a thing to Liz. What did matter was his evident penchant for honesty. Which only made him more likable.

"My brother," he apologized, "he's a bit of an Irish storyteller."

"Mmm." She feigned contemplation. "You *are* in the service, though, right?"

A slight smile returned. "After all our training, I sure as heck hope so."

"It's a good thing you went Army, then. I hear basic's a lot harder in the Navy and Marines."

At that, his mouth retracted, leaving him speechless. Liz tried to keep a straight face but failed.

Tentative, he shook his head before easing out a laugh. "Are you always this nice to fellas you just met?"

"Just the special ones." The admission rolled out before she could stop it. Oddly, however, she felt no need to backpedal; they seemed anything but strangers.

"In that case," he said, "I'll take it as a compliment."

Behind Morgan, an attractive woman in a WAVES uniform rose at the neighboring table. She linked arms with an airman, who bid farewell to his buddies, and the couple set off through the crowd.

It suddenly occurred to Liz that she had landed herself in the worst kind of room, one full of impending good-byes. Distant memories seeped about her. As she refocused on Morgan, words never far from the clutches of her mind spilled out. "So when are you leaving?"

He paused. The question ironed the crinkles from the corners of his eyes. "We're heading for our post tomorrow."

It was a reply she should have anticipated. Still, her heart sank.

"Wanna know the truth?" He leaned toward her as if passing along a secret, his forearm on the table approaching hers. "I'm still hoping they'll have second thoughts about trusting my brother with a loaded weapon."

She nodded as he sat back, and found herself equally disappointed and grateful he'd increased the space between them. "Well, that may not be an issue. Rumor has it, the war could be over any day now."

"Yeah, well. Whatever you do, don't tell Charlie. If he doesn't see at least one battle, he'll never speak to me again."

"Oh? Why's that?"

"I made him wait till he turned eighteen." Morgan traced the edge of the table with his thumb. "Even took a deferment to give him time to grow up."

"And you think that worked?" she mused.

"Based on what we've seen tonight, I'd say definitely not." With a wink, he turned to watch the dancers. Aside from the premature gray sprinkled above his ears, he appeared just a few years older than Liz. Only from careful observation of his eyes did she sense a forced maturity, a cheated youth. An accumulation of endured hardships intended for a man far surpassing Morgan's age.

"I swear," he said, "that kid has added ten years to me." He gave the side of his head a gentle scratch as if he'd read her thoughts.

"Sounds like he's kept your life exciting, at least."

"That he has." When Morgan faced her, their gazes did more than meet; they locked in place, forming an open passageway. Her natural reflexes should have intervened, broken the connection, but those reflexes were no match for the invitation in his eyes. Without reason or reservation, she felt her soul accepting.

"I'm done," Julia said breathlessly, materializing out of nowhere. Her presence tugged Liz back to reality, reminded her of the performance that had brought her here. She glanced at the stage. A tuxedoed soloist had replaced the trio. Betty must have been primping for fans in her dressing room.

"What happened to your partner?" Liz asked, not seeing Charlie.

"Oh, don't worry about him." Julia flicked her hand behind her. "He's already found a new victim. Thank goodness."

Morgan stood and offered the chair to Julia.

"That's okay, I'm not staying," she said, grabbing her beaded purse.

Liz's shoulders tensed. "You're ready to leave?"

"Suzie and Dot are here. We're going to Tasty's to grab a bite. Want to come?"

Morgan retook his seat, appearing watchful of Liz's response.

"You go on ahead," she replied. "I'll be home after the show." Even in her own ears, the words seemed to have come from someone other than herself.

Julia rumpled her brow, then extended a curious smile. "You two have a good night." Once out of Morgan's eyeshot, she gave Liz a look that said she expected a full explanation in the morning.

Liz urged her legs to follow—after all, what was she doing?— but then a series of notes overpowered the thought. A slow version of "Stormy Weather." A melody of her past, towed through every dramatic measure.

"This tune"—Morgan gestured toward the band—"reminds me of my mom. Sang it around the house all the time."

"Really?" Liz remarked at the coincidence. She tried to think of how many times she'd heard the original playing behind her mother's locked bedroom door. Must have been a thousand. Liz had every reason to hate the song, yet somehow it persisted as one of her favorites. "Mine liked it too," was all she added.

Eyes toward the singer, Morgan shook his head. A tender smile played on his lips. "Funny. She always made it sound so upbeat, I never noticed how sad the words are till now."

Liz listened to the lyrics, about gloom and misery, and realized she hadn't either. She verged on volunteering as much, but the glow in his expression stole her focus. Before she knew it, her gaze sloped down his arms, leaving her to imagine how they would feel wrapped around her.

When the tune ended, she jerked her eyes away, hoping he couldn't actually read her mind. Then another ballad began, "At Last," based on the opening bars. A horn sang soft and sultry and filled the silence between them. A silence that suddenly gaped for miles as he fidgeted in his chair. Staring in the other direction, he tapped his heel at quickstep tempo, as though antsy to reach the exit. She wanted to say something, yet nothing came to her. Their wordlessness dragged every second into a torturous crawl. Unsure of what to do, she peeked at her watch to verify time hadn't stopped.

"So, Liz," he said finally, "would you mind if I, um, asked you to dance?"

She was so relieved he had spoken it took her a moment to weigh his invitation.

It was a slow number.

She should decline.

Then again, he was leaving tomorrow.

"Sure—I mean, no, I wouldn't mind."

They rose and walked to the edge of the dance floor. As she slipped her hand into his, unfamiliar nerves rippled up her sides. His other hand cupped the small of her back and drew her close. She fought the trickle of a chill on her neck, willed moisture into her mouth gone dry.

This was a mistake, she warned herself. Still, she rested a palm on his broad shoulder, the starched fabric separating her from the skin beneath. At the shift of his muscles, the feel of his gaze, her heart pounded twice as fast as the beat. She didn't take in a single lyric, yet everything about the song was perfect. It seemed the spiraling combination of notes was commanding her emotions to lead; her body to follow.

She turned her head and closed her eyes. Vanilla, lemon, and cedar—the scent of his talc or aftershave was soft but masculine. The slight rasp of his chin brushed against her temple; a rush of warm breath passed by her cheek. She tightened her grip on his shoulder as subtly as she could. Cracking her eyelids, she noted goose bumps prickling her arms. She desperately hoped he didn't notice the effect he had on her. Unless he felt the same.

What was she thinking? They'd only just met. Sensible. She needed to be sensible.

Then his hand adjusted on her back. His fingers moved up slightly, pulling her closer. Never before had she been so aware of being touched. The air enveloping them thickened, a dense cloud, smothering sensibility.

She relaxed her neck, her shoulders, her rules. Unable, unwilling to stop herself, she angled toward his gaze. Her mind reached for his lips, and—

"Watch it!" a stranger's voice shrilled.

Liz startled back to the room, and to the sailor falling straight into them. Morgan tried to slant her out of the way, but wasn't fast enough to dodge the man's red drink. It splattered an S down the side of her dress.

"Hey, I'm soor-ry," the stocky guy slurred. He floundered off, rubbing his hairless head.

"You okay?" Morgan touched her bare arm.

Chills again. She pulled the damp portion of her dress from her legs. "I just need to clean up in the powder room."

"Take your time," he told her, and smiled.

She turned to hurry away, not from anxiousness to leave, but rather to return.

With the fog Morgan found himself in, he almost wondered if fumes from his brother's whiskey were to blame. Liz had disappeared into the crowd, yet here he was, grinning like a possum. He couldn't stop. He'd never met anyone so captivating. From her amber eyes that glowed and dimmed with her mood to the fragrance of a lavender field on her soft skin. More attractive still was the blend of her gentleness and outward strength.

But there was something else. A feeling of understanding, a comfort that defied reason. It was as though kissing her, a near stranger, would have made all the sense in the world.

He'd certainly had the impulse. Maybe he should have acted on it. Most guys at the dance would have done so without a second thought. At this very moment, his brother was likely coercing a smooch out of some girl in the room, a last favor before heading off to war.

The war.

How could he have forgotten?

Tomorrow they'd be at Union Station, one step closer to deploying to some country thousands of miles from home—and a world away from Liz.

Would a girl like that be willing to wait for a soldier she'd only known a single night? Or was he screwy to even consider the idea?

He drained a sigh heavy with doubt.

"Don't tell me you lost that dame already." Charlie's voice turned Morgan around.

"She's in the ladies' room." Promptly diverting, he said, "So what happened with the redhead? Not as irresistible as you thought you were, huh?"

"She was engaged. Doesn't count. Besides, Jack says there's a juice joint nearby, lots of gals there dying to show their patriotism."

"Hope they don't charge much."

"Hey, I didn't crack open my piggy bank for nothin'." Charlie beamed. "I'm guessing you're not going anywhere?"

"Think I'll stick around awhile." The answer formed so effortlessly Morgan almost missed the pricking of his conscience. When the town sheriff caught little Charlie drilling peepholes at Mrs. Herman's Lingerie Boutique, their father had made it abundantly clear Morgan was responsible for keeping tabs on his brother. A passage of years hadn't relinquished the duty; if anything, need for the role had risen.

But tonight, with the promise of Liz's return, how could Morgan leave?

"Now, if the skirt comes to her senses," Charlie said, "and decides to hide in the john all night, be sure to come looking for us."

"Yeah, all right. Stay out of trouble, though, you hear?"

"Absolutely." Charlie grinned and snaked off toward his buddies by the door.

"I mean it, Charlie!"

The kid raised his hand as if to affirm he was going to heed the order. Morgan knew better, of course. And he certainly knew better than to turn his brother loose with a flask of booze and their buddy Jack Callan on their last night in the city.

The thought ignited a flicker of regret, doused the instant Morgan's nose caught a residual whiff of Liz's perfume. Proof of her existence on his shirt. A reminder that he really had no choice.

Preparing for her reappearance, he spiffed up his necktie, then swiped his hands over his hair, due for another buzz cut. In the midst of sliding his watch down over his wrist bone, he halted at the color of red: a cluster of punch spots, spiked punch at that, tainting the cuff of his sleeve. "Ah, damn."

Liz had only been gone a minute or two. He still had time before she finished cleaning up. Although finding a miraculous stain remover was a long shot, he had to try. The last thing he needed was a commander's reprimand, followed by hours of scrubbing latrines. And more important, looking like a slob wasn't how he hoped to come across to the woman he wanted to impress.

At the snack table, a matronly volunteer extended her sympathy and set off to retrieve a bottle of seltzer. While he waited, a couple nearby Lindy Hopping caught his eye. The Marine tossed the girl around his back, then flipped her like a hotcake. His feet swiveled and scooted and shuffled. He may not have been the smoothest swinger in the room, but the fellow could pass as Gene Kelly next to Morgan's own less-than-snappy footwork.

Inwardly, Morgan kicked himself. He should have taken notes instead of heckling his brother when their mother used to lead Charlie in the box step around the kitchen. Then he wouldn't have wasted two songs mustering the courage to ask Liz to dance. Too bad he wasn't as skilled with a dance partner as he was with a plow.

"Hey, toots! How about a twirl?" The husky voice boomed from a few yards behind. No surprise, it was the same chief petty officer who had separated him from Liz, only now he was falling all over someone deliberately: the curvy blond singer appearing from a door by the stage. She swatted at the guy's hands, but his groping continued until she gave him a shove. Turning to break away, she lost her footing and stumbled forward. Morgan's arms swung outward, barely catching her.

"Gimme a chance, doll face!" The Navy man staggered closer.

She gazed at Morgan with big blue eyes. "Save me," she pleaded in a whisper.

His first instinct called for a harsh warning toward her inebriated fan, and, if that didn't work, an invitation to step outside. However, based on stories he'd heard while at basic, Morgan knew better than to tangle with a superior of any branch. He'd have to get creative.

"Excuse me, Chief." He positioned his body to guard the singer. "But I promised my fiancée, here, a dance."

The man pulled his chin back over his neck. He scrunched his face like a bulldog being challenged. "Fiancée, huh?"

Morgan straightened, inched a step forward. "Yes, sir. High school sweethearts."

The Navy man scrutinized the couple with his bloodshot eyes. His pulse visibly throbbed on the side of his head, bald as a billiard ball. Suddenly, he flared a grin and stuck out a swaying hand. "Well, congrad-julations!"

Relieved, Morgan accepted the guy's ironclad grip while leaning away from the smell of sweat and bourbon seeping from his pores.

"Let's go, honey bear." The blonde latched onto Morgan's arm. "They're playing our song." She pulled him free and towed him to the dance floor. The horn section, rocking in unison, blasted lively notes toward the high ceiling.

With no sight of Liz yet, he took the singer's hands. He did his best to spare her toes through the basic steps of a jitterbug. Thankfully, the tune ended within a few bars and the petty officer, though still in view, had about-faced. Seizing the opportunity to exit, Morgan released the woman's hands.

"Can't leave me yet, Private." She drew him back for the crooner's ballad. "We didn't finish our wedding dance." Her arms wrapped around his neck, guiding him into a close sway.

He swallowed a gulp of air. Obviously, city girls were bolder than the small-town gals he'd grown up with.

"Miss, I'd love to keep dancin', but—"

She peered at him with a seductive glint. "Oh, come now. I have to thank you for your help somehow. And you did promise me a dance." A smile slid across her lips before she rested her chin on his shoulder. Just then, the petty officer shifted his stance to face them. Upon catching Morgan's eye, the guy tapped an arm of the sailor standing beside him. "Hey!" they yelled raggedly, and raised their cups in a distant toast.

Morgan lifted his chin in acknowledgment. For the singer's sake, he'd wait for the song to end before leaving the floor discreetly—unless, that is, he glimpsed Liz's chestnut hair, her heavenly face.

"I'm Betty, by the way," the blonde said.

"I'm Morgan . . . McClain," he said in pieces. His gaze hopped back and forth between the drunken bookends and the far corner of the dance floor, the exact spot where Liz had woven into the crowd and would presumably emerge.

"Well, thank you for rescuing me, Morgan." Betty's fingertips grazed the small scar on the side of his neck, a permanent reminder of the day he'd saved Charlie from a fatal dive down a grain chute. Man, he wished his brother were here to repay the favor by cutting in.

Charlie would think he was nuts, of course. Betty had to be the most sought-after girl in the place. Regardless, there was only one woman Morgan wanted to be with.

Alone in the ladies' room, Liz felt a new chapter in her life unfolding. She was a six-year-old waking to her first snowfall, a kid in a general store given free rein over the candy barrels.

Calming herself, she set aside the hand towel she'd used to blot her dress. Looking in the mirror, she tucked in her loose hair. The makeup she'd applied that morning had almost completely faded. She pinched her cheeks and licked her lips. She felt like a starlet standing by for a knock on her dressing room door.

Five minutes, Miss Stephens, before we shoot the kissing scene with the soldier.

Suddenly Liz could see the world as Julia did, through a soft cinema lens where boy met girl and all lived happily ever after. Where obstacles fell away like mist, temporary and translucent. Where you were held accountable only for actions wedged between the opening and closing credits.

She could have that, couldn't she? A clean slate, a happily ever after?

Don't be silly, the skeptic in her sneered. Such a reality only existed in the movies. Her parents had taught her that. And what was she going to do? Jeopardize her relationship with Dalton for a GI she barely knew, one who'd soon be on his way?

Thank heavens for the sailor's interference. She could have ruined far more than her favorite summer garb had he not reawakened her sanity.

Embarrassed by her behavior, and even more by her ridiculous thoughts, she jetted from the lavatory and off to the exit. The doors were in sight when a twinge of guilt slowed her steps.

The least she could do was wish the soldier well, freeing him to mingle with other girls—available girls—who'd be worth his efforts.

She grumbled at the call to decency, an ironic notion at this point, and trudged back to their table. Yet there, she found strangers in their seats. She rotated slowly, her gaze circling the room. Another turn, and still no sign of Morgan.

Perhaps he had sensed she wouldn't be coming back. Some buddies could have whisked him away, moved on to another dance hall, a late-night diner.

Perfect, she told herself. *An easy way out.*

She ordered relief to take hold, though the feeling refused—until she glimpsed his profile. He had waited for her, after all.

Or so she thought, before a curtain of strangers divided, and the full scene came into view. Across the dance floor indeed stood Morgan, but with a girl in his arms. And not just any girl. It was *Betty*—eyes closed, cheek nestled against his neck, the slope of her hair pillowing his chin. Both certainly looked at ease, a natural pair.

This was a good thing. The best, actually, for them all.

So why did Liz feel a cinching around her heart? Why was a streak of anger sweeping through her, a sensation bordering on betrayal? The reaction was absurd. Morgan owed her nothing, and even if Betty had seen them dancing, there was no reason for her to question Liz's intentions, what with her already having a beau. Not that anyone here would have guessed.

"Elizabeth Stephens, is that you?"

She swung toward the voice. A tall man approached wearing Coke-bottle glasses, his suit a size too small for his gangly stature.

"Is Dalt here?" His lenses magnified the enthusiasm in his eyes. His name escaped her, but he was unmistakably a schoolmate of Dalton's.

"Um . . . no. He couldn't make it." Shame rushed through her, flooding every limb.

"Well, tell him I said hi."

"Of course." She smiled feebly. Whirling around, she bumped her way through the faceless mass. She needed to flee before any further harm was done, before her logical foundation could crumble beneath her feet.

She dashed out the doors and down the steps, not slowing until she'd boarded the "L" train destined for the seclusion of her suburban home. Stooped in her seat, she rested her head against the window. Summer clouds reclaimed territory above, draping a cluster of stars. No twinkling, no trace of existence.

If only mistakes were as easily erased.

At long last, the USO band played the final notes of the song. Until then, Morgan didn't think anything could seem lengthier than the Sunday masses he attended as a kid. The audience thundered in applause and a slew of dancers dispersed, concealing his brisk parting from Betty. Concerned that Liz still hadn't returned, he immediately strode off on a search.

For close to an hour, he scoured the place. He described the brunette's features and what he recalled of her outfit to more than a dozen random people. He'd gone so far as to ask ladies exiting the washroom if she was still inside, in the event she wasn't feeling well.

But his hunt was futile. It was clear she'd left.

Had he said or done something wrong? Or was it something he'd failed to say or do? He reviewed as many details as he could, and still no explanation.

Maybe it wasn't him at all; maybe she was too upset over her dress to stay. Could have been an emergency that sent her rushing off. Whatever the reason, he hadn't given up all hope. He wasn't about to. There was too much to lose.

God, how could he find her again? He hadn't even asked for her last name.

He scorned his thoughtlessness before taking another approach. Like a detective from a radio drama, he mulled over the clues. She mentioned studying, but where? And caring for the elderly. A hospital? A rest home? What about the redhead—which joint did she say she was hitting with her friends? He should have asked for specifics. Then again, if Liz had decided to follow them, she would have said so.

Wouldn't she?

A swell of doubt washed over him. All these questions with no answers. What a chump he was, pining after a gal he didn't know the first thing about. The assumption that her attraction equaled his now seemed laughable. Stupidity settled in his gut, heavy as a ton of coal. He blew out a breath.

Enough already. Time to focus on things that mattered: his brother, the war, his patriotic duty. A few days and he wouldn't even remember what she looked like. That's what he told himself. But then the feel of holding Liz swept over his arms, and already he knew she would haunt his memory long after she'd vanished.

2

Two knocks, yet no one answered. No sign of life through the door's smoky glass pane.

In the vacant corridor outside the instructor's office, Julia scraped at the side seam of her overcoat, desperate to get this over with. She must have arrived too early; Madame Simone was nothing if not punctual.

With no clocks permitted in the small fashion academy, usually a rule Julia favored, she moved to the hall window for a narrow view of the world outside. Her eyes strained through the sun's morning glare to reach the bank at the corner. The clock pinned to its brick forehead indicated 10:06. More than twenty minutes until their meeting. Twenty-*four* long minutes, to be exact.

"Splendid," she muttered.

Had nerves not rushed her, she could have relaxed at home longer, interrogated Liz more thoroughly. Sifting her friend's recount of the previous evening might have actually produced a juicy morsel. Perhaps, true to her claim, Liz had stayed at the USO merely to watch one last performance. But Julia would have at least enjoyed the chance to dig a little deeper, playing the role of a savvy investigator, before the clues turned cold.

Oh, why did minutes pass swiftly only when you wanted them to last?

A coffee. And an apricot fritter. Good time killers, she decided, recalling the bakery around the corner. Should her teacher be inquiring about Julia's delay in fall registration—why else would she have asked her here?—a place to hone a response would be helpful: *Thank you again for all you've done, for everything you've taught me. But I'm sorry, I simply can't.*

Julia pushed away an onset of guilt and hastened toward the exit downstairs. She felt pleading stares from the sketches of faceless models on the walls as she passed. In their bold hats and curly-strapped shoes, woven waterfalls of shimmery gowns, they silently called her back.

She averted her eyes, focused on her goal, just as a lineup of fragrances snuck into her senses: hemmed cotton, trimmed wool, raw imagination. They emanated from a slightly open doorway and blended in the valley of her lungs. As though on tracks, she found herself guided toward the scents, into her old classroom. Enticing and intoxicating as champagne.

A few more steps and apprehension dropped away. Light through a cluster of windows pronounced vibrancy in the bolts of fabric, poised at attention within the worn shelves. She trailed her hand over the spectrum of textures. As always, the French caretaker kept the materials organized by hues. They flowed like a rainbow, their divisions softened by the gradual transitions: from Persian blue to cornflower to cerulean to teal.

In this very space, like nowhere else, Julia had luxuriated in her impulses against the grain. For within these four boundless walls, the art of a woman's freethinking was demanded, rather than discouraged.

And still, she had spent the past two months telling herself that her parents were right, that funds from clerking part-time at the nursing home should be spent on holiday gifts, not a hobby taking bites out of her regular studies. The commute itself, to the downtown academy, had contributed greatly to the slip in her respectable grades. Only a slight slip, but enough to raise concern from parents whose eldest daughter, Claire, had yet to stray from a trail spun of tradition, trimmed with approval.

Sometimes Julia wished her sister weren't so dang likable. Had the girl been wretchedly competitive, or haughty in her seniority, like a typical sibling, Julia might have scuffed at Claire's exemplary footsteps. Instead, so flawlessly formed, they gave her little cause not to smile, curtsy, and follow.

With a sigh, Julia pulled her fingertips from the propped fabric. She hadn't expected a return to this familiar playground to cause such a tug on her heart. The thorny pulse of missing an old friend.

Loosening her grip on her handbag, she gazed at the pair of dress forms in the corner. Dashes of chalk acted as blueprints for the developing ensembles. She was trying to recall how many times she had used those very mannequins when a sight trapped her: Eggshell trim dangled awkwardly from the breast pocket of the maroon suit jacket. She scanned the tiled floor for the delinquent straight pin. Its metallic point sparkled, a beacon to her slender fingers.

Another's design was considered a personal expression. Soulful. Sacred. But surely a student would appreciate the unobtrusive remedy.

Julia quickly retrieved the pin and tacked the trim back onto the pocket. As she confirmed its levelness, however, she had a vision of the extreme opposite: the entire pocket at a slant. To test the idea, just for a second, she angled and secured the accessory. The hem of the skirt needed to be raised as a complement. She shimmied the fabric upward around the wire cage below the limbless torso. Then she stepped back, evaluating.

What a statement the garb would make with a sharp, lightning-bolt collar rather than a conservative rounded appeasement. And if the belt were an inch wider with, say, a square copper buckle—

A sound from the doorway whirled Julia around. Her teacher entered, a small box in her arms. Mismatched pattern pieces hung over its edges like a deflated circus tent. Julia's anxiety, instantly revived, sprang to attention.

"Ah! I see already you are here, *Zhoolia*." The same tough elegance permeating Simone's French accent encompassed her trademark appearance: dark hair slicked into an impossibly tight bun, no bangs to soften her angled features, slender arms pale against her all-black attire. Only wrinkles huddling around her eyes confessed her age exceeding fifty. And aside from her raspberry lipstick, the jeweled chain on the half-glass spectacles dangling from her neck provided her sole splash of color. "Have you been here long?" she asked.

Julia grappled for her thoughts. "I—arrived a little earlier than I planned." Even more consuming than the rudeness of her untimely arrival was her tampering with the suit behind her. She could think of no discreet way of returning the outfit to its original state. Inching to her right, she settled for barricading the view. "Did you end up visiting New York last month, to see your niece?" She flung the question across the room, a verbal sleight of hand.

"Mmm," Simone affirmed, moving toward a worktable beneath the windows, her posture and movement like a swan's. "Have you ever been?" She set down the box.

"Oh yes," Julia replied. "About once a year since I was little. My mom liked to take my sister and me there to holiday shop, see Broadway shows, and such."

"And you are fond of it? That big city?"

A memory floated toward Julia: the first time she rode an open carriage through Central Park, the glow of lanterns painting the drifting snowflakes gold before her eyes. She swore heaven couldn't be any more beautiful. "I think it's the most magical place on earth."

The teacher nodded, then nodded again. "Good." The right answer. Simone disdained wrong answers. And, as Julia had learned, a student never had to question into which category their response had fallen.

"May I help you with that?" Julia hurried toward her, pulling the woman's eye line to a safe periphery.

"Scraps," the teacher complained, her fist full of thin strips from the box. "Silk pieces, they promised. But no. Only scraps." She dropped them into a rejected heap on the long rectangular table, a fixture Julia knew well. On occasion, she had literally lived on the nicked and scarred slab—eating, sleeping, dreaming among the spools and yardsticks when a gust of creativity caught hold.

"Well," Julia offered, touching the coveted material, "hopefully the war will be over soon, and everything will go back to normal."

"Mmm . . . normal." The word entered the air, soft as a wish. A brief pause and Simone's wistfulness disappeared, shut down on command. *"Alors."* She straightened. "You are wondering why I called you here, *non?"*

Fresh tension snapped through Julia as she waited.

"Let me first say," she began, "the opportunity, at your level of experience, is an exception. However, I would prefer not to see a talent like yours wasted. Not to mention the effort and time I have contributed to your education."

This was even worse than Julia expected. The woman was obviously inviting her into the advanced design program. A wondrous offer for a one-year student, almost unheard of.

Regardless. Julia's answer would be the same: *Thank you for everything—but—but . . .* The words resisted, dug in their heels, as Simone said, "You see, you've been offered an internship."

"I'm sorry, I can't." Julia's decline toppled out before the last statement soaked in. "What was that?"

Simone's expression held at stoic. "An internship, *chérie.* At *Vogue.* Naturally, they'll want to interview you first, but I assured them you'd be perfect."

"I had no—that you—" All of the thoughts in Julia's head crashed into each other, landing in a pile of confusion. A single word crawled from the wreckage: "How?"

Simone shrugged one shoulder, as if both took too much effort. "During my trip to New York. I brought a file of your sketches, and two of the gowns you designed for the fashion show."

Though the showcase last spring was only class-wide, the rave reviews Julia had received sent her spirit gliding cloud-high for an entire week.

Simone went on, "A dear friend I studied with decades ago is now working in designs for *Vogue.* And she believes you have something special. A gift. As do I." That last sentence, above all others, lit Julia inside. Compliments from the woman were like collectible coins. Rare and priceless. "But," she pointed out, "you will have a lot to learn before then."

"When would it start?"

"They had hoped for this winter, but I told them of your studies. She would be willing to wait until late spring for you. And you would be expected to prove, at all times, why you were worth the wait." She paused a beat for emphasis. "The pay would be minimal, and you would be responsible for all your expenses. Although there would be other interns you could share a flat with, if you prefer."

Julia's mind was spinning. "And this is . . . for how long?"

"That is up to them," she replied. "Or you. At the end of the summer, you could decide to return to school, or remain. The choice would be yours."

Julia breathed against the enclosure of her excitement. She felt herself drifting once more toward the clouds. Grounding herself as best she could, she shook her head and said, "I don't know what to say, how to thank you."

Simone's reply came strong. "Don't prove me wrong." The teacher's reputation had obviously served as an ante in the gambling match. The shared pressure didn't go unnoticed. "Of course," she added, "you will need to do some preparation work, around your studies at the university."

"The university?" Julia barely grasped the familiar word.

A suggestion of a smile played on Simone's lips. "*Eh bien.* I have given you much to consider. They will need your answer by end of summer."

Carried by the irrational current of the moment, Julia embraced her. As could be expected, there was no reciprocal effort—the teacher treated hugs like a contagious illness—but Julia didn't care. She had been handed a throne, and she wasn't about to complain about the detailing of its cushion. Rather, she simply stepped back and said, "Thank you."

Simone nodded before returning her attention to her box of scraps. A cue that their meeting had ended.

"Have a good day," Julia bid, and headed for the hall.

"Mmm," she said. "And *Zhoolia.*"

"Yes?" She turned to find Simone's head still down.

"No playing with other people's designs while at *Vogue. D'accord?*"

Julia's gaze darted to the mannequin. She felt a poke at her side, the finger of guilt. "Yes, ma'am," she replied, and without another word, she ducked out the door.

Once outside, Julia strode down the sidewalk, bridling an urge to skip. She could hardly feel her shoes making contact with the ridges of city cement.

A streetcar of strangers clanged across the street. A hefty construction worker passed lugging two buckets of tools. Julia wanted to shout to them all, spreading the news. She wanted to pick up a phone, tell her parents. Race home and write Christian all about it—

Christian.

Her *fiancé.*

"I'm engaged," she reminded herself. And again, a near reprimand, "I'm engaged."

What was she thinking? They would be getting married as soon as the war ended. Which, after three years of America swinging punches in the ring, couldn't be far away. Next spring wasn't the time to go tromping off to New York, laying the foundation for a career she had no intention of pursuing.

Sure, the offer was amazing. Marvelous. Incredible. But for someone who wouldn't waste the opportunity. There was no sense robbing another girl of the internship, a girl whose dreams rested in the balance of such a springboard. Julia was, after all, going to be a wife, wedded to her beloved Christian Downing.

Her parents were right. She adored fashion, creating garments from pictures in her head. But it was a hobby, just for fun. Like moviegoing and shopping. Nothing that should interfere with the gay future that awaited. Marriage, motherhood, a charming home to fill with love and laughter. There was no comparison.

Slowly she wheeled toward the academy. Through the trees, she could see movement in the second-story classroom. A figure in black.

Julia already felt dread pluming from her ankles. Simone had gone out of her way to recommend her, even saw to it that exceptions were made. The least Julia could do was give the impression she had heavily pondered the offer. The delivery of a snap judgment, no matter how obvious, seemed outright ungrateful.

Indeed. She would give it a reasonable amount of time before letting the woman down.

At a decisive clip, Julia resumed her departure. Blocks away, the streetcar rattled into the distance, crammed with passengers who would never hear her news; nor would anyone else. At least not until she presented the inevitable answer. She had no desire to allow Liz, Betty, or even Christian to sway her choice. Of all the paths, she knew which was right—despite the unforeseen temptation.

❧ 3 ❧

July 5, 1944
Chicago Union Station

The minutes until departure were evaporating as briskly as steam from the locomotive's smokestack. Morgan gripped the vertical handlebar of the coach's entry step and shot another glance at his wristwatch, an heirloom willed to him from his father. Now more than ever, he wished it were running fast. The leather band was weathered and the crystal scratched, but the movement could always be counted on for timekeeping. Unlike his dim-witted brother.

"Come on, come on," Morgan said, imploring the kid to show. Missing the last overnighter to Trenton would mean a guaranteed late arrival at Fort Dix, and likely even a seat in the cargo hold of their transport ship. Or in the latrine, depending on their commander's mood.

Charlie was a marvel. Who else would pull a stunt like this after waiting nearly three years? And Morgan wasn't the only one he'd be answering to if he fouled this up. Even their uncle with rarely a word to spare had gone out on a limb, ensuring the two served together by calling in a favor from a war vet buddy with military pull. A few "adjustments" to Charlie's birth certificate and everyone was happy. Supposedly, the desk-planted appeasers in Washington carried a lighter conscience when cousins rather than brothers shared a unit.

Not that it mattered now. Morgan appeared to be going solo.

"All aboard!" The conductor's voice echoed off the darkened ceiling of the underground station.

With a determined eye, Morgan studied the bustling platform. Dolled-up gals waved to windows, shedding tears, blowing kisses. Mothers held hankies to their mouths as their husbands consoled them with an arm around their shoulders. But still no sighting of the dimwit.

"Dammit all," Morgan growled. What had he been thinking last night, letting his brother leave the dance without him? That'd teach him to steer clear of dames and to stick with stuff he understood. Livestock auctions and auto engines. Things that came with instruction manuals.

The locomotive lurched into a sluggish chug.

Decision time. Of course, he had only one option: grab his belongings and leap off before landing required a body roll over gravel.

"Hey, Morgan!" A voice cut through the commotion. "I'm here!"

Sure enough, there was Charlie's capped head bobbing through the crowd. In and out he wove, dividing paired travelers, his Army-issue duffel bag slung over his shoulder. He hurdled a trunk and the toe of his shoe caught an edge. His pace slowed for a moment while he regained his footing. Half turned, in motion, he yelled something to the shapely dame standing beside the luggage.

"Move it!" Morgan shouted, leaning out from the step. Charlie resumed his sprint alongside the train. His free arm pumped, his face flushed red. Once close enough, Morgan stretched out his hand and yanked him inside. A small stumble and Charlie planted his feet. Tailbone against the wall, he hunched over to catch his breath.

"Un-believable." Morgan smacked the back of his brother's head, a punishment so often delivered since childhood the kid scarcely flinched.

"Not my fault," he gasped. "Army time still confuses the hell out of me." He wiped his sleeve across his forehead and flipped a grin. When he straightened, his service shirt showcased its unevenly fastened buttons, a perfect complement to the dark circles under his eyes.

Morgan was about to ask where he had slept last night—assuming he'd slept at all—then decided he'd rather not know. "I swear," he muttered, "I may shoot you before the Nazis get a chance." With a sharp turn, he led Charlie through the coach packed with noisy servicemen and an undercurrent of nerves. A craps game ensued in the corner. As the train increased speed, a cross breeze through the open windows lessened the lingering smell of sweat.

Frank Dugan, facing their two vacant seats, glanced up from his magazine, his leg stretched in the aisle. "Good of you to join us, Chap."

"Thanks, Rev. Always nice traveling with a man of the cloth."

At basic, word had spread quickly that Frank was a ministry dropout whose call to arms had come into conflict with his call to religion. And lucky for their platoon. Built like an ancient redwood, he brought practical fighting know-how from the tough streets of Brooklyn.

"Shit, you're coming after all?" Jack Callan smirked at Charlie while fanning a deck of cards. "Thought maybe you'd chickened out and gone home to play with your barn animals."

Charlie tossed his bag up onto the luggage rack. He pushed and shoved the bulky contents into place as if the clothes inside were putting up a fight. "Just had to make a quick stop on the way, *Jack*-ass."

"Why, you forget to pack your underwear?"

"Actually, I left them in your sister's room last night."

Jack glared. He slid the toothpick in his mouth from side to side. "One pull of the trigger, Chap. That's all it takes." And that was the truth. The lean, red-haired kid from Wisconsin was a crack shot with a rifle.

"Ah, c'mon, Jack," Charlie said. "You wouldn't do that. You need me around."

"Yeah, what for?"

"How else you gonna get any broads to notice you? Other than your mother, that is."

Frank looked to Morgan, who had just settled into his window seat. "Mac, your brother ever shut up?"

"Not without a big piece of tape." Morgan smiled, remembering the day he'd taped Charlie's mouth closed and tied the rambunctious grade-schooler to a pole of their mother's clothesline. It was the most effective way to stop him from telling a girl in class that Morgan wanted to "milk her udders." Their father cut a whimpering Charlie loose an hour later, in full agreement with the punishment.

Morgan almost wished he'd packed some tape for this particular trip.

"Forgive me, Reverend Frank, for I have sinned. Again." Charlie genuflected like the devout Catholic his mother had hoped he'd become.

Frank scratched the crook in his nose and continued browsing the latest issue of *Yank* magazine. He didn't bother to fake interest. When it came to Charlie's racy tales, Jack always showed enough for them both.

"Okay, Chap, let's hear it," Jack said, a smile in his eyes. "Which one of the twins did ya end up with? The one with the knockers or the long stems?"

"Are you kiddin'? I was too much man for them dames. Scared 'em off with these enormous cannons." He flexed his biceps as if he had the physique of Captain America. When Frank tossed the magazine at his head, Charlie sank back into his seat and grinned. "Did some neckin' with the broad from the coffee shop, though."

Jack crumpled his face. "The one with bad teeth?"

"No, you dumbbell. The tasty dish with glasses."

Frank turned to Jack. "Well, that explains it. She needs a new prescription."

"Ha, ha. You're hysterical." Charlie removed his soft garrison cap and rubbed his hair with both hands.

If only their mom could see him now. She used to say that someday girls would go wild over his golden waves. That they'd even be willing to pay to run their fingers through them.

It's funny the things you remember. Morgan regretted not paying more attention, regretted not seeing the truth behind his father's lie. Charlie had only been eight, but Morgan, at eleven, should have known better. Farm families avoided doctors like the plague. When he watched his parents climb into their old pickup truck that cold January night headed for the hospital, he should have realized their mother was never coming back.

"Hey, speaking of hysterical," Jack said, pulling Morgan from his thoughts. "Went to a tattoo joint last night. Rev ended up knocking the owner's lights out. You gotta see it—the stupid sap put 'Joan' instead of 'June' in the big ol' heart on Rev's arm."

Frank's lips flattened into steel rails, his dark eyes trained on Jack. "And you think that's funny, do ya?"

"Look at the bright side," Charlie interjected. "Instead of Joan, it could've said *John.*" He punctuated his wisecrack with a grin.

Frank picked up his magazine from the carpeted floor, still eying Jack. "At least mine don't make me look like Mussolini's branded cattle, ya dope." A jab at the unfortunate birthmark on Jack's collarbone, shaped like a sideways stamp of Italy, was one of the few ways to ensure the last word with the guy.

"So, uh, Mac, what about you?" Jack shifted the spotlight. "Get chummy with the brunette you went after?"

Morgan coughed into his fist, the question taking him off guard. "Nah. Not really." Considering how Liz had given him the brush-off, their encounter was the last thing he wanted to discuss. "How about you fellas? What else you wind up doing?"

Frank crossed his arms. His expression lightened. "Chap, I believe your brother's trying to change the subject."

"It's all right, Mac," Jack assured him. "You shouldn't be ashamed. First time getting lucky can be a scary experience for any young man." He grinned, impressed by his own sarcasm.

"What a coincidence," Charlie said to Jack, "I've heard that dames think *every* time is scary with you."

"Can it, both of ya." Frank angled to Morgan and jerked a nod. "Go ahead, Mac. You were sayin'?"

Morgan suddenly wished he'd jumped off the train after all. "Really, there's nothing to tell. She just had to skip out early."

"You're saying she ditched a McClain?" Jack asked in mock disbelief.

"Not his fault," Frank said. "If I was her and knew he was related to Chap, I'd double-time it outta there too."

"Oh yeah?" Charlie said. "Well, it just so happens that last night—on account of yours truly—my brother reeled in a broad any fella would give his left nut for a chance at."

Morgan tightened his eyes at him. "What are you yappin' about?"

"You have an admirer," Charlie sang out in a taunting voice he never outgrew.

"Sure it was a girl?" Jack smirked.

"Not just any girl," Charlie said. "That looker from the USO."

In an instant, Liz's face flashed in Morgan's mind, clear as rain. Wary, though, of being a sucker in one of his brother's juvenile pranks, he played it cool. "You're full of it," he muttered.

"I'm serious. Said she was searching all over for you."

"Yeah? Where'd you run into her?"

"At the dance. Where else?" Charlie's tone indicated he wasn't horsing around. "I went back to find ya. She heard me asking about you. Told me you two had twirled some, but then you flew the coop."

Morgan straightened, his thoughts racing: How could he have missed her? Did she come back after he left?

"Well, spit it out. What'd she say?" Morgan demanded.

"Said she wanted to keep in touch. So," he said, "being the dutiful brother I am, I gave her the Army address for forwarding." He reached into the chest pocket of his shirt and produced a small rectangular note. "Here, this is for you."

A broad grin latched onto Morgan's face as he retrieved the gift. A scribbled message spanned three lines. His heart pumped like an oil rig as he imagined her voice delivering the words.

> *To Morgan,*
> *Take care of yourself.*
> *Betty Cordell*

Morgan's mind pinched in confusion. *"Betty Cordell?"* He flipped over the paper and discovered it was a photograph, a black-and-white close-up of the girl from the dance. Just not the girl he was hoping for. He managed a closed-lipped smile as angst revisited his gut.

"Damn, Chap," Jack said, "you didn't say it was the foxy blond singer." He snatched the wallet-sized keepsake from Morgan's fingers. "I can't believe you got a dance with her, you lucky bastard. Where the hell was I?"

"Doesn't matter," Charlie said. "She only wanted Fred Astaire, here. Must have a thing for his fancy promenades and do-si-dos."

Morgan flicked his brother's temple. "Dry up, why don't ya."

"Man, that's so unfair," Jack grumbled, ogling the image until Frank swiped the photo.

"No need to get jealous," Charlie told him. "I'm sure she's got a few friends who would gladly talk to you outta pity."

"All this from a kid who hasn't hit puberty." Jack launched his toothpick with a puff. "Enough of this shit. Are we playing cards, or what?" Not waiting for an answer, he began dealing them out, each card featuring pinup models in garters and brassieres.

Morgan gazed out the window at the passing urban scenery. It was his first trip to the East Coast, his first journey out of the Midwest. Across the ocean, a battle-raging continent awaited their platoon, but all he could think about was Liz.

❧ 4 ❧

July 15, 1944
Evanston, Illinois

All day, Liz had avoided opening the envelope. She sat on the rumbling bus, staring at her name and address penned in Professor Emmett Stephens's meticulous longhand. Like the best of carnival fortunetellers, she could report what was inside before even breaking the seal.

> *Dear Elizabeth,*
> *I trust life is keeping you well. I was extremely*
> *pleased with your academic marks from last term. Your*
> *decision to take extra classes this summer is*
> *commendable.*
> *I leave tomorrow for New York to guest lecture at*
> *several universities. I shall return to Washington D.C.*
> *in approximately three weeks. Should you need to reach*
> *me in the interim, my secretary at Georgetown will*
> *have my itinerary and contact information.*
> *Please congratulate Dalton on my behalf. From*
> *what I have heard, he is running a powerful senatorial*
> *campaign for his father. I wish them continued success.*
> *Respectfully,*
> *Your father*

Respectfully. Such distance conveyed in a single word. A sad reflection of the fissure between them that had widened into a canyon.

Liz turned to the half-open window and closed her eyes. A gentle breeze swept over her sun-drenched face. Once again, she was eight years old, poking her head out the window of his shiny black Ford Victoria. Zooming past the California palm trees, she and her daddy would talk, laugh, and improvise silly songs, their excursions drastically warmer than those spent with her mother.

Isabelle.

In Liz's memory, she embodied a caricature in a household appliance ad, her cool disposition offset by her grace and beauty. How close their family could have been had Isabelle exuded the warmth and affection of a mother like Julia's.

Then again, ruminating on the impossible was as useless as deferring the blame.

A jolt from the bus's brakes brought Liz back to the present. Familiar landmarks and rising passengers reminded her of her stop. She stuffed her father's form letter into a skirt pocket and dashed down the aisle, her grocery bag slipping in her arms.

Around the bend of Kiernan Lane she pushed against the humidity. Sweat rolled down the slide of her spine as she passed the string of contemporary bungalow homes. The sharpness of newly cut grass clung to the air, blocking pollutants from the bordering city of Chicago. Service flags paraded in window after window; their proud stars of blue outnumbered the dreaded gold symbols of loss.

Willing herself to smile, she returned waves from neighbors relaxing beneath their shaded porches. Sun lovers basked in the late afternoon rays and giggly children played tag through the rainbow sprays of sprinklers.

Liz adjusted the bag, ripping the bottom corner. She cupped the protruding soup can to keep it inside while crossing the street to reach her house. Her favorite accents on the modest, brick-red structure remained the same since her childhood visits: a small garden of irises, a large picture window in the kitchen, facing the street, and a two-person swing her grandfather, "Papa," had built for the covered porch. Best of all, a towering cherry tree shaded the east side of the house, a finishing touch as sweet as the turnovers her grandma used to bake from its abundant fruit. Papa had purchased the home more than twenty years ago for his wife, his "sole reason for living." It was a claim he literally proved after she lost her battle with cancer.

"Your grandfather's had a stroke," Liz's father had announced. "We're moving to Illinois." The triangular plane of his face had concealed all emotion, a defensive mask not unlike her own. It was one he'd acquired six months before, the day her mother left their lives forever.

Correction: the day Liz sent her away.

And so, with Isabelle gone, there was no discussion, no call for a vote. By the eve of Liz's fourteenth birthday, they had packed up their boxes, along with their unspoken feelings, their devastation and sorrow too potent for words.

The paving of Liz's regret had stretched clear across the country, permanent as concrete. And there it took up residence, beneath Papa's roof, where she and her father coexisted for the next four years. The cordial but mechanical nature of their exchanges, maddening as a blackboard screech, gripped even his farewell words after her graduation: "I'll send your tuition payments directly to the university and quarterly allowances to the house. We'll touch base once I'm settled at Georgetown." With a nod, he'd grabbed his suitcases and left her on the front porch. It was at that moment she had realized: Abandonment struck in degrees.

Standing now on that same rickety platform, Liz squeezed the grocery bag to her chest. She closed her eyes and gave her head a brisk shake, as if emotional wounds were cold droplets she could simply cast off.

When she lifted her lids, the memory prevailed.

Liz placed the food items on their designated kitchen shelves. Cans of Scotch broth soup and corned beef hash, Mello-Wheat cereal, bread, oleo, and a splurge of Cocomalt. With the sleeve of her blouse, she dabbed her temple while washing her hands with a bar of lavender soap. The thick, purple lather failed to soften her calloused mood, and the dry texture in her mouth—like flavorless cotton candy—only irritated her more.

She tossed some ice cubes into an empty glass, a ricochet of clinks.

"Liz?"

She cringed at the distant voice, not in the mood for company.

"Liz, is that you?" Betty called again from her bedroom, a room Liz would have to pass to reach her own.

Reluctantly she answered. "Yeah, it's me." She poured herself the last of Betty's freshly squeezed limeade and downed half the glass. Sourness puckered her cheeks, stung the corners of her eyes. Of all the items rationed for the war effort, she missed sugar the most.

"Hurry up and get in here!" Betty's trademark impatience.

"Hold your horses, I'm coming!" She dragged herself down the narrow hallway lined with framed photos of deceased and twice-removed relatives.

"Come on, slowpoke." Betty reached through the doorway and tugged her inside. Liz nearly tripped over the girl's old teddy bear doubling as a doorstop. His lone button eye hung by a thread, his cream fur matted and stained. Clearly he had seen better days.

Yep, buddy, she wanted to tell him, *you're not the only one.*

Julia sat at the vanity. "Hey, hon," she mumbled around two bobby pins between her pursed lips.

Liz returned the greeting before daring to ask, "So what's the crisis?"

Betty tsked. "Now, why does it always have to be something bad?" She spun around so fast the white polka dots on her violet sundress streaked into lines. Grabbing an envelope from atop her pillow, she belly flopped on her bed to face the vanity. "Fact is, it couldn't be keener. Just wait till you hear Christian's latest."

Thanks but no thanks. Liz had read all the letters she could handle for one day. "I'd love to hear it, gals, but I really have to get some work done."

"Oh, don't be such a fuddy-duddy." Betty reached across the path created by the nightstand to pat Julia's mattress. "Sit, sit, sit."

Liz groaned, then stopped short; she did not want to hurt Julia's feelings. Christian's posts were, after all, among the redhead's prized possessions.

"Believe me," Betty told Liz, "it's even better than those Emily Dickens letters you like."

A smile crouched behind Liz's lips. "Dickinson," she corrected, speaking the author's name with reverence.

"Yeah. Well, this is better."

A sacrilegious comparison, no doubt. Though who was Liz to deny any writer a fair swing at the title?

"Fine," Liz conceded. "But only for a minute." She strode over to the wrought-iron bed she had given up when she moved into her father's former bedroom, and started clearing space to sit among Julia's fabric swatches. *Vogue* pattern pieces and celebrity shots torn from *Silver Screen* magazine added to the fashion hodgepodge.

"Did you happen to pick up some bread at the market?" Julia asked.

"Yeah," Liz said, settling in. "I noticed we were out when I tried to make toast this morning." She should have known then what kind of day she had ahead of her. "Speaking of which, when did Hillman's start charging eleven cents a loaf? It's outrageous."

While Betty sorted pages from the envelope, Liz glimpsed Julia's pearly face in the vanity's oval mirror. The crimson-haired girl contorted her expression at an uncooperative spit curl. Limited reflection space further challenged her efforts, with a mural of photographs covering half the mirror: a graduation picture of the three of them amidst her family snapshots, a sepia-toned portrait of her and Christian, and a new photo of her sailor leaning on a signal lamp of his ship, with *Love you Red* penned across the bottom.

"'My dearest Julia,'" Betty began, letter propped before her. "'Only another week has passed, but it seems an eternity since last seeing you. You'll have to send a new picture soon. I've looked at the one I have so many times, my eyes are wearing your image right off the paper. Unfortunately, thinking of you for hours on end only makes me miss you more. The weather has been sweltering, so I've taken to sleeping out on deck. To cool off, some shipmates and I had liberty yesterday and headed for . . .' Yeah, yeah, yeah, boring, boring."

The letter was a typical one from Christian Downing, sweet and smooth as butterscotch. *Enough to give you a toothache,* Dalton would say; and though from the start, he and Liz had agreed mushy offerings of the like weren't necessary between them, Liz suddenly found herself wondering: Had the ban been her idea or his?

"Ooh-ooh, here we go." Betty resumed reading. "'Although I am proud of the job we are doing for our country, already I am eager for the day we will hear that we've won the war and that it's time to sail back home to you, my darling, the beautiful woman whom I will soon make my bride. Well, I best drop anchor for tonight. Sending oceans of kisses from your loving husband-to-be. Eternally yours, Christian USN.'" Betty rolled onto her back. She pressed the papers to her chest, tight enough to embed the prose into her heart. "This is sooo romantic," she said dreamily.

Liz turned and caught Julia running her fingers over her fiancé's latest photo, losing herself in the gray tones of their separation. That same look of hers, a pensiveness in her eyes, had made appearances more than usual lately.

"It really is lovely, Jules," Liz agreed, feeling the coarse edges within her smoothing.

A quick nod and Julia abruptly rose. She headed for the wardrobe closet, as if sadness were a garment she could shed at will. Since the three girls had become fast friends in high school, lab partners in freshman science, Liz had only once seen Julia cling to an unpleasant emotion for a notable stretch: It began the morning Christian announced he'd up and joined the Navy. Julia had been beside herself. He'd already planned to enroll in the Naval officers' program at Northwestern so they could be together, but decided he couldn't wait to enlist, not even for an officer commission. Then a week before his fleet's departure, Christian earned her forgiveness; specifically, the moment he knelt and slid the engagement band on her finger.

"Why don't I get letters like this?" Betty sighed.

Julia tipped a smile. "Liz *is* the poetry pro here," she reminded her. "Why not ask her to write you a love note? She could even sign it from Clark Gable—oh, wait, that's *my* fantasy." She giggled.

"That's it!" Betty perked.

In the midst of a swallow, Liz sputtered drops of limeade. She wiped her chin. "Betty Cordell. I am *not* writing you a love letter."

"No, no, that's not what I meant." The blonde shifted onto her knees with a slight bounce. "Seriously, I do need your help. Please say you'll agree."

Liz blew out a stream of air. She was all too familiar with the plea; Betty had used it for myriad requests over the years—everything from French kissing instructions to leg-makeup applications due to the silk and nylon shortage, an act Betty considered as her contribution to the war effort. In other words, Liz had learned to ask for details up front.

"What *exactly* do you want me to do?"

"Well, you see," she said, "there's this soldier I met." Her opening hardly launched a shock wave through the room. "He's not the usual kind I date. I mean, he's handsome enough. But he's sorta shy. The mysterious type."

"And you need my help with . . . ?"

"Oh, right," Betty said. "The point is, we met at the USO, where we danced and had a grand time of it. Sadly, the next day he shipped out with his brother."

The USO?

His brother?

Oh God. With Liz's luck, she was certain to be talking about Morgan. But why now? Ten whole days had passed since the dance, and not once had Betty spoken of him. Liz had hoped to forget all about that night, all about where foolishness might have led her had she not witnessed Betty and Morgan dancing. Which, incidentally, was the best thing that could have happened to Liz.

So why did she find herself hoping, with everything in her, that Betty was referring to another guy?

Liz interjected, "Who is he, this soldier of yours?" She managed a casual tone.

"I just told you," Betty said, as if she hadn't been listening. "He's handsome and mysterious and—"

"I mean his name. What's the fellow's name?"

"Oh. Sorry. It's McKall—no. McLew—wait . . ."

Liz restrained herself from volunteering what was undoubtedly the final syllable.

"McClain," Betty remembered. "It's Morgan McClain."

"Morgan McClain?" Julia paused in the midst of changing into her mauve blouse. "Liz, isn't that the same guy you—"

"Yeah, he's the one we met," Liz cut in.

"You know him?" Betty exclaimed. "Oh, that's perfect. Then you *have* to help me write to him."

Write to him? This couldn't be happening. Fate couldn't be that spiteful.

Liz arrived easily at her answer. "I'm sorry, Betty, but I don't have time."

"It'll only take a few minutes," she insisted. "Pleeease, I promised. And it'd be rude to keep him waiting any longer."

As if he didn't deserve it. The guy was plainly out for one thing: one night of fun, one roll in the hay before deployment. An obvious deduction in hindsight.

Then again . . .

If a one-night companion was all Morgan had wanted, he wouldn't have bothered asking Betty to write. Maybe he wasn't as insincere as he'd appeared. Perhaps his initial attraction to Liz was genuine, but a single glance at the stunning blonde had cured his interest.

Another reason to decline.

Liz was about to do just that, more firmly this time, when Betty continued her plea.

"I already started his letter. I just need your help with the ending, and to make sure the rest is okay." She pouted her lips. "You know what an awful writer I am."

Liz couldn't argue. Had she not rewritten all of Betty's essays in high school, the girl would still be there.

"And since you've met him," Betty went on, "you'll know exactly what to say."

"Wrong," Liz countered. Clearly she had no clue what he wanted to hear.

Betty held up her right hand, taking an oath. "If you help me with this, I'll never ask you to write anything for me again. Scout's honor."

Julia chimed in, "Don't you have to be a Scout to make that pledge?" She smiled, straightening the seams of her stockings.

"Come on, Liz." Desperation spilled from Betty's eyes. "You and Julia already have beaus. Don't I deserve to be happy too?"

Liz groaned helplessly. How could she dispute that kind of logic?

"Besides," Betty elongated the word, "need I remind you about an incredibly boring play I attended for a certain friend?"

Liz narrowed her eyes. "You mean the one you slept through?"

"One measly act," Betty snipped. "Even so, I went, didn't I? And without a solitary complaint."

Truth be told, Liz herself had come close to drifting off during the student-directed play; verses from the overdramatic actors had dripped like sap off their tongues. More relevant to Betty's request, however, was Liz's unwillingness to explain the real cause of her hesitation. Which left her little choice.

"All right, I'll do it," she gave in. "But just this once. No exceptions."

"Thank you, thank you!" Betty dropped Christian's letter while clapping with glee. Julia swooped up the pages from the floor and carefully added them to the drawer of her nightstand.

"I'm not fooling, Betty." Liz mustered the sternest voice she could. "No V-mail, no notes, nothing."

"Okaaay. I'll even write my own obituary."

Julia giggled as she slipped into her black pumps and fastened the ankle straps. From her lace collar to her tailored mid-length skirt, she was as stylish as Ava Gardner. "I'm heading out, girls. Either one of you want to join me and Dot for a triple feature? The Tivoli's playing *Cover Girl* again."

Ah, yes. Hollywood's cure-all for the perpetually glum. A perfect example of why talkies weren't always better than the silent pictures. At least in *Casablanca* the tragic ending was scripted out of realism, and the stars didn't belt out lines in melodramatic show tunes.

"I wish I could," Betty moaned. "I swear, if I have to take Vera's shift again this week, I'm quitting once and for all."

"What about you, Liz?"

Any activity sounded better than ghostwriting a letter to Morgan, even suffering through a silly musical. But completing the task, purging the soldier from her system, also had its appeal.

"I'll take a rain check," Liz replied with eyes that told her, *Thanks for getting me into this.*

Julia grabbed her pillbox purse, missing the glance. "See you tomorrow, then," she said, and turned for the hallway.

By the time the front door slammed, Betty had sidled up to Liz, cross-legged, pillow on her lap, armed with a pile of stationery. "Here's what I have so far." She held out the page for Liz to read along, and cleared her throat as if preparing to give the State of the Union address.

> *Dear Morgan,*
>   *It was nice talking to you, you seem like a terrific guy. I definately wish we could've spent more time together. Where did the Army ship you to?*

The glaring grammatical and spelling errors seized hold of Liz's eyes. She fought every urge within her not to seek out the nearest colored fountain pen to circle what her father would call "blasphemous mistakes."

Betty looked up. "What do you think?"

Liz aimed for diplomacy, a specialty of Dalton's. "It's, um . . . not bad."

"I knew it," Betty whimpered. "It's dreadful." She buried her face in the pillow.

"No. It's not dreadful. It's just that—" Liz chose to limit her critiques to the misguided content. "I don't think the Army will let him say where they're going."

"So what *can* I write?" Betty rumpled the letter into a ball and pitched it at the woven wastebasket, falling a foot short.

Liz set her glass on the nightstand. She reminded herself this wasn't a hundred-page dissertation. With just a few intelligible sentences, life could return to normal. "How about something like . . ." She threw out the simplest opening that came to her. "Dear Morgan. Although our time together was brief, it was a pleasure meeting you at the dance—"

"Oh, that's perfect. I love it!" Enthusiasm shot through Betty like an electrical current, straightening her posture, widening her eyes. "Now, what was that again?" She held up her pen, a stenographer ready for dictation—with no knowledge of shorthand.

Already Liz felt exhausted. She opened her mouth to repeat the phrase when the tinkering notes of her grandfather's cuckoo clock rang out from the living room.

"Cripes. What time is it?" Betty rotated the alarm clock on the nightstand. "Shoot, I'm gonna be late." With the speed of a fireman preparing for a five-alarm blaze, she jumped into her carnation-pink diner dress and pinned on her name tag. At the vanity, she smoothed Julia's styling lotion over her pageboy hair.

Relief and aggravation rivaled within Liz at the postponement. Now that they had started, she wanted nothing more than to rid her thoughts of Morgan McClain; him and all the "what-ifs" that had tangled her mind like ivy.

"I really gotta go," Betty addressed Liz's reflection in the mirror, "but could you please finish the letter while I'm gone?"

"Finish?" A laugh of disbelief snagged in Liz's throat. "We haven't even started it."

Betty applied her Victory Red lipstick in one circular motion. "I wouldn't ask, but I won't be home till late. And then I'll be with Suzie all weekend visiting her family."

Liz was about to refuse, needing to draw a line somewhere—wavering and faint though the line may be—when Betty produced a scrawled address on a napkin.

"Pretty please?" She knelt by the bed with clasped hands. "A couple more lines is all it needs."

This was ludicrous. "Don't you think he'll know it's not from you?"

"He's a guy. He won't have any idea," Betty said, as if reporting the sky was blue. "Besides, what's the difference? I'd just be writing down everything you say anyway."

If gender and academics weren't a factor, the gal would have made a great trial attorney. After all, it was her indisputable case that had convinced Liz's father to allow his daughter not one but two roommates in his absence, an arrangement for which Liz was grateful. At least on most days.

Betty glanced back at the clock. "Piddle, I gotta fly." Scurrying toward the doorway, she motioned to the bed. "Stamps and envelopes are in the drawer. Just toss it in the mail when you're done."

Liz's mouth dropped open. "You don't want to read it first?"

"I trust you," Betty called as she rounded the corner. "The sooner it goes out, the sooner I'll get a letter back, right?" Her footfalls sounded down the hall and out the front door, leaving Liz alone. With a pile of stationery. Shackled.

She should have escaped with Julia when she had the chance.

"I must be going mad." Liz snatched the pen and paper and tramped across the room. Seated at the vanity, she scowled at the page and debated reneging on the deal. This wasn't what she'd agreed to.

The heck with it.

She tossed the pen down. Grasping the edge of the table, she began to rise, but a memory stilled her—the memory of Morgan's face. She'd tried so desperately to erase him from her mind. Yet there he was, as vivid as if they had shared a dance yesterday. She could almost feel the tenderness of his breath gracing her cheek, the heat of his hand pressed to hers.

Why couldn't she forget him? And why did the mere idea of him cause her pulse to quicken even now?

Her grip loosened. Her body lowered. She settled her gaze on the empty page, its fibers beckoning the beautiful stains of the written word. And she sighed.

"All right, I'll do it," she repeated her verbal assent.

Really, it was just a short note. A small favor for a friend. What was the big fuss?

At that, she placed the tip of the pen on the stationery, and surrendered her thoughts to flow through the ink.

≈ 5 ≈

July 15, 1944
Chicago, Illinois

"It's about time!" As usual, the greeting flew out of the kitchen, over the diner chatter, and into Betty's ears before she could even clock in.

"Yeah, yeah, so fire me," she meant to mutter to herself, yet a look from the grizzled chef indicated her retort had made it through the pass-through window.

"You straighten up, or that's precisely what I'm gonna do. You got me?" A cigarette bounced against his bottom lip as he spoke.

"Hey," she said coyly, "I can't control the bus schedule. But give me a raise and I'll happily race down here in a cab." She blew him a kiss, a standby tactic to alleviate his mood.

Today, however, he wasn't having any of it. He shook a fistful of his mottled dish towel in her direction, an especially deep scowl carved into his face. "Don't push me, Betty. You're this close—*this close*—to gettin' the ax. Now, get to work!" With a grumble, he returned to his grill, which crackled like the invisible eggshells he'd erected beneath her feet.

So much for a warm welcome, she wanted to say. Instead, she buttoned her lip and snagged an order pad. She wasn't up for yet another career hunt, specifically when she'd just spent money intended for her shared living expenses. But then, who could blame her? That keen aqua dress from Goldblatt's was to die for.

Tucking a pencil behind her ear, Betty assessed the status of business. Her jitters kicked in as she played her customary game of catch-up. Holding a job all the way down by the Loop wasn't the most convenient, but there was nothing like being in the thick of things. And the Loop was certainly that.

Betty threw on a wide smile, cocked her hip. Accentuate your assets, she had learned, and no one noticed your troubles. "How about a warm-up, gentlemen?" She raised a coffeepot, interrupting the three guys parked at the counter sparring over the same old topic—the war, what else?

"Thanks," they said, voices overlapping. Hands calloused, fingernails smudged, they were as blue-collared as the pedigree she strove to hide.

She filled their mugs, committing small splatters she deftly hid from the chef's view. She swiped the mess away with a rag. "Let me know if you need anything else," she told them. As she sauntered away, she could feel their gazes latched to her backside, coupled by murmuring about a nice ass. Her first instinct was to admonish them, given that their ages approached her father's—how old she presumed he'd be, anyway. But she needed their tips. For the time being.

And so she continued on, relieving the frazzled busboy from serving her tables. Mostly regulars dotted the room, plus a few additions. She topped off their mugs, took some orders—only two of them wrong—and delivered dishes back and forth, wearing a trail into the chessboard floor. Hours from closing and already her feet begged for a soak.

By the time she hit a break in the dinner rush, the sun had excused itself for the evening. Scribbled bill in hand, she ventured back toward Irma, rooted in the back booth, same as every Friday. A subtle indentation in the black cushion permanently reserved her spot. Aside from rather wide hips, her frame was of medium size. Her silver flapper hat and gaudy brooch, a firefly with tarnished wings, dated her peak years to be more than a decade past.

"Enjoy your dumplings, Irma?"

The woman, gazing distantly at the empty seat across from her, replied with a nod. Rarely saying a word—not even for her order; it was always the same—she carried the perpetual grief of a widow. The familiar reserve of a lonely child.

Betty forced a smile. "Can I interest you in a slice of pie? We got banana cream tonight."

Irma declined with a slight shake of her head, already unsnapping her worn velvety clutch.

"Well. Next time, then." Betty presented her tallied check.

The woman's hand trembled, more noticeably than ever, as she emptied all her coins onto the table. She seemed to be struggling with counting them. Given that Irma's bill never fluctuated, Betty swiftly noticed there wasn't enough money. And something told her the lady's purse didn't have a reserve compartment.

Betty glanced back at the kitchen, where the chef's mood remained stuck in a ditch of aggravation. He didn't believe in running tabs, and was far from the charitable sort.

"Here," she told Irma, "let me get those." She scooted the change off the edge and into her hand, whispering a pretend calculation. "Forty-five, fifty-five, seventy . . ." Then, "Perfect!" She dropped them into her uniform pocket. Her tip from the last table would provide just enough to compensate for the shortage. "Be sure and try our dessert sometime. A girl's gotta treat herself once in a while."

A smile brushed past Irma's dry, wrinkled lips, but only a shadow. A memory. An echo of her withered beauty.

Betty didn't know why she was helping her out exactly. Maybe it was an offering to the universe, a bribe to prevent her from ending up the same. Or worse, like her own mother, an old maid whose scandalous life had been the infection of Betty's childhood.

"Order up!" The chef's voice jerked Betty back to greasy paradise and her mouth into a frown. She deposited Irma's bare dinner plate in a bussing tub. As she headed for the kitchen, someone called out, "Excuse me? Miss? Over here."

"Be there in a minute," she shot back; she couldn't be in two places at once. But then she registered the new customer's appearance. An Army sergeant, all alone, dark and suave. Fit in his sharp uniform, he boasted looks as dreamy as they came.

Her shoes did an automatic U-turn, straight to his table. Cosmetics undoubtedly needing to be refreshed, she tilted her face to its most flattering angle and asked, "See anything you like?" She inserted a deliberate pause before gesturing to his menu.

His mouth slid into a grin. His eyes glinted.

And she knew she had him.

"Hey, I know you," he said. She would have taken the phrase for a tired old pickup line, but his tone sounded of genuine discovery. "The USO," he explained. "A few weeks back."

Had she danced with him and forgotten? Surely she would have remembered a guy like this. Crud, she hated when a fella had the upper hand.

"You were one of the singers," he added. The connection seemed to end there.

"You've got quite a memory . . ." She drew out the last word, a prompt for him to volunteer his name.

"J.T.," he said. "And you're Betty."

"How did you—" she began, then glanced down at her name tag. "Oh. Right."

"Pleased to finally meet you."

"Likewise." The feel of something sticky between her fingers prevented her from extending her hand. As a cover, she yanked the pencil from her ear and notepad out of her pocket, posed them in order-taking position.

"Well, Betty, I think you got a fan club started by some of the guys in our office."

"The office?" she asked, milking the compliment.

"Army recruitment, down off Jackson." He reclined in his seat, one arm draped across the top of the neighboring chair, as if accustomed to claiming ownership and space at will. His posture launched a wave of arrogance stronger than his spicy cologne. "You should come by sometime. We could use a smart, beautiful woman like you in the Women's Army Corps."

A giggle bubbled through her. "You see me in the *WAC?* Marching around all day in khaki?"

J.T. gave her figure a brief scan, no doubt picturing her out of a uniform rather than in one. "Just think about it, sweetheart. You could help out our soldiers by doing more than singing to 'em." The implication might have been offensive had he not continued so smoothly. "Besides, you seem like the kinda girl who'd like to travel, see the world. Sydney, London, Rome. Maybe Hawaii? White sandy beaches, luscious palm trees. Water so blue and clear you could spot a dime at the bottom."

His pitch sounded as rehearsed as that of a Fuller Brush salesman, but the vision towed Betty's mind into a drift regardless. Life could certainly be worse than living in a tropical haven. Too bad military enlistment was a requirement. She'd sooner become a lumberjack than run around playing soldier. Why, for the love of Mike, some women tried so hard to swap roles with men, she had no idea.

"I said order up!" the chef bellowed.

She pushed out a sweetly appeasing voice. "Coming," she answered, abruptly reminded of her unglamorous servitude. The chef's call should have taken priority, given his grumpiness tonight, but she couldn't bow to another command before enlightening someone, *anyone,* of her overflowing potential.

Posture lifted, she peered down at the sergeant. "Thanks for the offer, but I already got plans," she stated, as though he should have expected as much. "I'll be traveling with the USO, soon as a spot in a touring group opens up. So I'm sure I'll be stopping in all those places you mentioned." She added with a wink, "Even drop you a postcard if I have time." In reality, all the Hedy Lamarrs and Marlene Dietrichs took overseas priority. But the possibility of joining the tour was the main reason Betty had auditioned for the USO, and she wasn't about to give up the chance at a better job—a better life—no matter how slim.

"Well, if things don't work out," he said, "come on by and see me. Or, even if you wanted to chat about other things, besides the military . . ." He trailed off, inviting her to fill in the blanks.

"Wessel, there you are!" A GI appeared at the front door beside two rather refined-looking girls. To top it off, they were knockouts, which J.T. seemed to note in less than a blink. "We're hittin' O'Toole's. Ya comin', or what?"

The girls whispered to each other, then giggled, a sound that drew the sergeant from his seat like a snake to a flute. Not until reaching the exit did he rotate back, as though suddenly recalling Betty was there. "Like I said, you oughta come by."

She layered on a smile. "Yeah, sure." *In your dreams,* her mind added. Jerks like this reminded her why she'd be better off with a real gentleman—like Morgan, that soldier from the dance. Because mysterious and chivalrous deserved to beat out suave and dreamy every time.

Not that they always did, of course.

As J.T. and his gang strolled gaily past the diner windows, Betty tried to imagine a hundred ways to put the nitwit in his place if given the chance. But before she could come up with a solitary one, a gruff warning from the chef took another stomp at her pride.

✺6✺

"Charlie! Where are you?" Morgan screamed, pain grinding his throat. He rubbed his eyelids with the back of his hand and strained to focus. The gray smoke of mortar explosions burned his nostrils.

"Charlie!" His voice melted into the bursting of artillery shells and hammering of machine guns. He fought off a cough. The taste of tar coated his tongue. He spat and missed the water, hitting the sleeve of his fatigues. Black, grainy liquid.

Waves were riding him mid-thigh. Ocean waves. But he couldn't feel the chill. Too numb, too filled with terror. Too confused by how he and Charlie had ended up separated.

He clutched his M1 rifle to his chest and plodded through the bloody sea, the water like a flood of molasses. Leaning every pound of his body forward, he pushed toward the hazy beachhead. German bullets zipped past his ears. He ducked his face away, grasping his net-covered helmet. Behind him, miles of Allied ships, now tattered floating tombs, dappled the ocean. Infantry hung like soiled rags off bow ramps. Uniformed corpses plugged jagged holes in landing craft.

Morgan refocused and resumed his march, until something bumped his knee. He gasped at the sight. A swarm of dead bodies hovered beneath the surface of the water. Their unseeing stares reached for him, pleading for help too late. Boys, all of them, too young to be soldiers. Still, here they were, cut down by machine-gun fire. Drowned by the weight of their own field packs.

Staggering from dizziness, he trudged onward. He searched for pillboxes camouflaged in the trees overlooking the shore. Not a bunker in view, but he knew they were there, preserving the merciless rage of Wehrmacht troops awaiting his approach.

Once at water of knee-high depth, he hurdled the waves with his weighted boots. The suction of wet sand suddenly yielded. He stumbled out of the ocean and onto a quilt of fatigues covering every inch of the beach. Was he the only GI left standing?

The question retreated as he plowed through the patchwork of helmets and weapons, of crumpled bodies lying facedown in the gritty sand. A mortician's waiting room for fallen heroes.

He dropped to his knees in a bucket-sized gap, tossing his rifle aside. He yanked back on jacket collars for a glimpse of their faces. Blood trickled from their gaped mouths. Gashes, bullet holes, missing pieces. The stench of death seared his senses, folded his stomach in quarters. And their eyes, their glassy eyes, shining hollow, like tinted doors entrapping their souls.

"Morgan. . . ." A hoarse whisper seemed to cry out from the heavens.

He flew back on his knees. "Charlie?"

"Morgan. . . ." The voice drew nearer, echoing as if spoken from the base of a well.

"Charlie!" he shrieked, searching, searching. "Where are you?"

A fatigue-clad arm shot up from the pile of bodies. The sandy hand grabbed hold of his shoulder and shook him.

"Morgan, wake up."

The unexpected words jolted him back to their French campsite. From the milky light of the moon, he could see his brother, wrapped in a blanket an arm's length away.

"You okay?" Charlie asked groggily.

Yeah, Morgan mouthed without sound. The terror of his dream tapering, he forced a dry swallow and nodded.

Charlie yawned as he rolled onto his other side, adjusted his head on his elbow.

The duty had always been Morgan's, waking his brother from nightmares. All those months after their mother's death, he would climb up the bunk-bed ladder to interrupt the kid's tossing and turning.

When had things become so backward?

Morgan blew out a quiet, shaky exhale, his muscles as taut as tucked Army bedding. He swept a glance over the mounds bivouacked around him: his slumbering squad, spread throughout the pasture like grazing cattle.

He rested the back of his hand on his forehead and inhaled the familiar smell of dewy meadow. He'd find it soothing if not for the distant barrage of artillery fire, or the vengeful explosions of Hitler's "Buzz Bombs." Not quite the sounds of summer nights on the farm.

From star to star he drew imaginary lines, struggling to erase the haunting pictures flipping through his mind. Considering how many images there were, it was hard to believe only two months had passed since their troop transport ship left New York. For twelve days they'd sailed in the dank, creaking chamber, zigzagging to avoid wolf packs of German subs. Poor Charlie had rarely been sick a day in his life, but the Atlantic's unforgiving pitch and roll made up for lost time; his waistline shrank two belt loops before the ship had anchored.

"Good thing we didn't join the Navy," Morgan had joked. Charlie hadn't laughed.

Looking back, Morgan almost laughed himself, remembering how eager they'd all been to reach the living nightmare that waited across the English Channel. His squad had arrived on the Norman shore well after the D-Day invasion, but the gruesome crime scene still invaded his dreams. Even now, the memory of bodies washing ashore sent a chill zipping up his spine.

Then again, the thought of death sometimes offered a strange sense of peace. A morbid notion, perhaps, until you're at the tail end of another twenty-mile march beneath the hot French sun, with sixty pounds of gear bound to your chafed, raw back, your feet swollen and bleeding, your stomach knotted from K-rations. All elements of an Army conspiracy, Morgan decided, to make battle an appealing prospect.

An effective strategy, as it turned out. At one point, he'd been suckered along with the rest of them. Like a kid awaiting a parade, he too had lined the road to welcome the tarpaulin-covered convoy. No one seemed to mind that the front line was the next scheduled stop.

Over winding roads, their truck had bumped and groaned. They'd snuck through the black of night with taped-over headlights, getaway cars preparing for a heist. By the time they unloaded in Brezolles, Morgan was certain the torturous hours of marching or waiting for action would surely rival those spent in combat.

The theory didn't last.

In three-foot-deep foxholes, he and Charlie had dueled trapped members of the German Panzer army, closing the Falaise Pocket like a tube of toothpaste. Though tens of thousands of Kraut soldiers had been captured, a hefty number escaped through the gap. Both a success and a failure. The essence of war.

The battles were far from over, but the amount of bloodshed Morgan had already witnessed could soak the earth to its core. He'd learned there was no limit to how violently men and their machines could deconstruct the human anatomy. How desensitized people could become. How barbaric it all was.

Now, studying the dirt road cutting through the meadow, the road they'd be tackling at daylight, he feared what other lessons war had in store for them.

"Charlie," Morgan said in a loud whisper. Unable to sleep, he wanted someone to talk to. He tapped his brother's shoulder. The kid didn't move. Not even a break in the rhythm of his heavy breaths.

How was it that he rested so peacefully?

Maybe in Charlie's dreams they were somewhere far away. A safer time, safer place, where the air brimmed with warmth and the lullabies of crickets. They were kids back in their dad's Iowa fields, dozing out in the open, naming shapes made of stars in the sky. A sky that offered them promises, futures as limitless as the universe.

A sky that lied.

❧ 7 ❧

Late August 1944
Chicago, Illinois

The gilding of the room amplified the stiff formality at Liz's table. In the corner, a string quartet played Rachmaninoff over silverware clinking on fine china. A tuxedoed host at the entrance relieved a woman of her fur stole while waiters slipped in and out of the kitchen that smelled of grilled steak and spices. Diners nodded and murmured and lobbed laughter back and forth like a tennis ball in a never-ending match.

"All done here, miss?" The waiter gestured with his upturned hand, the movement as groomed as his mustache.

Liz opened her mouth to decline, but Dalton replied for her. "We both are, thank you."

Why on earth did he choose a place as fancy as this if he wanted to eat at drive-in restaurant speed? Had she known he was in a hurry, she would have bypassed the vegetables and savored the marmalade chicken first.

Liz pressed up a smile as the waiter retrieved their plates. The distraction of eating gone, she bounced her leg under the table-cloth, keeping time with the drumming awkwardness.

Dalton took a long drink of red wine. Tabletop candlelight traveled through his crystal glass and cast severe shadows across his face. With the chiseling of his features, it wasn't a stretch to imagine him draped in a toga, orating before the Roman Senate in another lifetime.

"Was your steak all right?" she asked, attempting conversation.

"Come again?"

"You only ate half your dinner. Was something wrong with it?"

"It was fine. I just had a late lunch." He offered a lean smile, then popped his second Rolaids of the evening into his mouth. If it weren't for knowing heartburn ran in his family, she might suspect she was the cause of his indigestion.

Sipping her lemon-wedged ice water, she glanced to her side. A middle-aged couple, necks adorned in a bow tie and pearls, sat silently at the next table. Engrossed in their meals, they sliced, chewed, and dabbed their mouths with white linen napkins. They had to have been married fifteen, twenty years. No children, Liz guessed. Just a small, yippy lapdog waiting at home. The woman would knit next to the radio while her husband read the paper before they retired to opposite sides of the bed.

Liz tried not to stare, but she had exchanged so few words with Dalton over dinner she began to feel as though they had more in common with the neighboring couple than each other.

Dalton drained his glass and contributed to their small talk, finally. "Did you end up with all the classes you wanted?"

"For the most part. I was hoping to take the one on Yeats, but it was still full."

"That's great." He glanced over his shoulder.

Had he heard a word she'd said?

"Dalton, I said I *didn't* get into the class."

"Oh, right. Sorry. I'm just looking for our waiter."

She hoped he was planning to ask for the bill rather than the dessert menu.

"Dalton Harris, how the heck ahh you?" A deep male voice encroached on their table.

Dalton shot to his feet, accepted a handshake. "Mr. Bernstein, it's a pleasure to see you."

A swath of the man's slicked gray hair fell over his temple as he slapped a palm on Dalton's shoulder. He reeked of cigar smoke and old Boston money, and the button closing his pin-striped suit jacket appeared ready to launch should he laugh too hard.

"Did you just arrive?" Dalton asked.

"Just finished up. Dinner meeting, you know. All hobnobbing and politics. Not a romantic evening like yours." He motioned his double chin in Liz's direction.

"Please," Dalton said, "allow me to introduce my girlfriend, Elizabeth Stephens."

Mr. Bernstein gave her hand a cordial peck. "Nice to meet you, missy."

"Thank you, sir."

"Her father is Professor Emmett Stephens," Dalton pointed out, "a recent transfer from Northwestern to Georgetown."

"Ah, yes. I believe my son, Warren, took one of his classes way back when. History, was it?"

"Classical literature," Liz replied, then risked a peek into Dalton's eyes to make sure correcting the gentleman was acceptable, an act she immediately regretted. When had seeking his permission become a reflex?

"Literature. Of course," Mr. Bernstein said. "Well, no time for amusing folk tales anymore. Right, Dalton? Not with law school keeping you as busy as it does my own boy these days."

Amusing folk tales? Liz's jaw coiled closed, and thankfully so. She was feeling less and less inclined to refrain from slinging retorts labeled "brash" by the charm school Julia had attended.

Dalton folded his arms, wholly absorbed. "Warren is in his second year at Harvard now, isn't he, sir? And already published in the *Law Review,* I believe."

"That's right," the man said, surprised. He looked down at Liz. "Sharp as a tack, this one is. You hang on to him, and you just might end up our nation's first lady. Right after Warren's presidential term, of course." When he chuckled, Liz dipped her gaze to the taut thread securing his coat button, hoping for a fracture in the monotony.

"I believe you mean his *terms,*" Dalton said. "Re-election would be a given."

Mr. Bernstein slanted a grin toward Liz. "What'd I tell you? Sharp as a tack."

Dalton delivered a low, hollow laugh that grated on her ears, one he had developed when the campaign began. It was an imitation, she now realized, akin to a man of Bernstein's build. Even Dalton's chest appeared slightly puffed to enlarge his medium frame.

"You two enjoy the rest of your evening." The fellow shook Dalton's hand. "And you stay on top of those studies. We're going to need men like you to lead when those boys get shipped back after the war."

"I will, sir. Thank you."

While other girls might, Liz never felt a bit embarrassed over her boyfriend's lack of uniform. She preferred his safety to the unknown. Apparently so did his father, who'd made it clear that the primary obligation of his only son was to carry on the family name. That the nation would best benefit from his political prowess, not the sacrifice of his blood. With Mr. Harris's connections, a deferment, or stateside defense job at most, was a surety should Dalton ever be drafted. A relief to Liz, on one hand; on the other, frustration that the decision wasn't viewed as his own.

"Good night, Elaine," Mr. Bernstein said to Liz while leaving. "Oh, and son"—he turned back, bumping a busboy in passing—"tell your father to give me a call. We'll see what we can do to get that man the seat in Washington he deserves."

Face alight, Dalton nodded. "Any support would certainly be appreciated."

Another shark reeled in.

Dalton was in the midst of sitting down when their waiter returned and set a dome-covered plate before Liz. She peered up at the man. "I'm afraid there's been a mistake. I didn't order any dessert." Her desire to get home squashed any craving for a decadent torte.

Without a word, the server removed the lid in a grand arc, the dome pinging above his head.

Obviously, no one was listening to her tonight. She would be better off skywriting a message. "Sir, I said I didn't order—" The objection died on a gasp, strangled by the sight of the small box on her plate.

A sterling box.

For a ring.

Dalton reached across the table and clasped her hand. "Elizabeth." He spoke slow, articulate. "We've known each other for as long as I can remember."

Her hands tingled with fear of where this was leading, of sentences resembling a life-altering speech. She focused to hear him over the quick thumps of her heart. Every word carried a pulse. She strained for each vital syllable, to confirm that merely an early birthday present lay before her. Or a Christmas gift—in August.

"Thanks to our grandfathers, you were the little pest I was stuck playing with every summer." Nostalgia seeped into his voice. "For years I thought of you as a kid sister. But eventually, it became clear our friendship was destined to grow into something more."

A proposal. It was a proposal. Too soon, it was too soon!

"Dalton," she stage-whispered, "I thought we were going—"

"To wait, I know. But there's no reason we can't make our plans official now. In less than two years, I'll have my degree and you'll have enough credits to graduate early. Still top of your class, knowing you. Then we can finally start our lives together. With my practicing law, and your professorship, we'll be . . . unstoppable." He smiled, eyes twinkling like sapphires.

"But my father—"

"He's already given his permission."

The statement clattered in her head. "He what?"

"He said so long as you had a degree in your hand first, we could sign the marriage license whenever we wanted."

Her life, in an instant, became a runaway train. The velocity left her breathless. "You spoke with him?"

"On the phone last week. Told me he was absolutely delighted."

Absolutely delighted. Did he use those very words? Ones that conveyed an actual emotion? The image of her father wearing an expression in the realm of happiness slowed her thoughts, lessened her alarm. His acceptance of Dalton, though established long ago, had never implied such zeal. Perhaps with the inclining prominence of the Harris family, their marriage could resuscitate her father's approval.

Certainly, she favored that possibility over the alternative: his delight but a form of relief, her wedding vows marking the end of his parental obligations.

Dalton slid from his chair and knelt before her. He picked up the box and creaked open the lid. "This ring has been in my family for four generations." He pulled the heirloom out of the turquoise velvet tuck. A beveled emerald shone at the center of the star etched into the gold band. Five small diamonds winked between each point. "If you'll have me, Lizzy, it would be my honor to pass it along to you."

Either the restaurant had fallen silent or shock was hindering her hearing. No tinking of silverware, no lobbing of laughter.

He peered into her eyes. "Elizabeth Stephens, will you marry me?"

The question burned in her ears, its heat stretched down her neck. Her tongue was cold, absent a reply. She glanced over Dalton's shoulder, stalling to produce her answer. Against a swagged velvet curtain, their waiter stood at attention. She wanted to ask him to open a window before the pressure bowed the fabric-lined walls. But the bottle of champagne in his hand, surely intended for her table, indicated his task card was full.

"Elizabeth?" Dalton said.

She returned to the ring, then to Dalton's face. When he leaned forward a fraction, candlelight brushed a caramel glow over his skin, erasing the hard lines on his forehead. Before her eyes, he reverted to the boy she'd grown up with. Dalton Harris, her childhood friend. The one who spent a week by her side when she had chicken pox, playing jacks while stuffing themselves with Baby Ruth bars. The same one who taught her how to ice fish and took her to her first dance. The guy who'd held her hand at her grandfather's funeral.

And now, here he was, matured into a man, offering his devotion and security. What girl in her right mind would say no?

Liz drew a breath. Under the gaze of the entire room, she smiled. Then nodded.

Applause erupted as Dalton guided the ring onto her finger. It was halfway on when her knuckle resisted the band. She winced from a second push. A feeling of self-consciousness stirred inside, an itch she couldn't reach. Was the coliseum of spectators interpreting the mismatched size as a bad omen?

"I think it might be a little small," she said quietly.

"It's okay, it'll fit." Determined as always, he twisted the band one way, then the other, as if the solution were a matter of angle.

"No, Dalton, really." He shoved harder, pinching her skin. "Ow!" she cried, halting him.

He raised his eyes, and his whole body sighed. "I'm sorry," he told her. "This isn't going the way I'd planned." His crestfallen tone released a rush of compassion in Liz, and, in its wake, regret for misjudging his behavior throughout dinner.

"It's no problem." She shrugged. "I'll just have it resized." Smiling, she shifted the ring onto her pinkie. "Until then, this should work."

Soon a beam returned to his face. He pulled her hand toward him and stood to embrace her. The audience caught a second wind and clapped louder.

"I love you, Lizzy," he said into her ear.

She closed her eyes, relished the familiarity of his arms, his musky scent. "Me too," she replied, holding him tighter.

This was right. This made sense. You didn't need chills or flutters or illusionary magic from a fleeting dance. Just the loyalty and devotion of someone who cared. Any other notions were better left as daydreams.

Of this she was certain.

8

Two Fridays in a row, and still no sign of her. That was the thought still scratching at Betty's mind as she waited at the bus stop on Michigan Avenue. Nobody at work could recall how many years Irma had been frequenting the diner, eating in that far booth—*Irma's* booth—but it was long enough to leave an arresting hole when she didn't show two weeks ago.

A cross-country trip. A visiting relative or a seasonal cold. These were the theories tossed among the staff like hamburger patties, kneaded and molded as reasons for her absence, shaped into the most tantalizing form. Yet as much as Betty strained to visualize the woman pleasuring in a lengthy train ride, or painting the town red with a long-lost cousin, she simply couldn't. The possibility of a severe cold, on the other hand, the flu maybe, was the only explanation upholding Betty's hopes after the first missed Friday.

Then a second one passed without the arrival of Irma. Dear, quiet Irma, who wore her aged solitude as elegantly as her silver flapper hat, her tarnished brooch.

Why did her absence bother Betty so much? She barely knew the woman.

Betty tried her darndest to flick the pointless concerns aside. It was Monday afternoon, the heat rising. Her feet were moaning from a morning shift that ran an hour over. Due to meet Julia soon for a matinee, she aimed her focus on getting home, peeling out of her diner uniform, lemon-washing the smell of grease from her hair.

But then an image of the young couple from that morning returned, another set of customers with the audacity to invade Irma's booth. The recollection stung like a slap.

Could it be that life was no more precious than a streetcar, trudging round and round on a loop? A schedule to keep, no time to grieve over a single lost passenger.

"Nice, eh?" A man's reedy voice came from beside her. A suited stiff, he grinned with teeth befitting a horse. "This weather we're having. Rather nice, eh?"

She glanced at the sky, surprised to find it endless in blue. Somehow an overcast gray seemed more appropriate. "Yeah. It's swell."

He pushed his glasses up the bony bridge of his nose. "So, do you live around here?"

Not a chance, buster. Especially not today. "Ah, look!" She threw a glance over his shoulder. "I see a friend, but it was great talking to you." Her feet were already in motion before she'd concluded the fib. Thankfully, only his reply chased after her as she zipped away to hide within the farthest cluster of strangers.

Safe out of his eyeshot, she checked her watch. Her standard impatience revved louder than the passing cars. A little boy halfway down the block, tap-dancing for change, wasn't helping; the quick ticking of his shoes contrasted the creeping speed of every second.

She should have taken the "L" train. No way would she have time to bathe before the matinee. If only she had the means to roam the city with speed and style—like the two older ladies there, emerging from the revolving door of a hotel. All pearls and white gloves, they radiated with an air of high-society Brits. From the side, the taller one looked so much like . . . could it really be . . .

Irma?

Betty's eyes froze wide as she studied her. It seemed an eternity before the gal turned toward an approaching taxi. A full view of her face clarified the lunacy of the notion. Still, just to be sure,

Betty watched while their doorman helped exchange passengers. Out of the cab, he guided the hand of an Army nurse, roughly Betty's age. The sun threw a spotlight onto her crisp white hat, her blue and red cape. The older women—neither of them Irma—smiled at the girl and nodded in approval.

No. More than that: admiration, respect.

Acceptance.

They looked at the nurse as though she were important, her purpose meaningful. As if people might actually care that she missed her Friday supper at a diner.

"Are you gettin' on or not?" a man behind Betty grumbled.

Her gaze swayed toward the bus that had instantly appeared, cloaking her in its shade. Exhaust fumes were like smelling salts to her senses. She awakened to discover the passenger before her climbing the stairs.

Betty rushed forward and closed the gap. Stepping onboard, she glanced down to grab coins from her pocket, its pastel fabric streaked with mustard and syrup and who knew what else. Same went for her pitifully roughened fingernails. Tough scrubs could wash away the grime, but not her station in life. Her mother, by example, had taught her that; had ingrained early on that Betty's ticket to prosperity lay in her beauty. All she needed was to groom herself like a rose and prepare for her prince to arrive, regal in his shiny gold buttons and polished shoes. After all, she was never going to be one of those college girls, like Liz and Julia, with the smarts and the dough. Girls who had so effortlessly attracted their Mr. Rights.

Thus she'd waited, in her mother's tiny rented room, ready to be plucked away, displayed in a crystal vase for all to admire.

But the prince had yet to show. Undependable, as all men were. Even that soldier from the dance, the supposed gentleman, hadn't bothered to write her back. It was high time she took control of the matter.

"Move your feet, will ya?" the man snapped behind her.

Her legs, she realized, had concreted on the middle step. As she paused to deposit her fare, the bus driver, too, appeared annoyed.

No question, she received better treatment when donning a snappier outfit. If the USO had provided a uniform—demanding respect, admiration—she'd wear it every day of the week.

From the thought, an idea chipped free. A brilliant idea. Utterly brilliant. "That's it," she murmured to herself. Floating, revolving, the solution came solidly formed, as if waiting all along to make itself known. Why oh why hadn't this occurred to her before?

"Hey." The creep behind her huffed. "I've got better things to do than stand here waiting all day."

A solid grin overtook her lips from the surety of her plan. She pivoted around. "So do I," she announced, then pushed past him and marched down the block.

ᑌᑎ 9 ᑌᑎ

"Get down!" the man shouted into the darkness.

Julia ducked a few inches in her chair. It took her a moment to realize the stranger was merely yelling at latecomers, silhouettes obstructing the movie screen.

She quietly laughed at herself. Apparently, she hadn't fully shed habits gained from those first jittery blackouts in the city, back when the war was a ubiquitous intruder crouched just outside the door. When, at any hour, another wave of General Tojo's planes was expected to hail greetings across America, a nation vulnerable in its paranoia.

On the home front, a gradual semblance of safety had returned. The battles were a million miles away. Or at least that's how far the distance seemed separating her from Christian.

She'd been used to his absence, before the war. With his living in Michigan, weekly letters and stretches of longing between visits became the standard after they met three years ago. He had been working in Chicago for the summer, a soda jerk in his uncle's drugstore, and she thanked every day since for a cherry Coke craving that had led her through those doors and into his life.

The very thought of him now made the seat beside her feel even emptier.

Oh, bother, where was Betty? The newsreel had already begun: Allied infantry streaming into a village, a drumbeat added to increase the drama. As if local casualty lists in the newspapers weren't dramatic enough.

Twisting around, Julia scanned the aisle in search of the blonde, then craned her neck to see the balcony above. Beneath the projector's tunnel of light, only a scattering of couples came into view, each in the midst of a thorough tonsil check. Couldn't they wait for the feature to begin? And why did all the guys appear to be sailors?

Julia flopped back against her chair. She should have met Betty at the house instead. It wouldn't be the first time the girl had gone to the wrong movie palace.

Usually, Julia had no issue seeing a picture alone. Only when Christian was the one beside her—bringing her undivided attention to his soft lips on hers, the shawl of his arm—could her focus be swayed from the featured films. All those glamorous characters, exhibiting the latest fashions, entangled in heart-melting romances. They wouldn't so much as jump off the screen as suck Julia in to enjoy them firsthand.

Today, though, even the riveting newsreel had to vie for her interest. She felt her irritation spreading like a rash. A mounting impatience, a clock ticking in her ear. The war should have been over by now, she thought for the hundredth time. She wanted the complications to end, the life she was building with Christian to resume and soar.

A reflection of the same thought played out in the images before her. Freed European villagers flickered in black and white. Stories poured from their eyes. They'd held on to but a thread of hope, and now they could finally grasp the tapestry of their future. With outstretched arms and gifts, they welcomed the liberating GIs. Young girls waved American flags. They were pretty girls, exotic in their features. Girls no older than Julia. Elation brightened their faces; their gazes swam with gratitude.

But just how far did their tokens of appreciation go?

A terrible thought.

Simply terrible.

But it was one Julia couldn't help dwelling upon now, surrounded by sailors whose groping hands and searching mouths bobbed like buoys in the shadows. If this was how they conducted themselves back at home, imagine how they acted after months at sea, after being welcomed by those young, exotic girls willing to twirl around far more fabric than a flag.

The room suddenly turned sweltering. Dots of sweat met the inside collar of her blouse, the lining of her skirt. The clasp on her garter itched. She needed to stand, to move. In an instant, she was striding up the aisle and out the theater. Sunlight choked her vision as she breathed deep of the city air.

She was being silly, letting her imagination scuttle away like this. She couldn't have asked for a more devoted beau than Christian. Regardless, with his handsome face and athletic shape, not to mention his dapper uniform, there was no question he would be tested at some point.

That's what this was: a test. Just like their long-distance relationship had always been. Just like the internship offer she had yet to decline.

Only days away from autumn, her deadline imminent, and still she had provided no answer. She'd savored the mere possibility weeks longer than she should have. This, she now realized, was the rash, the ticking clock. This was the test of their love. And the response she would give—today, she'd go there today—would determine if she passed or failed.

The brick academy loomed like a haunted mansion. At the base of the entrance steps, Julia's momentum hit a wall. On her way from the theater, her mind had flipped through article after article, recollections from *Woman's Day* and *Good Housekeeping*. Her husband would come first, above all. His needs, not hers. Christian, of course, wasn't ever one to limit her choices, which was exactly the reason she needed to do this. Because he wouldn't ask her to. Because love required sacrifice. And, if nothing else in this world, she knew she wanted to be a good wife.

"Are you going in?"

Julia tracked the voice to the gal behind her, lustrous with her sleek ponytail and crisscross dress. Tangerine fabric with snaking copper buttons billowed like foam at the upper edge of her hand-held bag. A daring new design.

Are you going in? the girl had asked.

Was Julia going in?

"I don't know," she heard herself reply.

Understandably, the stranger appeared confused.

Julia glanced at the doors, and a sudden fear came over her. Certainly, the idea of disappointing her instructor had prolonged the answer; Simone had put her faith and reputation on the line. But now it was the challenge—perhaps impossibility—of saying no, should Julia dare to step foot into her beloved classroom again.

Maybe that had always been her true cause of hesitation.

Julia turned to the girl. "Could you pass something along for me, to Madame Simone?"

She shrugged. "Sure. I'd be happy to."

Not permitting herself another thought, Julia pulled from her purse a small notepad. She scribbled the same words that had been waiting from the start.

> *Dear Madame Simone,*
> *Thank you again for all you've done, for everything you've taught me. But I'm sorry. I simply can't.*
> *Yours sincerely,*
> *Julia Renard*

Immediately, Julia handed off the note and walked away. A pound of angst dissolved with every step, and to her relief, she felt no urge to look back.

❦ 10 ❦

Late August 1944
Chicago, Illinois

Although vacant for lunch hour, the room felt full around Betty, gapless with her teeming eagerness. The fan oscillating on the file cabinet spread equal attention across the office. A futile attempt to loosen the knotted heat. From its ticking blades, a gentle gust ruffled a browning fern in the corner, stacked documents on the neighboring desks.

This was meant to be, she told herself while waiting in her seat. Having barely caught the sergeant on his way out was a sign: Her life would soon be turning around.

Giddiness, which had sprouted during her rush from the bus stop, flourished now as she studied the posters, an array of Army recruitment plastering the wall. She'd seen them a million times—the vibrant drawings of gorgeous gals in uniform, posed before waving flags, proclaiming a need for women with Star-Spangled hearts. Then there was the portrait of old Uncle Sam, in dire need of a visit to the barber, scaring boys into the service with his menacing eyes and accusatory finger.

Until today, though, it hadn't dawned on her that those messages were also meant for *her*. Not the way they were intended maybe, but in the same realm.

"Afraid we don't have anything stronger than water round here."

The uniformed sergeant approached with a pair of paper cups and handed one over. Easing into his desk chair, he reclined with the same cloying arrogance he wore when they'd met at the diner. He didn't deserve to be as good-looking as he was.

"Water's perfect, thanks," she said, and drew a polite sip.

"So tell me, Betty. What brings you down to my neck of the woods?" Smugness lingered in his smile. It was clear he believed she'd hunted him up in hopes of a rendezvous; no doubt plenty of other girls had done the same. Awaiting her answer, he took a drink, eying her as if examining a rack of lamb at the butcher shop.

That's when Betty realized why she had actually remembered his name: J.T. Wessel sounded remarkably similar to *Just a Weasel*. Fitting. She could have opted for another recruiter, but seeing J.T.'s reaction would be worth every second.

She straightened in her chair, and with her chin determinedly set, she reported, "I'm here to enlist."

His cup crinkled slightly in his grip. He pulled his water away and cleared his throat. "I'm sorry, did you say you—"

"Wanted to enlist." Evidently, his enticing pitches about overseas service had filled his little black book more than his enlistment quota. She grinned with satisfaction. "Why, yes, I did."

To his credit, he gathered himself quickly. "I see," he said. Then he scrounged a pencil from his torrent of papers. "Did you have a particular area in mind?"

"As a matter of fact, yes." Time to unleash her idea on the world: essentially, a civilian's role with all the perks. "I'd like to sing," she replied.

He went still for a moment before raising his head. "You . . . wanna sing. For the Army." Confusion stretched his words, his eyes. She was rather enjoying this.

"The Army has bands, doesn't it?"

"Well . . . yes . . ."

"Then it should have vocalists as well. Obviously, the USO sees the importance of singers in raising soldiers' morale. I think the Army would agree, don't you?"

He opened his mouth, but no argument formed, which only fed her confidence to continue.

"The military believes in promoting entertainment. Otherwise, it wouldn't have the likes of Joe DiMaggio playing baseball for the Armed Forces. And I for one don't see how this is any different."

J.T. nodded slowly, as if receiving the information through Morse code. Then a broad grin returned. "Betty, I'd be happy to look into that. For now, though, let's just get some basic paperwork going." He poised his pencil. "How about we start with your full name and age."

Right away, she rattled off her information, enunciated all but her middle name—"Betty Jo" sounded like such a hillbilly.

"So you just turned twenty?" he confirmed.

"That's right."

"In that case, as you probably know, you'll need parental permission."

"Say again?"

"Since you're under twenty-one." He scribbled and looked up. "Is that a problem?"

A problem? He could say that.

But how could she tactfully phrase that her father had been some married guy who'd split before she was born, and that her mother, the fool who fell for him, was the last person Betty wanted help from? Besides, her communication with her mom had slimmed to mere holiday cards years ago, after Betty was dumped on relatives in Evanston—supposedly a means to curb the high schooler's rebellious nature.

At least in the end, with all her aunt's plastic-covered furniture and earmarked Bibles, Betty had realized that living with a mother who was home every minute of the day, versus always out working like her own, could be just as miserable.

"My mother," Betty explained, "actually lives in Kansas." She couldn't say the state name without it sounding raspy and rushed. Like a sneeze from a cold she couldn't kick. "Do you need to see her, or is there any other way?"

"We do need her signature in person, but I could send a local recruiter to get it."

"Great," she said, before catching the disappointment ground into the word. She was about to divert with a peppier sentence when the clicking of footsteps interrupted, saving her.

"Afternoon, Sergeant," a uniformed female called from the doorway. She was hardly as attractive as the Women's Army Corps on the poster, but was just as magnetic. Everything from the shiny captain's bars on her shoulder loops to her authoritative chin commanded attention.

J.T.'s posture stiffened like a pole. "Ma'am."

"Busy recruiting, I see?"

"Yes, ma'am."

"Nice to see you've been paying attention." After a brief pause, the captain produced a chiding smile. "Back at it, then. We need every fine lady we can get." She tipped her billed hat at Betty and strode into her office, shutting the door behind her.

How fascinating to see a woman in power for a change, specifically over a man.

A down-to-business look tightened J.T.'s face, only an ounce of resentment leaking through. He glanced back at his document. "So tell me, is there any other area you might be interested in?"

"*Other* area?"

"Outside of singing, that is. An alternative you might consider."

She was about to say no—why would she need one?—when he added in a whisper, "Just have to put something on paper. A formality for the file."

"Oh. Oh, right."

He resumed his spiel. "You know, there's lots of exciting things you can do in the WAC, and with skills you already have. For instance, do you know how to drive?"

She shrugged. "Never been a need, with me living around Chicago."

"Sure, sure," he said, understanding. "How about cooking? You like to cook, don't ya?"

"Once in a while. Unless it requires heat."

He started to laugh, then stopped when he saw she wasn't kidding. Betty was tempted to explain. But there was no sense relating the hazardous brownie episode that could have burned Liz's house to the ground. She swiftly pointed out, "Cold things, though, are a breeze."

"Uh-huh." He dragged in a breath. "What about typing?"

"Mmm, not really."

"Shorthand?"

"Nope."

"You don't . . . speak another language?" The doubt in his voice made the question rhetorical.

She shook her head anyway.

"Didn't think so," he murmured, before shifting to a lighter tone. "Well, like I told you, there's loads of exciting duties out there. Everything from weather forecasting and glass blowing to working as a control tower operator. Even issuing weapons. Sounds pretty good, doesn't it?"

Not really, she wanted to say, but held back. The reply could come off as unpatriotic, which she undoubtedly was not. On the contrary, she was no less patriotic than, say, that nurse near the bus stop. What with her fancy cape, her white exclamation of a hat, both serving as badges from years of schooling.

Oh, there had to be another option. Something similar yet more appropriate for her personality. Granted, it was just an unlikely backup she was choosing, but Betty preferred not to have anything remotely ordinary in her file.

She then thought of her roommates. For extra spending money, Liz and Julia held jobs in a nursing home—a semi-medical field— and they'd never indicated it being strenuous.

"What about hospital work?" she asked him.

"If you mean the Army Nurse Corps, the Red Cross handles all—"

"No," she broke in. "Just something like it. But without the blood and mess. And not all that long, tedious training. After all, I *do* want to help out before the war's actually over." She smiled.

The fan in the corner ticked away the seconds. A useless breeze passed by.

J.T. gave his head a weary rub. Lacing his hands on the desk, he sat forward as though it took great effort. As though being back in action would be a relief in comparison. "Look, Betty. You're a nice, pretty girl . . ."

She cringed at the familiar phrase. It had been a favorite from her guidance counselor, a guy who smelled like pickles and always ended their conversations with a verbal pat on the head, a *why don't you run off and play with your dolls* conclusion.

Though tempering herself now, she interjected, "Are you trying to say that pretty girls can't be WACs?"

"Of course they can," J.T. countered. Then he threw a conspiratory glance around the empty room and continued in a hushed tone. "You already got a gig as a singer, right? Why not just focus on that, sweetheart, and forget about all this Army stuff. Didn't you say something about touring with the USO, trotting the globe?"

The USO tour. The aspiration she had so often boasted about. Suddenly, tossed back at her in the presence of her filthy diner dress, the possibility seemed stripped down, naked in its unlikelihood.

"But I wanna help," she managed to assert.

"And I'm sure you'd be great at . . . something. I'm just not confident the Army is the best place to utilize your talents."

Like serving malts and meat loaves was?

"Thanks for coming by, though. It was swell seeing you." That cocky recline again. "Hey, maybe we can go out to dinner some night, after one of your shows."

Disgusted by his nerve, she couldn't bring herself to reply. She stood up, head pressed against the ceiling of her crushed hopes, and started for the door. When she reached for the handle, however, a harsh truth slammed into her, one she never saw coming:

She needed this. Needed the change, needed to escape. Even if it didn't involve a stage. She was no Ella Fitzgerald, she knew that. But that didn't mean one patronizing heel should stand in her way of finding her prince—and how could she not in a tropical paradise? Plus, if she was able to help the war effort in the process, all the better.

Betty swung around and found J.T. flipping through a magazine. Hand posed firm on her hip, she smiled. "Sergeant," she sang out. "I was curious. Do I need an appointment to meet with your commanding officer? Or should I just knock and see if she's free?"

His expression bent. "'Scuse me?"

"I thought she might be interested in hearing how a recruiter, in this particular office, turned away a perfectly willing and capable enlistee. And how, instead, this same recruiter used his work hours to seek out a date."

He looked toward the captain's closed office, then back at Betty. Setting his magazine aside, he shoved on a tight smile. "Come to think of it," he said, "I might've been too hasty. Why don't you have a seat? I'm sure I can find the perfect assignment for you." He picked up his pencil. "A hospital, did you say?"

"That's right." She sat down with a triumphant smirk. "And I believe you mentioned something about palm trees. If memory serves."

❧ 11 ❧

September 1944
Belgium

"You ever gonna write the dame back? Or you just gonna keep reading that damn thing till she forgets she even sent it?" Frank's voice tugged Morgan from the wrinkled letter in his hand. Again, he was back to the stale-smelling grime of soldiers and warfare.

"Haven't decided yet," Morgan admitted.

"The gal's a bombshell. What's to decide?" Jack said, perched on his upturned helmet on the cobblestone road. Teamed up with Frank, he shuffled his worn cards for another round of euchre, their latest pastime between orders. "Hell, if you're not gonna write to her, then I will."

Charlie tossed a couple Lucky Strikes into the betting pile. "Now, there's some motivation for ya," he said to Morgan. "No girl deserves *that* much punishment."

"Here we go again," Morgan mumbled. Their very own Abbott and Costello.

"You know, Chap," Jack said, "it must be hard for you. Having to use humor to compensate for your physical shortcomings. And I ain't talking about just your height."

Morgan laughed along with Frank, who reached past "Mouse" to give Jack two pats on the shoulder for that one. "Ahh, Callan," Frank told him, "it's nice to have you back."

And that was the truth. The guy had gone missing after the chaos of a recent battle. In a leapfrog push toward the Meuse River, their unit had no choice but to continue on and hope for the best. Days later, Charlie's greeting upon Jack's return—*Glad you finally found your way from the Piggly Wiggly!*—seemed to aptly convey their unified relief.

"You planning to deal those cards anytime today?" Charlie prodded in return, apparently at a loss for a comeback. "'Cause I'd like to collect my winnings before sundown, if you don't mind."

"You hear this, Mac?" Jack puffed on his cigarette. "Your brother thinks he's actually gonna win one."

"Something changed we should know about?" Frank asked Charlie.

"Yeah." He grinned. "Mouse, here, has a few extra jacks up his sleeve." With a bantam frame and thick glasses, the new replacement had been a chess and pinochle champ back home, making the kid Charlie's new best friend.

Frank pinned Mouse with stone-cold eyes. "Is that right?" he demanded, the GI cowering.

"Y-yes, right. I mean, no. No, I ain't got nothin'."

"Swell." Frank winked. "Then we're gonna get along just fine."

Although entertained, Morgan felt his focus drawn back to the letter on his lap, the one he'd read at least a dozen times since its arrival.

When the company clerk had called out, "McClain, Morgan!" during mail call two days earlier, he was baffled—until he realized the sender had to be Aunt Jean, his mother's only sibling. Three years ago, the bank had foreclosed on the McClains' family farm just months after Morgan and Charlie's father was killed in a tractor accident. Stripped of their Iowa home, they moved in with Jean and her husband in Belknap, Illinois.

The couple's only child, a boy with angelic features, had drowned at an early age, taking their joy with him. So while Morgan never expected them to correspond, he couldn't think of anyone else who'd have dropped him a line.

Then he'd read the return address.

Betty Cordell
821 Kiernan Lane
Evanston, Illinois

Several minutes of racking his brain had produced a vague image of the USO singer he had met in Chicago. He'd been so focused on Liz, the brown-haired beauty whose face only recently began dimming in his memory, he had almost forgotten about the blonde he rescued from the drunken Navy man.

Morgan now pulled Betty's photo out of his jacket, took another look. She'd been popular at the dance for good reason. With smooth, pouty lips and long lashes framing her eyes, she was Hollywood material.

He uncurled the corners of the picture, regretting he had originally tossed it into his barracks bag without care. But how could he have known? Not until he read her letter did he realize how important the memento would become.

> *Dear Morgan,*
> *Although our time together was brief, it was a*
> *pleasure meeting you at the dance. Fate can be such a*
> *curious creature, bringing new people into our lives*
> *when we least expect.*
> *The disillusionment I had as a young girl, believing*
> *I actually possessed control over my circumstances, my*
> *loved ones, my feelings, should have ended long ago.*
> *Yet, still I find myself startled by the unpredictable. I*
> *suppose, in the end, all we can do is put our faith in the*
> *notion that our journeys, despite occasional rockiness,*
> *will be more rewarding than actually reaching the*
> *destination (or so I tell myself—sometimes even*
> *convincingly).*
> *I must apologize for my wandering thoughts. One*
> *might suspect that my pen has a mind of its own. I hope*
> *my message does not belittle the challenges you have*
> *surely faced. I can only imagine the uncontrollable*

*environment in which you now find yourself, fighting
in a foreign land against our enemies.*

*The amount I know of war is but modest. Through
tales of the Great War, however, my late grandfather
taught me much about life. He once told me it was in
the shadows of his darkest hours spent in combat that
he had discovered his most valuable lessons.*

*"Until you're gliding at 5,000 feet at the mercy of a
stalled engine," he would say, "life's small worries can
carry too much importance and your loved ones too
little." I do my best to remember this whenever I place
too much weight on my own petty concerns and need to
put them in perspective. Thinking of soldiers like you,
selflessly sacrificing for the good of our country,
provides me with another humbling reminder.*

*Such was the case when I heard Glenn Miller and
Lena Horne on the radio today. The carefree evenings
of dancing to a swing band or gathering around a
jukebox must seem faded dreams to you, having been
replaced by scenes of the unspeakable. Although I
cannot fathom what you are going through, please
know that I, as a citizen whom you now protect, am
ever grateful for the service you are providing our
country.*

*It is with heartfelt wishes that I send this letter, and
with trust that it will somehow find its way to you.
Please take good care, and godspeed for a prompt and
safe passage home.*
Sincerely,
Betty Cordell

Morgan studied the flow of the cursive penned on the pages.
The feminine loops and curves had managed to seep beauty into
this masculine, war-plagued existence. But her words, her words
were what truly moved him. Their kindness, their elegance. And all
in a message he so desperately needed. In the aftermath of battle, it

was too easy to forget that somewhere out there a compassionate world still existed. A world worth fighting for. A world waiting for their return.

"Morgan," Charlie called out, "you want writing tips, you let me know. Dames go wild over my poetry."

Jack smirked. "Ah, that's right. Chap here's that famous poet who wrote—now, how'd it go? 'Roses are red, violets are blue, your tits are so beautiful, thank God there's two'?"

"Hey, asshole." Charlie raised his voice. "You of all people ought to get my poem right, given that *is* about your last date. Goes like so. . . .

> "On the breast of a lady from Yale
> Was tattooed the price of her tail.
> And on her behind,
> For the sake of the blind,
> Was the same information in Braille."

The GIs chuckled while Jack dealt his cards to the tips of their boots.

Morgan had heard his brother recite the limerick on more than one occasion; the first, before an audience of church volunteers who'd stopped by their house to drop off a basketful of pastries. Evidently, not even a few whips with their father's belt had expunged the off-color rhyme from Charlie's memory.

"What about you, Rev?" Charlie asked. "Got any hymns to save our souls?"

Frank ran his hand over the dark stubble of his two o'clock shadow. "Well, I think we all know where *your* soul's headin'. But for these other God-fearing men, I do have a special verse taken straight outta the Good Book."

"Oh, man," Charlie muttered, as if dreading a sermon offering the spiritual guidance they all lacked.

"Gentlemen, a parable often overlooked in the Old Testament reads as follows. . . .

"In the Garden of Eden sat Adam
Massaging the bust of his madam.
He chuckled with mirth,
For he knew that on earth,
There were only two tits and he had 'em."

Charlie raised his palms to the mottled sky, crying out, "Amen! Hallelujah!"

Morgan rolled his eyes. "Thanks, fellas. Real helpful. I was thinking of wooing her with some Emerson or Whitman, but you're right, smutty poems about tattooed hookers are a helluva lot better."

"Here, catch." Charlie tossed him a pen. "Now, get at it already."

"Might be out of ink, though," Frank warned, "after the huge pile of dames' letters that Chap's had to answer." He paused. "Oh, wait. He hasn't received a single one, has he?"

Charlie glared. "For your information, Rev, I got a letter yesterday. It was a note from God. Said He knows you've been fornicatin', and He wants His Bible back."

Morgan blocked out the verbal skirmish and homed in on Betty's letter. He gave the stationery a discreet sniff. A trace of lavender. Maybe from her hand lotion. Maybe his imagination. Either way, how could he not write her back?

He tucked the pages into the envelope, stored them in his jacket pocket, and pulled out a blank folded sheet. He removed the pen cap with his teeth and steadily wrote his salutation: *Dear Betty.*

That wasn't so hard.

Now what?

Staring at the paper, he raked his mind for the first sentence, something worthy enough. Sure, he'd always been at the top of his class in high school, his head filled with dreams of going to college. Limited finances wouldn't allow such a privilege, however, no matter how many books he'd read or tests he aced. He'd accepted that fact long ago. Yet now more than ever, he wished that hadn't been the case. For even a paragraph of his best, most thought-out writing couldn't come close to the eloquence of Betty's post.

And what about his topics? What of interest could he possibly offer? He was a simple boy from Iowa, with little worldly experience to share—save brutal battle accounts destined to be blacked out by military censors if he dared put them to paper.

He needed a pep talk.

If you ever want another letter from her, you're going to have to send one back. So pull up your bootstraps and get it over with.

No more thinking, he told himself. Instead, he gripped the pen and commanded his hand to write the first words that came to mind.

❧ 12 ❧

October 1944
Evanston, Illinois

Liz ascended the porch steps at sloth speed compared to Julia. In the entry, the redhead dropped to her knees, schoolbag discarded, and scooped up envelopes from the metal door slot. She scanned them as hastily as a postal worker two days before Christmas.

"I don't think the mail was going anywhere." Liz giggled as she stepped around her friend's doodle-covered notebook. Though fashionable sketches adorned each one, the variants of Julia's future married name dominated in quantity and bold lettering—a visible reminder of how her priorities and Liz's differed.

"There's nothing from him," Julia reported. "Again." A grave catch in her voice turned Liz from unloading textbooks at the kitchen table. Darkness flashed in Julia's copper eyes. "You don't think . . ." Her words faded into a harrowing abyss.

"Of course not, don't be silly." Liz's standard consolation—despite her concerns. "Besides, didn't you get a letter last week?"

"It's been *ten* days."

"Well . . . military mail gets delayed sometimes, you know that. A few weeks ago you got three at once, right?"

"Yeah," Julia breathed. "I guess so."

"And," Liz added, "he's probably been busy with other little things like—oh, I don't know—keeping a destroyer afloat."

A thoughtful beat passed. Then Julia returned a smile, slow but full. "You're right. I'm sure he's fine." Rising, she brushed the dusty knee marks off her A-line skirt.

Liz nodded her assurance, and before it could fade, she made her way to the living room. The scents of vanilla and potpourri clinging to her grandmother's floral drapes made this her favorite part of the house. Nestled in the rocking chair, she kicked off her Mary Janes and rolled her feet around in the shaggy strands of the sage throw rug. "Nana's green spaghetti," Papa used to call it, just to make Liz giggle.

Through the window, she spotted a bird perched on a branch: a brilliant red cardinal. She closed her eyes. No sharp metallic chirping, only the rhythmic creak of the antique rocker. Little by little, she wiped the chalkboard of her mind, erasing lectures and equations her professors had crammed into the day. This was exactly what she had been waiting for, a quiet moment to relax.

"Hey, I got a letter from my sister!"

Liz groaned, squeezed her eyes. She thought about making a break for her bedroom and barricading the door, but realized that would require moving. Instead, she listened to Julia enter the room, then rip and rustle paper. Liz savored the silence that followed, brief as it would be, before the highlights began.

"Claire says to congratulate you on your engagement . . . says Mom's already buying out every store in the city for Elsie's first birthday, telling clerks she's the next Shirley Temple. Dad's been working his fingers to the bone as usual . . . and they'd love to hear from us both when I get back from Michigan."

Liz had nearly forgotten Julia would be leaving for Union Station within the hour to visit Christian's family.

"You're not sleeping, are you?" Julia demanded.

Liz gave up. She rubbed her tired eyes back to life and discovered Julia on the Empire love seat across from her. "How could I possibly sleep with all that world-changing news?"

In all honesty, she loved hearing about the bustling activities of the Renard household. The rapid growth of U.S. Steel, as a result of the war, had required executives like Mr. Renard to relocate to their central headquarters in Pittsburgh, a short car ride away from Julia's sister and her blossoming family.

Sometimes, Liz wondered if she missed having the Renards nearby even more than Julia did.

"Say what you will," Julia told her. "But deep down you secretly adore all my gossip. And you know that life without me would be dreadfully boring."

"Yeah, yeah, so you've said."

"Then we agree." Julia's voice vibrated with optimism. "You *have* to come to Flint with me."

Liz veiled her face with her hands. Why did her bedroom have to be a thousand miles from this chair? "I thought we covered this already."

"We did. But for some silly reason, you haven't said yes."

Liz lowered her fingers to peer at her. "That silly reason is called 'homework.' Perhaps you've heard of it?"

"Ah, homework, shmomework."

Easily said when you're among the "matrimonial scholars." For half the engaged females on campus, their degrees weren't a means to a career, solely proof of being a well-rounded wife.

"Liz, there's no reason to moon around here. Dalton's traveling with his dad all weekend. And since you'll be planning a wedding too, we could chat about the details."

Angst balled in Liz's chest at the thought of her ever-expanding checklist of nuptial duties, compliments of Dalton's mother—who, incidentally, would much prefer if Liz also belonged to the "matrimonial scholars" club.

"First," she told Julia, "Christian's mom is interested in *your* wedding, not mine. Second, I've got a lab project to finish and a huge exam on Wednesday. Not to mention over a hundred pages we still have to read for Professor Carpenter's class."

"The solution is simple. You could study on the train, like me."

Liz dipped her chin for a doubtful look. "That's precisely what you said last time. But with all *your* chattering . . ."

Julia sagged into the cushion, defeated. "Please, you have to come. Ian is back home. You know how much he hates me."

So that's what this was about. Christian's older brother. The infantryman must have finally been released from an overseas hospital after fighting in Italy.

"I'm sure he doesn't hate you," Liz offered.

"He thinks I'm a snob."

"Did he say that?"

"No," Julia said. "But I can feel it. He'll be joking and laughing, then I walk into the room and his mood completely changes."

"Have you mentioned any of this to Christian?"

"He says I'm imagining it."

"Well," Liz ventured, "maybe things will be different, now that Ian's been away so long."

Julia shrugged. "We'll see." She sounded unconvinced.

The draw of being needed, a near-forgotten sensation, would easily have swayed Liz's decision if her degree wasn't the only incentive.

"I'm really sorry, Jules. I wish I could."

"I know, I know. Valedictorian and all that." Julia rolled her eyes, bouncing back in her usual style. "Too bad Betty isn't here. She'd be packing your things as we speak."

"Ah, yes." Liz smiled. "Florence Nightingale to the rescue."

Both Liz and Julia had assumed Betty was kidding when she'd mentioned joining the Army. The idea of the fickle blonde climbing cargo nets, scrubbing floors with a toothbrush, and doing calisthenic drills had made Liz laugh repeatedly. Right up until the day she found Betty packing for basic training. Borrowing from Liz and Julia's occupational know-how, their roommate had finagled her way into a hospital clerk position, fast-tracked for a warm Pacific island. Obviously, the Army recruiter was of the male persuasion.

"So what else is in there?" Liz tried not to stare at the mail on Julia's lap. But the push-pull of dread and hope escalated as she waited to hear if a new note had arrived from her father.

"What else is in where?" Julia asked, before glancing down. "Oh, yeah." She laughed at herself, an ability Liz always admired, and began flipping through the pile. She listed them off one by one: utility bills, a postcard about a new store, standards from the college. Nothing personal.

By the stack's end, Liz almost felt more relieved than disappointed.

Almost.

"Oh, here's one more." Julia picked up an envelope. "It's for Betty, but it's hard to tell who from. The ink on the return is smudged." She squinted, deciphering. "Looks like it's . . . PFC . . . M. McCrann."

It took a moment for the right name to register. When it did, Liz's heart contracted, skipping a triplet of beats. "What'd you say?"

"I don't know. Something like that." She held out the post for Liz to read.

Oh, murder. It was *him*.

Private First Class Morgan McClain.

Nearly three months had passed since Liz had mailed him a letter. *Three months.* She had reached the clearing, crossed into the safety zone. They were never supposed to hear from the soldier, so why—

"Liz?" Julia said twice before Liz recovered her voice.

"It's, um . . . M. McClain."

Julia studied the name again. "Ah. You're right."

The fuzzy strands were now strangling Liz's toes.

"Hey," Julia said, "isn't he the one you helped her write to?"

Helped? That was hardly the accurate word. "One sentence and Betty was out the door. I had to come up with the whole stupid thing myself." Liz caught the telling hostility in her answer, and pulled back. "Anyway. That's the last time I write anything for her."

Julia eyed her with the slyness of a cat, ready to pounce. As she fanned herself with the envelope, Liz's neck tightened under the scrutiny.

"What?" Liz said, defensive, tight. A fist of a word.

"Do you know how much fun you could've had with that letter?" Julia asked. "Like making her out to be a German spy, using the USO as her cover. Or better yet, the former wife of a resistance leader who's hiding in Morocco."

Liz shook her head, shielding her relief. "You've seen too many Bogart movies."

"Maybe." Julia gazed downward, then back up with brow raised. "So what do you think *he* wrote?"

Liz didn't want to consider it. She had no interest in what the soldier had to say.

Not a whit.

Not at all.

"It's none of our business." The statement left an aftertaste, bitter as a lie.

"Liz, it's been eons since you wrote to him. Maybe something bad happened. Maybe that's why he couldn't write back until now."

The idea had certainly burrowed through Liz's mind, on more than one occasion.

"You can't tell me you're not the least bit curious," Julia pressed. "After all, the letter he got was from *you*."

"That doesn't change the fact that the one in your hand isn't addressed to me."

"A minor technicality."

"Minor?"

"Gee whiz. It's not like she'd care. She probably doesn't remember anything about him but his uniform. In fact, you know as well as I do that if the milkman wore khaki, she would've run off with him a long time ago."

Liz grinned, more at the truth of the claim than the outlandish image.

"So," Julia said, "just a peek, then." She teetered the envelope in the air. Eve showcasing the forbidden fruit.

Liz's expression dropped. *"No,"* she told her.

Julia flailed a loose curl with a puff of air, and relented. "Okay, you're right. It would be wrong, purposely opening someone else's mail."

Somehow Liz didn't feel the relief she should have felt. She was about to redirect the conversation—to Ian, to Christian, even to weddings—when Julia's hand flew to her nose, stifling a sneeze.

"A-a-a-chooo!" She doubled over from the force. "Excuse me," she said, then looked down and gasped. "Great Scott, how did that happen?"

Liz traced her friend's gaze to the now-unsealed envelope. "Julia. Frances. Renard."

"What?" Her eyes widened in shock. "It was an accident."

Liz glared. However, her impulse to put the redhead in the corner was only slightly greater than her desire to read the pages inside. Exposed, calling her name. Well. Not *her* name exactly.

"Shall I read the letter aloud, since it *is* open?" Julia's thumb rested inside the tampered casing, awaiting Liz's response. Not that her concession was required at this point.

Liz sighed. "Read it already."

Julia smiled, victorious. "Since you insist." She tugged out the letter and flattened the creases before beginning. " 'Dear Betty, I'm sorry for taking such a long time to answer. From your postmark, I see you sent—' "

Bang! Bang! Bang!

Strong-fisted knocks caused the girls to jump as though their seats were spring-loaded.

Julia glanced at the cuckoo clock on the wall above her. "Blast it, that's my taxi." She tossed Morgan's pages onto the coffee table and dashed around the corner. "Just need to grab my bag!"

Liz was halfway to the entry when the second set of knocks rattled a shelf full of Nana's porcelain Kewpie dolls. "I'm coming, I'm coming!"

At the door, she greeted the craggy-faced cabbie. His response of a grunt made it clear he preferred a short route to an extravagant fare. He skulked back to the North Shore cab parked along the curb with engine idling.

Julia came barreling out of her room, cloche hat over her curls, luggage tipping her shoulders. From the sides of her brown rectangular suitcase dangled swatches of colorful garments. She must have plunked her entire body down on the overpacked container to close it.

"Aren't you only going for three days?" Liz laughed.

"They'll be my in-laws soon," Julia reminded her. "I have to keep up a good impression." A quick hug and she tottered out of the house.

Liz waved good-bye as the taxi took off like a pitted stock car reentering the track. She hadn't so much as shut the door when a voice whispered in her mind: *All alone in the garden.*

The words led her thoughts to an image.

Morgan's letter.

Splayed bare on the table.

Perhaps Julia was right; maybe something had happened to him. He could have been hurt in combat. A wounded patriot sharing his woes. And who knew when Betty would be back to find out? Nobody could guarantee what "the duration" would be. Six months, a year, two years from now. Besides, with Julia gone, the duty of resealing the envelope fell to Liz. What difference would a quick scan make before rubber cementing it closed?

The letter *was* already open.

Grasping reasoning that would soon slip away, Liz sped back to the living room. She picked up the papers and hopped into the rocking chair. The cushion remained warm, as if expecting her return.

> *Dear Betty,*
> *I'm sorry for taking such a long time to answer. From your postmark, I see you sent your letter back in July. The only thing more amazing than how long mail can take to reach us is that it reaches us at all. I'm certainly glad yours did. Your words really lifted me up and reminded me of the world we left behind.*
>
> *It's funny what I've come to miss these days—the murky swimming hole by the old bridge or Sunday suppers of corned beef and cabbage. I remember hoping that just once we could eat something different on Sundays, that my dad would find another favorite meal that wasn't so Irish. Now, stuck in the middle of a war-blasted country, all I can think about is having it again!*
>
> *Of course, I'm not the only one reminiscing over food. Seems like all the fellas here have wish lists of*

what they're going to eat the second they get home.
We've spent hours on end talking about chicken 'n'
dumplings and glazed meat loaf and chocolate chip
cookies hot out of the oven like my mom used to make.
Probably sounds foolish to you—torturing ourselves
with what we can't have. Then again, if you too relied
on canned Spam and cold green beans to get you
through the day, I bet you'd jump right in. Boy, what
you miss when it's gone.

Some evenings over here while camped in a pasture
there have been moments I almost believed I was back
on our farm. And for a few seconds I get the old feeling
of relaxing on a tractor at the day's end, with the engine
off and my head laid back, just taking it all in. Did you
know you can actually feel the sun going down if you
shut your eyes and sit perfectly still? I never told
anyone that before. Guess I kept it to myself like it was
some big secret, since most folks only enjoy a sunset
with eyes wide open. Not that I blame them. The
evening sky can sure be calming with its mix of bright
colors. In the midst of battle, sometimes that sunset is
the only proof we've got that there really is a God. Who
else could make something so beautiful?

When I was a kid, my mom once told me that God
was an artist and how on occasion He'd throw a
bucketful of paint across the sky for us all to see. I
asked her why the paint disappeared by morning, and
she told me that if the sky was always like that we
might take it for granted. I suppose she was right.
Maybe that's what war is all about—so we can
appreciate times of peace.

These are just some of the thoughts that crossed my
mind when I read your letter. Those jukebox days and
radio tunes you mentioned—they do seem far away
now. Thanks to you, though, I'm reminded they're still
out there. I wish we could get back to them sooner than

*later, but unfortunately that's not up to me. As you
said, we're given little say-so in life. Now in the Army,
I realize that more than ever. Guess I'll just have to
focus on the things I <u>can</u> control, like keeping my
brother on track and sticking to the belief that we're
going to make it home in one piece.*

    *Anyway, I'd best sign off. Thanks a million for
sending such a wonderful letter. Already I look forward
to the arrival of your reply.*
Kindly,
Morgan McClain

Liz sat in silence. With such openness, his candor infectious, the
letter was unlike any she had ever read. His tender words channeled the memory of his voice. His descriptions, inciting mental
brushstrokes, transported her to another place. On that tractor
he'd held her in his arms, the sun gracing their faces as its rays descended beyond the fields. If only she could stay in that world, continue to see life's beauty through his eyes.

She hugged the page to her chest.

What was she to do? Allow a post like this to go unanswered?

A soldier risking his life for their country at least deserved a response. Besides, there was no question Betty would have retracted
her oath and begged for help in writing him back. The handwriting
needed consistency, after all. And if Morgan ever sent another one,
Betty would be thrilled that Liz had taken it upon herself to sustain
their correspondence while—

A sparkle interrupted the thought, the binding sparkle of an
emerald surrounded by five diamonds on her left pinkie. She ran
her thumb over the ring she had described to her father on the
phone.

I'm delighted. That was his response when she shared her news,
the expression almost identical to the one Dalton had relayed. No
yelp of joy or twenty-one-gun salute, but based on the scale of her
father's limited emotional range, he was pleased.

She placed Morgan's letter on her lap. Her eyes retraced his words. No doubt, her father would be far from delighted if he knew what she was considering. As would her mother, if she were around to intone her disapproval.

Then again, it wasn't as though Liz would be breaking any rules. She wasn't *lying* to Dalton. And composing a note on someone else's behalf certainly wasn't cheating.

Or was it?

~~ 13 ~~

October 1944
Belgium

"I'll do it!" Morgan replied so fast the words smeared into a single syllable.

Lieutenant Drake flicked an acknowledging nod. His gorilla-like build filled the dark archway that had once featured the front door. The house was one of the few in the Belgian village to still have the majority of its stone walls and roof. A relative mansion.

"No firearms or helmets! Only edged weapons!" Drake barked as if Morgan were a hundred feet away rather than ten. According to rumour, the guy's overpowering volume was the result of a grenade explosion in Saint-Lô that had deafened one of his ears. Morgan, though, suspected that the commander's inflated ego was just as much to blame. "Briefing outside the command post in five minutes, Private!"

"Yes, sir."

Drake spun around to leave.

Morgan rubbed his hands a final time over the potbellied stove. Glancing at Frank and Charlie standing beside him all nice and warm, he realized what a numskull he was, snagging the last spot for the midnight recon patrol. Out of instinct, he'd volunteered before his brother had a chance—for weeks the kid had been antsy for an assignment more exciting than message running and telephone guarding—but with the cold temperature and six-inch-deep mud, no way Charlie would have spoken up.

Too late to reconsider. Morgan wasn't about to say, *Hey, Lieutenant! Never mind!* He wasn't that much of a numskull.

He threw on his moist, mildewy jacket, wishing he'd laid it out to dry earlier. In the back corner of the room, he carefully unclipped a trio of pineapple grenades and placed them in his helmet, next to his propped rifle. Behind him, Jack was pilfering a pile of debris-smattered belongings—civilians' lone shoes, tattered books, jagged records. Abandoned normality.

"Hey, get a load of this," Jack exclaimed, approaching Charlie with his find. He held its serpentine handle, displaying the large white porcelain bowl brightened by a castle scene in colonial blue. "Thing looks like a big ol' teacup. Gotta be from the Brits, don't you think?"

"It's a thunder pot, *Jack*-ass," Charlie corrected him.

"A what?"

"You know. To take a crap in."

"No way," Jack shot back, studying the item. Then, "Shit."

"Precisely, genius."

Jack tossed it back onto the heap, his face contorted. The handle snapped off upon landing. The rim cracked.

At the wooden block near the doorway, Morgan paused to grab his only permissible weapon. He'd found the trench knife and worn scabbard in a cupboard, and the blade had proven razor-sharp at suppertime. Unfortunately, arming himself with the knife didn't lessen his unease; stripped of his usual gear, he still felt as naked and defenseless as a newborn.

"Be careful out there," Charlie stressed in his direction.

Morgan nodded once, a confident gesture.

"Goddamn it, Chap." Jack snatched his socks off the stovepipe. "You said you were gonna yank these off for me before they started smokin'."

"What am I, your mother? Watch your own damn socks."

"You just wait, ya little pissant," Jack said, inspecting them. "If I find one hole burned in these, we're swapping and they're gonna be *your* damn socks."

"You two ever shut your traps?" Frank growled. "I swear to God, it's like living with two old biddies."

These were the last words Morgan heard as he ventured down the cobblestone road.

In the center of town, the volunteers huddled around their commander, a quarterback calling a play. Drake gave explicit orders not to engage the enemy, just to scout the vicinity and report back before dawn. Simple enough.

Morgan joined in with another programmed *Yes, sir*.

After a few minutes of memorizing the lieutenant's map, they received their general area assignments and, not to be forgotten, the daily secret password. While it lacked the steel moxie of a loaded tommy gun, it provided the promise of safe admission into and out of their territory, patrolled by American sentries.

Personally, Morgan preferred to have both.

The group trailed behind Drake in a single-file column, silent surveyors. Shadows thick with memories draped crumbling houses and decaying orchards, blasted farm fields. While being pushed out by the encroaching Allies, a German army had poisoned the wells and crops, slaughtered every animal in sight. Apparently, if the Krauts couldn't have the Belgian territory, they'd make damn sure it had nothing left to offer.

At the village border, the men dispersed. Morgan knelt on the cold ground and began a long, taxing crawl reminiscent of the basic training drills he despised. He'd grown up in the dirt, entrenched in farming soil, never guessing he would loathe it as he did right now.

He slithered on his stomach through the muddy terrain of a heavily wooded area. Night creatures rustling, the smell of damp moss engulfed him. Fear festered inside, a low-grade fever, so constant he hardly noticed its presence.

"Laurel," a male voice rasped from the invisible outpost, prompting the designated password.

Morgan strained to see farther than ten paces ahead in the tar blackness. "Hardy," he lobbed back. Cleared by the guard, he continued on.

The moon glowed dim and yellow through a thin break in the clouds. Arms tiring, he alternated between a hunchback's walk and a crawl. He trusted his hands more than his boots to detect a trip wire.

Soon, from his left, came the distant gurgling of a stream. The sound revived memories of the creek near his uncle's farmhouse, of those summer afternoons he'd spent perfecting his rock-skimming pitches. He smiled at the image of Charlie hunting for crayfish, gathering a bucketful to toss into the hair of girls he liked at school. They were hot, humid, carefree days that Morgan now missed as his mud-encrusted uniform drank up pools of rain left from the daily downpours.

For hours, he edged his way through an obstacle course of rocks and branches, mounds and trees. Area assessed, he was ready to head back to the assembly point. Empty embankments and a couple rank, bloated bodies of dead Wehrmacht soldiers were all he'd found. Nothing significant to report, and he liked it that way.

He rotated and started to retrace his path toward the village. It took only twenty feet, however, for him to realize he had lost his way along with his sense of direction. Every tree, stump, and boulder he'd noted as bread crumbs on his outbound trail now appeared cursedly identical to all the others around him.

Focus. He just needed to focus.

With a steadying breath, he chose a route he wanted to believe looked familiar. He plodded warily through the woods. Darkness amplified nature's sounds, twisted them into a solid mass pressing against his neck; there it remained until he spotted a wide clearing. The invisible rope cinching his shoulder blades loosened a notch. In no time, he'd be slipping back into their heated palace, able to knock off some shut-eye before breakfast lineup at the mess tent. The thought of food made his belly growl.

"Yeah, yeah," he muttered to his stomach, just as men's laughter echoed through the forest. He hugged the ground as a precaution, listened for the sound of GIs chatting it up. The voices drew nearer, but the words came in slices and fragments. Nothing he could make out.

"Warte, ich komme gleich wieder!"

Holy Jesus! They were Krauts!

Morgan jerked his hand toward his belt to grab his loaded pistol.

No firearms or helmets! Only edged weapons! The lieutenant's words hit him like a sledgehammer.

Shit! Shit!

The chances of fending off more than one soldier with a hand-held blade were slim, and required a proximity that petrified him. But it would be his only option.

He reached for his trench knife, preparing for what he'd have to do if discovered. Across the throat, into the heart . . .

He patted the leather casing. Patted it again.

Empty! It was gone, the knife was gone!

His thoughts tumbled over themselves. It was there when he— but how did it—

No time for questions.

Pores opened on the back of his neck, the crown of his scalp. Sweat trickled down his face. His knife was out there somewhere in the mud and would soon be a German trooper's souvenir. Just like him.

Dear God, please help me, please help me.

The snapping of twigs closed in. At least one of the Jerries was headed in his direction. Morgan's heart pounded so hard he feared the enemy might hear it. He wanted to run. Oh Jesus, he wanted to jump up and run.

Body flat. Eyes down. Don't move. His father's calm but firm warnings floated up to the surface of his mind. The very same words had saved Morgan's life as a kid, the night he'd surprised a black bear investigating their family's campsite.

Closer and louder, more twigs snapping. With only a thick tree dividing them, he could feel the Kraut's shadowed form, the messenger of death.

Morgan clenched his eyes, willing his body to fade into the soil.

Our Father, Who art in heaven, hallowed be Thy name—

A sound entered the air: the splattering of liquid. He opened his eyes to a squint, saw no one. He cricked his neck toward the right edge of the tree and caught his first glimpse of the foe—a gray-uniformed German only a few feet away, taking a leak, gazing up at the branches.

Two Wehrmacht soldiers stood in the background. They slurred some comments to their comrade before staggering off. In tandem, the pair belted out folk songs as though Oktoberfest had replaced world war. The smell of their cognac sickened Morgan, not for the scent, but for proof of their arrogance. Celebrating, at a time like this!

Then again, drunkenness impaired coordination. A surefire advantage. Maybe the Kraut wouldn't notice if Morgan just lay still. Better yet, he could outrun him. But where to? He didn't know where the hell he was.

As he shifted his torso to keep out of sight, something jabbed his rib. He shoved his fingers into the mud and found a fist-sized rock. A caveman's weapon. He gripped the stone with every ounce of strength within him.

And he waited.

The soldier's stream seemed in contention for a timed record breaker.

Finally, the splattering trailed to an end. Morgan reaffirmed his grasp on the rock, a grasp for his life. When the buckle of the trooper's belt clanked, an exhale crept from Morgan's mouth. Hope was growing. Just a few seconds more. The enemy would leave and Morgan could flee undetected.

Then at last, the Kraut turned around. He stumbled a couple steps before his boot caught a jutting tree root. Arms too slow to react, he fell onto his side with a squish. He raised his head, two feet from Morgan.

Their eyes locked.

The Jerry opened his mouth wide. He was going to scream for reinforcement. From a dark cellar in Morgan's mind came a single word:

Survive.

He swung the rock with all his might, a blow to the Kraut's temple. He struck again, harder. The sound was nothing he was prepared for; it was empty, inhuman, like hitting a hollow log with a baseball bat.

He raised the stone once more. This time he held it suspended in the air. Panting, he awaited movement. Several minutes and still his enemy lay motionless, eyes open, head firmly planted, a cracked boulder in the earth. Adrenaline tempted Morgan to strike him again, but humanity grabbed hold of his wrist, lowered his shaking hand to the ground.

On the trooper's belt, he spied the nub of a pistol. A Luger. To hell with Drake's firearm policy!

He dropped the rock and reached for the weapon, like a starving man scrambling for food. If he were taken prisoner, possessing the Luger would bar any possibility of mercy. But he was willing to take his chances.

Now to get his ass out of here.

Slowly, he peered around the tree, keeping the loaded pistol pointed at the Jerry's head. A German camp had to be close by, yet the starless night swallowed the view.

In the distance, a light appeared. A flame, floating on a current of black air. Into its orange glow came a harsh-angled face. It was another Kraut, a sentry on patrol, igniting a cigarette. Muted voices indicated the guy wasn't alone, but still far enough away to give Morgan a chance to escape.

Aware of every muscle, he eased his right knee backward. Then his left, and—

Snap!

A twig split beneath him. Pulse thrashing, he buried his face in the mud. Terror froze his mind, his body. Thoughts hovered beyond reach. Only when his lungs threatened to burst did he allow himself a small pocket of oxygen. The metallic smell of blood and cognac strangled his gut.

He gradually lifted his head and listened. No murmuring, just the diminishing rustle of boot steps. He released a breath, unable to tear his gaze from the corpse before him. Its black, soul-spearing eyes stared at him.

And then the trooper blinked.

Morgan double-gripped the pistol. Beneath muddy eyelids, he

watched for chest movement, a twitch, a reason to pummel the German with the butt of his own gun. He waited on edge, nerves bunched, long enough to confirm he'd imagined it.

The guy was dead, soon to be worm food, his flesh eaten away underground. The vision launched bile up Morgan's throat. He muffled his dry heaves with the image of a Nazi firing squad.

Sure, he'd slain his share of Kraut troops. But not until tonight had he ever lain beside any of his victims. Not until now did he realize the detachment of shooting faceless, armed enemies from an anonymous distance wasn't a luxury extended to hand-to-hand combatants.

Morgan shoved down the pointless thought. What the hell was he still doing here? He had to move out before the others went searching for their friend. Soon dawn would lift the felted cover of night, hand-delivering Morgan to the Jerries on a breakfast platter. Black bread, sausages, and a lost GI.

Once more, he peeked around the tree. The area looked clear. If he was ever to make it out alive, now was his chance.

As he inched his way backward, his fingers snagged on canvas. He risked a glance downward and found a long strap beside his hand, connecting to a haversack. The trooper must have dropped the bag when he fell.

Making it out of here at all would be a miracle; who's to say there wasn't a flashlight or compass inside?

He slung the strap across his torso and continued his ebb, his gaze fixed on the blood streaked on the man's face.

No—not a man. A Kraut. Who would've gladly done the same to me.

The message looped in Morgan's mind like a scratched gramophone record. When he reached an estimated safe distance from enemy territory, he scoured the inside of the haversack, searched by feel. A book and pencil, a tin cup, candy wrappers, some bread. He opened the issue folder he'd found.

A map, it was a map!

If only he had enough light to make sense of the damn thing.

Morgan chucked the folder back inside and shifted the bag to ride piggyback. He crawled away as fast as his knees would shuffle, praying he'd sense a mine before discovering one the hard way.

The croaking of frogs and stench of stagnant water eventually led him to a sizable pond. He envisioned its placement on the vague map stored in his memory. Based on his recollection of the village's position—three o'clock from the murky pool—he angled his steps toward what he hoped to be the road leading back to camp. He mumbled profanities at the trees that invaded his straight path, the same obstructions he blamed for his detour.

An hour later, the sound of rushing water returned. The stream he'd passed at the start of his patrol was beckoning him home, sweet as the clang of his mom's rusty dinner bell. The world lightening to a hazy gray, he was able to make out more of his surroundings. He proceeded with caution until he reached the Allied border. Cleared by the sentry, he hurried down the GI-guarded roads of the village. Faster, faster, like a horse nearing the stable.

He half expected his roommates to be pacing with worry, but when he entered the heated dwelling, only quiet praised his presence, as if nothing had happened, as if nothing had changed. Except for him.

Around the room his buddies lay sprawled on makeshift beds: Sheets and towels covered the kitchen table, a mattress on the floor, a lineup of dining room chairs. They expelled the soft snores of peaceful slumber, forgetting the hell from which only sleep allowed temporary escape.

Morgan tucked the Luger into his belt, pulled off the haversack, and leaned against a stony wall. Caked with mud from head to boots, he slid downward until he was seated among the pebbles and dust. He clasped his hands, his fingers as tired and stiffened as the rest of his body.

And he prayed.

Dear Lord, I know I shouldn't be asking for more, especially now. But please, I'm begging You. I'll do anything, anything at all. Somehow, just get me and Charlie through this.

He mouthed *Amen* and dropped his hands.

Beside him, the contents of the bag peeked out as though trying to sneak away. He zeroed in on the Soldbuch, a treasure among booty hunters who collected the personal pay books—essentially wartime passports—like baseball cards. Another notch in their belts.

Though not sure why, Morgan wiped his muddied hand on the back of his jacket before picking up the book. An army eagle atop an encircled swastika marked the tan cover. Identity documents were rarely discovered anywhere but in a German soldier's tunic pocket. Did he want Morgan to know who he was?

Compelled by a morbid urge, he flipped through the pages that detailed the Jerry's military information. A life summarized in lists and numbers. A quarter of the way through, a black-and-white picture slipped out. He picked it up. A woman sat posed in a photographer's studio, hands layered daintily in the folds of her full skirt. At her side, two young boys boasted shorts and knee-highs, slicked hair and button-down shirts. The soldier, in dress uniform, stood proudly at attention behind her. They withheld smiles for the formal portrait, but an air of pleasantry shone in their expressions.

Morgan studied each of their faces, searching for features as evil as the blood he'd been convinced ran rampant through their Nazi veins. But there were no fangs or claws, no wicked snarls. They were merely a family. One just as easily from Duluth as from Dresden.

Feeling short of air, he rubbed his chest. He tried without success to pry loose the invisible grip on his lungs.

Maybe the trooper hadn't been celebrating, after all. Maybe he'd turned to liquor to forget the horrors he'd seen, to drown the loneliness and fear he suffered from leaving his loved ones behind.

The attack replayed in Morgan's mind, gruesome, irreversible. An act destined to bring a lifetime of grief to the German's unknowing widow—and for two now-fatherless children.

Tears channeled to the surface and poured down his cheeks, an unstoppable current of confusion and fear. Fear about himself, of what he'd become.

Suddenly Charlie stirred.

Morgan stuffed the picture into his pocket along with his emotions. Drying his stubbled face with his sleeve, he glimpsed a flare of color. Red. The reddest shade of blood. It clung to his wrist in droplets no miracle potion could erase. Each mark a gory reminder of the father, the husband, the man, whose life he had stolen.

Please forgive me, Morgan pleaded, eyes raised upward. It was then, in the numbing silence, when he finally dared wonder: Were prayers of murderers, when fighting on the "right side" of the war, ever heard—let alone answered?

⨳ 14 ⨳

October 1944
Flint, Michigan

Julia braved one last swallow, thankful her plate was empty. Her jaw might very well come off its hinges if she had to chew another bite of the cardboard-like meat.

"I do wish I had more roast for you, dear," Cora apologized, seated beside her husband, George, at the dinette. The slender woman had taken none for herself, a residual habit from feeding her boys first, and therefore hadn't discovered her baking-time miscalculation for the rationed portion. Julia wasn't about to tell her.

"Actually," she assured Cora, "it was more than enough."

George snuck Julia a knowing wink, then returned to mopping the seasoned meat juice from his plate with his biscuit. He too could have been made of dough, all of his features round and cushy.

"How about finishing off the peas?" Cora reached for a serving spoon, but Julia held up her hand to stop her.

"Thank you, Mrs. Downing, but at this rate, I'll never be able to fit in my wedding dress."

"Rubbish, you're thin as a rail. And it's your last dinner with us." Her wide smile accentuated the apples of her cheeks. "At least have a little more cottage cheese salad." She rotated the lazy Susan to reach the corresponding bowl. Daffodils adorned the ceramic she had painted with ladies from her quilting group. While the petals lacked finesse, all bore the same personal touch she'd infused throughout her modest home, a dollhouse assembled piece by piece.

"One scoop or two?" she asked Julia.

"Ah, Mama, stop your fussing." George leaned back in his chair and rubbed his hair-wreathed head, as if for luck. "She's the perfect picture of health. Just look at the girl."

"Of course she is." Cora waved him off. "Still, I wouldn't want her parents thinking I ran her ragged all weekend and didn't feed her proper."

"They'll think nothing of the sort," Julia promised.

Cora sighed, a reluctant surrender. "You did save room for dessert, I hope."

"But of course." Julia spoke as though stating the obvious. "Scientists have proven dessert digests in a completely different compartment."

"Now, that's the smartest thing I've heard all day," George said, and rapped his knuckle twice on the table. "No surprise our Chris snatched up such a winner. Keenest girl in the country. Not to mention the prettiest."

Julia shook her head, blushing. "So that's where Christian gets his Sinatra charm. No wonder Mrs. Downing couldn't resist you."

Cora giggled though her nose, a little girl's laugh that never faded. "Well, I can't say he ever sang like Sinatra. But he did try to serenade me once. That is, until the dogs in the neighborhood started howling right along. My landlady had a conniption fit." She directed her attention to the right of Julia. "You remember that story, Ian?"

For a few pleasant minutes Julia had forgotten Christian's brother was there.

"Ian?" Cora repeated. "You remember that, don't you?" Desperation for a connection filtered through her cheery tone.

Ian glanced at Julia. It was only a flick of a look, making clear she wasn't worth a full second of attention. "Yeah," he said, already returned to his plate. His shaggy umber hair fell over his eyes, his thinned form molded to the chair in a slouch. He moved his fork through his scattered peas, a cold link of circles. Every spiral drained more levity from the room.

Julia pinched the side seam of her skirt. Damn him. And damn herself for still wanting his approval.

"Ian, darling, you've hardly touched your food." Cora smoothed the base of her brown chignon. Her lips upheld a worn smile. "Would you like something else?"

The scraping of his fork was his only reply.

"Enough's enough!" George snapped. His low gruff stiffened Julia's spine.

Ian's hand ceased, his eyes down.

George leaned forward. "Lord knows how much trouble your mother went to making that meal for you. Least you can do is show some respect."

Cora shot to her feet and began gathering their plates. "Please, George," she pressed in a painfully light tone, "we have company."

George remained motionless, his gaze on Ian. The air gained the weight of molten lead, the stifling intensity of a Hitchcock film.

Cora touched her son's shoulder and directed her words to Julia. "Here I've been rattling like an old wreck, asking you one thing after another. And all the while there's a pie getting cold on the counter. Strawberry rhubarb, Ian's favorite. Even used the full amount of sugar." She laid her napkin over her son's plate, topping the stack built on the daffodil dish. "You all relax, now. Be back in a jiffy."

"May I be excused?" Ian murmured.

"Oh." Cora's disappointment showed only until George opened his mouth to answer. She jumped in. "Well, of course you can, honey. We'll save you some dessert. I'm sure your appetite will improve after a good night's sleep."

Ian stood and slowly inclined his head. His eyes, though turned down at the corners like Christian's, reminded Julia of a stirred-up pond. The green-brown mixture clouded the depth and truth that lay beneath the surface. " 'Night," he said to his father.

George released a breath, and nodded. "G'night."

Julia watched Ian cross the room. With silent footfalls, he floated toward the darkness of the stairs. A shaded figure, then a sketch, he gradually disappeared.

"Would you like your pie à la mode, Julia?" Cora asked.

"Um—yes, that would be lovely." She spotted Cora's full hands. "Let me help you with those." Rising, Julia reached for the impressively balanced tower, but the woman stepped away.

"You sit right down. You're our guest, dear." Cora smiled again and hurried off to the kitchen.

Left to tread in Ian's wake, Julia quickly mined for conversation. "So, Mr. Downing," she said, "how's everything at the factory?"

Not responding, he gazed at the small bouquet of orange mums on the table, long enough to count the infinite petals. Julia was about to repeat her question, but thought better of it. Perhaps she ought to excuse herself as well.

"I have to apologize," he said suddenly. "Ian hasn't been well. If it weren't for Cora prying him out of his room, he'd never come out."

Julia couldn't help feeling a dash of comfort knowing it wasn't merely her visit that had soured Ian's mood. She lifted her shoulders and offered, "Maybe once he settles in, after he sees his friends and starts working again . . ."

George shook his head. "My boss did me a favor, setting him up at the tank plant. A few weeks and he had to let him go. Ian kept staring off into space. Other times, banging metal would make him all jumpy. Even sent him hiding under grates or behind artillery parts."

He glanced at the wall dividing them from the kitchen, keeping his voice low. "Despite what Cora might've told you, he wasn't in the hospital for a combat wound. On his discharge papers they called it 'battle fatigue.' Another way of saying my boy's crazy—just like you must be thinking." He sighed and ran his hand down his face. His helpless expression tugged at Julia's heart. "I never should've let him join the damn Army," he said as if to himself.

Julia had heard rumors about soldiers being shipped home and discharged for similar reasons. Their minds had snapped after intense combat for extended periods of time. Temporary amnesia, blindness, paralysis—all psychologically based. Imagined pains in their own bodies where they'd stabbed or shot the enemy. The varying conditions often perplexed even doctors. And without the luxury of bandages to showcase their injuries, their heroes' welcome faded fast.

"Anyhow." George's tone indicated he'd delved too far into the topic for comfort. He lowered his ample chin and peered at her. "Chris is in the Navy, and they're taking good care of him. I can vouch for that."

Until tonight, her only fear had been that her fiancé might not come home at all. Now, after seeing Ian, she worried how different he might be once he returned.

"Don't you worry." George patted her arm through her sweater. "Chris has always had a good head on his shoulders. You ask any of his coaches, any teacher he's ever had, they'd gladly tell you: 'Christian's a shining star.' Biggest problem he'll have, when he comes back, will be needing another shelf for all his decorations."

Julia nodded before he'd finished. She was more than happy to accept the testament of a former sailor. Not just any sailor, mind you. A bos'n's mate who had been awarded the Navy Cross from the Great War. A war that *should* have ended all wars.

"Say," she said, redirecting, "why don't I go see if I can help in the kitchen. I have to do *something* to earn my room and board."

"You just being here is reward enough," he told her. "But while you're at it, you tell my wife I want a double scoop of vanilla. No need to be stingy."

"Aye, aye, sir." She saluted and set off to join Cora, in need of the woman's contagiously high spirit.

The sweet aroma of baked strawberries pulled Julia around the corner and into the kitchen. "Mrs. Downing," she reported, "your husband has decreed any piece of pie unacceptable without two enormous scoops."

Cora stood at the counter, an apron tied about her waist, her back to Julia. Three plates of lattice-crusted pie wedges awaited ice cream from the opened carton. She didn't answer.

Julia stepped closer. "Mrs. Downing?"

Cora jumped, yanked from the basement of her thoughts.

"Sorry," Julia said. "I didn't mean to bother you."

"Don't be silly, dear." She swiped her hand across her cheeks, erasing evidence of her private tears. "My mind was just wandering. Happens in old age." She tossed over a pleasant glance, almost brief enough to conceal her reddened eyes.

Julia hesitated before moving toward the counter.

"Oh no, would you look at that." Cora grabbed a dishcloth with her free hand and dabbed at the elbow of her lilac sleeve. "Here you've made me this beautiful blouse, and I'm ruining it by not paying attention." A slight shake altered her voice as she worked the fabric harder.

Julia touched Cora's hand that held a small ladle. "Please. Let me do this." The woman tightened her grip, a stranger to accepting help. But Julia waited patiently. At last, Cora allowed the utensil to slide from her palm.

A small nod and Julia began salvaging the ice cream, its top layer liquefying to malted milk. She was on the third serving when Cora's face angled to hers. Sorrow and frustration appeared in the woman's eyes, a longing to bring back the family she'd lost.

A lump lodged at the base of Julia's throat.

"Julia . . . I'm so . . . ."

Julia whispered her reply. "I understand."

Cora tucked her lips and nodded in gratitude. With a loving mother's hand, she brushed Julia's stray curls off her cheek. "Thank you," she said, "for being here. It's been a long time since we've had laughter in this house."

After a pause, Cora sniffed once and puffed out a breath. Then she opened a drawer and produced three forks, smile reattached. "What do you say we eat these before they turn to mush?"

Julia grabbed two plates and stood at attention. "You lead the way."

Lying in bed, Julia flipped this way and that. Her cheeks ached from giggling along with Christian's parents at the new radio show *The Adventures of Ozzie and Harriet,* a nice break from FDR's Fireside Chats or the nail-biting reports of casualties. Although she'd downed her glass of heated milk an hour ago, its warmth still flowed through her, massaging her spent muscles. She'd packed a month's worth of activities into a single weekend: tending a victory garden with Mrs. Downing and mothers of Christian's friends; carting tin foil and scrap metal to a salvage drive; attending a bond rally at a local park.

Julia had every reason to be out like a light. Well, except for one. The fact that the bed beneath her was Christian's. As was everything in the room.

He'd been away for months, but his scent clung to the fluffy pillow: a mix of mint soap and easeful sleep. Covering the case fabric were images of baseballs and bats, their colors faded from years of laundering in the kitchen sink. He had probably been using the same bedding since he was five. No wonder she could smell his skin, his hair, his breath, in the sheets wrapped about her.

She felt his indentation in the mattress, an impression from his usual side-sleeping position. Rolling onto her hip, she fitted herself within the curves. She closed her eyes and tried to imagine his arms holding her. Just as they'd done the last night they spent together, before she and his parents had seen him off at the station.

As was proper, she had been assigned to stay in his brother's bedroom next door, with Ian gone off to war. But not even a Nazi prison warden could have kept her from sneaking into Christian's room once darkness had settled heavy over the house. She'd poked her head in, afraid he had already fallen asleep. Instead, he lay there smiling broadly up at her, as if to say, *It's about darn time, Red.*

He slid back the quilt, inviting her to join him. Questions thrashed in her mind: What did this mean? What was she consenting to? Considering the ring he'd given her, though fresh on her finger, weren't they practically married?

Nerves skittering, she closed the door and tiptoed over the chilly wooden planks. She climbed into the warmth of his blankets. Her head on his arm, they gazed into each other's eyes. He ran his hand across her cheek, then down her chin and neck. His eyes followed slowly, as if etching every angle into his memory. Her heart picked up speed as he trailed over the shoulder of her nightgown and down the bare stretch of her arm. Her skin came alive with each inch traveled. When he reached her hip, her toes curled in anticipation.

Yet he went no farther.

He threaded his fingers between hers and brought their linked hands to his lips.

"Wait for me?" he whispered, and kissed her fingertips.

She smiled gently, tears welling, and she nodded. When he smiled back, she rested her head on his chest. Through his undershirt, she heard his heart beat in a rhythm of waves lapping the shore. Waves that made no promises in a sea of the unknown.

And so they lay in the quiet, unwilling to sacrifice the moment for sleep, hoping the sun would simply forget to rise. Not until the crack of dawn did she slip out from the covers and back into Ian's bedroom, only to hear his mother making breakfast downstairs. If his parents had wondered why her eyes drooped as much as Christian's that morning, they kept it to themselves.

Now, smelling him in every trace of the room, she felt the same inability to sleep—this time regretting that on that night, or a dozen others before it, she hadn't tossed decency to the winds.

Detouring the thought, she visually collected her surroundings. Moonlight between the curtains slatted lines over photos taped to the wall. The cluster of snapshots was already stamped in her memory: she and Christian rowing a boat at Jackson Park; the two of them on the Navy Pier, sharing the sticky mess of a candied apple; a group of his teenage buddies camping at Saginaw Bay; he and Ian in raggedy trousers as kids, proudly holding up a pair of catfish on a line. Except for their heights, it was hard to tell the brothers apart. Same oval faces, pointed chins, same sparkling smiles.

Her gaze continued to roam, pausing on the shelf of sports memorabilia. An autographed baseball rested in a dark leather glove Christian was always bending and softening. First-place ribbons hung on trophies from various competitions, faced outward and neatly displayed. She began to count them, then realized they could very well substitute for sheep. By the tenth time through, she'd most certainly be out.

One, two . . . three, four . . . five—

A noise jarred her. A muffled yell. She froze and listened.

There it was again. Louder this time. And a word, indiscernible, from the next room. Ian having a bad dream?

She tuned him out, resumed her counting.

"Stop!" he said through the wall.

Oh, bother. If he kept this up, she'd never get any sleep. And she still needed time to repack her suitcase first thing in the morning. Maybe Mrs. Downing could calm him down.

Julia scooted out of bed and into the hallway.

"Get out!" Ian cried.

She glanced down the hall toward George and Cora's room. No sounds of movement or light under the door, as dark and still as the inside of a hat.

"Good grief," she muttered. Resolving this herself would be the more sensible option. His poor mother deserved a peaceful night's rest.

Julia knocked lightly on Ian's door. Then a little harder to ensure she wouldn't have to get out of bed twice.

She waited.

Nothing.

Relieved, she turned for Christian's room.

"Help me. . . ." Ian moaned.

Of all the words he could have used.

With a sigh, she took hold of his doorknob. She modestly gathered the collar of her nightdress and tipped her head into the room.

"Ian," she stressed in a whisper. "Ian, wake up."

"They're up there! Behind you!"

He was going to wake the whole blasted house.

She scuttled into his room and closed the door. "Ian," she repeated, now at conversation level.

Back and forth he twisted in the sheet, legs and elbows jerking.

She moved closer, a cautious invasion of his private space. The moon's glow from the window outlined the muscles of his bare chest, increasing her discomfort. She nudged the back of his shoulder with her fingertip. "Wake up," she told him.

He rolled toward her, his breathing uneven. His eyes twitched beneath closed lids. Still dreaming.

A last resort, she reached down and gave his arm a shake. In an instant, a violent blur, she was hurled onto her back. Ian's hands clenched her throat as he straddled her on the bed. His eyes, stretched wild, trained on his own grasp, set on destroying the enemy. She battled to breathe, pushing at his wrists, at his chest. Pressure mounted against her skull.

"Ian," she choked out. "It's *me.*"

She clawed at his fingers as her throat convulsed. Her legs kicked worthlessly beneath his weight. Dizziness and horror nibbled the gray edges of her mind.

Abruptly, Ian relinquished his grip. Air flooded her lungs. Starved for oxygen, they drank in too much. Her hands guarded her neck as she coughed. Her heart slammed into her chest wall, an aftershock of terror.

Curled in a ball, she calmed her breathing while rubbing her neck. Sore but safe. After a long moment, with concerted effort, she forced her head up. On the corner of the bed, Ian sat in his boxer shorts, knees drawn, fists pressed to his temples.

"Oh God," he rasped. "I'm sorry, I'm so sorry." Choppy breaths flowed in and out. He looked at her with an expression of vulnerability unlike any she'd ever seen. The remorse in his eyes trumped her concern for her own well-being.

Slow with reluctance, she dared to reach for him. When her hand grazed his elbow, he jerked away, an animal wary of a trap. His body shook.

Lord Almighty . . . What had they put him through?

She leaned toward him, meeting his gaze. "I'm okay." She touched his arm again and spoke with conviction. "It's not your fault, Ian. Believe me, it's not your fault."

A silent beat passed before the ridges in his forehead began to fade.

Julia stood and lifted the top of the crumpled sheet. "Try to get some rest," she told him.

He didn't move.

She encouraged him with a smile and tip of her head. "Go on, now."

Gradually, he unfolded onto his side and into place. She layered him with the sheet, then the blanket. In a final gesture, she smoothed a wrinkle in his pillowcase. As she started away, he grasped her hand, tensing her arm.

"Don't leave," he whispered.

Still cautious, she turned to face him.

"I just . . ." Despair filled his eyes. "I don't want to be alone."

She glanced at the door, considered what his parents might think if they happened to come check on their son.

"Please stay," he pleaded. "Just till I fall asleep?" His tone hinted at embarrassment from having to ask. The sound tore at her heart.

She tightened her grip on his hand, a signal of agreement. When she reiterated with a nod, he relaxed his head into the pillow.

Perched on the edge of the mattress, she watched his eyes close, his worries drift away. Shadows graced his face, creating a replica of his brother. Comfort and serenity poured over her like a hot bath. By morning, reality would replace the illusion, but for now, in this moment, her dear Christian slept beside her.

With her thumb, she gently brushed his temple, verifying he was real. "Shh," she soothed as she stroked his hair, already knowing that against her better judgment, she would stay until the first sobering rays of dawn.

❦ 15 ❦

Liz opened the front door and took a tentative step into the bee-hive. Volunteers buzzed about the room on interwoven paths. Banners and posters streaked the walls in red, white, and blue. A carpenter on a ladder hammered repairs—alternating *tap-tap-taps* and *bam-bam-bams*—over the strident rings of a phone. From signage on straw hats to campaign buttons pinned to lapels, the credo was clear: *Harris for U.S. Senate—a vote for America.*

"Are you here to volunteer, miss?" The narrow woman with a large helmet of hair emerged from the swarm, clipboard in hand. Her wide-set eyes shone with such earnestness Liz hesitated in replying.

"Actually, I'm looking for Mr. Harris."

"Ah," she said, a sharp breath. "Which Mr. Harris do you have business with?"

"Oh, excuse me." Liz had forgotten to clarify. "It's Dalton Harris I was hoping to see."

"You have an appointment, I presume?"

Liz had the sudden feeling she'd broken a cardinal rule. "No, I'm—afraid I don't."

"I see." The woman peered down the slope of her pointed nose. "I believe Mr. Harris is on a very important call to Washington at the moment. So it might be a while before he can get to you." She exuded an air of being in the know, depositing Liz on the outside of that privileged circle. "May I tell him who's here?"

"It's Elizabeth. Stephens." Then, having second thoughts, she added, "But if he's going to be tied up—"

"Miss Stephens?" Her expression illuminated as if a revelation had shot sunbeams straight through the ceiling. "Well, why didn't you say so?"

"I . . . didn't know—"

"That you're only the most talked-about couple in Chicago?"

The dramatic shift in attitude left Liz struggling for a response.

"Your engagement announcement," the woman explained. "In the *Daily Times* this morning. It's been quite the topic today. Everyone gossiping over losing its most-prized bachelor." She shook her head and sighed. "And now I have the honor of meeting the woman responsible." Despite the gal's smile, Liz felt as though she were being sized up like a long shot at the Kentucky Derby.

Liz cleared her throat. "As I was saying, I'd be happy to stop by later, if it's more convenient."

She caught Liz's elbow, tilted her head. "For you, dear, I'm certain he'll make time. Come, come, follow me." She navigated a trail around boxes and tables. Paint fumes, from what appeared to be a parade sign, assaulted the air.

Upon reaching a door across the way, the woman rapped gently on the frosted glass panel. She peeked inside. Murmurs were exchanged before she pivoted, grip possessively on the handle, and swung the door open for Liz. "Please, go on in," she whispered.

Liz crossed the threshold to find Dalton seated at an oversized oak desk. The door rattled closed behind her.

Dalton lifted his chin at her in greeting, a handset pressed to his ear. "Definitely, sir. I couldn't agree with you more." He nodded as though the caller could see him. Then he laughed, a negotiation woven into the rise and fall of his voice. His sleek black tie swagged beneath two unfastened buttons. Rolled sleeves exposed forearms leading to hands that promised to sculpt the country's future.

"We stick to the plan," he went on, "and those suckers won't know what hit 'em."

Liz gripped the handles of her purse, feeling intrusive. She noted the engraved nameplate propped on his desktop, the official-looking documents splayed over the stacked file folders. The magnitude of his importance was never so palpable.

He concluded his conversation and dropped the phone onto its cradle. "Lizzy." Face brightening, he rounded the desk. He cupped her shoulders and gave her a kiss, an act so routine her lips barely registered the touch. "What are you doing here?"

He seemed tired but happy. Too happy for her to tell him the core reason she'd come.

"I had a few hours to kill between classes and work. If you're free, I thought we could sneak away. Maybe share a sundae or something." The suggestion conjured memories of swiveling on stools at Tasty's, the two of them playfully fighting over the prized syrupy cherry.

Dalton laughed as he glanced out the window, where a gray wall of chilled sky had blotted out the afternoon rays. "A sundae? In this weather?"

She rolled her shoulders. "Someone has to keep dairy farmers in business."

A look of serious consideration swept over his face. "Now, that"—he wagged a finger—"could be a helpful tactic if our points ever take a dive." He paused before boosting a grin.

Liz sighed, relieved he was only kidding. Although . . . the idea of gobbling Rocky Road for the benefit of the nation was awfully tempting.

She continued with alternatives. "We could get soup instead. Or just take a walk?"

A tap on the door preceded the reappearance of Liz's greeter. "Excuse me, Mr. Harris. I apologize for interrupting, but Mr. Field's office just phoned."

He perked. "What's the verdict?"

"His secretary said he could squeeze you in to discuss the commercial zoning bill, if you can be there in twenty minutes."

He checked his watch.

"And"—the woman charged forward—"the AFT's memo on teachers' wages arrived." She handed him a manila envelope, slicing the space between him and Liz with a whisper of effort. "Mr. Landis would like you to call once you've reviewed it."

He swayed his eyes to Liz, asking permission. As though the pettiness of her invitation, next to his substantive dealings, weren't painfully obvious.

"We'll do it another time," she assured him.

"You sure?"

Liz smiled. "It's not every day Marshall Field calls for a meeting. Besides, you do want to win this race, don't you?"

He regarded his assistant. "Tell them I'm on my way."

"Yes, sir." She gave Liz an approving nod, then jetted out the door.

Dalton slung on the jacket he'd grabbed from the coat tree.

"Your buttons," she pointed out, and helped by refastening the top of his shirt. "While you're gone, I could always stay and lend a hand. I still have time until work."

"Sweetheart, you're a doll to offer." He tightened the noose of his tie, adjusted the knot. "But you've seen it out there. It's a madhouse." He pulled his wallet from the inside pocket of his coat and crushed a dollar into her palm. "Why don't you go on and get that ice cream you wanted. Gotta support those dairy farmers, right?" He smiled before peeking at his watch.

"You'd better get going," she said.

He gave her chin a tender squeeze. "Thanks for understanding, kiddo."

Her pleasant expression held as he donned his hat. Once he melted into the bedlam, she turned to the window.

Dalton was right about the sundae. The day, she realized, had become much too cold.

❧ 16 ❧

October 1944
Dutch New Guinea

Betty death-gripped the base of her cushioned seat with her left hand. Her right fist clenched the jeep's small exterior handle-bar. Humidity and fear streamed sweat into every fiber of her herring-bone twill coveralls.

On rusty clay, slick as oil beneath the tires, they slid around an-other hairpin curve. Betty dared a side glance over the long, ragged drop-off. The absence of a guardrail punished her with an unob-structed view. The sight of the rocks below, a bed of daggers, shot a squeak from her throat. She lurched toward the motor pool driver, burrowed her helmeted head behind his shoulder. Eyes squeezed tight, she held her breath, as if that alone could spare her life.

Just as her chest began to burn, she heard the private. "It's safe to look now."

She exhaled, then squinted a peek. Confirming the vehicle wasn't sailing off the cliff, she shifted her weight upright, though she didn't slacken her grasp on the seat. Identical walls of jungle closed in on both sides of the mountain road. Steam rose from enormous ferns and tangled vines. The sun scalded pungency out of their ancient pores, a damp rotting smell worsened by the jeep's exhaust fumes. And all around, massive roots of banyan trees serpentined above-ground, exemplifying the island's backward existence.

" 'Bout halfway there," the private announced, his chinstrap unfastened, swinging like a pendulum. His tone and permanent grin reflected the cheerful leisure of a drive through the countryside—despite cockatoos screaming warnings above. "So where you from?"

She strained for the answer. Her mind was still rattled after the enemy hits her C-47 had barely dodged en route to Humboldt Bay. "Near Chicago," she recalled at last.

"Chicago?" He slapped his knee. "I'm from Indiana. We're practically neighbors. In fact, my pop's been trucking me up to Cubs games every birthday since I was six."

Betty briefly wondered how many games that totaled. With his lean frame and round boyish face, the golden-tanned kid didn't look a day past sixteen. No wonder the guys at the airstrip called him "Junior."

"You a fan?" he asked.

"Sorry?"

"Don't tell me you root for the 'Black Sox,' doll. You just might break my heart."

Sports statistics made about as much sense to her as chemistry equations. She shrugged, tried for a knowledgeable response. "I'd say they have the nicest uniforms."

He chuckled. "Yeah, well. If you got a fondness for uniforms, you've come to the right place."

An insect the size of a muskmelon buzzed near Betty's cheek. She frantically batted it away before a bump in the road launched her like a rumble seat several inches into the air. Her grip reclaimed the handle as her field shoe braced against the opening of the jeep.

"Watch your toes there," Junior warned. "They got forty-foot pythons round here that would love to chow on those."

Betty jerked her foot inside. "Did you say *forty?*"

He nodded. "Must be something in the water. Bats, rats, lizards, even grasshoppers. Everything here seems to grow twice as big as back home. Well, except for in Texas maybe."

Edging out a reciprocated smile, Betty cut to another subject. "Is it usually this hot?"

"Ah, no," he assured her.

Thank heavens.

"Should get even hotter," he said, "once we hit the peak of summer next month."

Her scalp beaded within the oven of her helmet, releasing another rivulet down her chest. She had a sudden flashback of the sweaty old marching drills at basic. If not for her commanding officer allowing her to slack off due to shin splints, Betty might never have survived.

"Hang on to your hat." Junior cranked the wheels around a sharp bend. Once straightened out, he ground the gears and reduced speed. Dark-colored natives strolled toward them down the center of the road. Many wore GI shirts dyed brilliant yellow and purple. A handful toted large curved knives waist high. Barefoot and dusty, the men trailed women balancing bundles on their heads.

"They're Melanesians," Junior explained. "They live in the nipa huts, built on stilts back there over the water."

Relief fluttered inside her, realizing these unfamiliar beings wouldn't be residing next door to her civilized barracks.

The pedestrians moved aside as the jeep neared. They waved and smiled—with red-stained teeth.

Betty pushed out her question before horror could take hold. "Is that blood? In their mouths?"

"Nah. Teeth just get that way from chewing betel nuts."

"Of course," she replied lightly, grateful Junior hadn't laughed at her.

A few more zigs and zags, more distracting idle conversation, and soon they arrived at a compound of tents. An armed soldier waved them through the entrance. Stumps outlined the area that appeared to have been freshly bulldozed smack in the middle of the jungle. Perhaps a shortcut through a camp to reach their destination.

Junior brought the jeep to a halt and swung around to her side. He unhooked the thin, flimsy strap that served as her door.

Why was he extending his hand? Did she need to get out?

Seeds of terror sprouted. "You mean, this is it? This is the hospital?" She couldn't move, her body paralyzed.

He gave a nod. "Home sweet home."

This was all wrong. It had to be a mistake, another foul-up like the one days earlier. While disembarking with other WACs in Australia, a country founded by convicts and far from the exotic island she'd been promised, she had gone straight to a handsome officer about the error in her destination. And sure enough, New Guinea was listed in her file. Once her imminent transfer had been confirmed, she even offered silent thanks to her recruiter on Jackson for honoring his word. . . .

Her recruiter.

Sergeant *Weasel*.

And now everything became clear.

Oh, she was going to thank him all right. The minute she got home. First, though, she needed to straighten out this mess. All she had to do was find the hospital commander. A little eyelash batting, an arousing smile, and she would have this "misunderstanding" solved in no time.

Girding herself, she accepted Junior's hand and carefully stepped down into the mud. While he unloaded her backpack and footlocker from the rear of the vehicle, she removed her helmet. She went to work on her bound hair, smoothing and tucking strands into a style that didn't suggest she had come through a hurricane.

A drawn-out whistle caught her ear. She turned to find Junior shaking his head in wonder.

"I tell ya, who needs sulfa? The boys laid up here get one look at you, they'll be feeling like a million bucks lickety-split."

Confidence stretched her lips into a smile.

"Well," he sighed. "I'd best be getting to the base. Got supply runs to make." He pointed to her luggage piled on a stump. "Need a hand with those?"

"No, no, I'll be fine." She wouldn't be staying long. "Thanks for the ride."

"Pleasure was all mine." He grinned, then stopped mid-turn. "Say, uh, Betty. Assuming we manage to crush the Japs in time to get home by spring, any chance you'd do me the honor of, oh, coming to senior prom with me?"

She giggled, lowered her chin. "Wouldn't you want to take a girl your own age?"

"Heck, no. Not when I could bring Betty Grable herself."

The comparison was flattering, specifically in light of her present appearance. "How about I give it some thought?"

"Hey, that's better than a no." Beaming, Junior hopped into the jeep and sped off.

Once he vanished from sight, she shed a deep breath. Duck soup—not a thing to it. A little persuasive conversation with the hospital commander and he'd help rid her of this nightmare in nothing flat.

She maneuvered through the carpet of red sludge collecting on her shoes. Outside the nearest tent, she undid a top button of her shirt and widened her collar. Nothing indecent, just casual and friendly. Pressing her lips together, she salvaged what was left of her lipstick, among the few cosmetics permitted under nonsensical Army rules.

She pulled aside the net screen covering the tent entry and stepped inside.

"Hey, angel, which cloud did *you* fall off of?" a bedded soldier called out in a raucous voice.

"Boy oh boy, a real American gal," said a second one. "That or I'm dreaming with my eyes open."

At the far end of the tent stood a ward man shaking out sheets. Betty made her way toward him, through the center of the lined-up cots, three dozen at a glance. Nearly every spot was filled with a bandaged patient, some wounded worse than others. She trained her eyes on the dirt floor, hiding her shock at seeing the obvious absence of limbs. A few guys paused their checkers game to toss her a catcall. The stewing reek of blood and antiseptic and male sweat attacked her senses.

"Excuse me, Corporal," she said.

The man faced her. Cheeks drawn, he had a strange yellow tint to his skin. "Can I help you?"

"There's . . . been an error in my assignment. This isn't where I'm supposed to be."

"You wind up at the wrong hospital?"

"Wrong island, actually."

"Say it ain't so," hollered a patient nearby. "We ain't all as ugly as Elroy over here."

"Ah, pipe down, ya rebel meathead," retorted another.

Betty's gaze remained on the ward man.

"Have you seen the first sergeant yet?" He was referring to the chain of command she had every intention of bypassing for efficiency.

She discreetly crossed her fingers, immunity for minor fibs, and nodded. "I was told to speak to the commander."

"You're a WAC?"

She nodded again.

"Then it's Kitzafenny you're looking for. Should still be in the pharmacy, three tents thataway." He gestured to her left.

"Thank you."

"Good luck to ya."

Heading out, she heard him mumble, "You're gonna need it."

She huffed to herself and marched on with vengeful determination. He'd never had the pleasure of seeing her charm in action.

As she approached the third tent over, a gruff voice boomed from inside. Betty slowed her pace. A tall, broad-shouldered woman stomped out, followed by a private.

"I don't know what to tell you, ma'am," he said.

The lady rounded on him. Her fists indented the hips of her ill-fitted men's khaki trousers. Their pleats were as plentiful as the lines in her face, her skin lemony beneath her short mud-colored hair. "Well, I'll tell you what you *can* do. You march on up to MacArthur's bungalow and you tell him he'd better scrounge me up some decent uniforms. My gals are getting dermatitis left and right. And I don't want to hear any more cockamamie excuses about the supply chain in the Pacific being mucked up for everyone. Not *everyone* was shipped here with Arctics and earmuffs. My girls are being roasted alive in their winter ODs, while you boys are ironing your half dozen khakis. You got that?"

A tense pause. "Yes, ma'am." The futility in his tone indicated he could already predict how the "brass" would respond. Prior to hustling away, he saluted her. The motion marked her as an officer, though her uniform lacked insignia.

Her hard brown eyes snapped to Betty. *"Yes?"*

Betty straightened and shot her hand up in a salute, which the woman returned and released.

"Ma'am, I'm trying to find . . ." Cripes, what was the hospital commander's rank? Had she missed it? With little choice, she finished her sentence with "Commander Kitzafenny."

"That's *Captain* Kitzafenny," the gal corrected. "And you found her."

In that split second between confusion and embarrassment, Betty realized her blunder. She'd failed to clarify, and had been directed to her *company* commander. "My apologies, ma'am. I didn't mean to bother you—" She stopped there. No sense in placing herself on the military chopping block for attempting to bend the rules.

"Let me guess," the captain said. "You're the transfer from Sydney. The one with hospital experience."

Suddenly terrified of being caught in a lie, Betty felt perspiration pour beneath her twill. "Well, sort of, ma'am. It was a nursing home that I worked at."

"I see," the captain said. "Private . . . ?"

"Cordell, ma'am. Betty Cordell."

"Well, Cordell, you'll fit in perfectly here. Between giving enemas and changing bedpans, your med tech duties will feel like an old hat."

Med tech duties?

As the implication sank in, Betty gleamed inside. She couldn't have wished for an easier solution.

"Ma'am, I believe there's been a mix-up."

"Wouldn't that be the shocker of my day."

"You see, I'm not a medical technician. I don't have any nurse's aide training. I'm a medical clerk."

"How's that?"

"A medical clerk, ma'am." Betty racked her brain for a list of Julia's duties. "Even at the rest home, all I did was file papers and answer phones and such."

Two litter bearers approached, carting a moaning GI. His pants were charred, burned away up to his knees. Shins stripped of skin exposed a red meaty rawness. Betty covered her nose with all the subtlety she could, the acrid smell wringing her gut.

"Excuse me, Captain," one of the soldiers said. "Got another burn victim. Electrical wires. Where'd you like him?"

"Has he had plasma and morphine?"

"Yes, ma'am."

"Take him to the shock ward. We'll get to his surgery soon as we can."

Betty averted her eyes as they carted the stretcher away.

"Now, where were we?" the captain said.

Betty forced herself to refocus. She stood tall, neck lifted, confident. "About my station, ma'am. I think it would be best if they sent someone else, someone more qualified for your needs."

"Listen, Private." Irritation raked her voice. "I agree this is another fine Army mess. But we're just gonna make do, 'cause I certainly don't need any more help filing records. You *have* taken first aid, haven't you?"

"Uh, yes. I have, but—"

"Then taking temperatures and pulses shouldn't be an issue."

"But Captain Kitz—"

"Look. I don't have time for a national conference on this. The U.S. government seems to think the European Theater takes medical priority. As if the patients in this hellhole are somehow going to heal themselves. So if you can tidy a linen closet, and know a medical term or two, you're staying put. Last week alone, I had three orderlies shipped home for malaria and jungle rot." She arched a thick brow. "Are we clear?" Not a question.

"Y-yes, ma'am."

"Good. An armed escort will take you to your quarters to settle in."

Armed escort? "I thought—ma'am, I was told New Guinea was secure."

"Still have isolated patrols of Japanese guerrillas raiding up there." She jabbed a finger toward the mountain range that spanned the massive island, an unbroken spine of greenery topped with fluffy mist. "Private Taylor will give you a full briefing of restrictions. No dating, no leaves, no travel passes, strict curfews, et cetera." She stepped away, then paused. "And, Cordell, you'd be wise to button up that uniform. Daytime mosquitoes spread dengue fever like it's going out of style." With that, she strode off around the corner.

Betty felt her insides shrinking, her body withering in the equatorial sun. Her balance swayed as she closed the gap of her shirt.

"You okay, there?" The mustard-hued corporal stood before her, a small crate in his hands. "Miss? You all right?"

"Yes," she replied, finding her voice. Of course she'd be all right. Sooner rather than later, she'd work out another transfer—off to a civilized island, even back to Australia. That's all there was to it.

"Looks like you could use some water," he offered.

Before she could respond, an air-raid siren pierced her eardrums. She cowered, wrapped her head with her arms.

A hand touched her shoulder. "Not to worry," the ward man yelled over the wailing alert. "They sound the dang things all the time. But our own buzz-boys are the only ones doing any swoopin'. Usually when you gals are showering in the open drums, coincidentally."

She sighed, relaxing.

"First day on the islands?"

She nodded.

"Well, well." He snickered. "Welcome to Hollandia."

Yeah. Some welcome.

Just then came the boom of an earth-shattering explosion. Instantly, Betty's body was propelled into the air. Time floated in a separate dimension, stretching like a rubber band, lengthening an eternity. Until it snapped.

She cracked her lids. She was facedown on the ground. Something heavy covered her—the corporal in a protective huddle. She heard quickened breaths, her own gasping. Pressure behind her eyes bulged in their sockets. Her ears rang and body swelled.

A faint voice. The ward man's. She tilted her face up and stared at his moving lips. He was asking if she was all right.

She tested her hands, her legs. A glance confirmed she was coated in clay but physically intact. She managed a nod.

He took off running toward a distant pyramidal tent. Its roof boiled with flames. Shards of hot orange reached for the sun, devouring the air. Soldiers and nurses sprinted frantically between structures. Thick smoke hazed the camp, blocked out the sky.

And there in the center of hell sat Betty, muscles tremoring, arms clenched around herself, rocking, rocking, whispering, "My God . . . What have I gotten myself into?"

17

October 1944
Belgium

"Man, I miss that house in the village," Charlie said through chattering teeth.

Morgan agreed, but he didn't reply. He was too consumed with trying to locate the source of the leak in the poncho covering their two-man foxhole, a challenging task in the dark.

"So how cold you think it is?" Charlie asked.

"There's the damn thing." Morgan adjusted the fabric and secured it to the logs overhead. No more white flashes of explosives or crisscrossing of tracer rounds. In the musty blackness, he held out his palm and waited for a drip to sneak through. Showers were expected to fall until morning, and he preferred to wake up covered in dirt rather than mud.

"Did Sarge say when we're moving out?" Charlie asked.

"Nah."

"How long you think the blackout will last?"

"How should I know?"

The strict blackout, for fear of night raids, allowed them to build outdoor fires during the day, but not after nightfall when they were needed most.

Morgan crouched down beside his brother. He fumbled his hand over the damp straw floor until he located the flashlight and switched it on.

Charlie squinted against the beam.

"Why you yakkin' so much tonight, anyway?"

"No reason." Charlie answered so fast something was obviously eating at him.

"You okay?"

He shrugged with a dim smile. "Just wish we could've taken the stove from that house, is all." He rubbed his palms together to warm his hands.

Morgan settled in, adjusting his legs. "I don't know what you're complaining about. You grew up in Iowa, for cryin' out loud."

"Yeah, but this is a wet cold."

"Here," Morgan said, flinging his extra blanket at his brother's chest. "Now stop your whinin'."

Charlie unrolled the wool fabric and drew it around his shoulders.

Morgan propped the flashlight upright against his hip, projecting shadows through the fingers of roots. Eerie faces stretched to the ceiling. From his jacket, he snagged a D-ration chocolate bar, hard from the cold. Out of habit, and with some muscling, he broke it in half for his brother. The kid accepted, but then stored it in a pocket instead of digging in. Another sign something was off.

Morgan started into his own portion. He only got a couple nibbles off the corner, though, before giving up. It wasn't worth a chipped tooth.

"Can I see it again?" Charlie asked.

"What's that?"

"The Luger."

Reluctant, Morgan sighed a billowing cloud. "I suppose." He pulled the pistol from his cartridge belt and placed it in his brother's hand. As Charlie examined markings on the firearm, a string of images flickered through Morgan's mind: the coal-black eyes of the German, the trail of blood on his face, the photo of a now-fatherless family.

"So what was it like?" Charlie said.

"What?"

"Beating down that Kraut."

Morgan's gaze folded. "I dunno."

Charlie flipped the pistol over and ran his fingers along the barrel. "At least you got a good souvenir, right?"

"Yeah, right." The words lacked the sarcasm they deserved.

Morgan had planned to toss the Luger into a trench a few days earlier, but at the last minute couldn't do it. Discarding the weapon was like giving himself permission to forget that night, and while he found the memories as burdensome as his field gear, he wasn't ready to let them go just yet.

The real irony was that most guys in their outfit treated the pistol like a badge of honor. They'd slapped him on the back and congratulated him, first for acquiring the coveted weapon, then for delivering the muddied papers from the German's bag. Lieutenant Drake had even spared a fractional smile when Morgan handed over the map indicating a Panzer division's movement plans.

"Ya did okay," Drake had said, pulling a cigar from his mouth. On a pungent exhale of smoke rode the mention of a merit recommendation. As if smashing a rock into a drunken man's skull warranted a reward.

All those war heroes Morgan had studied in school, how different they seemed now. Probably just regular frightened men, like himself, who were lucky enough to survive their ordeals. He wanted to know if they too struggled to sleep at night plagued by the crimes they'd committed, or if the belief that their actions served a worthy cause allowed them to rest peacefully.

"How many times you slug him, you think?" Charlie persisted with an aggravating eagerness.

"Don't remember."

"Was it one time? Five times?"

Morgan shrugged. "A few."

"He see you before you whacked him?"

A burning sensation crawled up Morgan's neck, roughened his tone. "I guess."

"So how did you—"

"Look. Just did what I had to do, all right?"

"Yeah, I know, but—"

"Goddamn it, Charlie!" Morgan exploded. "I'm just trying to get by like everyone else! Can't you see that?"

Stunned at first, Charlie cowered his gaze to the wall of plastered dirt. Shadows pulled at his features, emphasizing the sullenness in his face.

Immediately Morgan felt like an ass. He wished the kid had yelled back, even taken a swing at him. But Charlie just sat there.

Morgan tempered his voice. "Listen," he said, "it's not something I'm proud of, okay? It was an accident, getting lost, being there." He tipped his head back on his jacket collar, his eyes on the slight swag in the roof. "Was nothing but a lousy mistake."

The pattering rain was the only sound in the foxhole. Same rain as home, different sky.

"Like Mouse gettin' it," Charlie said vacantly, raising Morgan's head.

A few mornings ago, the squad had been strolling through a deserted town. No one spotted the Kraut sniper until he opened fire from a church bell tower. Charlie barely missed taking a bullet, but Mouse wasn't as fortunate; he dropped facedown in the dirt, never knowing what hit him.

"It shouldn't have been him," Charlie murmured.

What the hell was Morgan supposed to say to that? If he agreed, did it mean his brother should have been killed instead?

Gauging his reply, he insisted, "It wasn't your fault." The phrase, once released, sounded pathetically clichéd, but he couldn't come up with anything better.

"He was talking about his girlfriend when it happened." Charlie rambled, as if not hearing. "God, I can't even remember her name."

Constance, Morgan recalled. Her name was Constance.

"Mouse was telling me about how they met. And that's when I reached down. I was just picking up a friggin' coin. Heads up for luck, right?" He spurted a laugh, dark and humorless—as was everything about war. Then he shook his head and his mouth tensed. "He was lying there, and all I could think about was heading for cover, to save my own ass."

Morgan swiped his hand over the back of his head. He tried to imagine what thick-skinned response his father would use. How do you make sense of something that makes no sense at all?

He turned to Charlie. "Look here," he told him. "There was nothing you could do. That bullet went straight through his heart. Died right away. You heard Doc. Said he didn't have a chance."

"But I should've grabbed him. At least pulled him outta there."

"And you'd be dead too."

"I'm just sayin' I should've tried."

"Charlie, I was there," he argued. "He was out in the open. You did what you were trained to do. What we were all trained to do."

"Oh yeah?" Charlie burst out. "Then why do I feel like such a goddamned coward?"

Morgan was taken aback by the notion his brother might break into tears. He canvassed his mind for words of comfort. He recalled the old standbys from the nights he used to calm the youngster from bad dreams. But nothing seemed appropriate anymore.

Charlie looked away, his breaths wavering.

The minutes froze between them, an ice block of silence, until Charlie spoke. "Just never thought I'd be so damn afraid," he rasped. "I didn't think it'd be like . . . this."

"I know," Morgan said. The flashlight's beam glimmered on tears striping his brother's ashen face. "You just keep doing what you're doin', all right? You stick by me and we're gonna get through this. Soon enough, we'll get that ticket home."

Charlie angled and searched Morgan's eyes. "You really think we'll make it home?"

"Damn right we will," he answered without hesitation. "Then you and me are heading back to Iowa. We'll pool every dime the Army gives us, work ten jobs if we have to. Then we're gonna buy back Pa's farm, or one of our own, just like we planned."

Charlie nodded slowly.

"Morgan," he said after a long beat. "I'm sorry."

Morgan blinked. "For *what?*"

"For getting you into this. And for . . . well, for everything."

Charlie had never been one for dealing out apologies. At least, not the serious kind. Morgan felt pride stretch inside, realizing the kid might actually be growing up. A smile started on his lips as he threw out, "What makes you think I wouldn't have enlisted on my own? Only waited 'cause I wasn't about to leave you by yourself. You would've burned the whole farm down by now."

It took a few seconds, but a subtle warmth returned to Charlie's face. He dashed his tears away with the heel of his hand. "Just the barn maybe," he said.

"Too bad battle hasn't knocked the wise guy outta ya." Morgan chuckled. "Get some rest, it'll be morning soon. And give me that Luger before you shoot me in your sleep."

Charlie handed over the pistol. He laid his head back in the straw and shut his eyes. Morgan watched as his brother's breathing turned heavy and deep. It was strange how shadows could add such age to a boy's face.

Against their roof, the rain fell harder.

Morgan pulled Betty's picture out of his watch pocket. With his thumbnail, he scraped a few specks of dirt off the edges before once again admiring her flawless features. Had he known how much her letters were going to touch him, he would have taken more notice when they danced together.

He set the photo on his knee and retrieved his latest post from Betty. By the glow of the flashlight, he began to read.

Dear Morgan,

I was terribly delighted to hear back from you. So much so, I am responding only minutes after first reading your letter. (If I am breaking a rule of proper etiquette, please don't report me to the authorities. It is, after all, your moving writing that is to blame.)

As of yet, visiting a zoo is the closest I have ever come to experiencing a farm. The way you described it was magical. Your words painted such a vivid picture of evenings spent amidst the quiet cornfields and blazing sunsets. In fact, the scene reminds me of a Byron poem my father taught me as a young girl:

The moon is up, and yet it is not night;
Sunset divides the sky with her—a sea

Of glory streams along the Alpine height
Of blue Friuli's mountains; Heaven is free
From clouds, but of all colours seems to be
Melted to one vast Iris of the West,
Where the day joins the past eternity.

I had not thought of those verses in years. It seems a lifetime since I studied literature of the like with my father. Such was a time when I, myself, felt as free as the heavens, when all was simple and the word "impossible" held no meaning.

Until your letter, I had nearly forgotten about the splendor found in everyday wonders, like a sunset, or "God's artwork," as your mother so poignantly referred to it. She sounds like a lovely woman, who, along with your father, must be enormously proud of their sons' bravery.

I smile now recalling occasions on which I, too, had made my father proud—the day I received a gaudy blue ribbon for my first short-story contest; and, of course, the evening I debuted in a school play as a singing pine tree. (An off-key one, at that. Though, from his applause, you would have thought I had performed the lead in "Romeo and Juliet.") They were silly things really, nothing as noteworthy as your current service. Yet I remember his face beaming, his pride speaking at full volume without his saying a word.

I would be lying if I denied how saddened I am by the distance that has grown between us over the years. Nevertheless, fond memories like these have helped me through many challenging times, times when I have felt far from confident in who I am, or regretful of acts I would change if given the chance.

I mention all of this in the event that you ever need an added source of strength, as well, particularly during this war. It might be simpleminded of me, but I hope my message will inspire your own recollections for moments when comfort is difficult to come by.

> *With both roommates away and my father on*
> *extended travel, the house feels terribly empty. I*
> *suppose this is another reason for my impulse to write*
> *back without delay. Somehow, reading your words and*
> *putting my own thoughts to paper has left me feeling*
> *less alone. It is as if you were here with me, telling me*
> *about the old bridge and your father's Irish suppers.*
>
> *I imagine that you, always being surrounded by*
> *fellow soldiers, are likely burdened by the opposite. As I*
> *complain of loneliness, the idea of having a quiet*
> *evening to yourself must sound so very appealing. If,*
> *however, that is not the case, I hope my letter brings*
> *you the same sense of warm company with which you*
> *have provided me.*
>
> *Please take good care, Morgan. I wish you and your*
> *brother a continued safe journey.*
> *With tender regards,*
> *Betty Cordell*

Morgan stared at the pages, warmed by words that evaporated the cold. How was it that a girl he barely knew, one living thousands of miles away, could feel so familiar? As if they'd known each other for years. From her sense of loneliness, to yearning for her parent's pride, even the strained relationship with her father, he could relate to every emotion in detail. The thought of finding a person who truly understood him sent a heated shiver up his arms.

But then a drop splashed his hand, bringing him back to the foxhole.

He stored the folded letter in a dry portion of his jacket. Safe. Protected.

This time there was no postponing a response. He held up the flashlight over a blank piece of paper. And through the ink in his pen, he offered a confession, which, if not for Betty, he would have taken to the grave.

❧ 18 ❧

November 1944
Chicago, Illinois

Liz wrung out the washcloth in such a hurry she entirely missed the porcelain basin on the nightstand. The water splattered off the glossy floorboards, dampening the ruffled bed skirt and the legs of Liz's chair.

"Lordy, Lordy, would you look at the mess you're makin'."

"Sorry about that, Vy."

"Oh, applesauce. I'm just giving you fits." Viola smiled, adjusting her thick bifocals. Seated against a mountain of pillows in bed, the seventy-four-year-old woman appeared deceptively frail. Her slight frame swam freely in her floral print nightgown.

Reducing her pace, Liz stood and draped the rag over the edge of the bowl.

Viola fluffed her short silver hair and said, "So, we're being sneaky, are we?"

Liz inhaled as sharply as if she had hiccupped.

"You thought I wouldn't notice?"

"I—don't know what you mean."

"Well, if I didn't know better, I'd say you're trying to slip out early for a little something special."

Liz giggled nervously. "Why would you think that?" She slid

her hand over her apron pocket, relieved the contents hadn't fallen out.

"It would certainly explain why that was the quickest sponge bath I've had in the six years I've been here. A romantic evening planned with your beau?"

Liz sighed inside. "Nothing like that. Just have some extra chores today." She promptly crossed the room to avoid Viola's scrutinizing gray-blue eyes. A former grade school teacher, Viola Knowles often bragged about being a living, breathing lie detector. One with "fading batteries and a bad hip," she would say, "but still in working order."

At the supply table, Liz glanced out the half-open window outlined with plum curtains. An old Ford Model T honked while rumbling away, and in the park across the street, an evening breeze blew a shower of leaves off branches. The room upstairs that used to be Papa's shared an identical view. Inhaling the same reminiscent smells of disinfectant and medications, Liz almost expected to hear his low belly chuckle behind her. But only a moment passed before a whistling gust of wind swept his presence away.

"Want me to close the window?" Liz didn't know why she bothered asking; she knew what Viola's response would be.

"No, thank you, dear. Fresh air clears the cobwebs."

Liz stepped back toward the bed with a cloth and bottle of rubbing alcohol.

"Careful, now," Viola said. "Water'll make that floor slicker than a log in a millpond. You fall, and you'll be my new roommate."

"Goodness knows, we don't want *that* to happen." Liz smiled. When she settled in her seat, Viola outstretched her arms as if welcoming an application from the fountain of youth.

"And what, pray tell, shall the court be feasting on this eve?" Viola asked.

"Chef's special, milady: mashed potatoes and steamed carrots, delivered by horse-'n'-carriage all the way from Windsor."

"Well, if it's good enough for the queen, it's good enough for me."

Liz smiled again while running the dampened cloth over the woman's baby-soft, wrinkled arms, trying not to ponder the time.

After a quiet moment, Viola released a sigh, shaking her head. "My oh my. You do remind me of your grandfather." She had voiced the same remark many times before, but Liz never tired of hearing it, especially from someone who'd known Papa as long as Viola had. Together with their spouses, the two had played in a bridge club for years and formed a lasting friendship.

If it weren't for Viola residing at the nursing home, Liz would have insisted Papa live out his final days in his own house, despite his need for round-the-clock care. Instead, Liz had simply applied to work at the facility in Lincoln Square, a community area on the far North Side of Chicago. Already, she'd virtually been a daily visitor, chatting away whenever Papa had felt up to it, reading to him when he hadn't. They were halfway through *This Side of Paradise* when he died peacefully in his sleep. Without a single utterance, Viola had offered Liz more comfort than anyone. No words were needed to express how much they both missed his company.

"You're all set," Liz said, helping Viola into her frilly robe. "Gorgeous as ever."

"Thank you, sweet pea."

"My pleasure." Liz glanced at her watch. She could still manage it if she hurried.

While Viola fished through a canvas knitting bag, Liz dried the floor and bundled the used towels in her arms. Excitement built with every step as she headed for the door, disrupted by the sight of crayon drawings on the bureau. She'd almost forgotten.

"Would you still like me to hang up your new artwork?" Liz motioned her chin toward Viola's personal gallery: a wall covered with school projects and pictures from her grandchildren.

"It can wait. You skedaddle off," Viola replied. "To those *chores* of yours." Her mouth split into a suspicious grin.

Liz gripped the towels tighter and made her escape. The aroma of baking bread and boiling carrots from the nearby kitchen warmed the air.

She had just deposited her supplies in the laundry room when the grandfather clock chimed. Fifteen minutes until meal service.

She sped around the banister staircase and into the front sitting room, where she dropped into the Victorian chair. The evening sky's indigo glow provided ample light through the massive window.

At last. An opportunity to read Morgan's reply without interruption.

> *Dear Betty,*
>
> *Thank you so much for your last post. To say its arrival was the highlight of my day doesn't do it justice. It's no surprise your writing has won awards, if your letters are any indication. I've read both of them so often that many of the words are smudged. With all the endless rain, marching, and nights spent in foxholes, they've definitely been a welcome escape.*
>
> *I'm actually writing to you tonight crouched in one of those soggy holes. My knee sure doesn't make a great desk, but with a grain of luck you'll still be able to read most of this. Of course that's assuming I can keep the paper clear of the rain and mud that covers us all from head to toe.*
>
> *The sound of drops hitting our roof is getting louder. Sometimes I think the only thing longer than a cold night spent in the dark is a cold wet night spent in the mud. Funny. Never thought I'd be one to complain about weather I was so fond of as a kid.*
>
> *So many times, I would wake my brother up in the wee hours. I'd drag him over to the window to smell the thunderstorm rolling in. There was something electric and wonderful about the scent of those clouds. When the rain did come, Charlie would stand on the covered porch and tell me how nuts I was splashing this way and that in my long johns and boots. I swear, my dad would have knocked some sense into both of us if he'd known—although I imagine even a good belt whupping wouldn't have stopped me from going right back out there. And now here I am, wishing the skies would just plain dry up.*

As for my brother, already conked out beside me, somehow he's now the one who doesn't seem to mind the rain and muck. Or maybe he's too tired to care. Amazing how a person can change over time. For me it was when my mom passed away that I had to grow up and become the responsible brother. At least I tried my best to be. Meanwhile Charlie turned into the daring one, convinced he could conquer the world. But now with the threat of death hiding behind every tree and in every bunker, fear seems to have changed him back into a little boy who still relies on his older brother for direction. God help us both.

I do my best to be strong for Charlie, honoring what I promised Mom before shipping out. In prayer, I swore to her I'd do everything in my power to be the son and soldier that would have made her proud—someone Charlie could always look up to and lean on. But truth be told, I share his same fears, maybe even more, about never making it home. Not exactly the picture of courage and valor I'd hoped I'd be. For his sake, I keep those thoughts to myself. Can't see what good it would do either of us.

The one saving grace is that Charlie's worries don't stop him from sleeping as sound as a baby. Tired as we are, with only a few hours between orders, you'd think I wouldn't have any trouble falling asleep either. But closing my eyes these days usually means seeing horrible pictures I can't erase—ones that rob me of needed rest night after night.

Not sleeping must be part of why the last three months of hopping from one battle to the next feel like three years. The war is certainly taking its toll. Sometimes I wonder if I'll even recognize myself when it's all said and done. I just hope my folks are watching over us from heaven, keeping us out of harm's way and on the right path so they can be proud of their boys.

Lord knows, I've had plenty of times through the

years when I've been too busy doubting myself to stand up straight. Then I remember what my mom used to tell us—"All the yardsticks in the world couldn't measure the love and pride of a parent." I'm sure this is a saying your father would agree with.

Obviously I have no idea what happened to separate the two of you. What I do know is that life is too short not to say how you feel to the people you love. Believe me, it's a lesson I've had to learn the hard way. My mom was only thirty-one when her appendix burst on the way to the hospital. Dad told us not to worry, that it was just a sideache troubling her. Had he let us know the truth, Charlie and I could have told her the things we needed to.

That being said, I do hope you can find a way to mend your ties before it's too late—especially if you still care for your father as much as I gathered from your letter. No doubt such a distance is causing pain for you both. Well, enough of my preaching. Better close now or I won't be able to fit these pages into the envelope.

Please write again soon. Your letters mean more to me than I can tell you. And be sure to include more of those beautiful poems. They're definitely better than the rhymes the dogfaces tell around here.

Thinking of you.
Yours truly,
Morgan

Liz released a breath she'd been unconsciously holding. Again his words had reached inside, touching her more deeply than any Shakespearean sonnet. And knowing he too had lost his parents only confirmed he was someone with whom she could share her feelings. A man whose utter honesty about his weaknesses and fears made her long to reciprocate the gift.

Could it be he was right about her father? Was it possible he was hurting as well?

Though the suggestion seemed improbable, Morgan had once

more given her a thought to ponder—the same as he had at the dance. They'd only but met, and still he had prompted her to examine her life. He'd raised questions in her mind about her mother, and Dalton, and even her career path—questions that had never occurred to her. Or ones perhaps she had been afraid to ask.

Somehow, with Morgan, her heart felt like an unedited book, its content speckled with imperfections. The fact that he continued to earnestly turn the pages, in both the figurative and literal sense, equally comforted and terrified her.

Yours truly, Morgan

She ran her fingers over his valediction, forward then backward. As her skin absorbed the words, a fluttering sensation filled her: a swarm of butterflies taking flight. She recalled the curves of his shoulder, the feel of his palm melting into hers.

Lowering her lids, she sank into her chair. Beneath an Arthurian sky dotted with stars, the soldier stepped toward her. His jeweled eyes and gentle smile arrested her senses. He wrapped his arms around her waist, his fingers caressing her back. Her yearning heightened from the memory of his scent, rich with lemon and vanilla and cedar. The heat of his body, his touch, blocked out the cold, blocked out the world. They were like Lancelot and Guinevere, they were Tristan and Isolde—meeting in secrecy, defying duties. Passion drawing their lips close, she tasted his sweet breath entwining hers. He guided her chin toward him, and at last their mouths met. . . .

"What is this, a love letter from Dalton?"

Liz's eyes shot open. Panic flared as Julia lifted the pages off her lap.

"Give it back!" She reached out, but Julia took them hostage behind her.

"My goodness, it *must* be something good."

"Jules, I mean it." She thrust forth her hand.

"I let you read all *my* letters," Julia complained, forehead scrunched.

"I know," she said. "Just not this one, all right?"

Julia studied her intently. Then she shrugged. "Okay," she said, and brought the letter back into view. Liz prepared to accept it, when Julia added, "Right after a quick peek," and darted into the entry.

Liz scrambled behind. "Julia, *don't.*"

"*'Yours truly, Morgan'?*" she read aloud, shifting the papers. "'Dear Betty, thank you so much for your last letter—'"

Liz managed to snatch them back without tearing them. She wanted to evade the pending inquisition, yet the accusation in Julia's eyes welded her shoes to the floor.

Julia folded her arms and waited.

The quiet was deafening. Liz couldn't stand it anymore. "Okay, I wrote him back," she said. "But it doesn't mean what you think it does."

Julia said nothing.

Liz felt heat rising to her face. Thoughts in a flurry, she threw out an excuse. "I just didn't have the heart to tell the poor guy that Betty up and left. And with her doting on some pilot from Australia, you know she's already forgotten all about him." She was shamefully reaching with her next appeal, but nothing else came to mind. "You of all people know what it means to a soldier to get a letter from home."

Julia's expression made it clear she wasn't buying it. "What exactly went on between you two after I left that dance?"

"*Nothing,*" Liz said before her conscience gave a nudge. "We just talked. And danced a little."

"And then?"

"And then I came back from the ladies' room to find him and Betty dancing. So I left. End of story."

"But it's not," Julia pointed out, "if you're still writing him."

Liz calmed herself and spoke evenly. "It's just a few letters, Jules."

"You're sure there isn't more to it?"

Liz parted her lips to say no, yet hesitated. And in that moment of hesitation, doubt about everything in her life returned. Everything but how she felt about the pages in her hands.

"Dalton," Julia called out over Liz's shoulder.

The warning whirled Liz around. Indeed, stepping through the front door in a black overcoat and fedora was Dalton Harris.

The hallway cinched about them.

Liz threw on a smile, reining in her nerves. "What are you doing here?" She blindly slipped the letter into her apron pocket.

"I had a meeting with Bernstein in Uptown. Thought I'd swing by on my way back."

"Oh, great. That's great." Everything was great—so long as she didn't say *great* one more time. "How'd the meeting go?"

"Fantastic." He removed his hat, his face still aglow from his father's recent electoral victory. "Nothing set in stone, but looks like he's landed me a clerkship with Judge Porter."

"Judge Porter? Wow. I'm so happy for you."

"Happy for *us,*" he corrected her. "All groundwork for our future, right?"

Liz maintained her smile.

"Hey, you dropped something." He bent over to pick up the folded stationery on the floor.

Perspiration opened up on Liz's palms as she realized the pages had bypassed her pocket. She quickly reached down, but Julia nabbed them from Dalton in time.

"Thanks," Julia told him, covering the writing with her hands. "You'd think I'd take better care of Christian's letters than that."

"I doubt he'd hold it against you." Dalton grinned. "Now, where was I? Oh yeah, the reason I'm here. Thanksgiving dinner's been changed to four o'clock. That way Congressman Blaine and his wife can make it. Hope that's not a problem."

"Fine by me," Liz answered. "Jules?"

"No argument here."

A small relief. Without Julia there, Liz would have no one other than Dalton's mother to talk to once the gentlemen retired to the parlor. And the tedious subject of acceptable wedding guests was certain to be the main topic.

Dalton glanced at his watch. "Dang, I'm late for my study group. But I'm glad I caught you." He grasped Liz's hand and was about to stamp her mouth with a kiss when he pulled back. His gaze dropped, fixed with concern. "Lizzy, where's your ring?"

She looked at her hand before remembering. "Oh, it's at home, in my jewelry box."

He blew out a breath. "Scared me." Then he tilted his head, the lines on his forehead deepening. "I don't understand, though. Why aren't you wearing it?"

She ushered lightness into her voice. "Because, silly, it's too valuable. With all the solutions we handle, I didn't want it to fall off." And that was the truth. So why were her hands slickening with a second sheen?

He didn't look convinced. "If you don't like it, sweetheart, we could find something else."

"Absolutely not," she insisted. "It's gorgeous. Once it's sized, I won't be worried about losing it."

"Do you want me to go with you, to the jeweler?"

"Well, sure I do. But goodness knows you don't have time right now." He didn't argue. Not that she expected him to. Still, something deep inside her crumpled. "Besides, you've got more pressing issues. I'll just take care of it after the holidays."

His mouth suggested a smile. "That's my girl. Wouldn't want people thinking you were stepping out on me, right?"

"Of course not," she said, which widened his grin.

He nodded to Julia. "See you Thursday?"

"Wouldn't miss it."

He replaced his hat and tipped the brim. "Enjoy your evening, ladies."

"Good night," they responded in unison.

When the door closed behind him, Liz felt as if she'd finally come up for air. Out of the corner of her eye, she caught Julia staring at her.

"It's only a few letters," Liz affirmed.

"If you say so."

Confining tension rose around Liz like bars. The pressure of standing trial emanated from the unspoken. She angled toward the hall. "I have to help with dinner." On her second step, a hand touched her elbow.

"Liz, wait," Julia told her. "I'm saying this as your friend. If you have feelings for another fellow, you owe it to Dalton to be honest. An engagement is a serious commitment."

As opposed to what? A passing fancy?

"I *know* it is," Liz replied, stronger than she'd intended. She softened her tone. "I know it is, Jules." Had her life been buttermilk smooth like Julia's, Liz would surely have been just as disapproving. Her friend wasn't off base; she simply didn't understand.

Julia paused before handing over Morgan's letter. "See you after work," she said, and turned for her office. A caution lined her thin smile: *I hope you know what you're doing.*

Left to her quandary, Liz leaned against a wall. She thought again of Tristan and Isolde and the tragedies that befell them, all for a forbidden love, doomed from the start.

Was she so naïve to think she could win fate's favor, when a couple like that had lost? A voice inside responded, said her deceptions would only lead to heartache—not just for her, but for everyone involved.

Perhaps it was time she listened.

～⊱ 19 ⊰～

November 1944
Dutch New Guinea

Slouched on a stump just outside the ward, Betty pinched her nose and fought a gag reflex. She tried to imagine nice, chilled limeade in the cup at her lips, but was failing miserably. The only drinking water at the hospital spent its days hanging in Lister bags beneath the merciless sun, intensifying the rubberized, chlorinated flavor of the liquid moving down her throat. Another highlight she wouldn't be writing home about. No need to burden her friends with details best left forgotten. The genuinely positive elements were the only tidbits worth sharing, their quantities few enough to fit on pocket-sized postcards.

That, however, would all soon change.

After weeks of Betty's diplomatic, systematic prodding, Captain Kitzafenny had agreed to swap her out with a trained medical tech, as soon as one could be spared from Port Moresby. Betty had heard conditions at the major supply port, located on the southeast side of the island, differed drastically from her primitive encampment in Hollandia. Insect and climate issues, though present, would be vastly more tolerable in a developed area with rec hall dances, day-rooms, and beauty shops. Rumor even had it WACs there cooled off in the afternoons by swimming in crystalline waters off sandy beaches shaded by coconut-garnished palm trees. Precisely what she had signed up for.

Now all Betty had to do was keep tight to the rails and not give her CO any cause to nullify their agreement.

"Knew I'd find ya at the bar." Rosalyn Taylor's velvety drawl reflected the mischievousness in her smile. The South Carolinian private, slight with high cheekbones and short black ringlets, stooped out from the ward's entry of mosquito netting. She secured the screen back in place, protecting patients suffering odorous wounds from being eaten alive.

"I was just so parched," Betty explained sluggishly, preparing to rise. "Did someone need me?"

"Ah, relax, honey. You've been working your fanny off."

Betty plopped back down. Her feet throbbed in her shoes.

Rosalyn lit a cigarette, took a drag, and blew the smoke off to the side. She wiped her glistening face with her sleeve. "I declare, if it isn't hotter than a blazin' bin of cotton."

The midday temperature felt like two hundred degrees to Betty, thanks to the impossible humidity and her sweat-dampened twill. She dropped her head back and stretched her gaze to the scattering of clouds, her mind reaching for the coolness of higher altitudes. "Cripes. Is it *always* going to be this hot?"

"Supposed to taper some by January."

"January, huh." Betty pulsed the chest of her shirt to create a pseudo breeze, then gave up. The movement did no more good than rocking before a coal stove. "So, a couple months and my clothes might stay dry for five whole minutes."

Rosalyn chuckled through another stream of smoke. "Reckon you shouldn't get your hopes up too high, darlin'. Monsoons will be here before you know it."

The bulletins just got better and better. Maybe one of the active volcanoes on the island would simply erupt and put them out of their misery.

"Afternoon, ladies." Tom, the first ward man Betty had befriended, approached with a bundle. Accustomed to the altered shades of everyone's skin from anti-malaria tablets, she hardly noticed his yellow hue anymore. "Ambulance driver dropped it by."

Betty thanked him for the package as he continued on. She perked up and set her cup aside, never too tired for a gift. From the scrawled words, she already knew who'd sent it.

To: Miss Grable
From: Junior

Rosalyn shook her head. "Gotta hand it to the poor boy. If nothin' else, he is determined."

Averaging twice a week, Junior had employed the help of soldiers whose regular runs to the hospital made them ideal couriers for her diverse presents: shelled jewelry created by natives; collectible currency from the Japanese occupancy; fresh apples bartered off ships in the harbor—like manna from heaven compared to their greasy canned mutton and dehydrated rations, the only food that didn't mold in the humidity. Not that Betty could tell, from the taste of them.

"What's your guess?" she asked Rosalyn. "Two tickets to Hawaii this time?"

"If it is, Junior will have to buy himself another one. 'Cause that second seat there'd be mine."

Betty smiled and opened the package. On top, bound in tissue, reading *For the prom,* was a handmade corsage of white orchids and red hibiscus blossoms. She brought the cluster to her nose. In contrast to the usual jungle-hospital stench, the floral fragrance was grander than an entire bottle of Chanel No. 5.

"Bless his heart," Rosalyn said, "that boy *must* be head over heels. Only way of getting orchids round these parts is fetching 'em from the highest treetops." She took the corsage and gave it a long whiff. "I do hope you humor the kid, for outright riskin' his life. At least a peck on the cheek, regulations or not."

Kid was certainly the appropriate title.

"Well, I don't know about that." Betty's thoughts dissolved at the sight of the remaining item in the wrapping. The most splendid treasure on the island. Men's khaki trousers!

Utter joy sprang Betty to her feet. She hugged the thin slacks to her chest and barely contained a squeal that shot from the base of her lungs. "He deserves a kiss, all right!" She bounced childishly on her heels, not caring how foolish she must have appeared.

"Thank the Lord," Rosalyn said. "Now I don't have to worry about you up and stealing my only pair while I'm snoozin'."

Betty shook out the creased pants and held the top edge to her waist. Back home, she wouldn't have been caught dead wearing men's clothing, and this was far from the uniform she'd envisioned when enlisting. Yet here she was, celebrating as if the baggy summer trousers were spun from twenty-four-karat gold. Already she felt several degrees cooler.

Rosalyn rubbed the fabric between her fingers. "You split these seams apart, top to bottom, and you can stitch 'em up to fit ya just fine."

Sewing was a laborious skill Betty had yet to acquire. Her aunt had tried to show her how to mend socks once, but Betty's disinterest cut the lessons short. Julia hadn't even bothered. And what need was there? Even now, a better option stood right beside her.

"Thing is, Roz, I'm not much of a seamstress," she began with a slight pout. "But if you're interested in, say, a trade, I've got a *beautiful* shell necklace I'd be willing to part with."

Rosalyn exhaled a gray plume while retaining a knowing smile. "Tell you what, sugar. I'll do you one better than that. Before lights-out, you come sit on my cot and I'll teach ya how it's done. A little thread, a few loops, and you'll be off and runnin'. How'd that be?"

"Well, I suppose I could." Betty sheathed her disappointment, still hopeful. "But wouldn't it be easier, with me staying out of the way? Maybe I could just watch this first time."

"Honey, I was a high school home arts teacher. By sunrise, you'll be able to make yourself up a whole wardrobe if you like."

Betty was about to scrounge up another tactic, then reminded herself that gaining the reputation of being a goldbrick could roughen her pathway to Port Moresby. Besides, in this heat, if it meant a break from her loathsome winter coveralls, a needle prick or two was a meager price to pay.

"It's a deal," Betty agreed as she shooed a mosquito scouting the landing pad of her hand. She watched the bug drift away on nonexistent wind.

Rosalyn blew more smoke. "You hear about the fresh casualties coming from Leyte?"

Betty nodded. Another endless night ahead. She rubbed her eyes at the prospect.

"Best get movin', then. Don't want *Kiss-her-fanny* to catch us resting on our laurels." Kitzafenny's near miss with a scorpion's tail in the latrine had recently landed her the secret nickname, one that fit in more ways than one.

Betty finished up her water and handed over the empty cup, a makeshift ashtray. In exchange, Rosalyn surprised her with an envelope. "Kept a little goodie for ya. Reckoned you'd like to pass it along yourself."

Betty bit her lower lip, suppressing a grin that rose like a welt at the sight of his name: *Flt. Lt. Leslie Kelly.* She shrugged casually. "What makes you think I'd want to deliver this?"

"Mercy. I have no idea." Rosalyn smirked before rounding the tent.

Left alone, Betty studied the name in the return address: *Nellie Miles.* Yet another of his female correspondents with a surname differing from his own. Evidently, he'd established girlfriends in a chain of ports. A tomcat she'd be wise to steer clear of.

His quiet reserve, however, failed to match. A mystery. One that had caused her mind to spin with possibilities, of who he was, who he'd been before the war. On the rim of sleep at night, she'd let her imagination fill in the gaps. As a child, she had created a make-believe father in the same manner, her mind assembling him like Frankenstein—but with better looks and a nicer outfit, military stripes riding the sleeves. Girls with fathers who'd died in the Great War, she had learned, spurred sympathy rather than gossip.

Betty laid the lieutenant's letter atop her bundled gifts. She headed toward Ward Four, on the east end of the complex. One step after another, she told her heart there was no need to flutter. He was just another pilot. In the Royal Australian Air Force. With the palest blue eyes she'd ever seen.

But no need for fluttering.

In a fluid motion, she swooped around the netting and entered the tent.

"Heya, Betty," the burly lumberjack called from the first bed. "My bathwater ready yet?"

"Still looking for a tub big enough."

"Well, if you're doing the sponging, it's worth the wait."

She shook her head while strolling away.

Right on cue, the Tennessean banjo player whistled his standard—"Pistol Packin' Mama"—in ode to her arrival.

Next came the father of newborn twins, beaming at a fresh photo.

"They gotten any bigger, Grady?" she asked.

"An inch a day, according to the missus."

"Be outgrowing you before long."

"Ain't that the truth." With the Pacific's poor evacuation system, the possibility wasn't all that far-fetched.

On the sixth cot to the right was the paratrooper with one leg missing from mid-thigh. As was his nightly routine, he meticulously polished both his high-laced boots to a perfect gloss.

"Evening, Sergeant Doyle."

A nod. "Miss Betty." Then back to shining.

Finally, up on the left sat the ever-reserved Flight Lieutenant Leslie Kelly. Sketchpad on his lap, he moved his pencil around fairly well in spite of the casts on both forearms. Quick thinking had saved his entire crew, though his forced landing of their Beaufort had earned him bilateral wrist fractures and deep lacerations on his leg and chest. A chest she'd repeatedly dreamt of exploring, mapping every ridge and plain with her hands.

"Afternoon, Lieutenant."

His gaze brushed over her face before returning to his drawing. Earthy brown bangs fell across his broad forehead. "G'day," he said quietly.

Her nerves rose beneath her skin. And for what? The man's scruffy jaw and rugged build portrayed nothing better than a lawless explorer of the outback.

Channeling her energy, she tucked in a loose corner of the sheet at the bottom of his cot. As she stood, a stray lock flailed like a mast from her head. She shoved the strands into her loose hair roll, noting the odd shade of her arms—an orangey combination from red dust and the yellowing effect of her Atabrine. No longer would she gripe about the camp's absence of mirrors.

Compensate with your poise, she told herself.

Free hand on her tilted hip, she stretched her lips demurely. "I see you're an artist."

His attention held to his paper. "Just passin' the dyes."

It took her a moment to realize he meant passing the "days." His accent only swelled her intrigue, as did the way he grasped the pencil with his left hand rather than his right. Another unique characteristic.

She glimpsed the picture he was fashioning in lead. A squinty animal. Round and furry. Quite good, actually. "That's a lovely koala," she said.

He halted and raised his glacier blue eyes. See there? A simple stroke to the ego was all it took. Typical male traits clearly knew no national boundaries.

"It's a wombat," he corrected her with a slight edge.

"Oh. Right." She kept her smile while thinking, *What the heck is* that?

Back to the mission.

She presented his envelope. "They missed this one, during mail call." She set it next to him on the sheet and added in a playful tone, "One of your many lady friends, I suppose." She waited for a reaction, a denial or affirmation.

He returned to his drawing pad. "Ta," was all he said, tossed out like last week's funnies. A bone to a whimpering dog.

Her jaw gaped for only a moment before she sealed it shut, hiding her simmering frustration.

Admittedly she wasn't in top form, but she'd still declined enough date requests from patients to know she deserved a warmer reception. After all, most men on the island had gone without seeing a civilized female for over a year. It hadn't taken her long to figure out that barbed wire surrounded the girls' barracks more to protect the nursing staff from their own soldiers than the enemy.

So what reason could he possibly have for snubbing her outright? And what did he think made *him* so special?

The one thing she did know: She wasn't going to stick around to find out.

"Good day, Lieutenant," she said through tight lips, and strode off before he could reply.

∼ 20 ∼

November 1944
Chicago, Illinois

Julia snatched a napkin from the tabletop dispenser and wiped the chocolate shake dripping down her chin. She narrowed her eyes at Ian and tried for a scowl. But her giggles swiftly broke through and blended with the clamor of the hamburger joint—the sporadic dinging of a service bell, the prattling of customers, a Tommy Dorsey tune on the nickelodeon.

Ian reclined in his white booth seat with a cocky grin.

"You did that on purpose!" She hurled her wadded napkin at him.

He showed his palms, a poor feign of innocence. "Not my fault you took a drink right then. I was just telling a story here."

Contemplating his tale, she eyed him dubiously, scanning for truth. "Did you and your buddies actually do that?"

"You wouldn't blame us if you knew the sarge. He was a real boot." Ian chomped on the last of his fries.

"So, then what did he do," she challenged, "when he found the poor animal in his bed?"

"That's the topper of it all," he mumbled around his food, then washed it down with a slurp of malt. "Sarge was so drunk, he rolled over and gave the goat a smooch on the kisser. Sobered him right up when he realized the hairy thing wasn't his wife."

The image sent giggles again flowing out of Julia. So many this time, her stomach muscles revisited the weariness of a hike around Devils Lake from her Girl Scout days.

"Whole prank was my bunkmate's idea. Sarge had it in for the fella since day one. And all because Marv's last name was Sir. He'd scream in his face, 'I hope you don't expect me to call you Sir, Private!' " Ian shook his head. "Marv must've had double the amount of duties, on account of that blessed name."

Recovering, Julia dabbed her happy tears with a fresh napkin and leaned back to catch her breath. Exaggerated or not, his stories were keepers.

"Are you sure you were in the war all this time?" she said. "Sounds more like a fraternity party to me."

The broadness of his smile withered unexpectedly. Memories seemed to pass like a stream beneath his cloudy hazel eyes. "Had our share of both good times and bad, I suppose." His words came out heavy, almost muffled. He rubbed his thumb on his beveled malt glass, then shifted his gaze to the darkened window.

Julia regretted the insinuation of her quip. Awkwardness had dangled between them when they first reunited at the bowling alley tonight, but by the fourth frame enough laughter and ribbing had brushed the discomfort away. So much so, in fact, the incidents from her visit the month before—his family dinner quarrel and nightmare manifestation—had slipped into the outskirts of her mind. Only once during their game had she witnessed him jolt at the cracking of bowling pins. And even that was easy to dismiss, given his smart appearance. The pressed slacks and button-up shirt, the Brylcreem-slicked hair. Though still leaner than he was prior to the service, Ian's face had gained a healthy fullness, increasing the warmth he now exuded in her direction. At last, an air of acceptance for his brother's girl.

And she wasn't about to lose it.

Julia aimed for a sly expression. "So what do you think Christian's going to say? You know, when he hears I whipped his big brother at bowling."

Ian smiled as he met her eyes, his outer glow returning. In the reflective glass, he was again the spitting image of her fiancé. "Well, he might have some trouble buying that one."

"Oh, and why's that? Because no male Downing could possibly be beaten by a girl?"

He moistened his lips and leaned forward, elbows on the table. A curling motion of his finger invited her closer. She obliged, eyebrow raised. The intimate space between them felt cozy as flannel. A space reserved for Christian that only his sibling could borrow with ease.

"Truth is," he said quietly, "I might've understated my usual score by a bit." A likely excuse to protect his male ego.

"Are you claiming you *let* me win?"

He sat back. Another grin settled on his face. "You really did bowl a decent game," he assured her. "If it's any consolation, it's one of the few sports I still beat Chris at."

As she analyzed the remark, her pride began to cower. She knew firsthand that Christian's athletic abilities didn't exclude the art of bowling. Which meant, if Ian was being as honest as he sounded, he indeed had purposely fumbled tonight's game of tenpins.

She flew back in her seat and crossed her arms, feeling her cheeks flush. "I did a victory dance for five minutes, and you never said a word."

"I didn't want to interrupt," he said, and winked. "Besides, the pinsetter loved your dance."

Julia huffed with a glare. "Okay, that's it. I want a rematch. Right now."

"Are you out of your tree?" he asked, incredulous. "The bowling alley's closing soon."

"Not bowling. . . ." She pondered alternatives that leveled the playing ground.

"What, lagging pennies?"

"Backgammon," she announced. "Unless that's too intellectual for you."

A smile caught his lips. "We'll find out, won't we?"

At that moment, she realized how much youthful feistiness was still within her—like a pair of mittens she had thought she'd outgrown, yet was still a perfect fit.

Ian gestured to the pile of fries in her burger basket. "Gonna finish those?"

"Be my guest." She slid the basket toward him. "Cheater."

Grinning, he reached between the salt and pepper shakers for the bottle of ketchup.

"Here, you missed one." She lobbed a stray fry toward the basket, but overshot and hit Ian in the chest. His mouth fell open in astonishment.

She did her best to stave off laughter. Regardless of how it came across, she never would have done such a thing intentionally. "I'm so sorry. Honest, I didn't mean to."

"Uh-huh," he said, tongue pressed against his inner cheek.

"No, really. It was an accident."

He grabbed a handful of the flimsy potatoes. "Did you say you were still hungry?"

Her amusement dropped off. "You wouldn't dare!"

"How rude of me not to offer you some." He retracted his elbow, preparing to pitch.

"Ian—"

She tried to duck sideways in time, but the cluster hit her square in the cheek. She wiped the moisture off her face. A glob of ketchup. He exploded into laughter, emanating pure, unbridled joy, a sound she could revel in all evening—if not for retaliation taking precedence.

Julia lurched for the oval basket, catching only the rim as Ian raised it up.

"Let go!" she ordered.

"Not a chance, peach."

A tug-of-war for the ammunition ensued, back and forth, lone fries diving this way and that. Both held firm, taking care not to yank too hard for risk of receiving a lapful.

"I take it you kids are done here." A stern female voice came from the side.

Ian and Julia froze. They tentatively turned their heads up toward the waitress, whose dimpled elbows led to fists on apron-stretched hips. Clearly her wages didn't justify mopping up after the outbreak of a diner-wide food fight.

"Real shame you won't be staying for dessert." The woman confiscated their baskets and grunted as she ambled off. Once she'd disappeared through the swinging kitchen door, Julia returned to Ian. Muffled laughs snuck from their guts until finally tapering off.

"Still up for that rematch?" he asked.

"So long as I get the ivories."

"We'll see about that." He tossed a few crinkled bills onto the table. Then he helped her into her winter coat and extended his palm. She accepted with a smile. Hand in his, she followed him toward the door, every cell in her body soaking warmth from their unexpected connection.

The scent of roasting almonds wafted from a vendor's cart in the shadows. Rubbing her arms against the crisp night air, Julia surveyed the ground that surrounded the massive oak tree. Late November, and its branches remained dressed, denying the inevitable.

"It's somewhere overrr . . . there." She pointed toward the flowerbed beside the long runway of hedgerow lining the park. A street lamp fingered shadows over the secret spot, a hand protecting the treasure of her youth.

"I take it you got a permit," Ian said, "with this being city-owned property." He looked at her askance with a hint of a smile.

Funny, it had never occurred to her she might have broken the law by burying her shoe box. A bona fide criminal at six years old. The very idea tickled her. "I suppose I was a bit of a rebel at times." She continued leisurely on the walking path speckled with leaves like an autumn stew.

"Sorta figured that about ya," he said, joining her.

She wasn't sure how to take that, but it sounded like a compliment.

In the background, the "L" rattled a melody on its tracks. Julia rubbed her gloved hands together, noting how quickly summer had passed. The heat she had absorbed at the diner was escaping through her stockings. She would have worn a longer skirt if bowling hadn't been among their planned activities.

"This your way of delaying the rematch?" he asked. "Or you just wanting a stroll down memory lane?"

She tossed him a semi-glare. "We're taking a shortcut to the bus stop."

"Thought maybe you were getting nervous, thinking of backing out."

"If anyone's turning chicken, it isn't me."

"Dandy," he said. "Although you should probably know that in high school, I was president of the Backgammon Club. Genesee County champ, three seasons running."

She halted at the news. "Are you serious?" Of all the games she could have chosen.

His mouth split into a slow grin. "Nah. Just giving you guff."

Chuckling, she lolled her head back. Then she pushed him from the walkway and onto the shadowed grass. "You're evil, you *know* that."

"Guess it makes sense that we get along so well, then, doesn't it?"

She shook her head as they treaded onward, their first wordless moment of the evening, comfortable as childhood friends.

At last, angling toward his profile, she said what she'd been waiting to all evening. "All joking aside, Ian, it's really good to see you. I know you said you'd come out here sometime, but when I didn't hear from you, I thought you'd changed your mind."

Seriousness crept over him, drawing his shoulders down. "After what happened, I wasn't sure you'd want me to." He dug his hands into his pockets, gave her a sideways glance. "By the way, thank you," he said. "For not telling my folks."

She replied simply, "There was nothing to tell."

Quiet billowed as they passed a pair of picnic tables, empty and gray in the night. She thought of George and Cora, and the gray emptiness that lurked in the corners of their home. There, Ian remained an unsettled ghost, stuck between worlds of who he used to be and who he'd become.

Julia's sympathy for all three of them spilled over. "They love you, you know. Very much. They just need time. Same as you."

He didn't speak, but she heard his thoughts like a distant voice: *Maybe so . . . maybe so.*

Careful not to push too hard, she continued, "Are things getting better? For you, I mean. Because you seem so much better."

He shrugged a little. "Comes and goes some days. But yeah, it's been better," he said. "Since your visit."

In the tinged glow of another street lamp, he sucked in a breath and projected a smile, the kind that took effort. "So what's in it? In that time capsule of yours?"

She honored his redirection by summoning the old images. "Well, if I remember correctly . . . I threw in a kazoo, the front page of a newspaper. A '31 Lincoln penny, and a handful of candy, I think. Oh, and a whole wad of hair ribbons."

"Hair ribbons?"

"Every color of the rainbow," she said. Then she confessed, "I actually only put them in there so I wouldn't have to wear them anymore."

"Did it work?"

She rolled her eyes. "I wish. My mother ended up buying me two new sets."

"I see," he drew out. "So you were the tree-climbing, world-explorer type."

"You could say that." Julia smiled. "My mom had a heck of a time forcing the tomboy out of me." As soon as the words escaped, she realized how terrible her admission might have come across. How it could rule her an ill-suited match for his younger brother, or an improper mother if they were to be blessed with baby girls. A tip she'd snagged from *Ladies' Home Journal*.

Amending the comment, she added, "Now that I've grown up, though, I just want to be the best wife I can for my husband."

Ian bent down and picked up a few large pebbles without breaking stride. He side-armed one down the path, skimming as if on a frozen lake. "And what about your career?" he asked.

"Well . . . my job will be looking after our home."

"But I thought you'd been offered an internship. Something in New York. In the fashion biz."

She slowed her steps, taken aback. "How did you hear about—" she started to say, then concluded: His brother must have written him, informed him of the flattering but impractical opportunity. She'd only told Christian in a brief mention, buried in a string of the usual updates. Withholding the information, after all, would be dishonest.

"I turned it down," she said with finality. "With us getting married, there's no reason to go."

"Did Chris say you couldn't?" Ian threw another rock, harder.

"*What?* No, that's ridiculous." Her laugh came out short, nervous sounding. "He wouldn't have—he didn't have to. I made the decision on my own. For the two of us." Somehow, when she wasn't paying attention, the casualness of their discussion had ended. She found herself in a minefield, navigating right and wrong answers.

"It's something you enjoy, though, right?" Not a question; a statement with an underlying chill matching the air.

"Yes, I suppose. . . ." Shame tinted her thoughts—from how long she had waited to decline the offer, how she'd responded cowardly with a note. Flustered, she answered now with the only truth that mattered. "But I love Christian more."

Leaves rustled, a car engine coughed, and the conversation died. Yet the thoughts it propelled in Julia didn't.

Had she said something to Ian earlier to bring this on? When she'd spoken about Liz's teaching plans, had Julia implied she regretted her decision?

No. That couldn't be. Because she didn't regret a thing.

Why, then, did she feel the smothering anxiety of an inquisition? As if he were looking for something, a mistake, a flaw.

Their pace climbed, along with her defenses. She glanced at him, at the guarded expression she knew all too well.

Of course.

How could she have missed it? The way Ian had been so charming all evening—like Clark Gable as a spy in *Comrade X*—relaxing her so she'd spill her secrets. She wanted to ask what it was he held against her. Yet before she could craft an appropriate phrase, Ian huffed. Perhaps meant only for himself, but too blatant, too derisive, for her to ignore.

Her legs froze. "What does *that* mean?"

He faced her and regarded her expression. "I didn't say anything."

"But you were thinking something. So say it."

He paused before replying. "It doesn't matter." When he tried to walk away, she tugged the elbow of his sleeve, sharply.

"It matters to *me*," she told him.

He turned toward the cars traversing the grid of the city, his focus on a theater glowing pink and white neon. His feet shuffled in place as though itching to flee.

In her periphery, she noticed a silhouetted couple on a park bench a few yards off the path. When Ian's gaze panned the necking teenagers, he muttered, "C'mon, let's go." He set off without waiting for her.

"Ian, wait," she said, trying to catch up. "What is it?"

"Nothing."

She couldn't contain her frustration a minute more. She was through with being judged. "If you don't think I'm good enough for your brother, you should just say so!"

He stopped as if hitting an invisible wall, and wheeled. A look of genuine astoundment contorted his face. "Julia. That's not it."

"Then *what?*" She charged up to him. "What were you thinking?"

"I don't—you're just, you're—"

"What? I'm what?"

"Perfect, all right?" he burst out. "You're one more perfect thing in my brother's life!"

She stared, stunned. "Ian," she mouthed.

"Everything comes so damn easy for Chris, and now he's got *you!* Someone who's willing to sacrifice anything for him."

He jerked his face to the side. The tremble in his breaths, the strain in his neck muscles, all revived the intensity of the night in his room. She could feel the hungry sorrow inside him clawing him back down. She scraped for a reply, something to soothe him, to keep him from retreating. Instead, she simply touched his wrist.

He didn't pull away.

"Ian," she told him, "any girl would be lucky to be with you. You're amazing, and funny, and . . ." She strengthened her assertion. "You're going to find a woman who makes you happy, I just know it." She tilted her head, seeking eye contact, to confirm he was listening.

His gaze lowered and locked with hers. The sheer desire pouring from his eyes caused her heart to seize, a shiver to race down her back.

"I've already found her," he said, a wisp of a voice.

Before she could think, he hooked the nape of her neck with his hand and drew her close. The mist of their breaths mingled as he leaned in, eliminating the final inches separating their lips. The raw passion of his kiss sealed her eyes, drained her strength. He swept his tongue across hers. His fingers slid through her hair. A flash of a moment and his mouth was on her neck. Primitive, strong, wanting. She could feel herself slipping away, her head drifting to the side, an invitation for more. As he pressed his body forward, heat from his skin burned through her clothing. The moisture of his lips traveled downward, and the whispering of her name rose, spoken against her collarbone. Julia. She was Julia. And he was . . .

Ian.

Senses sobering, she lifted her eyelids.

Jesus, what were they doing? What was *she* doing?

Stop! her mind screamed as his mouth again covered hers. Confusion and panic rode her veins. Her hands tunneled up between them to reach his chest. He held her tighter.

"Ian, don't!" She shoved him away with a desperate heave. From her mouth came a spearing gasp of regret. "What just happened?" she whispered into her glove-covered palm, a barricade raised too late.

"Julia," he said, and reached for her, but she yanked herself out of the way.

She couldn't be touched. She couldn't look at him. "I have to go," she said, and spun around to leave.

The clicking of her heels kept time with her thumping pulse. Behind her, she could feel Ian's eyes like scorching needles on her back. Hatred for him swelled with every step, every thought—not merely for what he did, but for the poisonous seeds of doubt he'd planted within her.

✥ 21 ✥

December 18, 1944
Belgium

A stab to Morgan's ear jarred him awake. His arms shot out of his sleeping bag. Reflexively, he snagged the Luger from the field jacket beneath his head and sprang up to a sitting position. He pointed the pistol forward, heart pounding, vision straining.

"Mac, don't shoot! He's unarmed!" Jack's voice.

Morgan let loose a breath and relaxed his finger on the trigger, just as laughter cut through the frosty air. He rubbed his eyes with his left hand and identified the predator: a scrawny, tattered chicken, the last original resident of the barn where the eight GIs were billeted.

As he shooed the bird away, he felt spider legs run downward from his ear. He shuddered a small convulsion. He frantically swatted at his neck and he discovered it was . . . bread crumbs? How the hell—

"Baaawk! Bawk, bawk, bawk, bawk!" Jack's mimicked squawking answered the question. The human birdbrain clomped over the tainted straw, bent elbows flapping, pecking the air with his nose. On a hay bale in the corner, Frank sat wrapped in a blanket, his smirk as broad as Charlie's across the room.

Morgan lay down, muttering, "Bastards." He gazed at the abandoned bird nest on the rafter above, irritated that he was suddenly so awake. Until today, ever a light sleeper, he'd been exempt from their nighttime pranks. Come to think of it, his stint of sleep just now had been remarkably deep. Must have been his body's self-reward for the two-hour guard duty he'd posted during last night's blizzard. Back and forth, back and forth, no breaks in his pacing. Not for military diligence, but because nodding off and freezing to the ground was a quick way to earn admission through the Pearly Gates.

"Runner just left," Charlie told him. "Said chow's up for grabs."

"See you soon, Sleeping Beauty," Jack called out before clucking again. Charlie laughed while following Jack and two other GIs toward the doorway, all bundled in long brown overcoats.

Morgan wanted to throw something heavy in Jack's direction, but decided it wasn't worth the effort. What's more, knocking out one of the tag-team breakfast fetchers would mean having to hike to the mess tent himself.

When Jack slid the door open on its track, snow-reflective light flooded the dim barn. Morgan jerked away. His eyes ached as though he'd stared straight into the sun.

"Oh, and Morgan," he heard Charlie say, "try not to scare the chicken off while we're gone. Gonna need her for supper later."

"Why, Chap?" Jack said. "You looking for a date tonight?"

The door rolled shut.

Morgan blinked away the white spots floating before him like lightning bugs. Gradually, clarity of the weathered walls returned, the boards grooved and faded, gouged from horses' hooves and equipment, peppered with lone rusty nails. He then made out the figure sitting hunched against the opposite wall: "Geronimo"—one-quarter Apache, full-blooded rancher from Lubbock. Reserved as always, he appeared engrossed in a Wild West pocket novel from a Red Cross volunteer.

Morgan settled back in and closed his eyes. He tried to clear his mind, tried to sleep. He covered his ears with his jacket-turned-pillow to quiet the rustling of Geronimo turning pages. Finally, the start of grogginess fingered toward him, until a loud crack came from outside. He snapped upright.

Frank afforded the small filthy window above him a two-second glance, then back to his letter writing. Geronimo simply flipped another page in his story. Neither showed concern, but Morgan still found his body rising to investigate. Better safe than sorry.

Cocooned in his blankets, Luger at his side, he used his sleeve to wipe a circle clean on the glass pane. Flawless white snow covered nearly every inch of the country road outside.

Then came another crack.

This time he saw the source: a pine tree bough collapsing under the weight of that pretty, harmless-looking snow. In nature, he'd learned, everything had a breaking point. And beauty could be deceiving.

"A little jumpy today?" Frank asked him.

"Gee, I wonder why."

Frank grinned as if reliving Jack's stunt in his mind. "Looks like you had a nice nap, at least."

"Yeah," Morgan said, still amazed at the fact. "Actually slept like I was back home."

"You farm boys always sleep in barns?"

"Only on special occasions." The answer conjured a flashback from Morgan's early teens, he and Charlie passed out in the hayloft. They'd spent half the night flexing their rebellious muscles with a fifth of cheap whiskey and a hand-rolled cigarette. A long day of fieldwork with brutal hangovers had served as their father's most effective punishment.

Morgan grabbed a seat on a bale, set his pistol aside. Until he could quell his jitters, sleep would be a lost cause. "So where's Boomer?" he asked.

"Pneumonia." Frank's tone was matter-of-fact. "Sarge came to get him while you were sleepin'. Sent him to a rear field hospital."

The Florida-native firefighter never stood a chance against the weather. "Poor guy."

"Yeah, but at least his hackin' won't keep us up anymore. I could use the rest."

Not long ago, Morgan's first inclination would have been to protest the coldhearted comment. Instead, he found himself nodding in agreement. "Wish I'd jotted down some of the guy's punch lines."

"He had some whoppers, I'll give him that."

"Five bucks says he's showing off his 'girlfriend' as we speak."

"Ten bucks says the docs will find her more amusin' than the nurses."

Morgan smiled, imagining their reactions to the pinup model tattooed on Boomer's forearm jiggling and dancing as he wiggled his knuckles.

It was always rougher losing the funny ones.

"Writing June?" Morgan motioned toward the scrawled paper on Frank's lap.

With a shrug, Frank replied, "God knows when mail's coming around, but might as well keep scribblin'." His hands, swollen from cuts, evidenced a recent night of preparing barbed-wire apron entanglements minus the hindrance of gloves. The skin was chapped and cracked, painful for sure, but the guy was never one to complain.

"Now, Rev, you need any poems for June, you be sure and tell me."

Frank grinned. "Thanks, but I'll stick with my standards."

"Suit yourself," he said. "So long as you don't forget to rave about all your high-class buddies here."

"Always do. Right after I give her the dope about our gourmet food and fancy hotels."

Despite the lighthearted delivery, Morgan knew there was truth in his friend's clowning; no doubt the majority of soldiers packed their letters with similar falsehoods. All well meant, but Morgan had yet to find comfort in the fibbing-out-of-love principle. Even with his father, it had taken years for Morgan's resentment to dissipate over the lie that stole the meaningful good-byes he and Charlie had deserved with their mother. A moment they could never get back.

Morgan flinched at a thud on the barn roof, then a sliding sound. Another branch. He huffed solid breaths into his cold, cupped hands. "So," he said, "you marrying this girl, or what?"

"Better believe it, Mac." Frank pulled a small photo out of his pocket, rubbed the edge with his thumb. "We get home, first thing I'm gonna do is get down on one knee and pop the question."

Morgan glanced at the snapshot, already familiar with her sweet doe eyes and long black hair. The photo had accumulated no fewer wrinkles than Betty's from periodic peeks.

"And what about *your* gal?" Frank asked.

"What do you mean?"

"You know, the blonde who sends those letters you can't put down?"

Morgan felt his ears redden, yet his nerves calming at the thought of her. "Not sure, just have to see. It's not like you and June," he said. "I really hardly know her."

Frank slanted a smile. "You sure trade a lot of mail with a dame you hardly know."

Morgan's gaze dropped to the floor. Was he completely off his nut to fall for a girl he'd exchanged all of a dozen words with in person? The question had been passing through his mind more and more frequently, always disappearing before logic could respond.

Ah, what the hell. If anyone would give him a straight answer, it was Frank.

"Thing is," Morgan admitted, "I barely spoke to her when we met. But now, I just . . . I think she might be the gal for me." He scuffed his boot in the dirt. "Sounds pretty stupid, huh?"

"Nah, not a bit. The second I first saw June walk into that diner, I knew right then." Frank hesitated and his eyes darkened. "You wanna hear stupid, it's me being stubborn. Telling her she has to move to Chicago to be with me, rather than stay in New York where her family lives." He pointed his pen at Morgan. "I tell you this much. When we're back stateside, I don't care if it's New York or Mars, wherever she is, that's where I'm gonna be."

The door squeaked open, severing the discussion, one Morgan suspected would never continue.

Charlie stomped into the barn and shook off his snow-covered overshoes. The other GIs trailed directly behind. The chicken made a sad attempt to flap out of their way.

"Breakfast is served, ladies." Charlie handed Morgan the standard special of the week: a canteen of chilled coffee and a mess kit filled with cold oatmeal and flapjacks. Not a brass-worthy spread, but a step up from another can of pork 'n' beans. "Gonna have to wolf it down, though. We're movin' out."

"How soon?" Frank asked.

"Didn't say." Jack passed along Frank's meal. "But convoys should be rolling in any minute."

Frank slid his paper into the coat pocket where he stored letters from June. When he caught Morgan's eye, they exchanged a swift look of understanding. Neither was about to tear up his most treasured items, regardless of the policy for GIs headed to the front.

While their buddies gathered up, the two of them joined Geronimo in shoveling down their food. They ate their pancakes as eagerly as if they were hot off the griddle and slathered with maple syrup. Morgan had barely swallowed his first spoonful of the bland, pasty oatmeal when he heard wheels crunching snow outside. An icy siren calling them back to war.

All seven soldiers, packed and layered in combat gear, raced out to put dibs on a wooden-bench spot in the rear of a cold truck. Much like the Army slop lines, seats were obtained on a first-come-first-served basis, the tailgate favored for its fresher air and convenient escape route. Somehow, it was a seat Charlie always managed to nab.

The convoy soon set off for an undisclosed destination.

Over slippery roads, the trucks crept along. They stopped intermittently, waiting for signals to continue, occasionally heaving vehicles mired in the semi-frozen mud. Rounding the sixth hour, Morgan studied the haggard GIs seated across from him—noses as red as their bloodshot eyes, bodies hunched, faces drawn. In eerie silence they swayed, like passengers in a hearse being driven to their own funerals.

The way Allied troops had been storming across Europe, rumors that the war would be over by Christmas had flurried. Fellas in Morgan's outfit had gone into great detail describing the turkey dinners they planned to devour with their families and the evenings they'd spend singing along with tunes on a Victrola. Thus, enthusiasm had plummeted like never before when the news arrived: Kraut paratroopers were dropping throughout Belgium; disguised,

English-speaking saboteurs were infiltrating American camps; and Allied infantry were retreating westward in masses.

If not for telling Betty he'd hold firm to the belief of making it home, surrendering his hope might have been an option.

After ten long hours, the convoy came to a halt, this time with orders to proceed on foot. In a single column of human dominoes, they marched thirty feet apart as a defense strategy.

Morgan stared at the muddy trail ahead. Lining the road, GI helmets topped bayoneted rifles planted in the ground; each acted as a "litter" marker for the frozen soldiers lying in the ditches awaiting proper burial. Horse and cow carcasses lay half buried in the snow, adding to the smell of decay and despair. In the opposing direction, a drove of refugees and civilians marched endlessly to nowhere. The feeble travelers, forced to abandon their homes, hauled only their lightest and most valuable belongings.

Morgan hardly batted an eye at the gruesome scene that would have sickened him before entering the war. Death and devastation had since become the norm. He was, however, surprisingly troubled by another sight: a little girl crying over a doll she had dropped in the dirty slush. Strangers carelessly trampled what must have been her last cherished possession, her pleas ignored like those of countless innocents wracked in the enemy cross fire. He watched the child being tugged away. Her desperate wails compressed his heart.

He wanted to chase after her and wipe her tears, tell her it would all be over soon. But he couldn't; word had it Hitler wasn't about to relinquish his throne. Even now, in a massive counter-attack, the Führer's armies were penetrating thinly defended areas through the Ardennes forest, entrapping GIs and pushing battle lines back toward the English Channel. With Allied troops stretched too far away from supplies, the tide of the war could clearly turn in Germany's favor.

Morgan tried not to dwell on that possibility once he'd reached Slevant. But it was easier said than done. In spite of the U.S. Army's need-to-know restrictions, something told him their impending confrontation would be their most crucial yet. And rumors of a massacre of American POWs in Malmédy only magnified his nerves.

"Spread out and dig in!" shouted the second lieutenant, fresh from West Point.

"We expecting backup?" Frank asked.

"That's a negative. Orders are to hold the line, whatever it takes. Shoot anything that moves." With that, the guy jumped into a jeep and careened away—far away, Morgan hoped. In battle, rookie officers often proved the greatest liability.

As engineers rushed to lay mines, Morgan scouted the darkening town for tactical stationing points. Going with his gut, he led Charlie to the top of a hill overlooking a steep-sided valley and a large portion of the village. The location sandwiched them between two heavily armed teams. To the right, an embankment sported a pair of antitank bazooka GIs separated from their company; to the left, Frank and a band of machine gunners held the roof of a two-story brewery.

The ground too frozen for them to excavate, Morgan and Charlie forged a foxhole by scooping snow with their helmets. No sooner had they finished packing their mound than a message reached the hill: A Kraut armored column was headed north, directly toward Slevant.

The countdown had begun.

❧ 22 ❧

December 18, 1944
Chicago, Illinois

Liz gripped the creaking ladder as she reached out in a rush, but her reflex had kicked in too late. The glass sphere skimmed her fingertips and shattered at the base of the tree.

"Oh, murder," she groaned.

She ought to quit her job this minute. Surely someone else on the nursing home staff could have handled hanging the ornaments. Not everyone was preparing to head out like Julia. Or baking meat loaf like the chef. Or cataloging medications like her supervisor.

Besides, Christmas was only a week away; in no time they'd be taking all the garish decor down again. Whatever survived that long, anyhow.

She descended into the moody shadows created by the fire in the hearth. Kneeling on the cherrywood floor, she gathered the large triangular shards and tried to ignore the pungent smell of tree sap. The noble pine, fully loaded with blinking lights and shimmery garland, showed like a display at Macy's, only feeding her annoyance. In fact, the whole sitting room could have been a Norman Rockwell sketch. Even snowflakes feathered the corners of the window with their clingling, taunting crystals.

Liz had aimed, once again, to make it through the Yuletide season without untucking old family memories. Yet what chance did she have when tomorrow marked the official anniversary? The afternoon of their quarrel. The night her mother packed her bags, leaving behind only a single wrapped present beneath the tree. *To: Elizabeth,* the small gift tag read. Characters from *The Nutcracker* on red matte paper covered the square box. A thin solitary white ribbon ran through the middle of the Sugar Plum Fairy. For months, Liz had fallen asleep staring at that wrapped gift on her dresser, bartering her hopes like a little girl—as if not opening the box, a demonstration of the restraint that had escaped her, would have brought her mother home.

To this day, buried in Papa's basement, the package remained sealed.

"It's beautiful." Julia's voice pulled her back to the tree-in-progress. The redhead stood between the open pocket doors, dressed in her navy winter coat with a curly lamb collar. Her notoriously heavy suitcase rested at her feet.

"Thanks," Liz replied. She tried for a smile that fell flat when the velvety voice of Bing Crosby drifted into the room. "I'll Be Home for Christmas." The king of all merciless holiday tunes. Lyrics about snow and mistletoe caused her chest to ache, straining to uphold its weakening walls.

Liz stood and placed the glass fragments onto the claw-footed table. "I just hope they don't take this one out of my wages," she said, forcing a joke.

Julia didn't smile. She seemed preoccupied, as though engaged in another conversation in her head and deciding which snippet to share aloud. With her reserved demeanor over the past several weeks, she was clearly storing up comments regarding the moral dilemma of Betty's letters.

Not that it mattered anymore.

For several weeks nothing but bills and Christian's weekly posts had arrived in the mail. The accumulation of gold stars in neighborhood windows continued to compound Liz's anxiety. If something had happened to Morgan, how would she know? Would her last letter to him be returned, or added to a bin of the forgotten?

"I've been meaning to talk to you," Julia said finally. "About Morgan."

Precisely as Liz figured. Only she wasn't up for this tonight. Even the mention of his name moistened her eyes. "Please," she interjected. "I know what you're going to say."

"No. You don't," Julia told her. "I was going to say that—that I . . ."

"Yes?" *Spit it out already.*

Julia exhaled. "That I'm sorry," she finished. "I was wrong to have judged you."

Liz's response stalled. She hadn't seen that coming. Her eyes connected with Julia's. In them, she found a fresh level of understanding. So much was said in a glance, Liz needed only to respond with a nod.

Then Bing's solemn melody wedged between them, breaking the moment.

"Anyway." Julia flicked her hand, as if batting away the song. "When did you say your father's arriving?"

Another swell topic. Perhaps they could cover flood and famine next.

"Christmas Eve," Liz replied lightly. "And leaving right after New Year's."

"Oh, good. Then you can still make it to my parents' in time, right? For Elsie's birthday."

"Are you kidding? I'm dying to meet the next Shirley Temple."

"Well, don't worry about a gift. My mother's bought enough for Elsie's next *ten* birthdays." Tugging her white gloves on, Julia glimpsed her watch. "Jeepers, I gotta get to the station." She wrapped a cashmere scarf over her tresses and lugged her suitcase toward the front door. "By the way, Viola wanted you to stop by when you get a sec."

"Will do. Travel safely," Liz said, wishing her own trip to Pittsburgh—or to anywhere else in the galaxy—were sooner.

The fine soprano humming of "Silent Night" flitted through the hall. Following the notes, Liz scraped for a convincing smile. She wasn't in the mood for a heart-to-heart chat or analysis of her love life. And even if she were, the sweet woman, at no fault of her own, couldn't possibly relate.

"Excuse me, ma'am," Liz called from the door, "but a resident upstairs is complaining about someone singing off-key."

"Is that so?" Viola retorted in bed without looking up from her knitting. "Then the person must be tone deaf."

"Obviously," Liz replied. Now to speed their visit along. "Julia mentioned you needed something?"

"Do me a favor, sweet pea. Fetch me the ball of pink yarn on the bureau there."

And Julia couldn't have done this? was Liz's first thought. But that was merely her annoyance talking, sharpened by her reluctance to move into close range of Viola's all-knowing sensors.

Liz snatched the yarn, placed it on the mattress, and started away. "Well, if you need anything else . . ."

"What, is there a fire you gotta put out? It's a rest home. Take a rest." Viola indicated a spot to sit beside her blanketed knees.

Liz wanted to decline, but any believable excuse eluded her. To prevent suspicion, she perched on the bed as ordered. Viola's knitting needles continued to dance in their silent rhythm. "So, what's the latest project?" she asked, deflecting the focus from herself.

"A little somethin' for my newest grandchild."

"My goodness. How many does that make now?"

"Fourteen and a half. Danny's wife is expecting right after the holidays."

"Well, that should be fun, seeing the whole family next week."

"Fun?" Viola clucked. "I'll be lucky to make it out alive."

A giggle almost snuck past Liz's throat.

"God love 'em, but they've all got more kids, pets, and toys than Carter has Pills. Why do you think I live *here*?"

No doubt there were heartfelt reasons as well, with her late husband's gravesite a short distance away.

"Speaking of holidays," Viola said, "I actually did ask you here for a purpose." She set her supplies aside and reached for her nightstand. From the top drawer, she drew a long bronze scarf. "Finally put the finishing touches on your Christmas present this afternoon. Found the perfect shade to bring out the color of those pretty eyes of yours."

Liz sighed at the meticulous needlework. "Oh, Vy. It's divine."

She dragged the fuzzy fringe across her cheek, her whole body warming at the touch.

"I know it's a smidge late for your engagement, so this is my one stone taking out two birds."

At the mention of her nuptials, Liz's delight shrank as fast as it had risen. She pulled the gift from her face, let coolness retake her skin, and doubled the scarf around her neck. "Thank you," she said, and leaned in for an embrace. It was in that moment she realized just how much she needed one.

"Pardon me, ladies."

Liz turned toward the familiar voice, surprised. "Dalton, hi."

He stood at the door, pinching his hat against his side. His smile appeared as thin as the pinstripes in his suit.

"Well, if it isn't Prince Charming," Viola said.

"Nice to see you, Ms. Knowles."

"It's been a while since I've seen you round here. Everything Liz has been saying about you must be true."

"I guess that all depends on what she's told you." Sternness bound his voice, squeezing each syllable into a jagged point. "Liz, may I speak to you?" He motioned behind him with his hat.

"Of course," she said, and turned to Viola. "If you'll excuse us."

Viola gave a few waves of her hand. "Shoo, shoo, off you go."

As Liz moved toward the hallway, she picked through possible causes for Dalton's demeanor: a negative ruling in his mock trial, his article rejected by the *Law Review*. However, neither seemed likely, nor urgent enough to bring him down here at this hour. So what could it be?

Her cheeks flushed at the conclusion: He'd found out. About Morgan. But how?

Oh God, how could she explain? And how could he understand why, or what she was feeling? *She* didn't even understand as much.

In the hall, she swallowed her nerves, forced them down like cod liver oil. Casually clasping her hands, she faced Dalton and smiled. "To what do I owe this honor?"

"Liz, I know we haven't spent much time together lately, but how could you?" He rubbed the back of his neck in aggravation.

The thudding in her chest grew, moving to her throat and on to her temples.

"I thought—" he started. "No, I *know* I told you how important tonight's banquet was to me."

Banquet?

Relief drifted over her, relaxing her from the outside in, until she grasped her error. His first prominent speaking engagement, she'd missed it completely. "Dalton, I don't know what to say. I meant to ask for the night off, I did."

"I waited at your house for half an hour. I barely made it in time. Had to tell everyone you got sick at the last minute."

"I'm so sorry. I know this meant a lot to you."

Lips tucked, he stared at the wall, contemplating.

"Dalton."

He didn't respond.

"Dalton," she repeated, and gently guided his cheek to face her. "I'll make it up to you. I promise."

After a quiet, indecipherable moment, his look of anger slackened. He glanced down and closed his hand around hers. His thumb rubbed the base of her bare fourth finger, as if smoothing a pathway for her ring.

"Lizzy . . ." He raised his head, searched her eyes. "Are we in trouble?"

Her first instinct was to tell him he was being silly, but the intensity of his concern melted away her nonchalance. The time had come to spill the truth.

Yet was she ready to let him go?

She glanced at his hand holding hers, a hand that had been there when few others were, and realized she didn't know. What she did know was she loved him and didn't want to hurt him. He was a kind, decent man. A man of whom her father approved. A man whose future made sense with hers. And most important, a man who would never leave.

"We're fine," she told him. "Truly, everything's fine." She kissed him tenderly, gave his fingers an affirming squeeze. In a matter of seconds, his manner warmed, his creases softened. He gleamed again with certainty.

"All right, sweetheart." He brushed her nose with his finger. "I have to get back. But how about dinner this weekend?"

"Sure thing," she said, smiling. As he turned to leave, she added, "I swear I won't forget."

His mouth split into a grin. "I'll hold you to that." He waved farewell with his hat.

The panic humming inside her faded with his departure. A head-on collision barely missed. She felt fortunate, weary, ashamed. As if she'd consciously driven in the oncoming lane yet was surprised when she needed to swerve.

How long could she press her luck? In the end, would she look back and believe it was worth it?

Uncoiling the scarf around her neck, she reentered Viola's room—where the elderly woman sat with crossed arms and a shrewd glower.

"Heavens to Betsy, girl, if you don't have some explaining to do."

Liz tensed, suddenly aware they'd had an audience. "I don't know what you mean."

"My vision may be fading, but I've got ears like a deer."

"It was nothing. Just been busy. And the event slipped my mind."

"You certain that's it? 'Cause for a bride, you sure aren't doing much blushing."

For a second, Liz considered sticking with denial, but she couldn't drum up the energy. Even if she could, the look in Viola's eyes made clear who would win the battle.

With a sigh, Liz reseated herself on the bed. She plunged her elbows into her lap, buried her face in the bundled scarf. And through the fabric, she mumbled her confession. "I've met someone else," she said. It was as good a start as any.

"And?"

Liz turned to Viola, coaxing herself onward. "He's a soldier I've been writing, ever since he shipped off to Europe. And although it seems crazy"—she shoved the phrase from its hold—"I think I've fallen in love with him."

There. She had said it.

Yet she didn't feel any better.

"He has the same feelings for you, I take it?"

"Well, yes . . . and no."

"I'm listenin'."

Bolstering her courage, Liz answered. "He thinks my letters are from another girl."

Viola squinted. She nodded slowly, processing. "Let me see if I got this right. You've taken a liking to a boy, one you've kept hidden from your fiancé, through letters you're trading while pretending to be someone else."

Summarized aloud, the situation sounded utterly despicable.

"Yes," Liz replied, light as a gasp.

"Mmm," Viola said. "And now you're worried you're making a mistake with the fella you got."

Liz was about to skim by with a "maybe," but then, somewhere inside her, a drawbridge dropped and out the words surged. "I love Dalton, I just don't know if I'm *in* love with him. When I think of us together, my life is a blur, like I'm lost in a crowd. But with Morgan, everything's clear. As if he's the one person who understands me."

From Viola's silent stare, Liz felt the scrutiny of a patient's exam. It seemed hours until Viola spoke. "I believe I've got the perfect story for this situation."

Liz smiled wearily. "Why doesn't that surprise me."

Clasping her hands over her nightgown, Viola reclined into her pillows. She took a deep, measured breath and began. "I was barely sixteen when I met the most dashing boy I'd ever laid eyes on. The moment I saw him standing at the door, you could've knocked me down with a feather." Pink eased a youthful radiance into her cheeks. "We went on a double date, to the carrot festival, of all things. He was there to escort my friend Lorraine, so naturally I didn't let on how I felt." She shook her head, remembering. "He was a stitch, he was. Always doing things to make people laugh. He'd walk on his hands till his face was beet red. And boy oh boy, could he imitate people's voices. He'd do it so well you'd think the mayor himself was talking behind you till you turned around."

Viola paused and her expression dimmed. "It wasn't long be-fore his daddy got fired from the mill. That man was a downright mean drunk, couldn't get any other work in town. Decided to pack up and move cross-country. 'Course, I was crushed by the news. Thought for sure I'd wave good-bye to the boy, and that'd be that.

"But then, one night, he and I ended up at a bonfire together. And that's when he confessed it all. Told me how smitten he was. How he'd been hiding his feelings on account of not knowing I felt the same. I couldn't help myself. Handed him a platter full of truth right back. He was leaving the next morning, figured I had nothing to lose."

Somehow, all these years, Liz had never thought to ask Viola how she'd met her dear late husband, Merle, and now wanted every detail. More than that, she needed confirmation that true love actually existed. "Then what happened?" she asked.

"He kissed me," Viola said proudly, and traced a quivering fin-ger over her bottom lip. "It was a kiss more breathtaking than the sky on the Fourth of July. And there, sitting in front of that blazing fire, he asked me to run off with him."

"Well, what did you say?"

"I said yes, of course. Then I threw as many belongings into a knapsack as could possibly fit. Met him by the railroad tracks just like we'd planned—although we didn't get farther than the county line when we had to turn back around."

Liz felt a tinge of disappointment. Running away sounded so lovely right about now. "Did a sheriff catch you? Or your parents?"

Viola shook her head, a tender smile on her lips. "The decision was mine. I couldn't leave my family, everything I'd ever known to follow some big dream in the clouds. We didn't have so much as a plug nickel in our pockets, and I knew we couldn't survive like that. That wasn't real life. We had been fool-headed to think it was."

All right, so they'd taken a more practical route. Things had still worked out somehow. "Merle didn't move away, then?" Liz asked, yearning for a happy ending.

"Merle, move away? Oh, no, he never left. Not till we got married, anyhow, and settled in a charming place about five miles from here with our two youngest. But Merle, well—he's not the boy in the story."

Liz wrinkled her nose, confused. "I'm not sure I follow you."

"The boy in the story was Nathan James. Morning after the bonfire, he left with his daddy. New Mexico, some folks said, though I'm not positive. Never did hear from him again."

The recount had taken an unexpected twist. However, when Liz identified the applicable lesson—the repercussions of not following your heart—she smiled. "Do you have any regrets?" she said.

"Oh, sure. I have my share. Same as anyone, I suppose. But if you're asking, Do I wish I'd gone with Nathan? the answer's no. I did the only thing that made sense. And despite an occasional tribulation, I've lived a pleasant life all in all."

Liz felt her heart sinking in stages. This wasn't the tale, or the advice, she was hoping for.

"Of course," Viola added, "that doesn't change the fact that Nathan James was the most dashing boy I ever met. And I will remember that kiss till the end of time." She gazed at Liz with gentle eyes. "Honey. You get what I'm telling you?"

Yes, she understood; but in this case, it was Viola who didn't understand.

"I appreciate what you're saying, Vy. This isn't the same, though. The way I feel about Morgan, it's . . ." How could she put indescribable emotion into words? "It's stronger than any feeling I've ever known. It's like I can tell him anything. Like we truly know each other."

Viola lifted a brow. "You certain about that? About telling him anything?"

"Yes," she insisted.

"Like who you actually are?"

The question blindsided Liz. It pierced all her supportive arguments in a single shot, rendering her speechless.

The wrinkles on Viola's chin softened. "Might not seem like it right now, but I *am* on your side, sweet pea. I just think you'd be doing yourself a real injustice by not taking a long hard look at the path you're considering. It's not often we're allowed to shimmy backward once we take those first steps." She moved a strand of Liz's hair aside and looked at her lovingly. "Could be there's a mighty good reason you haven't told that fella who you are."

Sure, there were a rash of reasons: Dalton, her father, her tidy plan for the future.

But those, Liz now realized, were not what had truly stopped her. The greatest reason for her deception remained from the start: A false name served as a last-line defense, an epistolary shield, given that in person, as herself, she hadn't held his interest.

And lying about her identity had hardly been a way to change that.

"You're right," she admitted to Viola, to herself, her voice a pinched whisper. "It's not real." The acknowledgment sprang moisture to her eyes, feeding tears that soon slipped away.

Viola reached out and enfolded her in the wings of her arms. "There, there, now," she said, and patted her back.

Liz wanted to remain like this forever. She wanted to stop time from moving, to avoid making a choice. But the choice, she knew, had already been made. And there was no use drawing it out. Even without the ominous lapse since Morgan's post, she'd been kidding herself, thinking they could actually have a future together.

All things considered, and painful though it would be, Liz accepted what she needed to do. Eyes squeezed shut, heart crumbling, she said good-bye to Morgan for good.

❦ 23 ❦

December 19, 1944
Slevant, Belgium

As darkness slid into dawn, Morgan battled his shivers with warm thoughts: hot coffee by a campfire, the tool shed in July, Betty's letters. Yet nothing could stop the chill from invading his bones.

Scrunched in the snow, blanketed knees beneath his chin, he strained to hear the first hint of a rumbling tank. But all he detected was his brother smacking chewing gum beside him. Its wintergreen scent only added to the cold. The kid soon spat out the wad, surely too hard to chew.

"They're comin'." Anxious whispers rushed from one embankment to the next. A bucket brigade passing fuel to feed an explosion.

Following Charlie's lead, Morgan kicked off his blanket. He yanked the bulky gloves off his numb hands and grasped his rifle as tightly as he could. His pulse was gaining speed. He crouched farther into their icy hole to keep his helmet and misty breaths out of possible enemy view. Shoulder to shoulder, they awaited the signal to attack.

An uneasy stillness. Then a muffled rattling. Tanks grinding over the snow, drawing closer and closer with every turn of their bogies.

Morgan turned to his brother, whose eyes were rimmed in red. "Ready?" he asked in a cautious undertone.

"You bet." Though Charlie spoke in a whisper, there was strength in his voice. Even his jaw appeared boldly set, projecting maturity, a steadiness free of fear.

Morgan felt a pinch in his chest, rooted deep inside. The sensation, he quickly recognized, was something resembling . . . loss.

The growing rattling refocused his thoughts. He edged his head up. Through the fog, he counted three Panther tanks entering the village. The Allied troops held tight, waiting for the juggernauts to reach the center of the battle stage.

Suddenly, a Kraut officer yelled an order and the armored vehicles halted.

Morgan hunkered down in the hole. *C'mon, c'mon,* he urged in his mind. But there was no movement. No sound but the faint howling of wind.

Maybe they'd changed their minds. Could be they knew the GIs were there, and were deciding on an easier route across the Amblève River. Imagine. Morgan's squad left fully intact, saved to battle another day, even allowed an entire day of rest.

No sooner had the rosy thoughts formed than the tanks resumed an onward charge.

Boom! Boom!

The first antitank rockets were fired from the remnants of a theater on the other side of the village. The curtain had been raised and the show was under way.

Morgan joined Charlie in stretching his neck to take another look over the embankment. More armored vehicles rolled into town, angling around their casualties.

One of the bazookamen signaled a warning to Morgan, then brought binoculars back to his face. Morgan tried not to blink despite the breeze stinging his bleary eyes. Aware of the white ski suits Krauts often wore as camouflage, he flexed his trigger finger, gearing up to pick off anything in motion larger than a snowflake.

Another signal, and he and Charlie teetered their rifles on the edge of the packed mound, the butt ends shoved into their shoulders. They trained their barrels on the Waffen-SS Panzer troops weaving through the village. On Morgan's mark, the two plucked their triggers, a percussion of fire in the violent chorus. The blasting of shells from American howitzers and Kraut tanks added to the cacophony of battle. And up above, an Artist brushed the sky with majestic red and white flashes.

Clink!

In one swift motion, Morgan pulled a new eight-round clip from his ammo belt and shoved it into the receiver of his rifle, then continued where he left off.

Swoosh!

A German Messerschmitt 109 plane swooped down through clouds. It released a bomb that obliterated a steepled church. Weather had grounded Allied planes, but somehow the damn Luftwaffe pilots always made it into the air.

Ack-ack-ack-ack!

An antiaircraft battery sent a second Messerschmitt twirling to its smoke-trailed fate. Despite its proximity, Morgan barely felt the ground reverberate when the plane slammed into the earth; his focus had turned to the detonation of American bombs on the village's strategically coveted bridge. Now, with the arched structure destroyed, he hoped the Germans would call for a retreat.

At the base of the hill, amidst the fog and billowing smoke, something moved. Morgan took aim at the figure. About to shoot, he glimpsed the soldier's face. It was Geronimo!

The Texan, layered with a hefty supply of ammunition bandoliers, sprang out from an emplacement and raced toward the brewery. He sped through a hailstorm of bullets, head held high, as though granted mystical armor by his Apache ancestors. Morgan watched wide-eyed, almost believing the GI's invincibility, before a Kraut's rifle cut him down a few yards from the doorway.

Morgan scanned the area. Medics must have already had their hands full. There was no one running to help Geronimo, no hero to complete his mission.

Then Charlie started to rise.

"Where *you* goin'?" Morgan shouted, grabbing hold of his brother's jacket.

Charlie tried to wrench away. "Somebody's gotta help."

He was right, but it wasn't going to be Charlie. No matter how much the kid wanted redemption for Mouse.

"Stay here," Morgan told him, "I'll go."

"I got it!" he protested, but Morgan yanked him down.

"I said: *Stay. Here.*" Morgan didn't release his grip until Charlie gave half a nod.

Preparing to reload, Morgan fired his rifle incessantly and emptied his clip. He expelled his fear in a deep puff. As he hugged the loaded weapon to his chest, the heated barrel stung his palm.

Three . . . two . . . one.

"Cover me!" he said to Charlie, and climbed out.

A series of shots popped like a John Deere behind Morgan, confirming his brother had taken his order. Thanks to years of racing Charlie home from school through winter drifts, he made his way to the bottom as easily as if the knee-deep snow were only ankle high. His legs were slower than they used to be, but the chatter of machine guns and belching blasts of German "burp guns" were damn good motivators.

He dropped behind an empty embankment and carved out his three objectives. The first was reaching Geronimo.

Through the sulfuric air and trodden slush, he ran hunched over toward the fallen GI. A swarm of bullets whizzed this way and that. Adrenaline enabled Morgan to flip Geronimo face-up with little effort. Two fingers pressed to the Southerner's neck and he knew. A form telegram would soon announce the loss of another good man.

Morgan felt a stab of grief, but paying his respects would have to wait. Instead, like a vulture, he stripped the ammo off the soldier's body. With the town's Allied blockades and maze of tanks, Kraut infantry were about to be streamlined directly past the brewery. There, the rooftop gunners needed all the firepower they could get to maintain control of the village, a stronghold that could bring them one victory closer to home.

Supplies bundled in his arms, Morgan sprinted into the brewery. He hopped and maneuvered his way up the debris-covered stairwell. On the roof, he found the GIs plugging away with bipod machine guns.

"I'm out!" one yelled in a panic, his stash depleted.

Morgan handed the ammo over to a grateful sergeant, then wheeled and headed back down.

On the homestretch.

As he emerged from the building, a Panther tank across the road exploded. He grabbed his helmet, hit the ground. Rubble peppered his face. The smell of gasoline was so pungent he could taste it, the fire so hot he nearly forgot it was winter.

He spat cobblestone particles out of his mouth. A screech that sounded like a banshee's lifted his head. Flames engulfed the vehicle's mounted cannon. A Kraut trooper dangled from the turret hatch. An Allied shell had found its mark.

Ears ringing, Morgan jumped to his feet and blasted his rifle aimlessly while weaving his way to the hill. He cowered down as he stomped up the slope. The nauseating stink of burning flesh was enough to maintain his speed, a tougher trek going up. Halfway to the top, he saw Charlie scurrying to their ditch.

What the hell was he doing? *Get back in the hole! Get back in the hole!*

Morgan intensified his dash. The kid was exposing his position like a new recruit at basic. Or worse, a daredevil with something to prove. After the battle, Charlie was going to get an earful.

Tat-tat-tat! Tat-tat-tat! Staccato fire flared up above. Morgan flattened on the ground. His cheek stung against the frigid floor. At a break in the firing, he resumed his plod upward.

The crest of the hill only a few yards away, he raised his head, and froze at the sight. They were darker than black, colder than night: the penetrating eyes of a stone-faced Kraut. In the enemy's hand, a submachine gun glinted its barrel. A barrel pointed straight at Morgan.

Instinct took charge, pitching Morgan backward. As he tumbled down the hill, he felt a stabbing in his left leg, like prongs of a red-hot pitchfork. His velocity slowed until he landed on his side at the bottom, dazed, empty-handed. He squeezed several blinks to clear his vision.

His M1! Where was his M1?

The butt of his rifle peeked out from the snow—yet it lay no closer than a tank's length away. Fear boiled in his chest. He prepared to leap for his weapon, just as the memory of an Irishman's voice returned.

Body flat. Eyes down. Don't move.

Breath held, he remained still as a corpse.

Crunch . . . crunch . . .

The faint sound of the enemy's boots intensified. The bear drew nearer.

Morgan prayed the trooper's desire to salvage ammo would prevent him from spattering more bullets at his motionless form. Not betting on it, he inched his right hand toward the Luger in his belt, half pinned under his hip.

Crunch . . . crunch . . .

Then the sound stopped. The Kraut was reloading his gun.

Go! Go! Go!

In a continuous move, Morgan arched, swung the pistol forward, and fired in succession. The trooper jerked from the impact and slammed onto his back. Blood oozing over the snow confirmed the match was over.

Within seconds, a thought clawed Morgan's mind: The trooper had gotten past the GIs up above. Which meant . . .

Charlie.

Morgan fumbled to stand. The throbbing in his leg told him a pair of bullets had pierced his flesh. Pushing down a groan, he once more clambered up the slanted path.

"Charlie!" he screamed against the blasts. "Charlie! Where are you?"

Atop the hill's plateau, he spotted the back of his brother's body, draped over the side of their ditch thirty feet away. The air went numb. The battle ceased. No tanks, no artillery, no pain from his wounds. Nothing but Charlie's inert form, and sheer terror propelling Morgan forward.

At the edge of their embankment, he dropped his pistol and fell to his knees. A sharpness surged through his leg. A confirmation of reality.

"Charlie," he said, tugging him upward. He cradled his brother's head on his lap. "Can you hear me?"

Don't be dead. He couldn't be dead.

Charlie struggled to open his eyes, and their gazes met.

A sigh shot from Morgan's mouth. "Thank God." He cupped his brother's chin with a tremorous hand. "You're gonna be all right, you hear? You're gonna be all right."

Morgan snapped his head up to call for help, but the bazooka-men appeared as lifeless as the SS trooper lying on the ground nearby. No one was there to save them. They were on their own. As they'd always been.

"Medic! I need a medic!" Morgan bellowed toward the village, praying someone could hear him. His attention flew back to his brother. Blood was dripping from the corner of Charlie's mouth. "Hang on. We're gonna get you help. You're gonna make it. Just hang on."

Morgan had to do something, anything, to keep him alive till a doc arrived. He ripped open his brother's jacket. His shirt was soaked red, holes torn from the fabric over his chest. Morgan pressed down with stacked hands, trying to dam the flow. But blood seeped between his fingers. It wouldn't stop, it wouldn't stop!

"Medic!" Morgan's head was pounding. "Man down! I need help up here!"

The blanket. He could use his blanket.

Keeping one hand on Charlie's chest, he grabbed the wool bundle from their ditch. He scrunched the fabric into a ball and held it firm to the wounds. "Please . . . please . . ." He begged the fibers to resist the outpouring of his brother's life.

Charlie weakly grasped Morgan's fingers with a shivering hand. He was trying to say something through his labored gasps. Morgan lowered his ear toward his mouth. "What is it, buddy?" He tightened his hold on his brother's hand, wanting to squeeze away the pain.

"It's okay," Charlie wheezed. "It's okay." His breath spread hot over Morgan's cheek, burned his skin with words that sounded too much like good-bye.

"Don't you dare give up," Morgan commanded. "You got me?

We're gonna get you outta here." Nose running, eyes tearing, he shouted again. *"Medic!"*

Then he felt Charlie's body relax.

Morgan looked into his eyes, tired eyes that were slowly closing. He nudged his brother's shoulder with a brisk shake. "Come on, kid, stay with me." A flutter of Charlie's eyelids sparked Morgan's hope, told him his brother was fighting. "That's it. Open 'em up. Look at me, look at me."

Another strained flutter and his lids drooped shut.

"Charlie," he said, clenching his brother's jacket collar. "Stay awake, goddamn it! You hear me? I said *stay awake!*" But Charlie's head drifted to the side in degrees, his soul slipping away. He yielded his final breath, left only a shell.

Horror torched everything Morgan possessed, his body and mind, the air in his lungs. "Charlie, no!" He shook his brother without restraint. "No! Don't you do this to me! Don't you leave me here alone, goddamn it!"

Morgan squeezed his eyes shut. This couldn't be happening. This was just a dream. A nightmare.

"Wake me up," he urged Charlie in a whisper. *"Wake. Me. Up."*

Yet he wasn't asleep.

And this was real.

"Charlie, no. No." Morgan pulled his brother's face to his chest. He rocked him forward and back, just as their mother had done to soothe them to sleep as children. This time, though, her sweet baby boy would never awaken.

Morgan pressed his cheek to Charlie's temple, sobbing with his entire body. Sobbing so hard he felt he might explode. How he wished he could burst into nothing, disappear into the space where his brother had been taken. Where everyone in the McClain family now dwelled but him. "Please," he choked out. "Don't go, Charlie. Please don't leave me."

Then a loud roar rang out from the heavens and the world turned to black.

❧ 24 ❧

December 24, 1944
Lincoln Park
Chicago, Illinois

Panic bloomed in Liz's chest. She strove for traction, running backward in place. Her arms fluttered in a frenzy until her tailbone pounded the ice, shooting pain up her back. Obviously, Sonja Henie made fancy spins seem much easier than they were.

Dalton's blades scraped as he braked beside Liz and knelt on one knee. "Are you all right?" he asked, touching her shoulder.

What a spectacle she must have been: graceful as a swan, before a bump in the surface transformed her into a turkey, flapping away uselessly. "You mean, other than my doomed skating career?"

He smiled above his plaid scarf, his nose stained pink from the morning chill. Shaking his head, he offered his gloved hand. "Come on, twinkle toes. Time for a break."

She wrung his fingers and coat sleeve to pull herself upright. Guided by prudence, she didn't let go until they'd coasted to the edge of the frozen lagoon, where she recalled the value of solid ground.

Fluffy snow blanketed an empty park bench. He cleared space for them with a swipe of his arm. Once they'd settled, he grabbed his thermos from under the seat and poured her a lidful of hot chocolate. She held the cup to her chin and warmed her face with the sweet, milky steam. Heat moved through her mittens, thawing her palms. As she took a sip, a little boy wobbled past on shoe skates, a pillow three-quarters his size strapped around his hind end.

"Now, that," she told Dalton, "is the way I'm doing it next time."

He laughed, his familiar youthful laugh. How she wished she could store that sound in a jar, like the butterfly she'd caught as a child, releasing it into the open when the need arose. Then again, there was no use holding on to something that wasn't hers to keep.

Together they downed their cocoa while watching the show go by. They took turns commenting on skaters of every age and size, all gliding counterclockwise in their bundled wool. In the eye of the whirlpool, a polished pair danced effortlessly to a song of giggles from rosy-faced children.

The melody relaxed Liz all the way down to her bruised behind. She was still smiling when a man several yards off the lagoon drew her focus. The father, she presumed, lifted his little girl to reach a snowman's head and helped her place the rock eyes, an old derby hat, a carrot nose. What a wondrous time in life that had been, believing in flying reindeer and enchanted elves.

Liz must have been seven when she first voiced her doubts about Santa Claus's existence. On the playground, a precocious schoolgirl had taken great pleasure in exposing the gift-giving conspiracy.

"That's preposterous," Liz's father had declared of the allegation. "And how sad for that poor girl who doesn't believe in Santa. It's a pity she won't be receiving Christmas presents anymore."

Years later, Liz had learned it was her father who stood outside her room that Christmas Eve, jingling a string of bells in the pouring rain. He'd even staged boot prints in a pile of ashes next to their fireplace to reinstate her faith.

Bells and ashes. How she wished it were that simple to restore her father's faith in her.

Apprehension rebounded at the thought of him. "What time is it?" she asked Dalton.

"We're not going to be late," he assured her.

"I just don't want to keep him waiting, with the holiday crowds at the station."

"And we won't. I promise." Dalton's gaze reflected the usual certitude in his voice. Then, as if to distract her, he reached into his pocket and produced a gift. A tiny box covered in glossy green paper, dashed with a silver bow. "Merry Christmas, sweetheart."

"Oh, drat," she said. "I left yours at home." When he'd surprised her with an invitation for an outing that morning, it hadn't occurred to her to bring his present along.

"There's no hurry. Technically, Christmas isn't until tomorrow."

Cup and mittens aside, she removed the wrapping with care, reluctant to damage the flawless display. Beneath the lid lay an intricate gold necklace. She dangled the chain in the air, inviting the cloud-filtered light to sparkle on the heart-shaped locket. "Dalton, it's lovely."

"Open it up," he told her, and smiled.

Liz used her thumbnail to divide the halves. Two photos had been cut to fit: on the left, a little boy in his Sunday best; on the right, a young girl in a queen's ruffled collar. She examined their faces, attempting to place them, then realized, "Oh my gosh, they're us."

Her mother had made that costume, sewn every stitch, every frill, for a week. How could Liz have forgotten? She'd adored that outfit. Loved it so much, she had worn the velvety garb whenever and wherever allowed, and only quit once the long strip of buttons in the back no longer reached the holes.

There were moments, she now recalled, warmhearted moments she'd shared with her mother. As rare and fleeting as they might have been, they had indeed existed.

"Where did you get these?" Liz asked him.

"I pulled mine out of an old scrapbook. Your father gave me yours in D.C. last month."

She knew the two had met for lunch, along with Dalton's father, but she'd presumed their exchanges had been limited to politics and academia—not a childhood snapshot her father had surprisingly retained.

"So what do you think?" Dalton asked, to which she wrapped him with a hug.

"It's perfect, just perfect," she answered. For it was more than a gift of a lost memory, more than a sentimental keepsake. Without knowing, he had provided proof that choosing him had been the right decision. The token, linking their history and families' blessing, served as tangible affirmation that they were always meant for each other.

"Let me get that for you." He leaned back, lifted the necklace from her hand. "*This* one ought to fit."

Smiling, she held up her hair. While he clasped the chain around her neck, she studied the pictures again. "I have to say, we were awfully cute."

"You think *we* were cute, just wait until you see our kids. They'll be the stars of Chicago."

In an instant, the balloon of happiness within her deflated. She first attributed the feeling to the obvious: the strained relationship with her parents, the fear of mimicking the distance with her own children. Then she moved onto the unease of living in high society's glaring spotlight.

Neither, however, was the case this time. Rather, what troubled her was the tone of Dalton's voice, a surety that encompassed even the unpredictable subject of raising a family. Wasn't there anything that caused him doubts? Anything at all, about his life, his future?

She replaced her mittens, trying her best not to dwell.

"Lizzy," he said with a gentle smile, "I didn't mean we'd be having babies *tomorrow*." He evidently sensed her mood shift. Exposing vulnerability in her letters must have left her careless with her expressions. "I know I jumped ahead on the proposal. But I'm still fine with waiting until our careers are settled to start a family."

Oddly, concerns over interrupting her profession hadn't occurred to her just now. And its mention, somehow, seemed insignificant. "No," she replied, "it's not that."

A herd of kids trampled past their bench. They launched into a snowball fight several yards away—laughing, chasing, pitching the frosty powder. The epitome of spontaneity, they were too busy living for the moment to worry about spring's rains that would melt away the magic.

"What's the matter?" Dalton asked her. "Just tell me and we can solve it."

She paused, seeking a means of explanation, of peeling back the armor covering his weaknesses, his fears. Or more important, to confirm he had any.

Subtlety seemed best. "You know I've always believed in sticking to a plan. But lately I've been thinking, maybe that isn't what life's about. Things happen all the time we don't see coming."

He squinted slightly, waiting to see where she was leading them.

"Let me ask you this," she ventured. "If you could have any job you wanted, live anywhere in the world, parents and pressures aside, what would you do?"

"Sky's the limit?"

She nodded.

"That's easy." He sat back and shrugged. "I'd be a lawyer, living in Chicago."

Her chest lowered, gapping her woven layers. A cold draft grazed her skin.

"Although," he added, considering, "I'd probably delve into civil rights from the get-go, instead of down the road. Help out the underdog straightaway." He quirked a brow. "But don't go spreading that around. Wouldn't want Judge Porter thinking I'd gone soft." He finished with a smile.

It was far from an ideal answer, but at least his altruistic aspirations were a nice discovery.

Dalton tilted his head at her. "Is that what's bothering you? Are you having second thoughts about teaching?"

Now that she thought about it, her chosen vocation was one more aspect of her life that had shifted from the "certain" category to "uncertain," all thanks to Morgan. Ever since he'd asked that ridiculous question of why she wanted to be a professor—ridiculous, given that the answer should have been a simple one involving her own desires, not someone else's.

There was no denying she had a passion for literature. Yet she didn't have to be a teacher to enjoy the classics. The power of the written word was what she revered, how thoughts on paper could change your perspective, and, on occasion, your life. Corresponding with Morgan had reminded her of the emotions penned prose could evoke—specifically when presented from the heart and free of fear over being judged.

In fact, authoring letters to the soldier had been just as rewarding as reading the pages he'd sent. As rewarding as scrawling the
sweet notes she used to trade with her father, and the journals of
poems, reflections, and short stories she'd created. All that had
ended, of course, when her mother left. And until recently, Liz had
forgotten the fulfillment of touching another's soul through ink.

Perhaps a truer part of her had been packed away all these
years, and had merely been waiting to unfold.

"Lizzy?" Dalton prompted.

Driven by her revelation, she blurted her answer. "I'd be a
writer." It then occurred to her that she'd addressed her own question, not his. "If sky was the limit," she explained. "That's what I'd
be."

"Huh." He nodded, taking it in. "I had no idea."

"I didn't either," she admitted. "Until now." A steadiness came
over her as she straightened in her seat.

"You know," he said, "there's no reason you can't. If you'd
rather write than teach, you should do it. It's not like we need the
money. And hey, if it means we could start a family sooner"—he
smiled—"then you've got my vote a hundred percent."

It was no surprise he'd be supportive. He always had been.
Even when it would make him the only lawyer in the city married
to a professional, he never challenged her ambition. And, naturally,
the timeliness of his becoming a father served as a rewarding draw.
In his eyes, she could already see the pride that would overflow the
minute he first held his baby son. He would tuck him into his
bassinet and kiss his forehead, warming him with a coverlet of security.

"I'll definitely give it some thought." She smiled back, just as a
fresh wave of giggles entered the air. A pack of teenagers had engaged in the snowball skirmish. Their voices rose with their laughter, but still couldn't drown out realism whispering in Liz's ear:
Best intentions aside, with Dalton's foreseeable path, he wouldn't
be home for family dinners by five. In many ways, their children
would be reliant on the guidance of one parent—the same as she
had been.

On the upside, at least Liz wouldn't be alone in her circumstance. For the betterment of society, Eleanor Roosevelt must have made her own share of sacrifices. And with a man like Dalton, a good husband and father, surely the sacrifices would be worth it.

"We still have some time," Dalton said. "How about giving that spin of yours another try?"

Her tailbone protested. "Better not. I'm saving up for my big performance in the ice ballet."

"Then I'd say you need a little practice before your debut." He set aside the lidded thermos and stood. "Come on, one more round. I want to make all the guys here jealous."

A smile settled on her lips. Conceding her will, she reached out and accepted his hand.

❧ 25 ❧

December 25, 1944
Dutch New Guinea

"I can't move," Betty moaned, limp as a rag doll sprawled across her cot. Her eyelids, resting for the first time in twenty hours, felt like shutters sealed for a storm.

Like many of the girls, she had formed a routine of sleeping in the nude, covered solely by a damp towel, and waking every thirty minutes to dip the fabric in a water-filled helmet. Tonight, though, despite her uniform being sweat-soaked and splattered with blood, she considered dozing off fully clothed. She'd only unbuttoned half her shirt, and doing more required exerting effort for little reward.

Another mumbled moan and her mind hailed three direct commands: *Sleep. Sleep. Sleep.* That's all she wanted to do. For days, for months. Whatever it took to resemble a human again.

In mere seconds, a magnetic pull drew her spirit into a fuzzy void. She swam in the watery grayness, suspended and free, before Rosalyn's drawl tugged her out with a start.

"I swear 'fore God, if I don't do another injection, infusion, or stitch for the rest of my life, it'll be too soon."

Static from Shirley's radio crackled through the small, mildewy barracks. The tent had been dubbed "Coconut Grove" by its four residents, who'd all assumed duties typically reserved for nurses.

With doctors having just completed weeks of forty-eight-hour shifts to the front lines, every available hand had been filling the gaps.

"I still can't find it," Shirley huffed. She'd once happened across a San Francisco station, and had hoped to locate it again in time for Christmas.

"Ah, just turn it to the usual," Rosalyn said. "Carols are carols."

A lethargic sigh. "All right."

How about off? Off would be nice, Betty longed to say, but even her mouth was too tired to function.

Soon an orchestral version of "Winter Wonderland" on the Jungle Network skirled in the muggy air. The pattering of rain on the roof served as further irony to the night's unrelenting heat.

"What in the Lord's name y'all got over there?" Rosalyn said, responding to their roommates' giggles.

Betty attempted to tune them out, but her curiosity, as always, triumphed. She eased open one eye. The candle stuck in a bourbon bottle flickered shadows across Shirley and Stella, seated side by side on a cot in their brassieres and undies. "SOS," the girls were called, stuck at the hip and so similar in looks and spunkiness, they could have been twins.

Stella drank another gulp from the hole in a coconut before replying. "It's a Christmas gift from Herb. Says it's called 'Jungle Juice.'"

"They put fruit and sugar inside," Shirley added, "and let it sit until the cork pops out three times. Then it's ready to drink."

"Why three times?" Rosalyn asked.

Shirley shrugged. "Don't know. But Herb's in chemical warfare, so I'm sure he's got a reason." She held out the coconut. "Want some, Roz?"

Rosalyn pondered for a moment. "Oh, why not. Bert's not here to say otherwise." She stretched from her bed to accept the cocktail, and tipped back a swallow.

"Who's Bert?" Shirley asked.

"My husband." Dreariness dragged her words.

The answer startled Betty from her daze, an icy splash to her ears. "You're married?"

"Won't be much longer. Just waiting for the paperwork."

Divorced.

Betty had never met a divorced woman before, at least not that she knew of. For a moment, she envisioned Rosalyn as an attraction at a traveling carnival. *Step right up and take a look,* the man in top hat and tails would shout. *A divorced gal in the flesh, ladies and gents. Rare as a bearded lady, scandalous as an unwedded mother. Keep those kiddies away, though, folks. Never can be too careful.*

Resuscitated by the image, Betty edged up on her elbows. "What happened between you two?" she asked Rosalyn. "Did he do something, well . . . *bad?*"

"Nah, nah. Nothing like that." Rosalyn waved her hand, then chugged down more of Herb's concoction. "Just got hitched too young. My meemaw saw it coming all along. Said Bert looked right stylish in a uniform, but didn't have a lick o' sense."

Yeah. Common sense did often seem in short supply among guys.

Betty accepted the coconut and managed to indulge without fully sitting up. Compared to Lister-bag water, the beverage was the best she'd ever tasted. Citric sweetness with only a slight tang of alcohol. A dangerous combination.

She wiped drips from her chin with her rolled-up sleeve. "Think you'll ever get married again?"

Rosalyn pursed her lips and shook her head. "Can't imagine it. Only fellas interested in a divorcée would come under the heading of wild oats. But then, well, you never know."

"You never know," Stella and Shirley repeated in dramatic unison.

As Betty took another generous drink, she focused on her transfer to Port Moresby. There, she'd finally land a respectable husband, taking her one step farther from the carnival of her past. One leap away from becoming her mother—or Irma from the diner. An old forgotten spinster with faded looks and faded dreams.

"What do you say, ladies?" Stella moved from her bed to the wooden floor. "Time for our gift exchange? It *is* officially Christmas." Kneeling, she reached under her cot and retrieved three small presents wrapped in rice paper, handy material left from the Japanese occupation.

Betty smiled a little. It seemed silly to swap personal belongings they each already owned, but mail orders from Montgomery Ward weren't on Santa's sleigh this year.

Just then, Stella split the air with a scream. She dropped the presents and hopped about as if on hot coals.

"What is it?" Shirley yelled.

"Rats! Rats!" she shrieked, reclaiming the elevated safety of her bed.

Two rodents the size of adult possums scampered over the planks, stirred from their dry shelter. Their shadows made them giants. Betty dropped the coconut as she and Shirley joined in the squealing. Juice splashed across the floor.

"Git! Git outta here!" Rosalyn used her Daisy Mae hat to swat the creatures through a gap in the canvas.

Area cleared, all four gals burst into hysterical laughter. Their eyes watered as they continued with the rib-aching release, feeding off each other's exhaustion and delirium at 0200 hours.

"Cordell!" Captain Kitzafenny stood in the entrance.

Their laughter stopped on a switch. The ladies snapped to attention.

"Yes, ma'am?" Betty answered.

"At ease," the captain said tiredly, flicked her hand at the group.

Rosalyn stealthily dropped her hat over the coconut as the SOS girls covered their bodies with towels. Betty clenched her open shirt together, as well as her teeth, preventing a smile over the scene.

The captain continued to address her. "Hate to break up the party, but there's a soldier at the hospital asking for you."

Inwardly Betty grumbled. She usually didn't mind late-night conversations with patients too uncomfortable to sleep, guys needing an ear to absorb their worries; talk about wives they hardly knew and babies they'd never met. Buddies lost along the way, and disfigurements that would gain more attention than their medals.

One night off, however, didn't seem too much to ask. Even the devil, according to Rosalyn, took a break now and then—particularly on Christmas, Jesus's glory day.

"Ma'am," Betty said, "with all due respect, can't it wait till morning?"

"An MP's here to drive you down. Ward Four." The captain about-faced and marched off.

Swell. Lieutenant Kelly's ward. Even better.

Betty allowed for a buffer distance before complaining. "Why me?" Her voice came out like the scraping of gravel.

"Well, now," Rosalyn suggested, "you could tell the MP you got yourself a bellyache."

Betty dipped into her reserve tank of energy and started on her buttons. "Oh, *shore*." She mocked Rosalyn's drawl. "And make 'Kiss-her-fanny' madder than an ol' wet hen?"

Stella and Shirley laughed some more.

Rosalyn primly crossed her arms. "It's about time my Southern class rubbed off on y'all," she said, pulling a smile begrudgingly out of Betty. "Don't worry, sugar. We'll wait on gifts till you get back."

While Betty threw on her wet hooded poncho, Stella celebrated the piece of luck that their coconut had landed upright, leaving plenty to enjoy. In galoshes borrowed from Rosalyn, Betty stepped outside. Wind moaned through the downpour, the sound of a weeping sky, a voice telling her to turn back as she made her way to the jeep.

Snaking below them was the only road Betty had traveled upon since arriving on the island. Torrential rain dumped from the blackened clouds. By the time the driver delivered her to the medical compound, a slight wooziness had set in from the homemade liquor.

She slogged through the gummy red mud, deep as a creek, then hurried down the boardwalk and into Ward Four, the planked floors all new additions.

The space was still as stone. Chaos from the day's emergencies had slowed at last. Every bed in the tent was occupied, along with the entire hospital. Candles bathed the room in a soft glow. The only noise was the drumming of rain on the roof and the plinking of drops filling a pair of metal buckets set beneath canvas leaks.

She hung her poncho from a pole and treaded toward Tom. Hunched beside a bed, he was administering an IV to a soldier with *TAT* inked across his forehead, a symbol of his tetanus shots.

"Tom," she whispered, turning him. "There's a patient asking to see me?"

About to reply, he hesitated. "You haven't heard." Graveness thickened his voice. He gestured his chin toward the middle of the ward. "He's down there. Waiting for you."

Her mind raced. Patients' faces and names that had taken up residence in her memory flickered past, an overflowing file cabinet. "Who is it?" she asked.

He shook his head before answering. "It's Junior."

She blinked. *"What?* What happened?"

"Hit a land mine. Doc took a look at him. There's just too much liver damage."

Her jaw clamped, buried the next question under her tongue. She forced out the words using only her lips. "How much time?"

He touched her shoulder. "Not much," he said. "I'm real sorry, Betty." His solemn glance set off a twisting in her stomach. Her arms swathed her middle as Tom stepped away to continue with his patient.

Light-headed, Betty blew out a ragged breath. She pivoted toward her task. She was a soldier, marching, preparing for duty. One step after the other, she released her selfish concerns, dropped them like crumbs that had no place in the hands of a medical servicewoman. Rosalyn was the one who had taught her: *Crying only inflames a soldier's wounds; good nurses reserve tears for private moments before dashing them away and forging on.*

Betty mentally drilled the phrases as she neared the GI barely recognizable as Junior. Gauze wrapped his eyes. Cuts and mud marked his round, boyish face. The split in his shirt, scissored open, exposed a stained bandage from the doctor's fruitless efforts.

"So, what's this I hear?" Her voice fought for levity that seemed miles away. "Someone's asking for Betty Grable?"

His cheek twitched as the edges of his mouth slid upward. "Hey, doll," he breathed. "Thought you'd never show."

Gently she sat down beside him. She grasped for words, came up empty.

"I guess this could put a damper on the prom, huh?" he said, fracturing the tension.

"Well." She smiled. "Just till you scrounge up a bow tie."

He puffed a laugh that his lungs immediately sucked back in, a reflex to the pain.

"Sorry, I didn't mean to . . ." She reached for his arm but stopped at a hover.

His breathing gradually returned. Each exhale sounded of heaviness matching the tropical air. Noticing the quake of his body, chills from blood loss, Betty pulled a blanket up and around his neck as if tucking him in for bedtime.

He gave her half a smile. "Guess I look pretty bad."

"Not so bad," she said. "For a kid from Indiana."

"Now, there you go—" he began to joke, but a dry cough drove through the rest.

On the neighboring table, she poured a cup of water and waited for his fit to wane. "Here. Drink this." Inclining his head, she tenderly guided his mouth toward the rim. A few sips and she eased him back onto the pillow. Her fingers unfurled, about to stroke his cheek, but she pulled them away, resisted within an inch. The act, Betty knew, could very well break her.

"So, I never asked ya." His voice sounded raspy, tired. "What'd you do, in Chicago? Before all this luxury?"

It took her a moment to remember. Life prior to the islands had become a distant dream, this now her only reality. "I was a waitress, at a diner near the Loop. And a bit of a singer, I suppose."

"See," he told her, "I knew you were a big star."

She smiled, shaking her head. "Not quite. Just sang for the USO a few times."

How important that stage and those lights had felt back then. The cheers, the whistles. As if the boys she'd been singing to were headed for a gala rather than war.

"Well, let me hear somethin'," Junior said.

She laughed tightly. "What, a song?" The idea of belting out a snappy jingle right then seemed even more ludicrous than inappropriate.

"C'mon, doll," he urged, fading to a whisper. "A dying man's wish." He stifled a quick moan, a testament to his claim. A dying wish was precisely what it was.

"Okay," she agreed, though regret balled inside; he deserved a better voice than hers. Still, she grabbed the first tune that came to mind. "Now, remember, it sounds a whole lot nicer with the band."

His chin trembled from the cold temperature rolling through his starved veins. Over his blanket, she dared to rub his arm, warming him. The lyrics of "Don't Sit Under the Apple Tree" gathered slowly on her tongue, like drops from a leaky faucet. She fed them out at the same speed, rationing the melody, her volume befitting a lullaby.

She made it through several lines—relatively smooth, unscathed—before singing about his long-awaited march home. The home he would never reach. Her voice splintered at the thought. A geyser of tears rushed to her eyes.

Keep going, she had to keep going.

She wrestled the moisture down as her mind yielded another lyric. A frivolous verse, about a stroll down Lover's Lane. Why couldn't she think of a more meaningful song? Surely she had more to offer him than—

A long flow of air came from the GI's opened mouth, deflating his chest. His chills ceased, chills that now crept over Betty's body.

"Junior?" She squeezed his elbow, spurred no movement. She shook his arm. "Junior?" Her fingers flew up to his neck, seeking a pulse. This couldn't be happening, not to him. He was just a kid. Tears rolled down her face and onto his. She searched again, desperate for even the faintest pulse.

Damn it. Why couldn't she find it?

The truth screamed at her, yet still she waited. For a heartbeat that wouldn't return.

Finally, with no other option, she surrendered. She tried to say good-bye, but the words dried and shriveled, invisible ashes on her lips. She leaned down and pressed a kiss to his forehead. His skin felt moist and warm.

Mustering her strength, dutiful mask reapplied, she rose to leave. But gazes, like spears, pinned her from every direction. She glanced from one soldier's face to another. Each had been watching her, listening to the tune of a life they barely remembered.

Something inside her cracked. Her emotions flooded through, filling her chest, pushing out her air. The pressure weighted every limb, threatened to crush her if she didn't escape.

She started down the ward. Her brisk walk turned into a sprint before she reached the exit. Once outside, her lungs heaved convulsively, ready to burst. She kept on running. Darkness caved in around her. She rushed against the current of muddy pools until her legs gave out, plummeting her to her knees. The will to move washed away in the rain, along with her tears. That's what she wanted. To float off to nowhere.

An eternity passed before a man's voice sounded behind her. "Up we go." He hooked her arms with his elbows to raise her. Here was Tom, saving her again. Except this time she didn't want to be saved.

"I don't belong here!" she sobbed. "I'm not supposed to be here!"

He didn't reply, just looped her waist and whisked her off to the closest tent. In a blink, she landed in a small storage room pillared with supplies. Dripping from the rain, she found herself being lowered onto the dry floor, her back against a wall of boxes.

She heard him open one container, then another.

"Here, mate." He passed down a folded blanket. "Dry yourself off."

His accent gripped her. Not until then did she realize her rescuer wasn't Tom. The man standing beside her, pajamas drenched, was Lieutenant Leslie Kelly.

She wanted to yell, *I don't need your help!* Yet humiliation stripped her anger, her pride. If he thought little of her before, what did he think of her now?

"Why are you here?" she rasped.

"Reckon your staff's shorthanded enough," he said, "without you blundering about in the rain, getting yourself sick."

She dismissed the worry with a laugh. "I could die of pneumonia and it wouldn't matter. I'm not helping anyone here."

He sat next to her, patted his mussed hair with a blanket. "And that's really what you think, eh? That you're not doing a touch of good?" His patronizing tone challenged her, a cold accusation of self-pity.

Regardless of whether he was right, the fact remained that she had no business in a medical role, one fit for those with noble intentions and capabilities far exceeding her own.

"I'm not a nurse." She drove her argument. "Truth is, I can't stand needles any more than I can stand the sight of blood."

"That makes two of us."

Her temper rode her cheeks. "You think I'm joking?"

Drying his casts, he flattened a rising smile. "Just seen you handle both without much fuss, that's all."

Of course, when lives were at stake, you did what was necessary. But that wasn't her point.

"I'm not cut out for this," she stated firmly. "I lied my way in, even forced a recruiter to enlist me when he didn't want to. And now I see he was right. I should've listened. Jungle or not, I can't do this anymore."

Leslie scrunched his chin, pondering. Then he gave a sharp nod. "Fair enough. Drop the bundle and go home. No doubt there's a heap of Yanks that'd be bloody delighted to see you again."

His merciless nonchalance stoked frustration in her gut.

"That's it?" she said. "That's all you're going to say?" After caring for his dressings, delivering his food trays, replacing and straightening his sheets, all she'd earned was confirmation of her dispensability.

He shrugged. "You want me yabbering on, pretending to fill your head with what you already know?"

She gritted her teeth, jerked her face toward the shadows. "Just leave me alone." Raindrops from her hair streaked over her ears. She wanted to dry herself, but her residual dignity forbade use of the blanket he had given her.

He sloughed a long sigh, aggravating her more. "You had a rough night," he said. "We've all had our share of those. And you know as well as I do that the war goes on. Whether you're here or not."

With two fingers, he angled her face to his, a slow, soft gesture. Defiantly, her eyes slanted away as he continued. "You don't need me telling you that the job you're doing's important. Blood and needles aside, for plenty of blokes round this place, your smile's the best medicine they can get."

A contrast to his usual demeanor, his sentiment confused her. As did his tone, tender with sincerity. She allowed her gaze to slide toward him, the words to slip from her mouth. "Just not for blokes like you, right?"

The look in his pale blue eyes burrowed through her, hollowed her defenses. "For me, more than anyone," he whispered. He smoothed her lips with his thumb, gliding over the moisture of her skin. Time twisted and stretched into nonexistence as he leaned in and pressed his mouth to hers. He tasted of earth and desire and rebellion. The hunger inside her smoldered and grew. He kissed her deeper, and a white-hot wave of fire swept through her body. Yet when the flames reached her chest, a bubbling of sadness seeped free. A tremble moved down her arms; tears escaped from her closed eyes. She fumbled with his shirt buttons, adding aggression to their kiss, seeking numbness to protect her, to keep her whole.

He covered her hands, squeezed them to a stop. And he drew his head away.

A pang of rejection should have struck, launching anger in defense. She instead melted into the warmth of his gaze, a look telling her she would be all right. An assurance that she wasn't alone.

"Come 'ere, now," he told her. He encircled her shoulders, guiding her to rest her back against his chest. Then he tucked her hair behind her ears and caressed her damp locks with his fingers. Every stroke further diminished the aches in her body, the longing to be anywhere else but here. "Just listen to the rain," he soothed. "All will feel better come morning."

She closed her eyes and absorbed the sound of raindrops dancing on the tent. The rhythm relaxed her soul. A song echoing tomorrow's promise.

❧ 26 ❧

December 25, 1944
Near Rheims, France

Morning had again become the most beloved and despised time of the day for Morgan. For a brief shining moment, the illusion of lying in his bed at home was so real he could actually smell his mother's cornbread, hear his father's tractor. He could feel the bed wiggle from Charlie stirring in the upper bunk. Then, as always, reality would come crashing down, drowning him in sorrow. And just as swiftly he would find himself hurled onto the rocky shore, battered and alone. Laid out in a makeshift hospital amidst the scents and sounds of loss.

His mind had grown all too familiar with the deceptive game after each of his parents had died. He had hoped he'd endured his fill of such torment, but alas, the cycle had returned. In spite of his heavenly pleas, Charlie was now but a memory—a brother and best friend resting with the angels.

If only Morgan had known. If only he'd run faster, or stayed on that hill, would his brother have survived? He had stopped Charlie from going after the ammo, even taken his place, in order to protect him. That was always the mission.

But could it be there was another reason, one he hated to face? That allowing his brother to go that night would have been Charlie's initiation into manhood. And where would that have left Morgan?

"How we feeling today?" Evelyn asked, approaching Morgan's bed.

"Fine." His voice was hoarse from lack of use. He kept his gaze fixed on the red and green holiday ribbons decorating the stack of school desks retired in the corner. Behind it, pockmarks streaked a dusty blackboard, the chalky remnants of lessons forgotten.

"Sorry I couldn't get to you sooner," she said, setting something on the foot of his mattress. The fragrance of her witch-hazel lotion was a welcome break from the pungency of disinfectant. She lifted the damp rag from his forehead, tested his temperature with the inside of her wrist, then flipped the rag over and replaced it across his hairline. The coolness was refreshing, though he wasn't about to say so.

Moving onto the lower part of his left leg, swollen and propped on rolled blankets, she peeked under the bandage. In silence, she studied the threatening wound. The bullet to his thigh had but grazed the skin, and the torn ligament in his left knee was expected to improve over time. The shot he took through his calf, however, had led to an infection that could cost him the limb. A minimal punishment, as far as he was concerned.

"Evelyn, have you seen a free bed?" A hefty nurse in the classroom doorway stood behind a wheelchair carting a German soldier.

Morgan eyed the guy's bandaged feet, assumed it was trench foot.

"Should be an open cot in the library," Evelyn replied. "If not, the girls in there can help you find something."

Morgan watched the moaning soldier being wheeled out of sight. Indeed, these monsters were human. Nevertheless, he appreciated the nursing staff's attempt to segregate the Jerries from the GIs whenever possible.

"Got a delivery for you," Evelyn announced. From the end of the bed, she retrieved a small rectangular box wrapped neatly in tan paper. "Just came down the chimney, straight from the North Pole."

A wave of sadness rolled in like the tide, pulled by a vague recollection of normality.

Morgan nodded and took the box from her sandpapery hand. His mouth tried for a smile but fell short.

In her tainted ward dress, she sank into a nearby chair. She smoothed her bobbed hairdo, chocolate brown interspersed with silver strands, and issued a sigh. Compliments of the Battle of the Bulge, the medical staff seemed to be on eighteen-hour shifts. Morgan had watched Evelyn assisting doctors, tending patients, and organizing the infirmary at a sprinter's pace. He wondered if the Army nurse ever allowed herself a decent night's rest. Such an indulgence, he figured, wasn't likely based on her frequently cited phrase: *If our boys don't get a break, neither should we.*

Morgan forced himself to sit up, letting the rag fall away. He stared at the package. A gift was the last thing he deserved.

Across the room, two nurses traveled from bed to bed, doling out similar bundles. Patients shredded their encasements to reveal groupings of candy and toiletries.

"Go ahead, open it," Evelyn suggested in earnest.

Not wanting to spread his misery, he honored her request. He edged away the tape to release the wrapping, one adhesive strip at a time.

"The paper isn't actually the present." Evelyn smiled. "There really is something inside."

His mother had insisted it was disgraceful when people neglected to reuse wrapping fit for future exchanges; therefore, minimizing tears had been a must.

"Old habit." Morgan shrugged lightly and slid the contents out onto his lap: a red cardboard cigar box. Spanning the top half of the container were three vertical ovals woven through the word *ZIFAT.* In large gold letters, *TERZETT* trimmed the bottom.

"Now, don't get too excited," she said. "It's not for smoking. Just a bit of a hand-me-down from Doc K."

K, Morgan had learned, was short for Kleever, a disconcerting surname considering the man's position.

"It's nothing extravagant," Evelyn continued, "but with the way you were carrying on about your letters when you got here, I thought this might come in handy for storing them."

Morgan had no recollection of his morphine-induced mumblings. His concussion and throes of pain had tossed him in and out of consciousness during his evacuation from Slevant—if nothing else, mercifully sparing him the sight of the Graves Registration crew hauling away Charlie's remains.

"Thank you," he told her, and ran his fingers across the case that still smelled of cigars.

"Got another surprise inside. Came for you this morning."

Puzzled, he glanced at her beaming face before flipping open the lid. Inside he found a crinkled envelope with Betty's return address. The November postmark indicated it had been shuffled around a bit, but thanks to the Army forwarding system, she'd managed to find him.

The start of a smile formed on his lips.

"I'm a letter fan myself," Evelyn said. "My husband's a major in the Pacific and all three of my nephews are paratroopers. So I know how special those pages can be. You keep them close to your heart, you hear?"

"Yes, ma'am." There was a quality about the woman, as comforting as a warm bowl of chicken soup.

"Well. Best get back to work before they fire me." She winked and pressed on her thighs to stand. "I'll change the dressing on your leg after supper. They say we're having a real turkey dinner with all the fixings, so be sure to save up an appetite." A few steps and she added, "Oh, and there's a pilot visiting some pals here before flying home to the States, taking a bundle of their posts with him. I'd be glad to slip something in if you'd like."

Morgan thanked her again. As she walked away, he picked up the envelope with both hands. He rubbed his thumbs over the wrinkles, imagining the softness of Betty's fingers beneath his. Then, craving the message inside, he broke the seal.

> *Dear Morgan,*
> *Once again, your words have brought me immense joy. I must confess that I, too, have read your letters*

more times than I can count. Please rest assured, your latest letter arrived legible, and the pages free of mud and raindrop stains (not that I would have minded in the least).

As a child, I was a rain lover like you, and still believe little in this world could rival the feeling of a warm summer sprinkling. Of course, I am sure my opinion would differ if I had to live in the muddy downpours you described. Aside from wishing those clouds away for you, I can offer only a relevant poem, as Swinburne's eloquence so greatly surpasses my own:

> *For winter's rains and ruins are over,*
> *And all the season of snows and sins;*
> *The days dividing lover and lover,*
> *The light that loses, the night that wins;*
> *And time remembered is grief forgotten,*
> *And frosts are slain and flowers begotten,*
> *And in green underwood and cover*
> *Blossom by blossom the spring begins.*

I know that verses, no matter how profound, are no substitute for dry shelter. Yet perhaps the poem's message will at least bring you a moment of comfort, just as my dear grandfather's same views used to provide for me. He taught me that to understand life's essential lessons, all one need do is turn to the wonders of nature; even the most violent of rainstorms will calm when afforded time. And if we were granted seasons without snow and sin, we would never know the blossoms of spring and hope; and from such hope, if we are in luck, comes peace.

Perhaps peace is what you, too, had discovered in the scent of the approaching thunderstorms you mentioned. Thunderstorms being quite rare in California, I myself was raised with other calming forms of nature: the sound of a breeze sifting through the branches of a palm tree, the crisp smell of the ocean

*waves crashing on the shore. In fact, among the most
cherished memories of my youth are the many nights I
spent sitting on a beach with my father, admiring the
changing tide.*

*I now recall that this tradition began on my fifth
birthday, when he gifted me with a lovely tale. He
explained how both the sun and moon were rumored to
share the morning sky, but on only one day of the year,
which so happened to fall on the date of my birth.
Supposedly, the phenomenon could best be viewed at
the break of dawn from a beach near our home.
Jittering with excitement, I begged him to take me
there the night before my birthday to witness the event.*

*For hours we waited, bundled in blankets on the
sand. We listened to the waves, counted the stars, and
talked about everything and nothing. Upon waking in
my bed the following morning, and discovering I had
slept through the anticipated show, I made him vow to
take me back on my next birthday. From then on, we
did just that, year after year, each time with my falling
asleep before the sun rose.*

*Eventually, I realized the occurrence was a common
one. Still, I insisted on our annual outings until we
moved from the area. I do wonder how long he
suspected my knowledge of the charade but, for my
sake, chose to play along.*

*Revisiting these memories, I admit that mending
our ties seems well overdue. I am not convinced a
resolution is plausible after so many years, but I
promise to consider making an effort in that direction.
Suffice it to say, I have taken your advice to heart, and
can indeed understand your view in light of your
parents' passing. May I add, in that regard, how terribly
sorry I am to learn they are no longer with you. Given
the sheer kindness in your soul, however, I have no
doubt they felt blessed to have had you, as well as your
brother, in their lives no matter the length of time.*

As for your concern about Charlie, I must first admit that I envy the bond you two have enjoyed since childhood. When I was little, the first item on my annual wish lists to Santa was invariably a baby sister, a sibling to whom I could tell all my jokes, stories, and secrets. (After two Christmases, I amended it to read "a sister or brother." As an only child, I was afraid my request had been too particular.) Though a newborn never did arrive down our chimney, years later I met my dearest friend, Julia. It is with her I am able to share many of my deepest worries—as Charlie does with you—and solely to lessen my own burdens, not transfer them onto her shoulders.

Now, in reciprocating your offering of wisdom, I would insist that neither your mom nor brother expect you to be a fearless role model, only the courageous man you already are. For, as my grandfather would insightfully say, "Courage isn't the trait of those trying to be heroes; it lies in the ones who, in spite of being afraid, find the strength inside them to continue on."

On that note, I shall retire for the night. Thank you, Morgan, for trusting me with your feelings and honesty, and for sending such beautiful letters. They have, unmistakably, become my most treasured possessions.

I long to hear from you soon. Please be safe.

Fondly,

Betty

Just when Morgan was convinced his body had completely run dry of tears, a light mist coated his eyes. How he wished she were here right now to console him with her voice, her touch.

He gawked at the letter, again astonished by Betty's ability to peer into his soul. She knew nothing of the tragedy that had taken his brother's life, nothing of the guilt that weighed on his heart and mind. But somehow she'd soothed him, as though she could read his thoughts and answer his prayers.

Morgan placed the pages in the cigar box beside him. Carefully, he grabbed hold of his field jacket from a pile of clothing on the floor. He slung the garment across his lap, the smell of dirt and war trapped in its stained fabric. Out of a pocket, he retrieved Betty's posts and picture, and traced her features with his fingertip.

How could pieces from two different puzzles fit so perfectly together?

Their worlds were nothing alike. Not just now, even before the war. She was a city girl, raised on the sunny beaches of California; until shipping out, he had never seen the ocean. She was articulate and educated, her options for the future clearly limitless; he was a hayseed with barely two nickels to rub together and had no certainty of plans now that Charlie was gone. All he had to offer Betty was himself.

And he couldn't help wishing it were more.

A current, again, shot through his calf. He grimaced, every muscle contracted. When the pain began to fade, he glared at his bandaged wound. He'd been prepared for what the doc might have to do, maybe even wanted it. An archaic penance for letting his brother die.

Yet now, with Betty's messages in his hands, he realized he'd have even less to give should he come home as half a man.

Telling her would be the right thing to do. But would she stop caring about him?

Could he blame her?

A compromise, fair enough for the time being: He'd come clean if his leg didn't improve. Until knowing for sure, he'd savor every one of her letters as if they were air, keeping him alive, giving him hope.

❧ 27 ❧

December 31, 1944
Pittsburgh, Pennsylvania

Julia anchored her hands on the cushioned armrests of her father's wingback chair, as if seated on a ship bracing for a squall. The envelope she'd freshly addressed lay in the center of the mahogany desk: *Christian Downing SM 2/C.*

A month of collecting regret like sea glass in her pocket had led to this moment. "Mermaid's tears," Christian had called the gems, while they'd strolled the shore together one unusually warm spring day. Ironic how now, after the confession Julia had at last penned to her fiancé, her own eyes were almost too dry to blink, let alone produce tears. Anxiety and heat from the den fireplace evaporated the moisture from her body.

She pressed the sealed letter to her chest and padded across the Persian rug. Peering through the French doors, she leaned against the ceiling-high shelves of leather-bound books. Snow trickled over the terrace, white with purity and innocence. Every flake perfect, unique, untouched—until meeting the stony ground and melting away.

Church bells tolled in the distance. Five chimes marked the evening hour. Five days had passed since she'd first attempted, without success, to purge her conscience in writing. Five weeks she had spent replaying "the incident" with Ian in her head, then deconstructing every component, every emotion, to make sense of it all.

Again and again, she had analyzed their mistake. A moment of weakness between two lonely people. Undoubtedly, to an outsider, their interactions all evening might have appeared romantic, their behavior misconstrued as amorous flirtation.

But never had that been her intention.

How could she have felt anything less than comfortable with Ian, a man whose very essence was directly tied to the one she loved? Had she closed her eyes, the similarities would have been indecipherable. His voice, his laugh, even his smell. Fragments of Christian had lured her into the trap. And the safety of knowing they were a marginal step from becoming family had served as enticing bait, dropping her defenses.

So why, then, was guilt corroding her soul?

Each visit to the question, to that night in the park, produced the same solitary answer: Despite her eyelids obscuring her view, she'd been aware they weren't Christian's lips on her body. And still, she had hesitated in stopping him.

For days after their date, she had debated on phoning Ian. The possibility of his telling Christian had writhed in her mind—a request for forgiveness, or worse, a lay of claim to her. Eventually, she'd reasoned neither would be the case. After all, to her relief, he hadn't pursued her further. No phone calls. No letters. Perhaps his guilt was as burdening as hers. One conversation and they could put it all to rest. Even laugh about it years from now. A plea of youthful insanity, sworn secrecy among in-laws. All she had to do was be the bigger person and reach out to him.

Yet she couldn't. Not until she knew for sure that his voice wouldn't send a shiver down her back, that his touch wouldn't seize her heart. That her darling Christian was truly her soul mate.

How presumptuous she'd been with Liz, believing she understood her friend's dilemma. The gray area of morality seemed so avoidable when one was perched on its solid black framework. But a single missed step and Julia had learned: Love posed just as many complications as war.

During their last talk at work, she had tried to tell Liz so, had verged on telling her everything. But she managed only an apology. Somehow, it seemed voicing her error, her doubts, would solidify them into permanence, irreconcilable and real.

"Miss Julia?" A woman's voice came from behind her.

Julia swung to find her parents' new housekeeper in the doorway. Dressed in uniform, the ebony-skinned woman looked on with a disarming gaze. Julia originally thought her to be a Hattie McDaniel replica, the beloved Mammy from *Gone with the Wind*. Now, though, there seemed to be little resemblance. One more mistaken notion. Another instance of trying to make something more than it was.

"Yes, Mabel?" Julia answered.

"Wadn't sure if you heard me knocking. The missus say guests be arriving soon. So's you might wanna get ready 'fore long."

Julia glanced down at her untucked blouse and pedal pushers. Time had slid around her since she had closed herself off in her father's study. Thankfully, the dress hanging on her four-poster bed had a throng of multifaceted beads, sparkly enough to detract from the pasted smile she would flaunt at the New Year's Eve celebration.

"Thank you, Mabel. I'll head up to my room right now."

"Yes'um." About to leave, she paused. "Oh, and missus say to tell you a gentlemen called for ya earlier. Mr. Downing be his name."

The hair on Julia's arms bristled. She knew full well Christian Downing, her sailor at sea, was not the caller who rang. She forced her voice to remain steady. "Did he happen to give his first name?"

"Can't say, Miss Julia."

"Did my mother mention why he called?" she pressed.

"You best ask her yourself, but I do believe he say he and his wife just wanna wish you and your family happy new year."

Of course . . . George and Cora.

Relief rippled through Julia.

"You wants me to post that for ya?" Mabel asked.

Julia glanced down at the envelope still clutched to her chest, her grip like a vise. "Thank you," she said. "But it's not quite ready."

With a nod, Mabel headed down the hall, humming one of her usual gospel tunes, rich in history and redemption.

Julia threaded around her father's large floor globe and crystal decanter bar. She centered herself before the fireplace mantel covered with framed pictures. Her sister's wedding portrait, various baby shots, a group family photo taken at the country club two Christmases ago. She drank in the smiles and special moments, the chronology of happiness.

And she made her unbending decision: She wasn't about to disrupt the joyful lineage merely to clear her conscience. This was just another test between her and Christian. A test she refused to fail over a meaningless kiss.

Bereft of hesitation, she thrust the corner of Christian's envelope into the blue-edged fire. The paper borrowed a small flame without a fight, as if knowing it would never reach another's eyes. She watched the casing smoke and flicker and curl. Ashes broke off as the heat crept toward her fingers. When only a scant portion remained, she tossed it into the fire and watched the evidence vanish.

❦ 28 ❧

January 2, 1945
Evanston, Illinois

Liz watched the dishwater in the sink funneling toward the drain, disappearing like the last of her family ties.

"Elizabeth?"

"Huh?" She jerked her fingers out of the suds and whirled around.

Her father stood in the kitchen doorway. He offered her a towel off the wall hook with a genial smile. "I just wanted to say good night." The wrinkles bordering his dusky brown eyes deepened behind his spectacles. She had noticed the gradual thinning of his russet hair, but not until that moment did she truly realize the toll time had taken.

"Thank you again for dinner," he said.

"I'm sorry the meat was so dry." As in Sahara dry, thanks to the butter shortage. Oh, why hadn't she pulled the chicken out of the oven earlier?

"Nonsense. It was fine. And the mashed potatoes tasted just like Nana's."

Unable to discern if he was being honest, she returned his smile. "I guess from working at the rest home, I've gotten pretty good at making food that doesn't require teeth."

He let out a low chuckle, the first of his visit. It had been a winter visit like so many before. Overly polite, excruciatingly civil. Radio shows and boughs of holly to pad the annual dues of Christmas.

Why couldn't her mother have chosen another holiday to leave? Groundhog or Columbus Day. April Fools'. One without the requirement of family bonding and outward joy.

"Well," Liz said, and set the dishcloth aside. With no words to follow, silence entered the room, clinging like guilt, a wall dividing them.

Her father angled a shoulder toward the hall. "I'll see you in the morning, then, before I head to the station."

Actually he wouldn't be seeing her, which wasn't necessarily a bad thing. "I'm afraid I'm covering the early shift. So I'll probably be gone before you're up."

"Oh. All right. Then I'll see you at your engagement party in April."

Ah, yes. The engagement party. Mrs. Harris's "intimate and informal gathering" soon to become a grand production.

Liz stowed the thought away and nodded pleasantly. "Have a nice trip."

At that, he raised his hand, reaching for her, as if to . . . hug her good-bye?

Anticipation stole her breath. Her arms began to lift—then swiftly dropped when he gave her a pat on the shoulder. "You take good care," he added like the afterthought she'd become.

"You too," she managed. Yet another opportunity for reconciliation slipped away as he turned to leave the room. She wanted to call after him. But besides the one incident that really mattered, was there anything left to discuss? They had already used up the usual topics: classes, students, weather. Always the Chicago weather. And, of course, they'd covered current affairs.

Several evenings ago while dining with Dalton's family, she had listened to her father talk about a fellow train passenger who'd boisterously delighted in the prolongation of the war, bragging of profits from stock market investments built on the sacrifice of soldiers. Disgusted, her father had apparently asserted his objections before an audience of concurring passengers.

It was a side of her father she never knew existed, a side she longed to know firsthand.

During the car ride home that night, the two of them rumbling along quietly, she had decided to express a side of herself that he, in turn, didn't know existed. She wanted to share with him her change in desired profession, a detour from his scholarly path. But before she could begin, her father proudly announced he'd been discussing her teaching possibilities with the dean of Northwestern's English department. To which she simply replied, "Thank you."

After all, there would be plenty of opportunities between now and graduation to express her plans. Plenty of chances to crush her father's dream, along with the remnants of his approval.

"Oh, I'd nearly forgotten." He now rotated back. "A post arrived for your roommate." He handed her an envelope from his sweater pocket.

"I'll make sure she gets it." Liz dredged up a smile and watched him stride down the hall, a hotel guest retiring for the night.

Once he sealed his door behind him, she hung up her apron. She reached for the light switch, happening to glance at the envelope in her hand—from Morgan.

From Morgan?

Her heart stopped. She felt the blood drain from her face.

He was alive! Thank God, he was alive.

Her fingers swiped open the seal before she remembered: She'd already said good-bye. No . . . *no.* She couldn't go through this. Not again.

Clasping her locket, she stared at his name on the envelope: *PFC M. McClain.* The same handwriting, same smudged fingerprints. Yet she had changed. She had moved on.

Hadn't she?

Reading his entire letter with emotional detachment would serve as her final test. A few insomnia reports and childhood anecdotes were all that stood between her and a doubtless future with Dalton.

She had to know for sure.

Steeling herself, she clicked off the light and headed to Julia's room. She closed the door and sat on the bed. A shakiness moved through her as she retrieved the pages from inside. Already she dreaded every dot, every line, that had been penned in the soldier's hand.

Dearest Betty,

I know it's been a while since you've heard from me. I apologize if I've caused you to fret. So much doing over here I'm not sure where to start. Figured the best I could do was to simply write down the thoughts as they come.

It's another bitter cold day and the war still drags on and on. Some of our mud-belly GIs have been fighting for three years now, but there doesn't seem to be an end to this foulness anytime soon.

My only rosy news to report is that the rain that nearly drove us all nuts over here has stopped. Unfortunately, slush and snow took its place and brought temperatures that chill us to the bone. Of course I shouldn't complain about the weather when I'm lying in a bed with a real mattress and clean sheets. Just too bad it's in a hospital ward thousands of miles from my room on the farm.

I don't recall much about how I got here. Only remember waking up from the pain in my leg and arm to find a nurse hovering over me, telling me where I was. Since then the docs have patched me up with bandages and penicillin. Funny that I've spent my whole life in the fields with heavy tools and machinery and never got more than some cuts and bruises. But only half a year here and I wind up in a hospital.

Lucky to be alive—that's what the doc says about me. Compared to all he's seen, I'm sure he's right. Just doesn't feel that way. Not after all that's happened.

*You see, Charlie died in my arms on December 19.
The last words he spoke were to tell me everything was
going to be okay. He's lying there, body pegged with
lead, and he's offering _me_ comfort. Maybe it's because
he knew me well enough to know how much I was
going to blame myself.*

*Over and over, every detail of that day comes back
like a movie running in my head, but in slow motion so
I can see all the mistakes I made. I keep thinking one of
these days I'll find a way to change the ending. All
along there hadn't been a single battle when I wasn't at
his side. So why is it that the one minute I leave him,
God decides it's time to take him back?*

*There are moments I almost expect Charlie to
wander through the door and gloat about how he
managed to put one over on me. That it wasn't really
blood covering his shirt, just ketchup he smuggled from
the mess as a dramatic touch to his prank. I'd give him
a good smack, then we'd both end up getting a laugh
out of it.*

*I think that's what I miss the most—his laugh. So
genuine it was contagious. More often than not, it was
at himself. That's a rare quality in a person. I realize
now it's just one of the wonderful things about him I
took for granted. His storytelling and humor, his free
spirit—they were all traits anyone with decent vision
and hearing could have sized up about Charlie from a
dozen rods away. But I was among the few who really
knew his other side. He had a caring nature, a solid
heart of gold. He would have given the shirt off his
back in the middle of a snowstorm to anyone who
needed it. Now that he's gone I wonder how many
people besides me were lucky enough to know that
about him.*

A chaplain named Father Bud passed through the

*other day, visiting guys in need of direction and
spiritual guidance. I must have looked like I needed
both, because he pulled up a chair right next to my bed.
A nurse had told him about me losing my brother, so he
tried to offer comfort. He told me how pleased I should
be for Charlie, knowing he's at peace and resting in a
better place, and that someday we'll be reunited in a
world without violence and hatred and suffering.
Truthfully it's hard to imagine a place like that about
now. Though I do hope he's right. It would definitely
make the rest of my time on this earth easier to get
through. Then maybe I wouldn't be filled with so much
anger over Charlie's death—anger at the damn Kraut
who shot him down, at God for stealing the only close
kin I had left, and at myself for not keeping it from
happening.*

*It's odd, isn't it? People die every day and the world
goes on like nothing happened. But when it's a person
you love, you think everyone should stop and take
notice. That they ought to cry and light candles and tell
you that you're not alone. Sometimes I feel so lost
without Charlie that my chest physically hurts. Like he
took part of me with him. After all, I can't recall a
single memory when he wasn't in my life. And now
here I am, some days searching for a reason to breathe.
What do I do if I'm not looking after my kid brother?
Guess only time will tell.*

*Although you couldn't have known it, your letter
helped me appreciate how lucky I was to have him in
my life at all, even if it was a shorter time than I
wanted. I'd give anything to spend one more day with
him. But at least those nineteen years were full of
memories I know I'll keep forever, memories even the
devil can't take away. And if there's truth to heaven
and the afterlife, no doubt Charlie's up there grinning*

*because he beat me to the answers. I tell you, I could
sure use some of those answers right now—like what
this war is really all about, and when, if ever, I'll be
leaving this hellish place and going home.*

*Home. It's such a simple word, one I never knew
would come to mean as much to me as it has. It once
was my dad's house, then my uncle's farm. Mostly it's
meant wherever Charlie and I were together. Now,
though, it's you. It's your letters, your words. They're
the place I go to with my fears, where I find comfort,
where I feel safe.*

*So thank you, my darling Betty. I would be one lost,
empty-hearted man without you. Please write soon.
Yours always,
Morgan*

Hot tears coursed over Liz's hand covering her mouth. Morgan's anguish invaded every inch of her heart—a heart that perhaps was never meant for anyone but him. She laid the letter over her chest, against the brittle-edged emptiness they shared. The scenes that haunted him were unimaginable, but she understood loss. And regret. And guilt from an irreversible act.

At the thought of replying, Viola's advice rushed back to her, though this time with little impact. For Morgan had offered Liz more than a passionate kiss or the admission of a teenage crush. More than a letter, even. This was a man's soul poured out on paper, real and precious as life itself. Names aside, his words were meant for *her*. And it was time she told him who that was.

Wiping her cheeks, she forged toward the stationery waiting in the vanity. She had never felt more ashamed of deceiving him. Yet as she gripped the drawer handle, a question halted her: How could she tell him now, in the midst of all he was going through?

What he needed above all was someone's support. What he needed was assurance he wasn't alone. And what *she* needed was . . . him.

It now dawned on her how hard she had worked all these years to avoid really needing someone. As though the moat she'd constructed with her independence could save her from getting hurt, shield her from loneliness in her locked-away tower. In the end, those very efforts had caused her to suffer all the same.

How ironic to think, it was Swinburne's poem she had presented to Morgan—about the beauty of spring's blossoms in the wake of winter's rains. And meanwhile, out of fear, she herself had been sustaining a life without seasons. Although scared, she wanted more. She wanted to start by revealing her identity. But would the truth hurt him as much as his father's well-intentioned lie? Perhaps it would cut even deeper in the aftermath of his brother's death.

Eventually, she'd tell him—of course she would tell him—once his grief lessened over Charlie. Oh, Charlie . . . full of such energy, such confidence. Like a shooting star, his brilliance glowed, and then he was gone.

The same as Liz's father would be one day.

Life is too short not to say how you feel to the people you love. The passage blared like a flashing banner, a phrase from one of Morgan's letters. Repeated readings, whether she liked it or not, had branded his words into her heart.

And he was right. If she didn't reach out to her father now, she could lose him forever.

Pen and paper in hand, she planted herself on the cushioned seat. Her mind hunted for a proper opening, leafed through her archive of profoundly succinct literary works. And somewhere in the tunnels of her thoughts, she mistakenly exhumed three sentences—the three sentences that had changed everything.

Go away! I hate you! Why can't you just stay out of my life?

She was only thirteen when she'd screamed the words at her mother, climaxing a year of constant arguments, but the memory returned with burning clarity. Her mother, Isabelle, had uncovered a note while laundering Liz's skirt. The note came from an older boy Liz barely knew, a schoolmate asking her to sneak out for a movie. Isabelle took the liberty of phoning his house. What kind of upbringing, she'd asked his mother, could the boy have possibly had to think Elizabeth was old enough to date, and that encouraging such delinquent behavior was acceptable? And by the way, a mechanic's son wasn't about to ruin her daughter's reputation and bright future.

That was the story making the rounds during gym class, anyway, before Liz had come storming into the house. Tempers flared, scorn flew, concluding with her three-sentence finale: *Go away! I hate you! Why can't you just stay out of my life?* From physical to personality traits, never had she and her mother seemed more opposite. Liz had fled to her room then, slammed the door, and fumed through the night. Come morning, she'd learned that Isabelle had taken the spiteful exclamations to heart.

"Your mother left," her father had explained in a voice as barren as the look in his eyes—a look that said she wouldn't be coming back. His next words had blurred in Liz's ears: Mother . . . unhappy . . . tried . . . blame. Everything she already knew.

Then unblinking, not breathing, Liz had watched him retreat into the seclusion of his pile-ridden study; the compassionate side of him never came out. She'd spent every night for weeks weeping in her room, where even the tiny yellow rosebuds on her wallpaper withered from guilt. All the while, she had brainstormed ways to locate her mother. But without maternal relatives to consult, and with the suspicion that no apology could lure the woman home once found, the search had ended before it began.

How strange that one little note—from a boy Liz hadn't even cared for—and the family she'd known was gone. No accumulation of dandelion wishes or coins in a fountain could reverse that day. Not even the enticement of a gift, addressed to Liz and wrapped in red *Nutcracker* paper, had brought Isabelle home to see the present being opened.

Perhaps Liz would never have the chance to make amends with her mother. But her father was still here, now, in this house. She would knock on his door this instant if she felt confident her mouth wouldn't fumble the words. No, she trusted her pen tonight to see this through. And if a scrawled message caused the mess, the same ought to end it.

Dear Father,

I wish I had the courage to say what I need to in person. Because I do not, I am pouring my thoughts onto paper.

Few days go by when I do not think about the closeness you and I once shared, or the sadness I feel, knowing we barely know each other anymore. And yet the widening gap between us is no one's fault but mine.

For the year that led up to my final argument with Mother, no matter what I did, I felt unable to earn her love and praise. In hindsight, I see how my acting out and talking back were merely attempts to gain her attention, even if that attention was no better than a scolding. I explain this not as justification, but to take responsibility for what I have done.

Please know I would do anything for the power to reverse time, anything to take back the hateful words that caused Mother to leave our home and lives forever. For this, and for causing you such pain, I am so very sorry.

I realize this letter cannot undo the damage I have caused. However, I hope that someday you will be able to find it within your heart to forgive me.
Your daughter,
Elizabeth

Not until Liz signed her name did she so much as pause. Forbidding herself the chance to read or regret her composition, she sealed the page in an envelope marked *Father.*

It was done.

Drained of all energy, she crawled into bed with her clothes on. She decided to make a wish—if ever she needed magical help, it was now. But before she could finish the thought, sleep shrouded her in its arms.

* * *

Only seconds seemed to have passed when Liz awoke. The lamp still alight but window dark, she strained to read the face of the bedside clock. 5:47 A.M.

She'd forgotten to set the alarm!

Panic shot through her body like lightning, hurling her out of bed. She had eighteen minutes to ready herself for work and sprint to the bus stop.

At the pedestal sink in the bathroom, she washed her face and teeth, trussed her hair into a ponytail. No time to change clothes. She shook lint off her sweater and skirt, then threw on her overcoat.

She tiptoed down the hallway, shoes in one hand, her father's envelope in the other. As she entered the kitchen, a sharp clank from the radiator gave her a start. Quietly, she reached into a coin-filled jelly jar on the counter and pocketed bus fare for her commute.

Nine minutes left.

The letter—she didn't know where to place it. What she did know was he couldn't discover the envelope until long after walking out the front door.

That was it! The front door.

In the entry, her father's leather satchel slumped against the wall. She slung her shoes on as she strode over to the bag and unfastened its wide center buckle. The first book she grabbed was co-incidentally the present she had given him for Christmas. *The Greatest Sonnets of All Time.* She hid the envelope inside the front leather cover. There it would remain until he happened across it while on the train at least halfway back to D.C., or perhaps in one of his classes, scanning for reference material.

Book in the satchel, she refastened the buckle and sped out the door. She forged her way down the slushy street, cloaked by dawn's early darkness. The jingling of her coins blended with the clinking of a neighbor's milk-bottle delivery. Her unbuttoned coat flapped as if preparing to soar.

As she barreled around the corner, the bus revved its motor and started to pull away.

"Wait! Please, wait!" Her volume surely woke a few neighbors. The wheels halted with a squeal.

Onboard, she collapsed in an empty row. Her pledge to Morgan fulfilled, she sat proudly gazing out the window. The transition of night to day would soon appear; twilight would rule the sky, utterly unstoppable. Just like the game she had set in motion. She'd moved the pawn, she'd tossed the dice. The next move lay with her father.

❦ 29 ❦

January 3, 1945
Dutch New Guinea

Unofficial word had reached Betty just after dawn. A med tech, her replacement, would be arriving within the week.

Despite her dizzying euphoria, Betty embarked on her usual morning rounds. Yet all she needed was confirmation of the news, and not even a full-fledged monsoon would be able to stop her from racing to the barracks. Faster than a person could say "Coconut Grove," she'd have her belongings gathered and clothing packed. Well, whatever the engulfing humidity hadn't literally devoured.

Until then, not wanting to jinx the transfer, she would simply go about her work. She would distract her mind with other things. That was the plan anyway. Nothing proved effective, however, before seeing Leslie Kelly seated in his bed.

"Perfecting your koalas, Lieutenant?" she asked, hugging her shield of linens.

"Not today." He hinted at a smile without looking up from his sketchpad.

"A wombat, then."

"Wrong again."

"Wallaby?"

He tilted his head at the drawing, pencil briskly moving. "This creature's a touch more rare. Wild as a dingo, with all the grace and beauty of a brumby."

"So let's see this wonder of nature."

He added a few finishing touches. Briefly hesitant, he flipped the notepad around, displaying the picture upright between his casts.

She recognized the features: the light hair, the rounded face, the dot of a birthmark high on the cheek. She brightened from the inside out.

"It's me," she said to herself. Then, downplaying her delight, she pointed out, "Except for the cockeyed smile." She set the linens on the empty cot beside her, and took the sketch into her hands for a closer view.

"Oh, but this one's a study on realism," he said.

"My smile is *not* crooked."

"Not always." He reclined against the wall. "Only when you're thinking of something that makes you happy, but you don't know anyone's watching."

The fact he'd analyzed a trait of hers not even she was aware of made her squirm beneath her skin. What other flaws had he catalogued? Dismayed, she reviewed the drawing again, focusing on the eyes. In them, he'd captured something—a vulnerability made of sadness and yearning—that all the giggles and flirtations in the world couldn't hide. At least not from him.

She glanced up timidly, discomforted by his x-ray gaze. Once again, like that night in the supply tent, she'd somehow shared with him more than she planned.

"Can I keep it?" she asked.

"Absolutely." He nodded. "For three bob."

"Bob?"

"Shillings."

She shot him an appalled look. "You're going to charge me for my own drawing?"

"A bloke's gotta eat."

She pursed her lips, tossed the sketchpad onto his lap. "I should've expected as much, from a descendant of the notorious Ned Kelly Gang."

He laughed, a delicious sound, a confection she could feast

upon for decades. "We're no relation to those Kellys, I assure you. Although my sister Nellie used to spin quite the yarn, telling her schoolmates otherwise."

The name snagged her thoughts: Nellie Miles, his most faithful correspondent. "Nellie—she's your sister?" Betty ventured.

"Eldest of the four girls. Ten years between Nellie and Caroline, the youngest."

Caroline was another name she recognized from his envelopes. Now it all made sense. He wasn't the Don Juan she had presumed him to be. Simply a beloved sibling.

But then, what did it matter? Even if fraternization with an officer wasn't strictly forbidden—although foreign military might be an exception—pursuing a relationship with him would be pointless. Australia was his home. If he ever made it back. There was a war on, after all, and in only a few weeks the removal of his casts would be freeing him for duty.

What's more, she herself could be leaving any day now. The transfer she'd begged for, fought for.

Earned.

She ought to be thrilled. Prickles of disappointment had no right crawling up her arms. Unfolding the bedsheet, she resumed her casualness.

"So are you the only boy in the family?"

"Got two brothers as well, both smack in the middle. Took a while for Mum to realize no babe could be as splendidly handsome as her firstborn."

"Don't tell me. You're the oldest."

"I am indeed," he replied, charmingly smug.

She shook her head, rolling her eyes. "With all that bravado, your mother should've named you Joe."

He scrunched his forehead, perplexed.

"As in Joe Byrne," she explained. "Ned's lieutenant."

He folded his arms, nodded thoughtfully. "I'm bloody impressed. You know some bushranger history."

Rosalyn had recently passed along a book on Australian historical figures. Of late, all things related to the outback had become fascinating to Betty. Specifically any chapter with the name *Kelly* in it.

"So what else do you know?" he asked as she leaned over to dress the vacant cot. She tucked the sheet's corners, perfect Army creases, but could feel his subtle gaze tracing her curves. Her mind battled to focus on relevant reading material.

"I know Mr. Byrne was an outlaw who thought himself a hero."

"Which he was."

"Sure. If you consider an opium addict a hero."

"Ah, merely a means for his poetry."

Betty laughed. "Writing drinking songs about himself didn't make him a poet."

"He penned more than that. One day I'll hunt down a book of his poems and prove it to you."

"Now, now, Lieutenant." She stood, smirking. "Don't go making promises you can't keep."

In an instant, his face darkened. Her sentence hovered like a thundercloud blocking the sun. A reminder that wartime promises were a dangerous commodity.

"Betty, there you are!"

She turned to find Stella and Shirley entering the ward. Cradled in Stella's arms was something that appeared to be a brown fur hand muff. The gal had clearly been sipping too many jungle cocktails if she thought the sweltering temperature warranted the accessory.

"You have to see this!" Shirley set down the bundle, which sprang onto its paws. The little dog's pointy ears reached Shirley mid-calf.

Betty knelt to pat its head. "Where did it come from?"

"Some GIs found her in a foxhole a while back," Shirley said. "Apparently she's been going on bombing raids with them ever since."

Stella added, "Dutch soldiers must have abandoned her after the invasion."

The mutt gazed up with sweet, beady eyes. A tiny pink tongue peeked from her mouth. She had a ragged look about her, but her fur felt silky and clean, fine as human hair. Betty scratched the dog's lower back and happened across a tickle spot that sent her hind leg thumping.

"What kind is she?" Betty asked, giggling.

"Doc Powers used to be a vet," Stella said. "Says she's a York-shire. Just about the cutest thing you ever saw, isn't she?"

"Hey, watch this!" Shirley stepped away as Betty rose, and called out, "Tell them how the war's been, Smoky."

"Ruff!" the dog barked proudly.

Soldiers sat up in their beds, drawn to the show.

Shirley fashioned her hand into a gun, her barrel finger pointed at Smoky. "Bang!" she yelled. The dog collapsed, spurring applause and much-needed laughter.

Betty was savoring the smiles in the room when, out of the corner of her eye, she glimpsed Kitzafenny speaking to an orderly.

Confirmation awaited: White sandy beaches. Shimmering blue water. Beauty shops and rec halls. The images flowed on an endless reel in Betty's mind as she took off down the ward.

She came to attention beside the captain as the orderly walked away. "Excuse me, ma'am," she said.

Kitzafenny mumbled something while scribbling on a clipboard.

"Permission to speak?"

The captain raised a hand, signaling her to wait, and wrote some more.

Betty watched the pen's erratic movements, the pages flip. Excitement tingled her fingertips as the seconds trudged on. Then a bout of laughter pulled her attention to the middle of the tent, and the sight overtook her thoughts. Leslie tossing a ball for the pup. The beaming smile on the pilot's face was the same she envisioned every morning when she woke, every night while drifting off.

Wasted efforts.

He was too incorrigible to be the prince of her future. Too frustrating to bear. Even now, she could visualize the look he would give her upon hearing her grand news. A look that said she had given up, abandoned her patients. That she'd let this place get the best of her. Worse yet, that she would so easily walk away from her team—Shirley, Stella, and Roz—the family she'd found in Hollandia. More of a home than she'd ever known.

And all for what? Fancy dances and glossy hair?

"Private?" The captain.

"What? Yes?"

"Make it brief. We've got supplies going a dozen directions."

Betty struggled to realign her question. "It's about my transfer . . . to Port Moresby, ma'am."

"Yes, yes, Cordell." She sighed, impatient. "I'm sure you've heard the latest. But the first sergeant will let you know—"

Betty interjected before sense could take hold. "Actually, ma'am, a transfer won't be necessary."

Kitzafenny squinted as though missing prescription glasses. "Oh?"

"I'd prefer to stay here, ma'am. If it's all right. That is, if it's not too late."

She angled her head, evaluating. "Any reason in particular for the change of heart?"

Betty swept a glance over the row of patients that she and the girls, her sisters in arms, had helped nurse back to health, and returned her gaze to the captain. "I just can't imagine wanting to work with any other staff."

"Uh-huh." Devoid of expression, Kitzafenny took in a breath, let it out. "It would take some calls and putting a stop to the paperwork, neither of which I have time for." She paused. "But . . . I suppose that can happen."

Betty hid a smile. "I'd appreciate that, ma'am." When the woman nodded, Betty started to pivot.

"And, Cordell."

She stopped. Fearful of an added task in exchange for the favor, she swallowed hard before answering. "Yes, ma'am?"

"Folks here, they'll be glad you're sticking around."

Gratitude spread over Betty's cheeks, curling the corners of her mouth. "Thank you, Captain." As the officer ducked out of the tent, Betty headed toward Leslie, slowing only when she heard a voice. It was her heart, whispering a warning. But before she could make out the words, she burst into giggles at Smoky. With a sparkle in her beady little eyes, the dog seemed to grin straight at Betty—while relieving her bladder on Lieutenant Kelly's cot.

❧30❧

January 3, 1945
Evanston, Illinois

Though struggling to stay awake on the bus ride home, Liz was thankful for her rigorous day at work. The nonstop pace had helped the time pass with few opportunities to gauge how far away her father's Washington-bound train might be. And how soon he would discover her letter.

She ambled up the pathway to her house. Each footfall brought her closer to an afternoon nap. A catnap, at least, before her evening rail departure to Pittsburgh.

She squeaked out a yawn while passing through the entry, headed straight for bed.

"Elizabeth." A deep voice lunged at her.

Liz grabbed her stalled heart. She sighed at the sight of her father off to the right, seated in the living room. But just as her pulse returned, it quickened from fear over his extended stay.

Don't panic, don't panic. He could have merely changed his travel schedule.

She smiled. "Father, what are you still doing here?"

"Elizabeth, sit down. We need to talk." His clipped tone and rigid posture alerted every nerve in her body that Chicago weather wouldn't be the core of their discussion.

"Of course," she replied, feigning casualness. She took her seat on the couch, opposite him in the rocking chair. Toes clenched in her loafers, she fidgeted her thumbs over clasped hands. A witty line to break the tension had nearly reached her lips when she spied the paper on his lap. Her eyes stretched wide; her temperature rose. The confession—not meant to be read until her father was at least four hundred miles away—had become the centerpiece of the room.

"Father, please. Let me explain."

"No," he said firmly. "I have something I need to say, and I want you to listen to every word."

It was already clear: She had pried open a vault her father wanted sealed, and now he'd be closing the door on her as well.

Bracing herself, she lowered her gaze to the copy of *Life* magazine on the coffee table. On the cover, Judy Garland offered empathetic eyes. How Liz wished she too could be transported into a magical world far from reality.

"The first time I ever saw your mother, I couldn't breathe," he began.

Liz blinked at his words. Tentative, she edged her head up.

"Beyond beautiful was the only way to describe her. She glided across the stage as if she were skating on ice. She wasn't the company's prima ballerina, but it didn't matter. Everyone in that theater was entranced by her." With unseeing eyes, he stared into the reflective glass of the china closet poised against the wall.

"I went backstage to meet her as soon as the show ended. When I found her in the corner untying her slippers, I just stood there. My mouth was so dry it was hard to swallow. Finally, I marched over and introduced myself." He smiled faintly and his voice lightened. "The second I heard her speak, I actually forgot my own name."

Liz couldn't imagine it. Professor Emmett P. Stephens, an esteemed scholar and speaker, intimidated by a ballerina.

A ballerina. *The Nutcracker.* On her mother's last present. The wrapping itself had carried a secret all these years. Before storing the box, Liz had memorized every figurine on that paper, unaware of their importance, their message.

Her father continued. "I'm not sure how I managed it, but somehow Isabelle agreed to go out with me. Once my nerves settled, it was as though we'd always known each other. We ate and talked and laughed. Then later that night, we were dancing at some back-alley jazz club, when a guy on the cornet starts playing a solo. It was Louis Armstrong himself, just a kid back then, but the song was like nothing I'd ever heard. It was a slow, moody tune, the kind that seeps under your skin. I remember feeling like we were the only ones in the room. And that's when I knew. I'd found the woman I wanted to spend my life with."

Liz understood completely. For that brief moment dancing in Morgan's arms, the notes had seemed mystical and perfect, powerful enough to evaporate the world around them.

"We talked for months, about the exotic places we wanted to visit, all the things we were going to accomplish. Your mother was so full of life. She had so much to offer, just like you." He paused, let the words take hold. "And, like you, she had big plans. She wanted to become a famed dancer in New York more than anything. But in the midst of all those dreams, we were handed a surprise."

Liz was still grasping that she and her beautiful yet aloof mother had once been anything alike, when he looked straight into her eyes.

"It was you," he said.

"Me?" she whispered, not entirely sure she'd voiced the word.

"When your mother told me she was pregnant, I didn't know what to say. My first thought was about all the sacrifices we'd have to make. Then I realized what a blessing we'd been given. I didn't waste another second. I ran out and bought the nicest ring I could afford. Our dreams would have to adjust, but we didn't have to give them up. We'd do it together, as a family. That's what I told her.

"But then, soon after, I was offered a good position in California. Since jobs were growing scarce, I didn't think twice." After a quiet beat, he moved the letter to the coffee table. Leaning forward, he clutched his hands. "Once we'd settled there and you'd grown up a bit, Isabelle auditioned for a dance company in L.A., but she'd become a little rusty. When she didn't make the final cut,

I encouraged her to try out again, that all she needed was practice. Yet she wouldn't. Said she'd missed her chance. And as time passed, your mother grew more and more resentful of a life that never suited her."

The fresh implication of blame seized Liz's thoughts. Filtering through in a murmur came the lyrics her mother had played endlessly in her bedroom. The phrases—describing the gloom and misery of stormy weather, of growing old and losing all she once had—gained a heart-wrenching meaning. Each line rolled and blended in an elusive spin, until all Liz could grasp was how little she knew about her own parents.

"So you see, Elizabeth, her leaving had nothing to do with some trivial argument between the two of you. Your mother loved you— even if she didn't know how to show it. She just finally realized how much of herself she'd lost along the way, and it terrified her. She was convinced that leaving was her only chance at salvaging what was left. That if she stayed for even one more day, she might never have the courage to go."

And there it was. The absolution Liz had spent years waiting to wrap her arms around.

Yet she couldn't. For she had just learned that her sole existence was the knife that had severed her parents' relationship.

"You're wrong," she told him, a quiver in her voice. "It *was* my fault. Don't you see? Things would've been so much better for you both, if only I were never born."

"Don't you *ever* say that." His stern tone verged on anger. "Elizabeth Marie, you are the best thing that ever happened to me."

She fisted her hands, struggled to withhold the emotions building inside. "But if that's really how you feel, then why have you been so distant? All this time, why?"

He sighed, his expression falling, his shoulders sinking. "Elizabeth," he said, "I never meant to hurt you. I was just so afraid of interfering with your life and your plans, afraid of letting you down. As I'd done with her."

The irony balled in Liz's throat. She fought her way through, tossed out her feelings. "I always thought I had disappointed *you*. I thought, if I became a teacher, if I married a man like Dalton, then maybe, just maybe I'd finally earn your approval. All I wanted was to make you happy." Her voice cracked, as did the dam holding back her tears.

"Oh, sweetheart," he told her. "*Your* happiness is all I care about. Whatever dreams you have, you follow them, and I promise, I will be there to support you. No matter what."

She nodded slowly, his words creating a bridge between them. And in his eyes, glimmering with moisture, she could see he'd at last met her halfway.

In a rush, she knelt before his chair. She hugged his waist, as she had as the young girl who never should have let go. "Daddy, I love you so much," she whispered.

Folding over her, he kissed her temple. "I love you too," he said. "More than anything in the world." There in his embrace, strong enough to carry her through a lifetime, Liz came to understand she had been wrong: Even two made a family.

After the tears ceased, Liz joined her father on the front porch swing. Side by side they sat, no invisible border dividing them. Just a daughter relishing the adoration of her daddy and wondering why she had waited so long.

They talked for hours. They spilled their hearts. And for the first time in her adult life, Liz felt as though her father really knew her.

Once evening had cooled into night, they bundled in wool blankets and sipped from mugs of steaming mint tea, swinging and talking until the early hours of morning. She wished she had the power to stop time. Part of her feared she was dreaming and the ring of an alarm clock would take it all away. Yet she quickly decided it mattered little. She was going to enjoy every bit of this feeling even if she had imagined it all.

"Elizabeth," a voice said as something tapped her arm.

She opened her eyes and discovered she had fallen asleep. When her vision cleared, she sighed. For seated beside her was her father. She had drifted off with her head on his shoulder, her hand resting in his. The corners of his eyes crinkled as he smiled, and without his saying a word, she knew she was loved.

"Honey, look." He pointed to the sun, its orange rays reaching up from behind the fortress of rooftops, painting the sky powder blue. She turned her head and found the most glorious sight before her: the fading image of a crescent moon, the kind out of storybooks. She closed her eyes, took in the crisp smell of coming snow. Through her eyelids, she could see the golden glow of the sun, and her face basked in its warmth.

Thank you, Morgan, she offered silently, and squeezed her father's hand.

✖ 31 ✖

Mid-January 1945
Near Rheims, France

Morgan increased his pace as he hobbled past bedded soldiers in the wide hall outside the gymnasium. The closer he got, the more certain he was about the identity of the guy parked at the end. He felt a smile coming on, despite the soreness in his underarm from the wooden crutch. Only for a second did he consider the topic their reunion could trigger, explosive as an S-mine.

At the foot of his buddy's hospital bed, Morgan sprang his greeting. "Those Dodgers gonna win the pennant again, or they gonna wait another twenty years?"

Frank raised his eyes from a worn issue of *Time* magazine. Gray light pushing through the frosted window outlined his freshly buzzed hair and clean-shaven face. "Guess they let anyone in here these days," he muttered.

"Hadn't you heard? Joint's under new management."

"Must be desperate for patients."

"They let *you* in, didn't they?"

Frank laughed and laid the magazine over his blanketed lap. He edged himself up to recline against the pillow cushioning him from the concrete wall. His undershirt hung loose over his dog tags and withered torso, verifying he'd lost as much weight as Morgan since their tour began. Good ol' Army rations.

"Take a load off, Mac."

"Yes, sir," Morgan shot back. He negotiated his way to the wooden chair beside the bed. Judging by the number of floor tiles between Frank and the next soldier, a lumped form completely covered in a blanket, this wing of the school had fewer patients to tend to. The smell of disinfectant, however, wasn't any less potent.

In the creaky seat, Morgan adjusted his bathrobe and propped his foot on the edge of Frank's mattress. His leg throbbed like a son of a gun, but he wasn't about to complain. Every sensation only reminded him the limb was still there. And how close he had come to losing it.

"So what'd they do," Morgan said, "find out you had the clap at the last short-arm inspection?"

"Not unless I got it from being near Jack." Frank grinned. "Doc says I got jaundice. Doesn't clear up soon, they're talking about sending me home."

It was then that Morgan noticed his friend's skin had a yellowish tint, as did the whites of his eyes. "Funny. Thought maybe you had some Jap in ya that you didn't want to admit to."

"Yeah, right." Frank ran his thumb over a wound dressing on his left biceps. "How ya like that? Six months of dodgin' Kraut ammo and I end up with a faulty liver."

"Well, it was bound to catch up with you sooner or later."

"How you figure?"

"From all that communion wine, while training for the minist—" Before Morgan could finish, a cramp attacked his calf. He muffled a huff as he massaged the knot through his rolled-up pajama pant leg.

"What are you doing walking around anyway?" Frank said. "Ain't you got the sense to stay in bed while you can?"

"Just following nurse's orders," he ground out. "Supposed to do a round through the place, till I either get too tired or collapse on the floor."

"Hope you don't think I'm carrying you back."

"Don't worry. I'm in no rush. The guy in the next bed's the biggest blabbermouth I've ever met." Morgan sighed as the cramp subsided. "They don't ship him out soon, so help me I'm gonna take this crutch and discharge him myself."

Fresh from the replacement depot, "Jabber" had allegedly been shot in the right buttock by an enemy sniper while crouching over a straddle trench to take care of his business. Yet by the twentieth time he'd recapped his dramatic "assault," Morgan wondered if his million-dollar wound had been compliments of a guy in Jabber's own unit.

In stark contrast, the bedded soldier to Morgan's other side was a young, stoic Air Corps gunner who'd survived a crash landing on the French-Belgian border. His bandages indicated that the flesh on his hands had been chipped away after freezing to his gun during the winter bombing raid. Deemed unfit for duty, he spent most days staring at the ceiling, ignoring Jabber's prattling and a stack of unopened letters from Oregon piled on a chair beside his bed.

Until now, Morgan's only reprieve from the morale-stifling duo had been brief visits with Evelyn and a run of cribbage victories against Father Bud. In light of his Catholic upbringing, Morgan had tried on several occasions to let his pious opponent win a single round, but not even cheating to tilt the game in the priest's favor could save him from constant defeat. Apparently, there was no telling whom God was rooting for these days.

"So what about Jack?" Morgan asked Frank, trying for a nonchalant tone. "He still in one piece?"

"Been a while since I've seen him. But you know Jack. Always pops up somewhere."

Morgan refused to consider the alternative. "Another conjugal reconnoitering mission?"

"That ain't no joke." Frank snorted. "You watch, by war's end, he'll have a hundred kids lined up from Paris to Berlin. All account of dames lovin' that uniform—and him loving their strudels."

Morgan chuckled. "Only a hundred, huh?"

"Hell, Ike just waits long enough, Jack Callan could dilute the Aryan bloodline by his lonesome. Then we could all finally pack it in and go home."

A draft brushed over Morgan's skin. He pulled the robe collar snug around his neck, rubbed his arms. "Hey, at least he found a better way to stay warm than the rest of our sorry butts."

"Yeah. By dodging rounds from pissed-off husbands gone home on furlough."

Morgan smiled, recalling Jack's story about getting hot and heavy with a leggy Hungarian gal. Supposedly, her blacksmithing father caught them in a stable and chased Jack two full miles with a branding iron. "I don't get it," he said. "How is it that *we're* in here, and he's the one without a scratch?"

"Beats me." Frank shrugged. "Downright miracle, with the smart mouth he's got on him. But then, same goes for that wiseacre brother of yours." The sentence stopped in midair, hung like a sheet pinned to a clothesline. No breeze, no sound. The stillness wrung Morgan's gut.

"Mac," Frank said. "I'm so sorry."

"It's okay."

"Yeah, but I didn't mean—"

"Really," Morgan told him. "It's okay."

Frank lowered his eyes to his grip on the magazine, his yellowed cheeks paling. The silence between them screamed for a full minute before Morgan decided they'd both be better off if he exited. As he reached for his crutch, Frank again slugged him with the unexpected.

"He saved my life, Mac."

Morgan raised his head. A patient's cough reverberated in the hall.

"What are you talkin' about?"

"Chap. He saved my life." Frank's voice was as solemn as his face. "Figured you didn't know, but he saved all of us on the roof that day."

The claim didn't make any sense. How could Charlie's recklessness be seen as heroic?

"I didn't know the whole story myself till afterward," Frank went on. "Right after you dropped off the ammo, Sarge starts screaming for us to clear out. A Jerry tank was about to blast us away. But then a rocket comes shootin' from the hill and blows the Panther all to hell."

Morgan narrowed his eyes at the revived image. The tank exploding across from the brewery, dirt and snow, the taste of gasoline.

"After it was all over, a couple of us hiked up the hill. And that's when . . ." Frank hesitated. "Well, that's when we found the two of you."

Morgan clenched his jaw, veered his attention to the tiled floor. He wanted to retreat now more than ever, but he couldn't. All he could think about was Charlie expelling his final breath as they lay in that icy foxhole, a gravesite with a charming view that Morgan had not only handpicked but helped his brother construct.

"Doc Gordon was patching you up," Frank said, "when one of the bazookamen up there came to. A round had ricocheted off a flask in his chest pocket, the lucky cuss." He cleared his throat, rustled his magazine. "Thing is, I tried to thank the fella for saving our asses. And that's when he told me what Chap did. Why the guy didn't keep it to himself, I don't know. Wiping his conscience, I guess."

Frank was obviously about to exaggerate, a way of memorializing the deceased. All with good intention, but Morgan wasn't in the mood for another eulogy. He looked up to stop him. "Rev. You really don't have to."

Frank persisted. "From what the guy remembered, Chap wiped out the Kraut who was shooting at him, then grabbed the bazooka. He launched a shell at somethin' below, just before the fella blacked out."

If Frank was telling the truth . . . if that's really how it happened, Charlie had sacrificed his cover—sacrificed his life—to save the rest of them.

Morgan paced his breathing, the wind knocked out of him. "So what you're saying," he managed to say, "is that he saved me too."

"He saved a whole lot of us," Frank told him. "I honestly don't know how it all would've turned out if Chap hadn't come through like that."

Morgan shook his head. "No," he insisted. "That can't—that's why I—" He tried for a complete thought, but all had fragmented inside him.

"I don't want to make things worse for ya. Just figured I'd want to know. If it was me."

Morgan strained to connect any words he could, hindered further by the squeak of a wheel. A nurse trundling a cart. He watched vacantly as she disappeared into the gym, leaving a clear view of a chaplain. Rosary dangling from his hand, head bowed, he prayed over a heavily bandaged soldier.

"Why?" Morgan said finally, still staring off. "Why would he do that?"

"Your brother?"

Morgan turned to Frank. "God," he replied, and was surprised at the calm in his own voice. He should have been outraged, yet he couldn't feel a thing. Like pulling water from a dried-up well, his bucket was empty. He was too tired to even blame himself. He simply wanted answers.

"Help me out, Rev. Tell me there's a purpose to it all. Otherwise, what are we doin' here?"

Frank opened his mouth, but then closed it. He slouched into his pillow and said, "I wish I knew."

Morgan angled his head back, heavy on its hinge. He stared at a spidery crack in the window beside him, too resigned to extend his view past the pane. "You gotta give me somethin', man. Anything."

Frank blew out a sigh. "My bet is you've got more answers than I do, Mac. I haven't said a prayer or stepped foot into a church since I was a kid. "

One syllable at a time, the statement sank in. Jarred by the implication, Morgan cut his gaze to his friend. "What'd you say?"

"Just that I'm not the best one to ask, is all."

"No, the other thing. About not being in a church."

Frank rolled his shoulders. "It's not like my ma didn't try. I was just such a terror to get out of bed on Sundays, she eventually gave up."

"But—what about when you were studying for the ministry?"

Frank's lips curved up halfway. "Seriously," he said, "can you picture me wearing a dress and preaching about religious virtues? With all my sins, I'm not sure any church would welcome me through their doors, much less ask me to lead one."

Morgan gaped as though his trusted pal, Reverend Frank Dugan, had just admitted to being Lucifer himself. Now beyond stunned, he struggled to grasp the second revelation Frank had handed him today. "Then why does everyone think . . ."

"Listen," he told him. "Here's the deal. The day I first met Jack, he asked me about what I did for a living before enlisting. I told him I was a clerk with Baptists—as in a *sales* clerk for Baptist's Hardware Store. Next thing I knew, word about me being a preacher had spread all over camp. I would've set 'em straight, but guys started passing me some of their food at chow time. Guess they thought they were racking up extra points with God, hoping for holy help to get them through the war. Figured I was better off keeping my mouth shut."

Morgan felt a rumble of emotion rising from deep inside, an irrational hilarity moving from his stomach to his chest. He leaned back, balancing his chair on its hind legs, and fought off a smile. "So let me get this straight. You're not a fallen pastor, just a Brooklyn kid who wanted extra scoops of Army slop?"

Just then, Morgan's chair crackled and a wooden leg gave out. He plunged to the floor. His bandaged calf struck like a full-swung hammer, sending a wallop of pain through his body. He grabbed his leg, stifled expletives by grinding his teeth.

"Hey, you all right?"

Morgan glanced up at Frank's concerned face. He was about to reply when his throat unleashed a peal of laughter. He tried to muscle it down, but like being tickled as a kid, the sound belted out against his will.

Frank's brow creased. "They give you morphine today?"

Morgan attempted to speak, but all that came out was pent-up tension through a stream of chuckles that soon proved contagious. In no time, Frank joined his state of delirium with quiet laughter that steadily grew. They were like innocent kids who had gotten the slap-happy giggles. Yet they weren't kids—not anymore. And their innocence had been stripped away, one layer after another. So how could they both laugh at a time like this?

The question was a sobering one. But no sooner did Morgan's

smile begin to fade than the answer surfaced loud and clear: Charlie wouldn't have had it any other way.

"All right, boys." Evelyn appeared at the foot of the bed. "Keep it down or we're going to have to separate the both of ya." A large box hoisted on her hip, she offered Morgan her free hand and helped him up. Once standing, he leaned on his crutch.

"Doesn't look like you need much spirit lifting," Evelyn said, "but I believe I have a delivery for one PFC Frank Dugan." She reached in the box and handed over a medium-sized package. Frank eagerly ripped into the tan wrapping.

"Got one for you too, Private." Evelyn displayed a similar parcel for Morgan. But still out of sorts, he didn't want to get his hopes up for nothing.

"You sure it's for me?"

"Sure as a juggler's box. Unless there's another Morgan McClain around here who'd like a package from Illinois."

He answered quickly, "No, no, I'll take it."

"Thought so." She smiled. "How about I leave it on your bed so you don't hurt yourself on the way back?"

Morgan studied the prop under his arm and ruled her suggestion a wise one. When he agreed, she nodded in reply.

"Just try not to destroy anything else today, all right?" Evelyn winked before continuing her zigzag mail drops.

Morgan turned to Frank. "So whatcha got?"

"Let's see here." Frank emptied the box onto his lap and adjusted the contents to lie label side up. "We got peach slices, animal crackers, fruit cocktail. Gum, M&M's, and a good ol' box of Cracker Jack." He cast Morgan a serious glance. "See now why I have to marry this girl the minute I get home?"

"They do say the way to a soldier's heart is through his stomach, right?"

"Certainly doesn't hurt." Frank patted his lean belly. Then he shook his head and said, "Man, I can't wait for you to meet her. The second you're mustered out, you gotta come see us in New York."

"You have my word."

"Good. 'Cause we'll be expecting you."

Morgan glimpsed the inked heart on Frank's right arm edging out from his sleeve. "Only question—do I call her June, or *Joan?*"

"Ah, shaddup." Frank yanked his sleeve down to cover his tattoo. "I'm getting the damn thing fixed soon as I get outta here."

Morgan shrugged. "Worst case, you could name your first kid Joan. Assuming it's a girl."

"A daughter?" he said. "You trying to give me an early heart attack? I'm working on recovering, here."

Morgan grinned, then remembered his awaiting delivery. "Listen, I'd better get back before I do fall down and break something else."

Frank shook the Cracker Jack box, loosening the caramel kernels. "Want a handful 'fore you go?"

"That's okay. You enjoy." Morgan adjusted his crutch. He tried to formulate a way to say thanks—for the details about Charlie, for the laughs, for his friendship. He settled on simply saying, "Happy new year, buddy."

Frank paused, and responded with a nod. "Yeah, Mac. You too."

Though Morgan's return journey to his bed seemed farther than his initial trek, the idea of opening anything from Betty motivated him to charge on.

Dog tired, he collapsed on his mattress, his unmarred leg dangling off the side. He took only a moment to rest before seizing the package from the bottom edge of the bed. Confident his mother would forgive him, he indulged in a ruthless shredding of the wrapping.

He set the dark gray shoe box he'd unveiled onto his lap and lifted the lid. A soft bronze scarf filled the top half of the container. He wound the accessory around his hand like a boxer taping his fist. Then he buried his nose in the knitted wool and drank in its lavender fragrance.

With his free hand, he pulled a red-and-white checkered bundle from the box. Untying the knot released an avalanche of golden brown chocolate chip cookies. He snatched up two morsels. Just like he'd done as a kid, he gobbled them up by alternating bites between the chocolaty pair.

Blanketed in contentment, he reached into the shoe box and retrieved Betty's envelope, the most precious part of the package. Already he knew he'd treasure this letter more than any other before it.

> *Dearest Morgan,*
>
> *I cannot begin to express how terribly sorry I am to learn of your brother's passing. Though I had the pleasure of meeting Charlie only briefly, the goodness of his character shone brightly through. His ability to make people smile, as well as his infectious zest for life, I will hold in my memory forever. Certainly even now, while in heaven, he is bringing immense happiness to those about him, your father and mother most of all.*
>
> *I would not dare to pretend I fully understand the deep sorrow you must feel. I do, however, recall the sadness that lingered inside me after the passing of my beloved grandparents many years ago. Missing their company dearly, I once composed a poem intended to celebrate their lives rather than mourn their deaths. While I have never shared the verses before, I humbly offer them now, hoping they will provide you with even the smallest bit of ease.*
>
> > *Mountain peaks and valley lows,*
> > *O'er sandy shores and streams,*
> > *I scoured the earth in search of you,*
> > *Yet only in my dreams*
> > *Did you come forth, a soul at dawn*
> > *Stolen by a Thief,*
> > *Torrential tears, an endless storm,*
> > *My heart awashed in grief.*
> >
> > *I cursed the Heav'ns for taking thee,*
> > *For plaguing me with pain,*

Denied a bid for one more day
To dance amidst the rain.
Lo, from the dark your glow appeared,
A star blazed in the sky
Shining down your love to show,
I carried you inside.

I believe with all my heart that your bond remains as strong as ever. Through his memory and love, Charlie lives on within you. And you can rest knowing, dear Morgan, that in his final moment of life, you were there for him. You were the courageous brother he needed to lean on while his frightful scene transformed into one of peace. Perhaps more purposeful than your protecting him against the uncontrollable elements of war was your presence as he took his last breath, eased by the assurance that he was not alone. For this reason, I hope you release any thoughts of self-blame, instead finding solace from knowing how deeply you touched your brother's life, just as you have mine.

Because of you, a door to new possibilities has opened. Heeding your advice, I at last reconciled with my father. Our emotional distance would have otherwise worsened, preventing revelations that have bettered our lives tenfold. Again, I am so grateful for your candidness, and for urging me to confront a situation that had weighed heavily on me for as long as I can remember. Thus, learning that I have provided you with comfort, support, and a place to call "home" brings me immeasurable joy, since I feel the same about you.

It seems incredible to me, how acquainted we have become almost entirely through a handful of pages. And already I cannot imagine my life without you in it. Although we are oceans apart, please know that you, too, Morgan, are not alone.

> *Well, I had better drop this in the mail, or the war might be over before it arrives. (Wouldn't that be wondrous!) Please enjoy the holiday gifts I have enclosed. The scarf, knitted by a cherished elderly friend, I pass along to you now, hoping it will provide protection from the harsh winter and, perhaps, a gentle embrace while you heal from your tragic loss. The cookies, though surely not as good as your dear mother's, are meant to remind you of the familiar comforts, and people like myself, awaiting your safe return in the new year.*
>
> *I wish you love, peace, and a speedy recovery. Carrying you always in my thoughts.*
> *Affectionately yours,*
> *Betty*

Morgan rested the letter on his lap. Taking in Betty's words, his feelings of loss and self-doubt all shriveled into nonexistence. In their place came her reciprocated affection, her understanding, and more than anything, his longing to be with her.

He smiled, reviewing her message. He felt proud that he had affected her life in such a meaningful way. That she and her father had been reunited due in part to his intervention. That he, in fact, had done something right.

Hand beneath his head, he lay back on his pillow. In his mind, he saw his brother. Polished in dress uniform, saluting during reveille. Private Charles Patrick McClain: a man, and a hero.

Morgan felt a loosening in his chest.

As he continued to sort his thoughts, his thumb grazed the inch-long scar on his neck, a reminder of the day he'd rescued his brother as a child. It was the mark of a debt he never imagined settling, but painfully, he realized: He and Charlie at last were even.

That night in the darkened ward, while the world around him slept, Morgan snagged two cookies from his shoe box. He quietly placed them beside the airman's mail on the chair dividing their beds. When he heard the kid nibbling on the baked treats a few hours later, he felt a hint of atonement.

"*A way to a soldier's heart,*" he murmured to himself, and closed his eyes.

Indeed, Betty's gifts, like her letters, possessed more healing power than she ever could have known.

❦ 32 ❧

Mid-January 1945
Northwestern University
Evanston, Illinois

Not until half the room emptied did Julia realize her mind had been roaming the entire hour of class. Haze clearing, she scooted out from her desk, grabbed her books, and drifted into the wake of the mob.

In the hallway, chattering students crisscrossed paths, a freeway of intellectuals.

"Julia." A man's holler rose from the collective hum.

She attempted to trace the voice.

"Julia," he called again. Ian's face and umber hair swam into view. In a faded peacoat, he was weaving through the crowd. A few seconds from entrapping her.

A breath rushed into her like a chill. Her gaze held at his smooth-shaven chin.

"There you are," he said, standing before her.

"Ian . . ." The name fell from her mouth, a pebble from a cliff. No sound of it landing. Instinct urged her to run, yet her legs remained planted, arrested by a reality she couldn't ignore. The reality of what they'd done.

"Look," he said, "I'm sure you've got—"

"What are you doing here?" she demanded, terrified of meeting his eyes, of what they might confirm.

"Hi, Jules," a girl said in passing. "See you at the Avalon tonight? Double feature?"

Julia flitted a smile as the student walked by. "Sure," she answered, not registering who it was. Her only thoughts were of the transparency of her interaction with Ian while out in the open. She hugged the books to her chest.

"Can I talk to you?" Ian asked.

"I can't. I have class soon."

"I'm only in town for the day. I just need a few minutes."

She considered his words. He wouldn't be staying.

Thank God.

"Julia, please."

"Fine. But not here." Her gaze circled the area and landed on a series of private music rooms. "Come on," she said, and led the way.

She skimmed the doors' narrow vertical windows. A flutist. A string quartet. A harpist. Finally a vacancy.

Once Ian stepped past her into the room, she leaned her back against the closed door. Her free hand gripped the handle behind her spine, unwilling to release her escape route. She settled her view on the clustered music stands beside the upright piano. The enclosed space felt no larger than a closet.

Ian sat on the edge of the piano bench, facing her. He leaned forward, forearms on his knees. His mouth opened, then closed, as if he'd blanked on a prepared speech. Silence between them drew out like an endless symphony, amplifying the muffled plucking of a harp in the next room.

What did he want, why was he here?

She wanted to ask, but a flashback of his lips on hers prevented her from speaking.

A trapdoor, that's what she needed, to rid herself of this confrontation. Or a secret tunnel behind a wall panel, like in that film—what was it called?

Oh, blast it, why did it matter? This wasn't Hollywood. They weren't hitting marks on a soundstage. This was real life, in all its confusion and complexity. And she was tired of putting on an act, pretending their kiss hadn't been eating away at her every day since that night.

"I brought something for you," Ian said suddenly, reaching into his coat pocket. He held out a palm-sized box.

A courting gift.

He was here to sway her affections. Away from his own brother, the man to whom she'd promised her heart, her everything.

Julia's eyes flared up to his. Her hands clenched. "You have to stop this, Ian. There's nothing between us. I love *Christian*. He's the most important thing in my life. I love him more than I could ever love anyone else." Truth, like steel beams, supported the core of her words. Against their strength, any doubt left within her crumbled away.

Ian retracted the box. He breathed out and replied, "I know you do, Julia." His tone surprised her, equally accepting and warm.

Guard lowering, cautious this time, she relaxed into his gaze, one that no longer held a threat. How strange, scanning his features now, that he appeared completely different from his brother. Could it be she had missed Christian so much that she'd morphed their traits, convincing herself they matched more than they did?

"I'm only here," he said, "to say I'm sorry. What happened was a mistake. My mistake."

She couldn't help feeling she was being released too easily from the hook, that the responsibility was mutual. But she nodded regardless, grateful for the gesture.

He rose from his seat. "Anyway, I know you gotta go. And I got someone waiting for me, long drive ahead of us."

Something told her he wasn't referring to a vacation. "Where are you going?" she asked, stepping toward him.

"A pal from my outfit, he got me a job in Montana. A cattle drive, if you can believe it."

"A *cattle* drive?"

His mouth suggested a smile. "Hey, it's something new."

Concern swooped through her as she imagined Cora's reaction to his decision. "What about your folks? What do *they* think?"

"That I'm screwy." He shrugged. "But that it just might be what I need. Plenty of time to get your head straight when you're staring at the rear ends of a hundred cows, right?"

She shook her head and laughed. "Thank you for the image."

Grinning, he again raised the box toward her. "An early wedding present," he explained. "Since I don't know how soon I'll be back this way."

A wedding present.

Now she truly felt silly.

She set her books atop the piano and accepted the gift. "What is it?"

"What, you gotta know everything? Open it."

She removed the lid. Inside was a compass wrapped with a long scarlet ribbon tied into a bow. The significance of the hair accessory was clear, from the tale about her time capsule. But the compass puzzled her.

"Are you afraid I might get lost?" she mused.

He peered at her thoughtfully. "Way I figure it, you may be the ribbon type now, but the world traveler in you is still there. So I suppose this is a reminder that it's okay to be both."

The sentiment tightened her throat. She fingered the ribbon, so red her skin looked nearly translucent in contrast. Perhaps Ian wasn't the only unsettled ghost. In some ways, they were all stuck between who they once were and who they'd become.

Ian hunched his shoulders. "Corny, huh?"

"No." She smiled. "It's the best gift ever." She extended her hand to shake his. No shivers or change in pulse. Just the comforting touch of a friend. "Thank you," she said, "for ... well. Just thank you."

"You're welcome," he said simply.

She eyed the box and twisted her lips. "I do wonder, though," she added in jest, "if you shouldn't keep this for yourself."

"Why's that?" He sounded afraid to ask.

"I'd hate to think of your getting lost out there in the country. My main concern being for the cows' sakes, naturally."

He chuckled. "Don't you worry. One way or another, I'll find my way home."

She nodded at him and smiled again. "I'm sure you will."

After bidding their farewells, Ian started down the hall. Yet as he reached the thinning mass, an afterthought found her. For peace of mind, Julia needed to confirm he wasn't going to tell anyone about their encounter—specifically Christian.

"Ian," she called, spinning him around. But before the words could form, she realized the request would only insult the understanding they had built. She replaced the thought with one that said everything.

"Don't forget," she told him, "you owe me a backgammon match."

"We'll get to it one of these days, won't we, peach?" he said with a wink. Then he waved and disappeared around the corner.

$\backsim$ 33 $\backsim$

Mid-January 1945
Dutch New Guinea

"Bloody hell, you've gotten us lost," Leslie chided a few feet behind Betty.

"No, I haven't," she lied while scanning for landmarks. Overhead, a roof of trees shuttered the moon, the jungle now an endless house of shadows. She ducked around a swag of vines bearing a disturbing resemblance to a python. Nerves doubled the beading on her brow.

A noise halted her. A rustling off to the left. "Wait," she whispered to Leslie, and gripped her blanket roll. The natives no longer alarmed her, but she couldn't say the same about Japanese guerrillas.

During the long moment of intent listening, she contemplated aborting the mission. A decent send-off for the pilot had seemed like a good idea, though not at the cost of their lives. Silently she cursed Rosalyn's directions. Then herself, for being willing to give up already, and in front of Leslie. She'd conquered bigger obstacles than this. She could handle a measly jungle. She could, she could.

Straightening, she gestured for them to continue and treaded forward.

"Leave it to the Yanks and their fancy maps." He sounded amused.

Betty was reaching for a comeback when something bit her calf, right through her pants. She shrieked.

"What is it?" Leslie yelled as she kicked and swatted. He rushed closer, just as she identified the assailant.

"It's okay," she said, relieved. "It was only a branch."

He puffed a breath and laughed. "Remind me never to take you camping in the bush. Mobs of deadly branches out there."

The vision of the two of them sharing a tent, alone in the Australian wilderness, launched a fresh streak of sweat down her spine. Fortunately, a fuzzy sight nudged the image away; the pair of C-shaped trees she'd been searching for appeared in silhouette.

"Almost there," she announced as if their looping and weaving had been intentional. The distant rush of a waterfall grew in volume. "I can hear the water," she thought aloud.

"What a relief. For a moment, I forgot we were on a bloody island."

"That's not what I—" She stopped, grumbled. "Oh, shush."

From one point to another she led him through the maze of secret clues, until finally they reached the drop-off. Six feet down, the rocky slope leveled into slate surrounding a secluded swimming hole. With sharp coral dominating beaches in the area, worsened by shallow salt water and vicious rip tides, this retreat was a priceless find. Mythical, it seemed. The waterfall sparkling like a silver ribbon. Moonlight pouring a white line across the surface. The pool as smooth as a Seabees airstrip.

She only wished she could have gifted Junior with a view like this—to thank him before it was too late.

"I'll go first," Leslie offered, and handed off a paper sack. "No peeking, now." His hands looked so powerful without his casts.

While he laddered down the protruding stones, she contemplated the weight of the bag. He didn't say she couldn't investigate the gift by feel. Her grip closed around the base of the items, rustling the paper. Two bottles of beer, from what she could tell.

"Leave it," he playfully ordered. Planted below, he demanded the bag and blanket before he'd help her down. When she neared the bottom, he grasped the sides of her waist from behind. She felt a slow burn beneath his fingers. Once lowered, she turned around, bringing their faces only inches apart. His Adam's apple rose and fell with a swallow. His hands didn't release, instead tightened a fraction. Almost enough to make her forget her thin layers of khaki.

Then, with a jerk, he snatched their supplies from the ground. "Shall we?" He gestured for her to take the lead.

Collecting herself, she nodded. She wasn't the least bit offended, actually, nor did she question her own appeal. He'd seen her at her worst—soaked in mud and rain and self-pity, blood on her cheeks in place of rouge, fragranced with antiseptic—yet his shielded glances had confirmed he found something to his liking.

Not that it should make a difference. They were, after all, merely friends. Friends who would be saying good-bye tomorrow.

"A bonzer spot for a midnight picnic," he said as they seated themselves on the blanket.

Crystalline stars speckled the black dome of a sky. A breeze from the waterfall, soft as an angel's kiss, swept over her face.

"I was wrong to doubt you," he conceded.

"Yes," she told him. "You were."

He slanted his eyes. "No need to get cheeky. If you hadn't finally noticed the wishbone trees, we'd be on our fourth circle right now."

She reviewed his words, the realization sinking in. "You already knew how to get here."

"A mate at the ward mentioned a detail or two."

When his mouth crept into a smile, she gave his arm a light smack. "Bastard."

"You do know that's a term of endearment to us Aussies."

She shook her head, giggling in spite of herself. "Open up the bag before I leave you here to drown."

"In a hurry, are we?"

She didn't respond, though the truth was, she couldn't escape a dusting of anxiety from knowing she was violating at least four Army regulations. While breaking rules had been something of a hobby of hers in the past, disappointing Kitzafenny, after everything it had taken to earn her acceptance, was an unsettling thought.

"Not bad, eh?" Leslie motioned proudly at the crackers, cheese tin, bag of nuts, and two bottles of Coca-Cola displayed on the blanket.

"No champagne for a farewell party?"

"Figured this was safer. Too afraid that if we got tiddly, I'd be tempted to take advantage of you."

She smiled over the jolt in her pulse and focused on the caps he was removing with his knife. When he passed her a bottle, a shiver surged up her arm, from more than his touch.

"They're cold," she said in disbelief. Coke was always a prized treat. But chilled soda of any kind, in a primitive world absent of ice, was a downright miracle. She wrapped both hands around the sweating bottle. "How'd you manage that?"

"I'm part of the Ned Kelly Gang, remember? Heaps of resources for us outlaws."

"I thought you weren't any relation," she reminded him.

He shrugged. "Depends on the day you ask." He clinked the neck of his bottle against hers, said, "Cheers," and brought the drink to his lips.

Sipping the beverage, she savored the caramel-flavored bubbles fizzing down her throat. It was the real McCoy, all right. By far, the most terrific beverage she'd ever had. Another long pull and she paused to roll the cool bottle across her forehead.

"I think I'm in love," Betty thought. She only realized she'd voiced the words when Leslie murmured, "Me too."

Picnic supplies depleted, Betty and Leslie sat in silence, peering out over the dark pool. The soft static of tumbling water alone should have induced complete serenity. But their time together was waning too quickly for Betty to relax. In mere hours, Leslie would be gone, perhaps forever. Considering how many life stories she'd collected from other patients, knowing so little about him didn't seem right. Not after the encounter they had shared in the supply tent, or the portrait he'd drawn, a peek into her soul.

"Is it harder for a pilot, being left-handed?" she asked, as if adding to an existing conversation.

He glanced down at his left arm, flexed his fingers, now free of plaster. "Been a mollydooker all my life. Reckon I don't know any different."

Ah, silly question. "So . . . what is it you like about flying?"

He rested the tip of his tongue on his bottom lip, thinking. "Hard to beat the rush it gives ya. And blowing things up isn't too bad either."

A reasonable answer, but nothing she couldn't have already guessed. "Well," she said, "what else do you . . . enjoy doing . . . ?"

Her words fell away when he brushed the loose hair from her cheek and smiled. A glimmer in his eyes told her he understood the reason behind her inquiries, and yet assured her there was no need for them. They already knew more about each other than any purge or interrogation could reveal.

At the thought, she found herself leaning toward him, toward the sensual roundness of his lips. But then he pulled his hand away. When he turned abruptly to the water, she sat up, shifted her legs to her side of the blanket.

His reaction was understandable, of course. Feeling so exposed would usually have frightened her off as well, sent her running for the mountains. Chances were high they might never see one another again, regardless of desire, and clearly he wasn't the type to promise the contrary.

"How about a dip before we go?" he mumbled, yanking his buttoned shirt over his head.

She averted her eyes to a nearby log—for her own sake, not his—as he tossed aside his shoes and socks, and stepped into the water in his uniform shorts. He pushed off with a breaststroke and glided across the surface.

Betty debated on following. Wasn't that why she was here—for a swim? She would be a madwoman not to enjoy the refreshing, clean water, particularly after all the effort spent locating the place. And since she was already risking military punishment anyway, she might as well make her delinquency worthwhile.

Rising, she slipped out of her footwear, then her trousers and shirt. She smoothed the white fabric of her bathing suit shorts and adjusted the cinched center of her halter top. Had it been a conservative one-piece, its stitch work would have made her aunt proud. No one back home would guess Betty herself had single-handedly created the stylish garment, and all from a silk bomb chute.

She unbound her hair and eased into the pool. With a gasp, she descended past her stomach, up to her neck. It took only seconds for the initial chill to subside. The temperature was that of a luke-warm bath. She floated on her back, casually scissoring her legs. The satiny liquid enwrapped her body, swaying her mane like an artist's brush. Eyes closed, she caught a scent of flowers and the freshness of springtime.

Any reason to be somewhere else ebbed away. The rustling in the jungle she'd heard earlier, while on their way here, could very well have been Kitzafenny on her trail, and still Betty would refuse to return.

"Find your own way back," she called to Leslie, who was tread-ing water. "I'm not leaving here, ever."

"Take to the trees and live off the land? You, all alone?"

"I don't see why not."

"Well, we know how handy *you* are in the jungle."

Righting herself, she shoved a splash in his direction.

"See, now," he said, "you can't even defend yourself from a brute like me."

She glared. "I'll hire a clan of natives to protect me, then."

"Oh? With what payment? Leaves and rocks?"

She inspected her resources, and spotted a cove mostly hidden by a waterfall. "Gold coins," she said triumphantly. "Pirates hid a chest full of them in that cave."

"Beaut idea," he replied. "If the treasure weren't already mine."

"Can't claim what's not yours, Lieutenant."

He nodded, pondering. "Then I'd say first one to find it is a rich man."

"Rich woman," she corrected.

"Fair dinkum." He grinned. "All contenders, on your mark, get set—"

She took off kicking, snagging a head start. Giddiness filled her as she scooped out waves with short but swift arm strokes. At the thick sheet of pounding water, she grabbed a gulp of air and ducked under to reach the pirates' lair. She broke the surface on the other side. Not two seconds later, Leslie emerged beside her.

"You dunny rat," he exclaimed, and ran a palm down his drip-ping face. "You cheated!"

"All's fair," she giggled, catching her breath. Her feet found the slick, mossy ground. Knees bent, she floated chest-high and marveled at their hideaway. Moonlight filtered through the waterfall in a foggy glow. Sounds of the beating shower echoed off the cave walls, a hypnotic melody. If only she could live here forever.

She swiped her hands down the length of her hair, draining streams over her shoulders. And that's when she felt the night change, the air intensify. She angled toward Leslie, their faces level, his mouth slightly parted. His gaze, charged with wanting, altered even the sensation of the water. Her eyes followed the definition of his glistening shoulders, settling on the broad chest she'd often fantasized caressing. An ache coursed through her.

Once more, her heart whispered a warning. This time, she heard the words: *It's now or never.* Not the caution she expected, but true all the same. If the war had taught her anything, it was how precious, how fleeting life could be.

Submitting to her instincts, she stepped forward through the mist. Moisture carried their unspoken passion into her lungs. Brazenly, tenderly, she touched the pink scar over Leslie's breastbone. His breathing grew heavier. She leaned down and kissed a trail over the raised line, a passageway to his yearning. He shuddered, rippling the water.

"Betty," he said. "We can't."

She lifted her face. Her hand on his tightened chest, she could feel his heart thundering.

He swallowed. "It's not fair to you."

With her fingers, she covered his lips, quieting him. "I know I may not see you again," she told him. "But we're together now. Somehow, nothing else matters."

Gently he moved her hand from his mouth. "But, Betty—"

"It's all right. You don't have to say anything more."

He held her gaze, consented through his silence, drawing her into the transcendence of his eyes.

A need sweltered inside her, to do what she hadn't dared during even the few sexual experiences of her life. With each of those boys pledging his undying love, she'd gone willingly, curiously, desperate to fill the emptiness. Then before they'd had a chance to discover the falsehood of her beauty—that the dresses and hair and cosmetics were but a diversion—she would move on to the next beau, sacrificing a lad's heart to protect her own.

However, tonight, for the first time, she wanted someone to see all of her. She needed to know that deep down she had the courage to expose herself as the pane of glass she was—with the cracks and smudges, the fragility—and not shatter beneath his judgment.

Pulse racing, she stepped back and straightened to her full height. The waterline dropped like a robe to her waist. She reached around to the middle of her back, never leaving his eyes, and unfastened the button. The strips separated and dangled, tickled her sides. With trembling fingers, she retrieved an end of the bow tied behind her neck. She released the binding in one fluid pull. The garment fell away, caught by the water's surface.

She felt the hands of Leslie's gaze sliding over her body. Seconds passed like hours as she allowed the terrifying exploration. Gleaming in wonderment, he rose to his feet and moved toward her. He placed a tentative palm on her shoulder, as though expecting to pass through a mirage. His fingers glided downward, following the path his eyes had traveled: over the outside contour of her breast, the in and out of her waist, the slope of her hip.

"My God," he whispered, "you're so beautiful." He spoke with such fervor, she finally believed she was.

She linked her arms around his neck. Her chest, then the flat of her stomach, melted into his skin. Her nerves settled and drifted away, natural as the tide. A tide she would surrender to completely.

He bent and kissed her shoulder, a long sensual movement. She lowered her neck to the side as his tongue journeyed upward. His hands stroked her back, sculpting her into the masterpiece she'd become in his arms. At last his mouth found hers, their forms merging into one.

Her final thought, before ecstasy blurred her world, was that if this were a dream, she never wanted to wake.

The meal cart had turned weightless. Betty effortlessly guided the wheels over the planks of the ward, still riding the crest of her bliss, still feeling the rapture of his body molded to hers. She coasted from bed to bed, taking meal trays. Her grin stretched from ear to ear. Only when she reached Leslie's bed did her joy wilt.

The cot stood empty, the sheets disheveled. His belongings had been packed and shipped out with him, proof of his existence erased.

A ribbon of regret twisted inside her, a knot for which she could blame only herself. She was the one who'd suggested they not see each other following their parting kiss near her barracks—easily done, since his pickup was scheduled for 0600 hours. She'd told him she wasn't a fan of sappy good-byes. The truth was, she wanted him to remember her as he'd seen her behind that waterfall, not as the blubbering wreck she might have been while watching him being driven away. The reality of his departure, she was determined to take in doses.

Now, however, staring at the bed soon to be filled by another wounded soldier, Betty would do just about anything to have seen him off that morning, to once more feel the sensation of his lips on hers. To declare she loved him.

Compressing her emotions, she focused on the chore at hand. She hadn't brought replacement linens, but she would strip his sheets regardless. Silly as it seemed, she wanted to be the last to handle his bedding. Her secret claim to the intimacy they'd shared.

Slowly, as if to prolong the remnants of his presence, she pulled the top cover loose and rolled it into her arms. The bundle smelled of earth and rebellion. For a second, she was tempted to hoard the fabric, a sachet to keep his image alive. But she knew that eventually his scent would fade like a whisper, until all that remained was a wrinkled ball of linen and the memory of one perfect night.

She set the sheet down and reached for his pillow. Hidden beneath, she discovered a folded paper. Scribed in pencil was a single word: *Betty.*

She caught herself smiling—a cockeyed smile, no doubt—and took a seat on the cot. Anticipation of the unexpected rushed through her. Yet when she opened the page, she realized the obviousness of his gift. It was the sketch of her face, plus a handwritten note.

> *No outlaw should be without a portrait. This one is
> on the house.*
> *Missing you already,*
> *LK*

Betty refolded the drawing and tucked it into her trouser pocket. She brushed away a single tear and stored her tangled feelings of happiness, worry, and longing. She would wait for a private moment to unravel each component, not yet ready to cushion their impact.

Standing, she resumed her task by gathering the rest of his bedding. In her usual turnover routine, she peeked under the cot, where she found the standard trail: gum and candy wrappers, a pencil stub, eraser shavings, shreds of paper from torn envelope seals. Occasionally, staff would find an item of greater value that would go into lost and found or, depending on the locator, fall under the category of finders keepers.

Betty couldn't help wishing Leslie had left yet another sentimental treasure behind for her—perhaps a book of poems by the infamous Joe Byrne. But alas she'd inherited mere litter for her palm.

About to rise, she noticed a wallet-sized photograph propped between a cot leg and the ward wall. Could it be a picture of him? A portrait of the uniformed pilot for her to keep?

All this time and she'd never thought to seek out a camera from someone on staff. Not that she needed proof he had been real. He'd left his imprint on her heart, invisible to others but with permanence she detected with every rhythmic beat.

She knelt and stretched her arm under the bed, then yanked the photo free. The image was clearly a family member, a memento he'd left by accident.

A disappointed sigh slipped from her mouth.

Although . . . it did make a great excuse to write Leslie first. Maybe he'd even dropped it there for that purpose. She wouldn't put it past him. The scoundrel.

Curious for details, hungry for anything about his life, she flipped the picture over. A note appeared on the back. She read the words, bewildered. The second time through, the implications materialized. Like the teeth of a vampire, they pierced layer after layer, sinking painfully into her being. She felt her soul being sucked away as she collapsed against the bed, the photo still clinging to her hand.

34

February 1945
Evanston, Illinois

"Jules, I'm home!" Liz tapped her snow-tipped shoes against the entry baseboard. She pulled off her damp black mittens and tossed them onto the heated radiator. "My group wanted to finish the whole project tonight," she called out. "Believe it or not, I was the first one to leave."

She shook the moist flakes off her braids as she headed down the hallway. The notes of "As Time Goes By" flowed from Julia's illuminated bedroom. Passing the kitchen, Liz flicked a glance at the rooster clock on the wall.

Late but doable. If they hurried, they could still catch the newsreel preceding *Lifeboat,* Hitchcock's latest, followed by some new Loretta Young flick even Liz had been wanting to see.

She rubbed her hands together and hastened her steps. Approaching the door, she stifled a sneeze. Infiltrating the air was the overpowering woodsy scent of the perfume Julia had recently received from Christian as a Valentine's gift.

Leave it to a guy to choose a fragrance that smelled like a campground.

Liz poked her head into the room. "Jules, do you have any gloves I could—" Her words broke off at the sight of the redhead adorned in her sheer, shoulder-length wedding veil, seated at the vanity. Again.

By now, it was a wonder Liz noticed the accessory at all. Since Julia's shopping excursion in Manhattan, the veil had been on constant exhibition around the house. Laundry, homework, dishes, dusting—no chore was too mundane for the display.

"You're not really going to wear that to the movie, are you?" Liz said. "You'll block half the screen for all the lovebirds sitting behind you." She marched over to the shortwave radio on the nightstand and clicked the power off. "Come on, let's scoot. I hate getting stuck in the back of the balcony."

Julia wasn't cooperating

"All right, Mrs. Christian Downing." Liz snatched the empty boutique box from the foot of the bed and held it out. "Either I'm going or the veil's going, but not both."

The redhead didn't budge.

"Hel-looo," Liz sang.

Julia gazed into the mirror, a stoic expression carved on her face.

A spark of concern pulled Liz to the vanity. "Jules, what's wrong?"

Slowly Julia handed over the folded beige papers from her lap.

"What is this?"

No response.

Setting the box aside, Liz combated a list of assumptions. Grief streaked each scenario. Hesitant, she knelt on the floor before unfolding the pages. An embossed emblem of a golden eagle with ropes and anchors appeared at the top. Recognizing the stationery as Christian's, she could already feel the hem of Julia's world loosening.

> *My beloved Julia,*
>
> *If you are reading this letter, darling, it means I will not be coming home. The mere thought of us not being together brings tears to my eyes. For as long as I can remember, I have dreamt of little more than spending every minute by your side. I have so looked forward to*

*the day when I would make you my bride, when I could
hear you declare to heaven and earth that you had
chosen me.*

*On nights like tonight when I can't sleep, I often lie
here in my bunk making plans for our future. I imagine
the home we would buy and the children we would fill
it with—sons who are strong but fair, daughters with
your grace and soft red curls. I can just see us, sitting on
the front porch many years from now, reminiscing over
memories of days gone by. Even in old age, I know you
will be just as beautiful as the day I first saw you walk
into my uncle's store, a day that changed my life forever.*

*If, for me, tomorrow doesn't come, this would be my
solitary wish: to spend one more day holding you in my
arms, kissing your lips, and telling you how much I love
you. No matter how short our time has been together,
please know that you alone have carried me through
this trying war, and given me the true reason to fight for
our country's freedom.*

*There is no question in my mind that our souls will
one day reunite at heaven's gate. However, until then, I
plead that you live a happy and fulfilling life, regardless
of my absence. As hard as it is on me to envision you in
the arms of another man, I will only rest peacefully
knowing you will someday marry a fellow who will
cherish you as dearly as I, and have a houseful of
children to bring you joy.*

*You have so much love to give, so much kindness to
share, that you must promise to follow the journey God
has laid out for you. I ask simply that you think of me
every once in a while and recall the teenage boy you
met one summer, who for a short time was given the
chance to touch your heart.*

*I do hope, above anything in this world, my dear
sweet Julia, that I have made you proud, a dutiful Navy
man who never faltered in deserving your love. Thank*

you for everything you have given me, darling. You are
the woman of my dreams. You are my best friend.
  I will love you with all my heart until the end of
time.
Christian

Tears rolled off the tip of Liz's nose. A hot rush of sorrow filled her, a cool sample of what Julia had to be feeling. Liz lifted her head against an overwhelming weight and gingerly touched her friend's arm.

"Julia," she said hoarsely.

An aching silence followed. No matter what consolation Liz could conjure up, nothing could bring Christian back. Nothing could change the fact that Julia's life would never be the same.

"Did you know I was planning to make my own?" Julia's tone was thin and detached. Her trance-like stare remained locked on her own reflection. "I'd sketched three different designs. But then my mother took me shopping. That's when I saw this one being carried from the back room. It was the most perfect veil I'd ever seen."

Liz swiped away her tears. What right did *she* have to cry?

"I was actually going to have a photo taken wearing the thing, so Christian could see it. But he wrote and told me not to. Said it was bad luck." Julia quickened, brow furrowed. "Why didn't he listen to me? All those times, he would never listen. The night he proposed, *I* was the one who said we should go to the justice of the peace. But no. He wouldn't have it. Instead, he insisted there was no reason to rush, 'cause he was going to be home *so soon,* and then we could do it right." With a head jerk, her gaze latched onto the photos lining the oval mirror. "And I believed you. I believed every word you told me!"

Liz's whole body flinched as Julia grabbed his pictures and threw them at the floor.

"You promised you'd come home! You promised we'd get married! I chose you over *everything,* and you lied!" She knocked over the vanity seat and stormed across the room. Anger transformed her into someone Liz barely recognized.

Dumbfounded, Liz looked down at the scattered photos. A film of tears distorted the collage of black-and-white images into a haunting kaleidoscope. Then a loud clanking yanked her attention upward. Julia was shaking the nightstand drawer, dumping the contents onto her bed. "You're nothing but a liar. I was actually going to marry a liar!" Her face flushed with rage as she hurled the drawer onto the hardwood planks.

Liz's forearms flew up to protect herself. "Julia, stop," she begged.

Julia swooped her hand across the bedcover. Her collection of Christian's memories flew through the room. "I'll never forgive you for this. *Never!*" She wrenched the pinned veil from her hair, struggled to rip the netting in half.

Unable to bear any more, Liz rushed over and threw her arms around her friend from behind. "That's enough, Julia," she ordered, but Julia fought to wiggle free.

"Leave me alone!"

"No," Liz told her. "I won't."

"Damn it, Christian. *Lemme go!*"

Against thrashing elbows, Liz squeezed tighter. "Jules, it's me. Look at me. Just look at me."

Still resisting, Julia swung her face to Liz. She halted as if slapped out of the delusion. Her eyes stared blankly, attempting to register the person restraining her.

At last, recognition flickered. "Liz?" she rasped.

"It's me," Liz assured her. "And I'm not going anywhere. I'm not leaving you."

Time suspended while devastation took hold, shedding Julia's defenses—her numbness, her fury, her dignity. She wilted in Liz's arms like a prizefighter in the twelfth round. Together they settled on their knees. Julia hugged the bundled veil to her chest, and a flood of pain poured down her cheeks. She spoke in a strained whisper. "He wasn't supposed to be there yet. It wasn't his turn to go." Body trembling, she gazed up with pleading eyes. "I don't want to live without him, Liz. I don't know how."

"You're going to be okay. We're going to get through this." Liz summoned more conviction than she thought possible. "Come here," she said softly. Julia sank her cheek into the shoulder of Liz's coat, a sponge for her muffled sobs.

"It's going to be all right, Jules. You'll see." Smothering her own tears, Liz stroked the wavy crimson locks Christian used to adore, and hoped with all her might that her words would ring true. For all of them.

❧ 35 ❧

February 1945—Later that evening
Evanston, Illinois

Every sound in Evanston ricocheted off the chilled night air, yet nothing was louder than the silence that hovered over the Stephens home.

Liz gripped the arm of the porch swing and stared at the bare cherry tree. The copper glow from neighbors' windows accentuated its features, as telling as the pages of a scrapbook: the trunk knobs she and Dalton had climbed as kids, the small crooked initials they'd carved, the weathered bark she'd leaned against when they shared their first kiss, brief and awkward in its innocence.

Moonlight sieved through the branches, creating a claw that reached across the snow-spotted yard. Liz shivered at the shadowed fingers. They gripped her heart as she waited for Dalton's response.

"And this is what you want?" He turned to her, his expression grim. "You're willing to throw away everything we have, for some soldier you hardly know?"

But I do know him arrived on her tongue. She swallowed the unnecessary words.

"Dalton," she said simply, "this isn't about him."

"There's a good chance he won't be coming home. You realize that, don't you?" His voice rose.

She paused, considering, accepting. "Yes."

"So you'd rather be alone than with me?"

She wanted to reply, but honesty would only hurt him more.

He emitted a sharp, humorless laugh. "That's great, Liz. Then why the hell did you agree to marry me? If this is how you felt, you should've saved us the embarrassment."

"Dalton . . . I'm so sorry."

"Just tell me why. If it's not about him, then *why?*"

Because after peeking over the wall of contentment, she couldn't reverse the ways in which the view had changed her. Yet how could she tell him that, and have him understand?

He slung his gaze toward the street. After a long moment, he relaxed, a revelation settling. "This is about the clerkship, isn't it?" he said, facing her. "It's consumed more of my time than I planned, I know."

She shook her head. "It's not the clerkship."

"Okay," he said. "It's school. Our schedules have been madness. But remember, we've only got a few terms left until—"

"It's not school."

"Well . . . if it's the wedding, if you feel like we're rushing—"

"That's not it either."

"Then what is it? What's changed?" His tone coarsened. "Is it because I'm not in the service? Because I'm not wearing a damn uniform?"

Thrown by the question, she hesitated.

His mouth tightened, then his eyes. "That's it, isn't it?"

"What? No."

"You think I'm a coward, because I didn't go off to war like your Army hero."

"Dalton—"

He cut in, nearly yelling. "Don't you think I would've enlisted if I could have? If a goddamn ulcer hadn't made me 4-F?" He stared into the air before him, his cheeks blotched from emotion. In the resounding quiet, Liz digested his words. His secret.

She was well aware of the stigma the 4-F classification carried, had read about guys who'd committed suicide after labeled medically unfit for the military. She'd just never dreamt that Dalton

Harris—the overachieving son, student, and future lawyer—adhered to anything less than perfection.

"Why didn't you say something before now?" she asked gently.

He raked his bottom lip with his teeth and released a weighted exhale. "Do you know what people would say? What it could do to my father's career? And my own?"

"But you could have told *me*."

"For what?" he said. "So you could pity me?"

Instinct urged her to embrace him, extending an apology, a retraction. Instead, she touched his hand resting on the swing's wooden grooves. "I would never pity you or think less of you for not enlisting. I just would've liked to have known the real reason why."

"Would it have mattered?"

She pondered the question, sighed. "I don't know," she admitted. "But I wish we'd been able to share more about ourselves with each other. Maybe we wouldn't have become so different."

For several seconds he closed his eyes, grasping her fingers. "Lizzy, please." He looked at her gravely. "Give me a chance to show you we're not as far apart as you think. Inside, I'm still the same guy you've always known."

"No," she said. "You're not."

"I am."

"Dalton, you're not. You've grown up. We both have."

"That doesn't mean we have to grow apart, not if we still love each other." He contracted his brow. "You do—love me, don't you?"

"From the bottom of my heart," she said easily. The next sentence would be harder. "The problem is, I'm not . . . *in* love with you."

He let go of her hand. "And you know this because of a few letters? I'm the one who's shared a history with you. Not him."

She nodded in thoughtful agreement. "You're right," she said. "And I wouldn't trade the years we've spent together for anything. You're a wonderful person. And you have an unbelievable future ahead of you—making stands, fighting for causes."

"You make it sound like *I'm* the senator instead of my father," he muttered.

Had he not seen what everyone else could? The respected leader he'd already become?

"I've seen you at political events. I've seen you on stage giving speeches. The crowds adore you. You belong in that world," she told him. "But I don't."

He hunched his shoulders, barely waiting to propose an alternative. "So we'll adjust. I can contribute in other ways. I don't have to be the guy at the podium."

"No, but you should be. It's what you were meant to do." All of a sudden, she viewed his military exclusion for what it was: a gift, not a misfortune. She balanced her next words, heavy in truth, to communicate why. "Maybe in all this craziness, there's a good reason you weren't supposed to go off to war. Because back here, at home, is where you're going to make the biggest difference."

He shifted in the seat, swaying them, his demeanor clouded with uncertainty. "Yeah, I guess. Maybe. I don't know." He shook his head, postponing the thought. Back to the puzzle, its solution just beyond reach. "Lizzy, tell me what you need to hear, what it would take to prove that we can make this work."

The conversation showed no signs of progressing, stuck on its circular path.

Growing weary, Liz glanced back at the house. She thought of Julia in her bed, asleep with her veil. The image reminded Liz why she couldn't put off her confrontation with Dalton another day.

She spoke only loud enough for him to hear. "Christian was killed."

"What?" he said, jolted.

"Julia got his farewell letter today."

"Oh God," he breathed. "Is she okay?"

"No. But she's resting now. I sat with her until she fell asleep." Liz met his gaze. "And that's when I knew I had to call you."

Confusion tugged at his face. He approached his reply carefully. "I'm sorry about Christian, honestly I am. I don't understand, though. What does *their* relationship have to do with us?"

"Dalton, there's no denying we feel deeply for each other. I'd be horrified if something ever happened to you. But tonight, watching Julia's heart being ripped out, that's when I knew—we'll never have what they had. We're a good match, we always have been. But we don't need each other like that."

He moistened his lips, as if to help craft a reply. "I know what you're getting at, Liz, but, given time—"

"Given time, we'll forget we deserve that kind of love too. Maybe neither of us will find it, but we have to at least try. Don't we?"

He went to respond, but faltered. No rebuttal. No deferral. In lieu of words, an unmistakable message glinted in his eyes: Although with reservations, deep down he agreed.

In a slow sinking motion, he reclined. They sat without moving for an endless minute.

Then Liz slid the ring from her pinkie. She handed the heirloom over with the care it deserved. "Believe me," she said, "one day you'll look back and realize this was the right decision."

The diamonds shone like the moon, gray from borrowed light, the emerald dark as an ancient gem.

"You think so, huh?"

"I know so."

He ran his thumb over the band before he gave a slight nod. Somehow, the gesture said it all. There was no need for anything more.

But when he grabbed his trilby hat from beside him, a final thought nibbled at her. An offering she should voice. She tried to push it away. She worried he'd heard enough, and perhaps it wasn't her place. As his friend, though, as someone who would always care, she softly submitted the words. "In case no one tells you, it's okay not to be perfect. You'd have lots of company, I promise."

They exchanged a look, an understanding stemming from history, tinged with the ache of loss.

Finally, rising from the creaky swing, he slipped the ring into his trouser pocket. Liz followed him to the stairs, as she always had to say good-bye. He stopped only one step down and shifted toward her. Sternness rode his eyes.

"When that soldier comes home, I'd better not hear about him mistreating you. You understand?"

A multitude of emotions whirled inside her, quivered her chin. Her one relief was that, this time, regret wasn't among them.

Dalton placed his hand on her shoulder and sweetly kissed her forehead. "See you around, kiddo," he said.

Then he walked away.

❦ 36 ❧

June 1945
Paris, France

Laughter and chatter bounced off the stone walls of the bar. In the corner, a U.S. Army regimental band traded eights in a battle of jazz. The reek of smoke and stale beer was overpowered only by the smell of victory. And more notably, Hitler's defeat.

From the doorway, Morgan scanned the dim room bulging with well-groomed GIs. They puffed on cigarettes and chugged down pints, flirted with the ladies swarming about them.

"I think I've died and gone to heaven," Jack mumbled through a mouthful of bread. His gaze traced the Mae West figure of a blonde sauntering by. She turned and blew him a kiss. Before he could catch it, a sailor grabbed her around the waist, squeezing a giggle out of her curvy frame.

"Sure you don't want to do more sightseeing?" Morgan joked.

"What do you think I'm doin' right now? Best sights in town."

On three-day leave from their camp in Germany, Morgan had towed his friend on a tourist race against the clock. The Notre Dame Cathedral, Eiffel Tower, Arc de Triomphe. Clearly, nothing had impressed Jack more than the majestic beauty of the Parisian female form.

"So many dollies, so little time." Jack sighed.

"Don't you ever take a break?"

"Can't. Too many dames would be disappointed." Jack chomped on the last bite of his baguette. "What about you, Mac? See anything you want for your birthday?"

"You offering yourself as a gift?"

"Hey, you know I would, but I'm saving myself for marriage."

Morgan smiled. "Listen," he said, "I still need to buy a present before we leave tomorrow. Why don't you grab a beer and I'll be back in two shakes."

Jack didn't answer, just nabbed Morgan's jacket sleeve as a stunner displaying more skin than clothing shimmied past. "Hoo boy, it's a tough call. I had Belgium in the lead, but now I'm thinking the French might have the hottest broads, after all."

Thank goodness the war hadn't changed Jack's youthful humor. Never a dull moment in his company. The one difference Morgan had noticed, however, was a look in his eyes. A dullness that said he had seen things he'd never talk about.

But then, who among them hadn't?

Already Morgan knew there were memories he too would never share. Not even with Betty. And to think, he'd actually believed he had witnessed the worst of war before visiting the liberated confines of Dachau. The satanic masterpiece housed such evil it should have collapsed into the molten center of the earth.

At the concentration camp, he and two other GIs, one of whom spoke fluent German, had trailed behind a skeletal inmate who spattered his accounts like a racing propeller. He'd toured them from one ghastly site to the next: crematorium with gas chambers, boxcars for corpses, a courtyard for mass executions. The laboratories for medical experiments were too heinous for a wax museum of horrors.

How were humans capable of imagining such atrocities, let alone committing them?

In a moment of needed solitude, Morgan had gripped a chain-link fence and bowed his head. It was then that he uncovered the single answer to his bitter questions of "why." Tears pooling, he peered into the sky and whispered, "This, Charlie. This is why we were here."

Morgan's first impulse had been to purge the encounter in a let-

ter to Betty. After all, she was the one person who was certain to believe his claims, not discount the speculative facilities as exaggerated propaganda—a crime he himself was guilty of before knowing
better.

Ultimately, though, he had spared Betty the recap. Rather, he'd
filled his pages with just about every other subject, each of their
posts growing in openness and affection. He felt there was nothing
they couldn't tell one another—except maybe a few romantic things
he would reserve for whispering in her ear someday. At least he
hoped for that chance. Until then, he would continue to share snip-
pets about himself, his family, and his unit, which he'd rejoined in
early February. With mixed emotions, he had already written her
about the Purple Heart he'd received from a colonel in a bedside
ceremony. And most recently, he'd described the surrealism of
civilians in an intact German town shopping and strolling the
streets. Such a display intensified his desire to resume his own normal life in the States, but as usual, he'd have to wait his turn in line.

"Jesus, Mary, 'n' Joseph," Jack exclaimed, "would you look
who's here." He pointed toward the center of the bar.

Through a small clearing, Morgan sighted their old squad buddy.
"I'll be damned."

Sure enough, there stood Boomer, with his black cowlick and
bushy eyebrows. One foot propped on a chair, he swooshed a pint
glass while undoubtedly reciting one of his humorous gems to the
GIs circled about him.

"No way you can leave now," Jack said.

Morgan tossed a glance at his watch. The stores would be closing soon, but he couldn't go without first saying hi. "After you," he
said, and followed Jack's lead.

On the way, Jack stopped at a table of flyboys. He snagged the
backs of two empty chairs. "Mind if we take these?"

"All yours," the larger guy said in a subdued tone, barely audible over Boomer's mock Irish brogue.

" 'Ah, Murphy,' " Boomer cried in a falsetto voice, " 'being that
it's yer eightieth birthday, yer friends hired me as a special treat. In
honor of yer big day, I'm goin' to give ya super sex.' " He lowered
his vocal key. "Confident that sex with the young lass would end his

life with a heart attack, Murphy answered the gal, 'Well, thank ya, miss. But, if it's all the same to ya, I'll take the soup.'"

His audience broke into laughter.

Jack parked his chair in an opening and said, "Any room for some *real* Irishmen here?"

Boomer's face beamed. "Well, what do you know?" He greeted both of them with a swift hug and slap on the back.

Morgan couldn't believe the chances of running into the guy. "Thought for sure you'd be basking in the Florida sunshine by now," he told Boomer.

"Nah. Just recooped in an evac before they reassigned me to G Company."

Jack settled in his seat. "So how's your girlfriend holding up?"

"Swell as ever." Boomer displayed his infamous tattoo. "Her jugs are little lopsided, but she can still dance." He shuffled his knuckles—Charlie used to love the shake of her hips— in a presentation that spurred more laughs. Then he guzzled his pint and turned to the bar. "*Madame, s'il vous plaît.* Another round."

Minutes later, a buxom French woman arrived toting a tray filled with pints of dark, foamy beer. The soldiers seized their glasses and bid *merci* while Boomer handed one to Morgan.

"Actually, man, got a quick errand to run." Morgan tried to give it back.

"What are you thinkin', refusing a perfectly good stout? Wanna piss off your ancestors?"

"Sit your ass down, Mac," Jack hollered. "It's your birthday."

"Birthday?" Boomer cried. "Now we really have something to celebrate." He raised his pint above the group. "To the birthday boy!"

"Hear! Hear!" they all chorused.

What choice did Morgan have? Besides, his bad knee was starting to act up after a full day of covering the city on foot. A short rest would do him good.

He sat down and took a chug of the thick, room-temperature drink that tasted like tree bark. A reflexive cough fought to surface, challenging his pride.

Boomer lifted his pint again. "To going home!"

"To going home," the group echoed, commanding Morgan to take a second but smoother swig.

Camp rumours had run rampant about the possibility of GIs being transferred to reinforce Allied offensives against the Japanese. Either word hadn't reached the guys at Boomer's table, or they'd chosen to focus on their homeward cruise regardless.

"Gentlemen." Boomer's speech began to slur. "May you all live to be a hundred years, with one extra year to repent."

For once, Morgan wished he'd followed Jack's example. Waiting to eat his own baguette would have been a wise decision, since the drink in his hand was markedly more potent than 3.2 beers at the PX. Another good reason to sneak out soon.

As he turned back to the table, the guys clanked his glass. He downed what was to be his last hefty swallow, but the thought took a backseat to the tingling in his legs, followed by his feet. Before he knew it, another round of pints had arrived. Then another. The soldiers swayed to "Bless 'Em All" and "Roll Me Over in the Clover," their volume growing with each serving.

Morgan was fairly certain he himself had made a couple of toasts, though he couldn't recall what he'd said. All he knew for sure was he couldn't feel his nose and mouth. While patting his lips to make sure they were still there, he felt two hands massaging his shoulders. He tipped his head back and slowly took in the hazy upside-down view of a ravishing young woman.

"*Allô, monsieur,*" she said in a come-hither tone. She swung around his seat, dizzying him as she slid onto his lap. A scanty black corset laced her tiny waist.

"Mac, this is Monique," he heard Jack say.

The girl smiled with red painted lips. She tossed her long black mane off her shoulders to reveal the paleness of her flesh. Before Morgan could speak, she ran her hands through his hair. His eyelids drooped closed. The lulling movements of her fingers hypnotized him. He breathed in the heady scent of her sugary-sweet perfume, even more intoxicating than the stout he'd consumed.

"Consider her a birthday present, m'friend." Jack's remark yanked Morgan from his daze.

He opened his eyes. Monique's generous cleavage stared back.

The sight caused a physical reaction that would have mortified him had he been sober enough to care.

Monique appeared amused. She wet her lips as she stood and guided one of his hands to follow her.

"Have fun, Mac." Jack grinned like the devil. His arm dangled over the shoulder of a brunette seated sideways on his lap. "Just don't forget to cover your rifle," he warned.

The Army was so paranoid about the spreading of venereal diseases, along with the image of immorality among soldiers overseas, they distributed packs of condoms like an infinite supply of candy to children. But other than rolling them onto the muzzle of his rifle to prevent the bore from rusting, Morgan had never considered actually using the prophylactic devices during his European service.

His body suddenly had other ideas.

In a passing blur, Morgan was swept out of the bar and into a dim, barren apartment. Lights from the street flickered through the window, waving shadows across Monique's curves and the sheeted bed behind her. Silently, they stood facing each other. With a seductive smile, she took his hand and placed it on her bare shoulder. She pulled his fingers across the shelf of her breasts and his legs turned to jelly. He'd forgotten what it was like to have a woman so close, to feel a gentle touch on his skin.

She stepped forward and pressed her lips to his neck. When she rubbed her thigh against him, he shuddered and closed his eyes. She trailed the tip of her tongue up toward his earlobe, stealing his air. He felt her hands glide down his shirted chest beneath his opened jacket. Every abdominal muscle tensed as she approached the waistline of his trousers.

"Oh, Betty . . ." The name drifted out in a gasp.

And with that, the fantasy began to slip away, towed by a feeling of betrayal against the woman he loved.

"Wait," he said meekly.

Either ignoring or misinterpreting the word, Monique knelt at his feet. She briskly unfastened his military belt buckle, demonstrating her familiarity with the accessory.

Carnal instinct implored his conscience to look the other way, to savor an act of pleasure that, for a brief passionate moment, could erase all that haunted him.

Still, his heart battled for control. "We . . . need to stop."

Her overpowering perfume throttled his senses. As she unbuttoned his pants, two words scratched at his mind: *Dearest Morgan.* His will returned with a vengeance. He jumped back out of Monique's reach, and her face clouded.

"Monsieur?"

"I'm sorry. It's not you. I just—have to go." He hightailed it out the door, refastening his pants and belt to the best of his impaired ability. On every corner, servicemen and their female companions embraced. To his left, to his right. Definitely not helping his cause.

A few wrong turns and several stumbles later, Morgan located Gare du Nord station. In a matter of hours the train would arrive to return them from their furlough.

He curled into a fetal ball on a wooden bench and clenched his eyes, desperate to fall asleep. Yet every creak and footstep reverberated in his ears. He tossed and turned, couldn't get comfortable. Which really made no sense. After months of dozing in the dirt, the bench should have felt like a lofty mattress.

It was useless.

He might as well journey back to the pub, despite a barrage of ridicule that surely awaited from the guys who'd been debriefed, in both senses of the word, by Monique. Not the ideal, but at least it would be better than camping alone in a cavernous station with too many noises and too many hiding places. Another night of trying to force sleep that refused to come.

He was about to sit up when an image stopped him. In his mind, Betty materialized. Her flaxen hair flowing in the breeze, her eyes shining like blue glass in the sun. She smiled her perfect smile, then offered her hand, welcoming him home. He folded his arms over his chest, imagining he was holding her, imagining their reunion, and before he knew it, he faded into tranquil sleep.

❧ 37 ❧

Mid-September 1945
Evanston, Illinois

"Ladies and gentlemen, it's official. The Japanese have surrendered. President Harry Truman has announced that the war
is over. I repeat, the war is over." On a beautiful August day, the
male broadcaster's voice on the floor model radio had sung like an
angelic choir.

Liz's father had dashed into the kitchen, swooped Liz up, and
spun her around until they'd spent every ounce of their laughter.
His personal reasons for jubilee needed no explanation. "Victory
Over Japan Day" marked a cease to the killing and maiming of his
former students and the safe return of those who had survived.

Finally, a period of healing began for those who had lost so
much. Veterans everywhere, no matter the color of their uniform or
skin, licked their wounds and headed for home. Prisoners of Japanese internment camps and Jewish concentration camps alike
lamented their stolen lives. And broken families around the globe
mourned the loss of a generation of young men: boys who became
men through valor but whose hair would never gray; soldiers who
would never bask in the glory of a victory parade, never smell the
warm, milky breath of their newborn babes; sailors who would
never turn their sweethearts into brides.

After taking a hiatus from the university, Julia had returned for summer school to catch up on her missed credits. Liz, oddly aware the roles had reversed, became a regular advocate of nonacademic activities: comedic film showings in the city or sundaes at a local diner. Anything to revive her friend's smile. In some ways, they'd become closer than ever; in others, they'd never been more independent. And while Liz wanted Julia beside her for support this particular evening, it was a task she had to conquer on her own.

Alone in the living room, Liz gazed wistfully out the open window. The natural creaks of her house harmonized with those from her rocking chair. Outside, purple clouds rushed over the sky as if floating down a river. She closed her eyes, inhaled the scent. Electricity and moisture. The smell of an approaching thunderstorm.

Begrudgingly, she lifted her lids and found it was still there. Atop her skirted lap, speckled with dust from the basement, the box waited patiently.

The gift from her mother.

Seven years, and yet it appeared exactly as Liz remembered. Against the backdrop of red wrapping, the Mouse King swung his sword. The Nutcracker stood stoically with his tall hat and narrow beard. In ballet tutu and pointe shoes, the Sugar Plum Fairy elegantly stretched her arms, her face a featureless blur. No expression, no clear identity. The box's skinny white ribbon, just as before, cut through her figure, dividing her in two.

Liz had spent countless nights back then peering at this very package, hoping to one day see her mother again—unaware Isabelle's image had been right in front of her the whole time.

And here they were, face-to-face once more.

It had taken months of internal debating for Liz to retrieve the gift. Who knew if it was still stored in the basement, or how long it would take to find the thing, or if a pile of clutter had crushed it beyond recognition or repair.

Of course, the real reason for her delay—as Morgan had seen straight through and told her so—was her fear of letting go. As always, and on more levels than he knew, he was right. Liz hadn't been ready to forsake her anger or resentment, not since fully grasping the selfishness of her mother's departure. The woman had left just before Christmas, and after an argument, no less. What else was a daughter to think or feel?

But when those emotions had subsided, a more challenging form of letting go loomed: the relinquishment of hope. A young girl's hope. The dream that a wrapped present could reverse time, or at least earn her mother's approval.

Touching the rectangular gift tag now, Liz flashed back to the rumored phone call that had ignited their fight, about a mechanic's son ruining her reputation, her bright future. And suddenly she realized: In all the years since, her check-off list of acceptable standards had been, in some odd way, linked to the possibility of Isabelle's return.

Which, Liz finally accepted, wasn't going to happen. Even if the package stayed sealed forever.

Nudged by the revelation, she stepped through her progression, first by untying the ribbon. Next, she carefully edged away the tape. The ripened adhesive detached with little effort and the paper fell away. No resistance at her touch. As if it had needed but her unspoken permission to unveil the lone brown box now resting on her lap.

At last, so close to its contents, she felt a youthful charge of anxiousness. She removed the lid and plunged her hands into the crinkled layers of matching brown tissue. At the bottom, her fingers closed on an object. A book. Before she could speculate further, she pulled it out.

A pattern of irises flowed over the cover, shades of purple and green. The flowers were her favorite, the same as she'd helped Nana plant in her garden as a little girl. Two imprinted words stated the title in white calligraphic lettering: *My Story*.

It was a journal filled with blank pages. Not a mark, save a handwritten note on the bottom inside cover.

An inscription.

She steadied herself with a long breath before reading.

> *Follow your passions, follow your heart.*
> *Create your own story in life, Elizabeth,*
> *and never stray from your dreams.*
> *Love and blessings,*
> *Mother*

Liz examined the precise script, startlingly similar to her own. She detected no trace of the quiet suffering that had spurred the message. No regrets or indication of her mother's ultimate plans. Yet the words sent unexpected warmth through her chest. It was a lesson hard won and offered none too late:

Never lose sight of who you are.

How alike they had been, breaking free of the logical molds that defied their hearts' demands—even when it required painfully leaving others behind. Liz had severed her relationship with Dalton, in spite of her deep care for him, due to her confidence that each of them would be better off in the end. Maybe her mother's intentions had been the same.

Maybe, true to her father's claim, Isabelle had simply loved both of them the best she knew how. And in accepting that, in allowing that bittersweet reality through the gates of her soul, Liz could finally let her go.

She traced the inscription with her fingertips. Her skin brushed every angled stroke. When she completed her mother's name, she closed the book, knowing she would soon take a pen to its pages.

Through the window, she again admired the streaming lavender clouds. A thin glaze of pink added a lining to their edges. The masses shifted and shapes reconfigured, and she now understood the scent. Electricity and moisture, energy and water. The symbols of change, and of strength.

After several minutes, her task complete, Liz rewarded herself by unsealing another gift. Morgan's latest post. The letter, as welcoming as a heated hearth, provided comfort before she'd read even a single line.

> *My dearest Betty,*
>
> *THE WAR IS OVER! I can hardly believe the news. Fellas over here have been so loud whooping it up that I wouldn't be surprised if you could hear them clear to Chicago. I, on the other hand, might be the only one who's afraid to cheer too wildly. Can't help thinking some colonel is going to break up the party and tell us it was a big mistake, that the war is still on*

*and we're moving up to the front. Just seems too good
to be true, sweetheart, after all this time. Even reading
the news and dirt in "Stars and Stripes" hasn't done much
to convince me. Guess I won't really believe it until I'm
boarded on a ship headed for the good ol' USA.*

*No surprise that the boys have already started
tallying up their rotation points—how long they've
been overseas, how many battles and decorations.
Apparently we've all forgotten how seasick we were on
the ride over. Although even I'd agree that two weeks
of nearly any illness would be worth suffering to get
back to American soil. And most of all, back to you.
With all the old-timers here, unfortunately, it will be
quite a stretch before I see our outfit listed on the
bulletin board.*

*Until then I shouldn't have much to squawk about.
The German apartment I'm billeted in is grander than
any place we've stayed in so far. With soft mattresses
and sheets, fancy drapes and paintings, and a real
working toilet! I know it must sound silly, but the
simplest things, like bathtubs and electricity, have
become the most appreciated inventions for us
doughboys. We've found so many storage rooms full of
fine china we don't even bother with our mess tins
anymore. Boy, what luxuries! I have to admit I'm
growing a tad tired of spud soup, black bread, and
kraut, but it beats Army chow any day.*

*Right now I'm sitting on a terrace overlooking the
town. How I wish you could be here with me. But then,
of course you always are. The warm sun is shining
down, making for an awfully quiet and relaxing
afternoon. Should be that way until the kids get out of
school and GIs start handing out chocolate bars.
Amazing how little it takes to bring a smile to a kid's
face. Not much different from the happiness a handful
of cigarettes brings to the local barber here in exchange
for a cut and shave. Guess we all have our indulgences.*

*Well, sweetheart, I don't have much in the way of
writing time today, so I best lay down the pen. There's
a USO camp show scheduled tonight that they say
Dinah Shore and Jack Benny will be performing at, and
I'll be on detail until it starts. Hopefully sooner than
later I will be spending an evening with you at a USO
club back in the States, dancing the night away
(dancing, I admit, being mostly an excuse to hold you
close). I so look forward to that day—so often dream
about finally being with you in person.*

Please write soon. Thinking of you always.
Yours forever,
Morgan

Liz read the closing again.

Forever. So much meaning conveyed in a word. But with such a word came conditions, the most essential being honesty. A trait he undoubtedly placed high value upon.

Since breaking off her engagement, she had been more anxious than ever to tell Morgan everything. But with the war still on, she couldn't help fearing her confession might be the last letter he ever read. And so she'd held off, selfishly, compassionately delaying.

Now, though, the battles were over, and she was out of excuses. It was time to tell him who she was. Or more notably, who she wasn't.

She made her way to the chair at the slant-front desk. The blank page before her called for a composition to the man she loved, quite possibly the last correspondence between them. Although any plea at this point seemed undeserving, she had to try.

She glanced at her mother's journal, a reminder of her own courage. Then she clutched the pen and scrawled as fast as her hand would move, hoping speed would lessen the sting.

Dearest Morgan,
*The words I am about to inscribe are among the
most difficult of my life. For so long, I have wanted to
tell you the truth. Yet with each of your posts, you have*

filled more of my heart, making a letter like this near impossible to write. Even now, I am more terrified of the consequences than ever before. Nevertheless, honesty is precisely what you deserve. So here, my darling, are the facts at last.

You and I indeed met at the USO club the night before your deployment. I am not, however, the beautiful singer with whom you made a promise of correspondence. Although our encounter sparked feelings within me I didn't believe could exist, it soon became clear that my roommate Betty, alone, was the one who had gained your interest.

Soon after, as fate would have it, I agreed to help her pen an initial letter to you, my repayment of a favor. In all fairness, I must admit part of me still had hoped to develop a connection, even through another's name. Thus, when your moving response arrived, following Betty's departure for military service, I could not resist sending a reply. And so it went, my feelings for you growing with each exchange, always with my intention to reveal the truth, but never was I brave enough to risk losing you as a result.

This far from excuses what I have done, dear Morgan. But I do hope more than anything that you can forgive me. You see, despite what you might rightfully presume, every word in my posts, apart from the signature, was honest and heartfelt, as is the tremendous love I carry for you.

The thought of not hearing from you again is an overwhelming one. Still, I would not blame you for retracting your affection. And so, understanding this note between us may well be the last, I now offer you a final confession: Not until receiving your letters did I understand what joy really was. Because of you, I will never again settle for an unhappy or content existence, merely for the sake of pleasing others. From you, I learned the value of family, the reward of being true to myself, and the beauty of caring for someone enough to need them—even if it means letting them go.

Above all, my darling Morgan, you have reopened my heart. For every way in which you have changed me, I am in your debt. Thank you for gracing my life, and for allowing me the privilege of getting to know and adore the kind, courageous person that you are. With all my love and regret,
Elizabeth Stephens

❧ 38 ❧

Mid-September 1945
Chicago, Illinois

Julia hesitated at the open door. Into the hallway wafted the same old fragrances of fabric and imagination, but now thick with motes of guilt. She left the buttons of her overcoat fastened. The academy seemed cold for a fall morning.

As she stepped cautiously into the classroom, a trickle of anxiety traveled through her. It wasn't the internal stampede she once would have felt, preparing for a figurative feast of crow; the limits of her emotions had since been stretched. Yet still, she found no voice to greet the woman.

Against the windowed backdrop, Madame Simone's profile appeared lean in black. Alone except for a lineup of mannequin dress forms, the French woman stood focused over the worktable, half-spectacles on the end of her thin nose. With measuring tape draped from her neck, pincushion nested on her wrist, she unrolled a rose-hued bolt. Her movements remained as sleek as the dark bun of her hair.

Had nothing changed in this place since Julia left? Constant safety could have been hers had she never abandoned this room.

"A little early in the day for a visit, *Zhoolia*," the teacher remarked. Her eyes didn't budge from her project. "Here to leave another note, are you?"

The question stung, despite Julia expecting something to the effect. "No," was all she managed to say.

"Mmm."

As Simone scissored fabric, continuing as if absent of company, Julia felt the full reach of the distance between them. She now wished she'd rehearsed her request, at least conjured a rough plea.

On the other hand, had she given herself time to second-guess, she might never have come back.

Simone stopped, looked at her. Her gaze held an edge. "Well?"

"I was wondering," she began, "I mean, I was hoping . . ."

"*Yes?*"

At the teacher's impatience, Julia shoved out the phrase gathering inside. "About the internship at *Vogue*. I'm sure the spot from your friend is long gone by now. But if there were another position, anything that opened up, I was hoping I could apply."

A humorless smile crossed Simone's lips. She reverted her attention toward her design, and sighed. "So this is how it goes, you think. That chances to work for a company like *Vogue* are handed out like baguettes on a street corner. Ready whenever your appetite calls, *oui?*"

Julia shook her head. "Of course not," she told her. Nothing in her life was coming out as it was meant. She commanded herself to continue, to not flee the school as she'd done before. Stakes that had seemed so high only a year ago were now almost laughable. She envied the girl she was back then, too scared to face even her teacher. To face herself.

"I'm sorry," Julia offered at last. "I should've explained in person. I shouldn't have waited all summer to tell you, not when I already knew my answer."

Unspoken thoughts soaked the quiet, broken by a sharp wave of Simone's hand. "No," she said. "I am to blame. I should not have expected so much. A girl your age, with so little experience, does not know what she wants. I assure you, it won't happen again."

In defense, Julia stepped forward. "But I did know." She tried for insistence, but her voice came out halfhearted.

Simone met her eyes. "Ah. Then you *must* have made the right decision. Which means there is no reason for you to be here. Hmm?"

What could Julia say, without saying too much?

"Things have changed—since then."

"How?" Simone challenged. Her clipped tone left Julia speechless.

The woman persisted with a huff. "What, may I ask, changed that would make me believe you truly regretted your decision? That I would not be making another mistake recommending you?"

"Well—because, I'm no longer . . ." The word *engaged* stuck to her tongue, throbbed like a bitten taste bud. Since the day she received Christian's letter, his final letter, she hadn't spoken of him. Not even at his funeral. At the service—a seeming rehearsal, lacking a body to bury—she'd held his mother's gloved hand, statues in their pew. Julia had nodded on cue when Ian took the podium, bowed her head as the pastor fulfilled his role. She'd consoled Cora with a gentle smile after George tore from the church, unable to complete his son's eulogy.

And through it all, Julia had survived the day tearless, safely detached, compliments of an internal bargain: So long as she didn't utter his name or speak of their shared past, their love, her eyes would keep moisture clamped inside. Each party had upheld the deal, which Julia perpetually extended. Fear of opening the floodgates had been worth the risk of forgetting. In fact, forgetting was what she had wished for. To diminish the pain that beat in an endless pulse.

Now, however, teetering on the edge of his memory, she uncovered the greatest scare of all: the reality of releasing him forever.

From the silence came Simone's voice, spiked with irritation. "If you don't know why you are here, perhaps there is somewhere else you should be." With that, she resumed her work, halving the material with a jagged slice.

The implied command for Julia to leave came clear as a tolling bell, yet the soles of her shoes had melted into the floor tiles. Her body refused to shift an inch. Not until she said his name—until she shared what he'd meant to her—to anyone who would listen.

She swallowed around her grief and blurted, "His name was Christian."

Simone slowly raised her head as Julia forced herself to go on. "I put our future first, our future together. We were supposed to marry, after the war. But then he didn't come home, and now I feel utterly lost.

"It's been seven months, and most of the time I still think he's the one who got off easy." That sounded terrible, she knew, but the intensity in Simone's eyes forbade her to stop. And so, out the truth flowed despite the rise of emotions, the blurring of vision.

"I walk around the city and every corner reminds me of him. The Pier, going to a restaurant, the movies. I can't get on a streetcar without seeing him in a crowd. Every sailor could be Christian from behind, and I think to myself, *They must've made a mistake. That he's still alive.* Until they turn their heads. Then I realize it's not him, and I have to face over and over that he's never coming back."

Simone straightened as she removed her glasses, let them dangle from her neck.

"You know," Julia said, remembering, "one day I rode the bus an entire afternoon. Just sat there for hours, not speaking to a single person, and I thought, *This must be what it's like to be a ghost. To watch everyone, but not talk or touch. Or feel.* And that's when it dawned on me: *That's what I am.* It's as if the world is moving around me, and I'm just going through the motions because that's what I'm supposed to do." She paused, thinking of Ian, the sketch he'd once become, the real person he'd found in himself again.

Then, suddenly aware how widely she'd exposed her heart, and to a woman whose veil of rigidity hadn't softened, a woman who couldn't possibly empathize, Julia charged to her conclusion. "So you see, I didn't come here today because I think I deserve a second chance, or because I took for granted what I passed up. I came because I thought, maybe by going back to something I was passionate about—a part of me I was sure of—I could find myself again. And then I might actually have a reason to wake up every morning. A way to feel like I'm still alive."

It was then Julia became aware of the tears gliding down her cheeks. No torrential flood, just streaks from drops as real as Christian had been. The bargain was over, and to her surprise, she was still standing. Fractured but not broken.

"Like I said"—Julia swiped the moisture away—"I'm sorry I let you down. But I don't regret the choice I made back then. Because I made the right one. I chose *him*." The declaration settled in her chest, spreading strength within. She turned and headed for the doorway, just as Simone beckoned her back.

"Zhoolia."

Julia tried to block her out.

"Zhoolia," she called again, then a gentle, "Please."

The single word, a rarity from the woman, halted Julia's feet. Had she imagined it? If Julia didn't respond, she would always wonder.

She gave her cheeks another finger-brush for dignity. Reluctantly, she swiveled around.

Simone perched on the corner of the worktable. Above tightly crossed arms, a dull shade of pensiveness eased into her face. She stared at Julia as she spoke. "My brother fought with *la Résistance*. The last my parents heard from him was in a smuggled note. That was three years ago." Her tone remained matter-of-fact. "You mustn't forget, *chérie,* they all fought for a purpose. My brother. Your Christian. They fought so others could live, so that *we* could live. You are here for a reason, even if you don't yet know why."

Julia reflected on the message, absorbing its painful truth. A tear fell from each eye when she nodded.

"Good." Simone rose, dropping her arms. "So, you will come by in a few weeks," she told her. "I cannot promise anything, but I will make some calls to New York, see what I can find. *D'accord?"*

Stunned, speechless, Julia stood frozen. Only two words climbed out in a hush. "Thank you."

Simone simply shrugged, already back to her garment.

Julia knew better than to stick around, pressing her luck. She strode toward the exit, and as she stepped out into the city, inhaling the fresh morning air, she felt a small tingling inside. Like a numb limb, a soul, regaining its feeling.

⏤⏤ 39 ⏤⏤

Seated cross-legged on the living room floor, homework spread about, Liz struggled to concentrate on her assignment. An analytical essay on Shakespeare's *Macbeth*. She'd attempted an opening paragraph four times. Each time she had crumpled the page and started over.

For most of her life, she had found such literary works glorious and poetic in their tragedies. But no longer. She had since discovered there was no poetry or glory in war, or death, or the loss of a loved one. What she yearned for today was a fairy tale, where the glass slipper fit and the couple lived happily ever after.

A *clink* interrupted her thoughts. It was the postal slot on the front door. That metallic noise, for the better part of a year, had been her favorite sound in the world. Thrill would bubble as she sprinted to the fresh mail pile, soaring on the wings of anticipation. An evolution of images had flipped through her mind, visions of a farmhouse on a wide stretch of golden land. Wrapped in a blanket that smelled of Morgan, she would scribble away on her first novel, while he and their children puddle-jumped in the rain.

Yet such a future, it now seemed, would never come to pass. The crawl of each passing day since mailing her confession, two excruciating weeks, told her as much. And though she wanted to believe hope between them remained, logic told her she would never hear from him again. That all she could do was pray her memory of him would fade over time. That eventually she would remember what life was like before Morgan and his letters.

Dread simmering, she slogged toward the entry. She had already prepared herself for the worst. There would be no response from the soldier. She didn't deserve one.

As she approached the entry, she spotted a single envelope front side down.

Could it possibly be—

No. It couldn't. So why were goose bumps forming on her arms?

To think there was a chance he'd already written back *and* accepted her apology was absurd. Such hopes would only pummel her with disappointment when she verified the delivery was for Julia, another card from Christian's mother.

Liz picked up the mystery envelope and promptly flipped it over. The addressee's name was . . . *Morgan.* She tensed at the recognition of her own handwriting, her stationery. Her confession had circled back like a boomerang.

A diagonal pencil line slashed through his address. *Return to Sender* had been stamped in a careless angle. Instinctively, she hunted for the additional notation of *Deceased.* She had seen the typed designation on a pair of unopened letters returned to Julia; they came within weeks of Christian's parents receiving official word. But that was all during the war.

Casualties at peacetime were unlikely, Liz assured herself. She would have assumed they were nonexistent if not for tales shared by the neighborhood air-raid warden, chatty in his retirement and lacking a social censor.

Liz breathed out at the absence of the military marking. Her mind turned to more minor causes: Had she forgotten the stamp? No, the six-cent airmail sticker was there. An error in the address? As if that were possible. She knew it so well she could recite the words and numbers backward.

As she scrounged for other explanations, she felt a sinkhole forming inside her. A deep hollowing from the possibility that he'd read her letter and, out of fury, pitched it straight back. But the seal, she confirmed, remained intact. There was no evidence the envelope had ever reached his hands. The only other difference was a scribble of three small letters: *UTF.*

She turned the acronym over in her head. *UTF . . . UTF . . .*

Her determination matched that of a military code breaker, not yielding until the translation emerged with terrifying clarity. The power a mere few words could possess shocked her yet again. For the grouping of letters could mean only one thing.

UNABLE TO FORWARD.

⋙ 40 ⋘

October 1945
Evanston, Illinois

Well past noon and still Betty lay awake in bed, gazing out the window at the tarp of solemn gray clouds. Even alone, she could feel the tightrope beneath her feet. It was a balancing act, looking forward, never backward, maintaining her sanity without a net. Most of all, hoping no one noticed she was treading on a wire.

Forced by thirst, she pushed off the covers, equally relieved to have a goal and agitated it took her only so far as the Frigidaire. In her closet, her green housecoat drooped on a hanger, cowering in the presence of her WAC dress uniform. The chocolate brown jacket hung stiff and proud, boastful with all of Betty's "fruit salad": campaign ribbons for show, overseas bars she'd earned, battle stars she hadn't. She ran her fingers over the pointed collar, starched from the day they'd dropped anchor in San Francisco Harbor. Fireboats had sprayed glorious colors; a band on a ferry played patriotic tunes. As the servicewomen had disembarked down the plank, a lion's roar of cheers exploded behind them. Covering every surface of the cruise ship were soldiers extending their heartfelt gratitude.

She released a sigh and threw on her full-length robe. Her thin white slip now served as her nightly wear; it most closely resembled the feel of sleeping in the nude, to which she'd grown accustomed.

En route to the kitchen, she passed an open closet full of dusty books, their smell reminiscent of the high school library she'd done her best to avoid. A rumor of something like vanilla added to the mix. The scents must have always been in the house, so how was it she'd never noticed until now? And why did she feel like an intruder in a place she used to call home?

Everything around her seemed different. Each furnishing and adornment was in the exact same spot as the day she left for basic, yet somehow the house felt altered. Smaller maybe.

She fetched milk from the icebox and sat at the table. She didn't stop drinking until every chilled drop had trickled down her throat, a much-missed nourishment that, incredibly, failed to satisfy.

Behind her, the radiator clanked, then settled. The quiet became unnerving. Already she missed the bustling of her barracks. They'd all been so excited about the prompt demobilization process, Betty hadn't considered what her life would be like once she returned, left again without a family, without purpose.

Could she really go back to taking food orders at some greasy spoon? From saving lives to serving burgers?

She had so much to say and no one to say it to.

Since arriving home several days ago, she had zipped in and out, exchanging idle talk with folks in town. Some praised her for her service; others looked at her askance, adding links to the slanderous chains of gossip. Evidently, people terrified of societal change found comfort in believing that the primary WAC duty had been to keep up the morale of male soldiers—by any means possible.

The ignorance of it all.

She'd come close to venting her frustrations to Liz, but the announcement of Christian's death had derailed her thoughts. She had barely absorbed the news when the phone rang. Rosalyn had called to share she'd gotten engaged to the combat photographer she and Betty had met after their hospital relocated to Manila. While Betty couldn't have been happier for her, the elation in Roz's words accentuated the dim undertones in her own voice, a sullenness that had taken root in her soul the morning she'd found the picture behind Lieutenant Kelly's cot. With a caption.

Beloved husband,
Can't wait for you to meet your son.
Enid

The caption on the back of the baby's snapshot left no room for doubt: *Leslie Jr. (3 mths)*

In that moment of devastation, the world had folded in on itself, trapping Betty within the confines of doubt about all she'd believed. Only from her girlfriends' persuading while in the Philippines had she slowly ventured out of her hermit shell to attend an occasional dance. And even then, her sole interest had been the tantalizing food spread. Keeping serious company with any man, uniformed least of all, had dropped to the bottom of her list.

Now, shifting her thoughts, she picked up the *Chicago Tribune* from the kitchen table. She skimmed the first few pages. War, war, and more war. It was over, yet there was still nothing else to report. She flopped the newspaper down, drummed her fingers.

Liz and Julia probably wouldn't be home from work until evening.

She stared at the wax fruit in the carnival glass bowl before her. The red apple reminded her of an old tune, about a girl sitting under a tree and a soldier marching home. About Hollandia and Junior, the last person she would ever sing for. Not because tears over their final moment together would accompany any melody from her mouth, which undoubtedly they would, but because singing for anyone else seemed insignificant.

A triple knock sailed from the entry.

"Thank goodness," she said, in dire need of distraction, and rushed to open the front door. A young, lanky man stood on the porch mat. His hat and uniform identified him as Western Union.

"Yes?" she said.

He stared with wide eyes and a slackened jaw. She traced his focus, directly to the lacy V-neck in her exposed slip. Cripes, she'd forgotten she wasn't dressed.

She gripped her bathrobe closed. "May I help you?"

He snapped his head up as if woken from a trance. "Yes, ma'am, um . . ." His freckled skin flushed while he nervously scanned the page on his clipboard. "I've got, um, a telegram, here for, uh, Betty Cordell."

"That's me."

"Yes, ma'am." He passed the clipboard and pen.

She signed for the delivery, and found his gaze back on the gap in her robe. She snatched the envelope from his hand. "Good day." She grabbed the door handle, demanding his exit.

"Oh yeah. Thanks." He stumbled as he turned and scampered down the steps. Spinning around, he added, "If you need anything else—"

Betty shut the door. "The nerve."

She reentered the kitchen and broke the seal, figuring the wired message involved her military discharge.

> BETTY CORDELL=
> 821 KIERNAN LANE EVANSTON IL=
> ARRIVING TODAY AT 1735. UNION STATION. PLEASE
> MEET ME. CAN'T WAIT TO SEE YOU AGAIN. FONDLY=
> MORGAN MCCLAIN.

Morgan McClain? Who was Morgan McClain?

The name was so familiar. Where had she met him?

Ah, yes . . . the USO. The GI who'd come to her aid. The one she had written to.

Gradually, a muted image of the soldier surfaced. As if being dusted off, the portrait gained definition. Dark hair, solid build, nice hazel eyes. Or were they brown? She wasn't sure. But she did recall his shyness, his mysterious nature. The same traits that had initially piqued her interest in Lieutenant Kelly—

Her thoughts stopped there. She didn't need to remember any more. And she wasn't about to make a fool of herself again.

She wadded the telegram, tossed it aside. The cable was no more welcome than the letter she'd received from Leslie soon after his departure.

On her bed she had sat that humid February day, tears trailing her face, streaks born of stupidity. His sealed envelope had called out to her, luring her with its concealed words. How her fingers had ached to break the seal, to feel the pages he'd held. Possible replies had raced through her mind: *I love you. I hate you. Come back. Stay away.*

A baby's picture, a single note, and he had broken her into pieces too jagged to fully repair. And yet the fault was hers. She should have seen it coming, with all those posts from girls presumed to be his sisters.

Had she refrained from asking, investigating their relations, because she didn't want to know? Or because she'd known all along but didn't want the truth?

Perhaps if she'd looked hard enough, she would have found the answers in his letter. The letter Leslie had sent her. Was it a confession? A declaration of love, an explanation for the facade? She would never know. With large black strokes, she had printed *RETURN TO SENDER* across the front and sent the missive back.

She never heard from the pilot again.

Back in her room, Betty closed the door, recoiling from a life that no longer fit. Like a woolen sweater she'd outgrown as a kid, she could tug at the sleeves, pull at the collar, and still the fabric wouldn't stretch. In the end, all that remained was an old garment she had once taken for granted.

She grabbed her tattered teddy bear from the floor, the one person who'd always stood by her, provided comfort, never judging. As she headed for the bed, however, a sight halted her. A woman she hardly recognized stared from the mirror. Although she'd managed to maintain most of her weight and the yellow had faded from her skin, the corners of her mouth had fallen and sadness had replaced the twinkle in her eyes.

Moving toward the woman, Betty discovered she was wrong. She did recognize the features; they were her mother's. Another person foolish enough to fall for a married man. Would her own ending be the same, no matter her efforts?

The question clung to her as she lamented the photos lining the oval mirror. Between gaps from Christian's missing images hung snapshots of the three girls together, an evening at a fair, another at graduation. In their caps and gowns, they smiled, aglow from their newfound freedom and the potential of their futures. She ran her finger over the picture, her makeup pristine, hair perfectly coiffed.

That Betty was gone.

Even Morgan McClain's telegram wasn't truly for her. He was inviting the person she'd been when they met, a person she couldn't get back—not without a time machine. Wouldn't that be nice? A few levers and blinking lights, and poof, the year never happened.

A year. Was that all? She almost laughed at the realization. Someday that year would be a speck, a piece of lint she had mothballed with her uniform, packed away, nearly forgotten. Oh, why couldn't she do that now?

Her mind snatched the rhetorical question, pulled it back for review.

Why *couldn't* she do that now?

If nothing else, her service in the Pacific had taught her anything was possible. Compared to what she'd survived, this was a cinch.

She padded over to her closet and extracted a favorite. The dress from her USO days, the one Julia had created for her. A Rita Hayworth knockoff, but better. Eye catching with its form-fitted blue fabric, the garb would inspire Betty's new outlook, her new objective. Now all she needed was Morgan, her time machine. With him, a guy who still saw her through the eye of his memory, she could substitute for the girl she'd lost—until she was no longer pretending.

In the mirror, she held the dress to her body. She forced her mouth into a smile, not resting until it matched her old one in the photo. Only someone who knew her well could differentiate between the two, and she wasn't about to allow any man that close to her heart again.

She could do this. She could be the woman, the wife, the socialite she was meant to be, and all in a life destiny was going to deliver.

Whether it wanted to or not.

October 1945
Nearing Chicago Union Station

A loud thud caused Morgan to jump. He jerked his head toward the sound. A paratrooper had yanked his bag from the luggage rack and dropped it onto the floor of the train car.

Morgan wiped his moist palms on his trousers. He exhaled a long breath, trying to relax, though not even a barber's blade could cut the tension binding his muscles. Too much movement in a small area, conjuring the franticness of a stirred-up anthill. His inability to see what people were doing behind him cranked his jitters up to a level bordering on nausea. Or perhaps it was simply the knowledge that he could soon be facing one of the most pivotal moments in his life.

In the aisle seat beside him, a pint-sized girl hummed away, five years old if he had to guess. Though indiscernible, the tune was a whole lot more soothing than the scuffling shrieks she and her toddler sister had let loose in the neighboring row before their mother divided them. He only wished the separation had occurred more than ten minutes earlier.

Evidently enjoying her newfound independence, the girl swung her legs as rhythmically as windshield wipers, keeping time with the rock of the creaky coach. She alternated licks between both sides of her lollipop, its green apple scent sweetening the smoky, wool-musty air.

So that's what it felt like to be young. Morgan could hardly remember.

He turned to the window and focused on the passing buildings, the huff of the wheels, the hiss of the steam engine. Crouched beneath the overcast sky, the city—no, the world—appeared different than he remembered.

"Are we almost there?" The girl's elfin voice and tug on his coat sleeve interrupted his thoughts.

"I'd say we're getting awfully close," he answered. Flashes of her kelly green tongue pulled his lips upward. "Are you heading home?"

"Yep, yep, yep," she twittered. "My daddy just got back from, um, the hospital. He was fighting bad guys, and, um, he's a big hero, so they gave him a pink heart. And they said he could go home 'cause Mommy said he took all his medicine."

Notions of which limbs her father might have permanently traded for his Purple Heart arose from the dark caverns of Morgan's mind. He immediately shoved them down and held tight to his smile. "Well, that's great news," he told her. "I'm sure he misses all of you very much."

"Do you know my daddy?" she asked expectantly.

Morgan's olive-drab dress uniform must have been a clear sign that he knew her father. After all, how many soldiers could there be?

"Not sure. What's his name?"

She beamed with pride. "His name is Butt Sergeant John L. Morris."

Containing his laughter, he considered teaching her the difference between "Butt" and "Buck," then decided her choice was better.

"I'm afraid not," he said, "but I'd bet a lot of other guys know your daddy."

She sat back, noticeably comforted. "What's your name?"

He was about to reply factually, but then thought better of it.

He leaned toward her, shifting into a hushed tone. "You can't tell anyone, but my name is actually *Superman*."

She tilted her head and studied his face, then let out a dismissive puff. "If you were Superman, you wouldn't need to ride a train."

Good point. Why hadn't he thought of that?

"Union Station! End of the line!" the train conductor bellowed before disappearing into another car.

The girl sprang onto her knees. She stretched her neck to peer out Morgan's window, her eyes the size of harvest moons.

Morgan's anxiety mounted with every rotation of the slowing locomotive's wheels. Minutes dragged in a marathon of time. *Tick, tock . . . chug, chug . . . tick . . . tock . . . chug . . . chug.*

The platforms of the underground station swelled as they approached.

"I don't see him." Distress twanged her munchkin voice. She turned to Morgan with fully pouted lips. "Do you think he forgot?"

"Mmm, something tells me he wouldn't have missed this day for anything."

A smile bloomed on her round face.

"Why don't you tell me what he looks like and I'll see if I can help out."

"Well," she said, "he's got, um, brown hair and brown eyes. And he wears a uniform and hat."

All right, that narrowed it down to half the station.

"Let's see if we can find him together." He turned his attention to the raindrop-smeared window. However, instead of hunting for the child's father, Morgan searched for the gorgeous blonde who had drawn him here. His pulse increased with each face they passed. When the train hissed to a final stop, his heart took off in a gallop.

"Mommy! I see him, I see him!" The girl bounced on her heels as if awaiting the pop of a pistol to unleash her from the starting line.

"Okay, sweetie bug, but you need to wait for Mommy." The travel-weary woman across the aisle returned to spit-shining the cheeks of the toddler on her lap, who wiggled as though seated on marbles.

Morgan's neighbor ignored the directive, launching herself through the coach like a self-navigating V-2 rocket. The ruffles of her lollipop-stained dress flailed as wildly as the hair that had fallen from her pigtail ribbons. She burrowed through the blockade of passengers who stood to collect their belongings, clearly unstoppable until colliding with her target. Within seconds, she lunged from the train car steps and into the arms of a uniformed sergeant with brown hair and brown eyes.

Now it was Morgan's turn.

He cocked his wool garrison cap on his head. Cane in hand, he tossed his barracks bag over his shoulder, his letter box stored safely inside. He took the full breath of a cliff diver about to plummet, then moved toward the exit.

By the time he reached the steps, the youngster was planted on the ground, gripping her father's hand. The sergeant grinned as he hugged her sister and mother with his other arm. Morgan maneuvered down the stairs, his knee stiff from the lengthy train ride. He was halfway around the family huddle when he made eye contact with the little girl.

"Bye, Superman," she stage-whispered.

He shot her a wink.

Leaning on his cane, he swiveled and scanned the buzzing platform. Plenty of gals, a speckling of blondes. But no sign of Betty.

The steam engine's mist thinned, as did the crowd. Fewer and fewer females were left unspoken for by the awaiting and arriving servicemen. His apprehension inflated like a balloon ready to burst.

Maybe she wasn't here. He'd barely given her warning. He would have alerted her earlier with a detailed letter, but the postwar mail system had gone haywire and he'd run out of that kind of patience. He also didn't want to jinx himself by putting his situation to paper, the situation being that technically he wasn't even supposed to be in the States yet. An Army miscalculation had prematurely landed him a slot on a Liberty ship. But, hey, who was he to debate an order?

Back at Fort Dix, life had fed him yet another dose of irony. There he'd learned he had been awarded the Silver Star for his show of bravery in Slevant, an honor that truly belonged to his brother. If there really was such a thing as a hero, Charlie was it. And one day, Morgan would return to Europe and take great pride in placing that star on his brother's grave.

Once discharged, Morgan had kept his promise and headed to the Big Apple, where Frank at last introduced him to June. By the end of their laughter-filled dinner, it was clear to him that when you found the one you were meant to be with, all the rest were details. Frank and his bride were living proof.

Now, however, while Morgan stood on the Union Station platform, the situation seemed a bit more complicated. What if she didn't get the telegram? What if he'd been presumptuous thinking she could up and drop everything to come meet him?

His questions fizzled away at the sight of a familiar face, a woman's profile twenty feet ahead. Couples shuffled back and forth between them. The universe slowed as the path cleared, giving him a full view of the knockout blonde clutching her pocketbook. The gap in her beige overcoat revealed a curve-hugging baby blue dress cut just below the knee. A matching large-brimmed hat rested atop her cascading locks.

How surreal to finally be so close to her. A sudden desire to exchange wedding vows flared through him, assuming their connection in person was even a fraction of what it had been in their letters.

So what was he waiting for? More important, what was he going to say to her?

He downed a dry gulp of confidence as he strode forward, trying his best not to limp. Ten feet . . . six feet . . . two.

"Betty?"

She turned to him.

"Hi, Morgan." She lowered her chin, accentuating her blue eyes. She was even more stunning than the image embedded in his memory.

"So you, um, got my telegram?" What was he saying? Obviously she did. "What I mean is, thanks for coming."

She smiled the gentle smile he knew like the back of his hand. "Thanks for the invitation."

When he opened his mouth but failed to speak, she giggled.

"I'm sorry," he said. "I just can't believe you're actually here, and I'm here, and . . ." He paused, then finished the thought simply. "It's good to see you again."

Betty nodded with a look of understanding. That's when Morgan realized there were no words for this moment. He dropped his bag and whisked her into his arms. She gasped and grabbed the top of her hat. Relying on his good leg, he spun her around in a move that even Gene Kelly would have found respectable. Her laughter filled the air, filled his heart, empowering him with the belief that together anything was possible.

Now if he could just find the closest chapel.

❧42❧

October 1945
Chicago Union Station

Liz flew through the labyrinth of Union Station—down the grand staircase and past wooden benches, through the underground passageway. Fear and adrenaline tethered her insides.

Roughly an hour ago, she'd come home early from work to prepare for her college awards reception, hoping for an opportunity to speak privately with Betty—about Morgan, about Dalton, about everything. Yet she'd found the house empty. Not until Liz happened across the wrinkled telegram in the kitchen did she understand why. The message had first induced shock, then panic, which only intensified during her race through the city.

Barely pausing, Liz tipped her neck back to check the station clock. A quarter to six already! The train was scheduled to pull in ten minutes ago. Her plan for gradual disclosure crash-landed in the realm of impossibility. She had never intended to face Morgan and Betty at once, always separately. But what option did she have? The sooner she presented an explanation, the better.

She ratcheted up her pace. Through the bright blur of Allied flags and war bond murals, she noted Morgan's track number. Fourteen. Fourteen was better than thirteen. She didn't subscribe to superstitions, but she'd cling to anything that could help her today.

Shooting stars, four-leaf clovers. She would have sought out both if she had the time.

Scanning for the platform gates, she angled around the ticket booth. Her thoughts of luck splintered when she collided with a wall of a moving suit. A man, paunchy and ruddy-faced, muttered around his limp cigarette, his newspaper pages parachuting into a heap. She registered a fraction of his words—something about dames watching where they were going—before she noticed her handbag on the floor. From its gaping clasp, contents stretched several feet, a trail leading to a shoeshine station.

"No, no, no," she cried under her breath.

She scooped up her purse, inventorying the spill in a flash: a handkerchief, some receipts, a couple of coins. Nothing worth stopping for. "I'm sorry," she called to the man, whose grumbling diminished as she scrambled down the concourse. She visually skimmed servicemen's faces while weaving through the bustle. The back of a blonde with Betty's frame broke into view, jarring Liz's heart. The gal turned and wiggled her fingers to gain the attention of a stout redcap toting a pair of suitcases. Middle-aged features revealed that the lady wasn't Betty.

Of course it wasn't Betty, because she'd just now be greeting Morgan at the train.

Liz scurried onward. Finally she reached the entrance to the tracks. But her legs stalled. This was it. Fate awaited on the other side of the wall. The path of her life could be determined by whatever should happen in the next few minutes.

Hands shaking, she smoothed the sweetheart neckline of her long black dress. She adjusted her pearls, then the collar of her open coat, having no idea why she was primping. Pristine attire would be irrelevant once the phrases began tumbling from her mouth. She could feel the words readying, rising in her throat. She pushed them down and stepped outside.

Track twenty. Eighteen. Sixteen. At fourteen, a steel locomotive rested after a tiresome journey, its bones creaking as they settled. Only scant groupings of pairs and families appeared on the platform. Her gaze hopped from one uniform to another, each face prompting elimination. She strained to hear voices, but none rang familiar. No sound from Betty. No sight of Morgan. *Where on earth were they?*

Countering her trepidation and heightened nerves, optimism mounted in drifts. Maybe he hadn't come off the train yet. And Betty was late, made a stop on the way. That's it. That had to be it.

But then, why was the platform so empty?

Liz looked around. There were other trains farther down. She must have misread the track number. He could be on four instead of fourteen. Or else his train was delayed, and the one in front of her was merely borrowing space.

She moved toward a dark, elderly station worker sweeping the ground nearby.

"Excuse me," she said.

He arched his neck up to see her, quirking his mouth to the side.

"There's a train scheduled to arrive at five thirty-five. Do you happen to know if it's late, or which track it might be on?"

He swung his glance toward the locomotive beside her. "That there'd be the one, ma'am."

She shook her head. Shook it again. He had to be mistaken. "No," she protested. "It can't be. There'd be more passengers out here."

"Train got in early."

"Early?"

"Yes'um. Twenty minutes ago, I'd say." He shuffled off, not waiting for a response.

As his statement replayed in her mind, the fresh consequences rained down, drops of iron on her shoulders. They rolled over her arms, wearying her limbs. Her handbag fell to the concrete.

Just then, a whistle blew on another train, the signal for its departure. At the sound, deep inside, Liz felt something shatter: It was the last bit of hope she had tried so desperately to keep intact.

∼43∼

October 1945
Chicago, Illinois

Morgan settled beside Betty on a city park bench overlooking the Chicago River. Ignoring the passing pedestrians and cruising motorboats, he studied her eyes. He searched for a deep sense of familiarity, yet even her powdery perfume seemed foreign. Everything about their interaction suddenly resembled the discomfort of a blind date.

But what was he expecting? They'd need a little time to warm up, to transfer their affectionate messages from paper into verbalized words. Words like: *Will you marry me?*

"So, Betty," he said, "how have you been?"

"I've been extremely well. Thank you."

He waited for her to elaborate. She didn't.

As he sought another conversation starter, he noted her eying his cane propped against the bench. No wonder she was so quiet. She was probably deciding on a proper way to ask about his injury.

"If all goes well," he assured her, "I shouldn't need this old piece of wood much longer."

"Oh?"

"Just went back to duty a bit early. The doc at Fort Dix thought it'd help the knee heal faster." The explanation seeped relief into her face. "I suppose I should've warned you. But I didn't want you to worry."

"Of course," she said, followed by an interminable pause. He fought the urge to fidget.

Awkwardness was firmly planted on the bench between them. To boot off the invisible, unwanted guest, all Morgan had to do was imagine what he'd write to her at this very moment. Before he knew it, his words flowed out. "It's hard to believe you're here. Truth is, you're even prettier than I remembered." And she was. Not even her starlet-ranking photo did her justice.

"You think so, do you?" She smiled, angling her hat with a tip of her head.

"Betty, I can't tell you how many times I've looked at the picture you gave me."

"My, my. You certainly know how to make a girl blush." She covered her cheek with her gloved hand, but then protruded her lips as if hit by a disconcerting thought. "To be honest, I didn't get the impression you were all that interested when we first met."

The USO dance, where it all began. In rapid flashes, his mind rounded up a scattering of scenes: his encounter with Betty, the swaffled petty officer, the captivating brunette with no last name.

"Sorry," he said. "Guess things were a little wild that night." He needed to keep the focus on Betty, let her know she was the only person who mattered now. "You definitely got my attention with your beautiful writing, though." An understatement, but the declaration appeared enough to refresh her spirits.

"Yes, well . . . I'm glad you liked it." She immediately fluttered a glance at the Army bag resting at his feet. "So did you bring me back anything special?"

The way she brushed past the subject of their letters surprised him. But at least the tension between them was dissipating.

"As a matter of fact, I did," he said, recalling the gift he'd been saving for months. Out of his barracks bag, he pulled a small paper sack, scarred with wrinkles from its voyage. Despite his growing anticipation, he downplayed the offering. "It's nothing as fancy as you deserve. Just a little something I found in Paris."

"Paris?" Excitement ripened on her face. He placed the bag in her expectant hands, slowly, to increase the buildup like a silent drum roll. With the giddy look of a child, she slid out the book and flipped it over to read the title: *Classical French Poetry.* In a blink, her expression fell.

"A book of poems," she breathed. An emotion he could only interpret as utter disappointment entered her eyes, soaked her voice.

"Betty?"

She veered her gaze to his. Her smile had changed. "Thank you. It's . . . terrific."

He'd been certain the souvenir he had purchased at a shop near Gare du Nord would be perfect for her. All this time, he'd refrained from mailing it, preferring to enjoy her delight in person. How could he have been so wrong?

"Guess I'm not very good at buying presents. I just assumed, from what you wrote, that you'd like this sort of book." Apparently, he didn't know her as well as he thought.

"Oh, no, it's grand," she insisted, and set the hardback on her lap, front cover down. "You'll have to forgive me. It's been a long week. I'm still travel weary."

He smiled as best he could. "I understand what that's like." He wasn't fully convinced that was the reason for her lackluster reaction, but he really had no way to read her yet. Not off the page. "Say, where'd you just get back from?" he asked, jumping on the next topic.

"Houston," she replied. "That was my last stop, anyway."

"Houston—as in Texas?"

"Actually, I should've said Fort Sam Houston. I was there to be processed out."

"Processed out? You mean from . . . ?"

She nodded proudly. "From the WAC. I was serving in the Pacific."

It took several seconds for what she'd said to register. "You mean the Women's Army Corps?"

"Yeah, I joined a year ago. That's why you never heard from me again. I suppose I should've written to tell you I was leaving, but it all happened so fast."

"Hang on." He held up his hand to interrupt, but additional words escaped him.

"I know," she sighed. "It's hard to imagine me slaving away in some hospital out in the middle of a jungle." When her lips curled upward, he mentally stepped back. Reviewing her claims, he felt a grin spreading, his confusion rolling away.

"Okay." He laughed. "You had me goin' there. For a minute I thought you were serious."

In an instant, the corners of her mouth dropped. Angry slits replaced her large blue eyes. It was a glare he recognized, a hardening for battle. "Don't tell me you're one of those macho dogfaces who think women in the military are nothing but a joke."

The stern comment knocked the props out from under him. "N-no, of course not. I didn't say that." He had no inkling what had just happened. Her expression, however, made it clear she wasn't pulling his leg, and that he'd better explain himself but good. "It's just that . . ." He struggled to assemble the mismatched pieces. "If you were overseas all this time, well, then, you couldn't have got my letters."

"*Letters?* What letters?" Her knitted brow shifted from irritation to a perplexity equaling Morgan's. Then her forehead relaxed as if a revelation came to her. "No wonder. I just got back a few days ago. I haven't had a chance to go through my mail at home yet."

He shook his head. "No," he told her. "I meant the letters you *answered.*"

She paused, again appearing baffled. "What ever are you talking about?"

"Your letters. The ones you've written me over the past year."

"Look. From what I remember, I only wrote you once before I shipped out."

That couldn't be right. The letters she'd sent weren't imaginary, nor was her photograph. So why would she say such a thing?

A pair of possibilities quickly formed in his mind, threatening to strip him of all he held dear. The loss would be unimaginable.

Yet he had to know.

"Betty, you don't have to make up a story." He strove for a smooth tone but could hear it roughening. "If you've met someone else, or are having second thoughts now that I'm here, you should say so. Just tell me the truth."

In the old days, he never would have been so blunt, but he simply didn't have it in him to waste time anymore. And he wasn't about to walk away from the best thing in his life without a fight.

"I am not *lying* to you." Her voice turned to ice. "Like I said, I only wrote you once."

Something within him was picking up speed, a tornado destroying everything in its path. He yanked the cigar box out of his bag and opened the lid. "You expect me to believe you didn't write all these?"

"I don't expect you to believe anything." She tilted the carton set sideways on his lap, barely affording the envelopes a glance. "But no, I didn't write them." Crossing her arms, she sat back on the bench. "You clearly have me mixed up with another girl."

He discounted the excuse, the impossibility, with a rigid shake of his head. If she didn't want to be with him, he at least deserved to hear it outright. "You're telling me there's another Betty Cordell? On Kiernan Lane?"

She opened her mouth to speak, but stopped. "Let me see one of those." She grabbed the top envelope and pulled out the pages. A moment later, she presented the expression of a detective who'd solved a crime yet wasn't pleased with the findings. "It's my name and address, all right. But I'm *not* the person who wrote these."

He peered at her, searching for the truth. What he discovered in her eyes was honesty, a frightening find. "If it wasn't you," he said, "then who did?"

"Based on the handwriting? I'd say my roommate's had some fun with you."

Roommate? But—that would mean—

At the conclusion, the city fell silent, the bustling disappeared. His body weakened under the pressure of air that now stifled him. He clutched the corners of his box as if it were a life raft, afraid to let go. Afraid to accept that his greatest love was an illusion, the result of a stranger's joke.

Betty rose and held out the poetry book. "I'm sorry about the mix-up," she intoned.

Morgan remained mute, motionless, paralyzed. As if part of him had died.

She waited, placed the book beside him. "Take care of yourself, Private." Her voice dipped with a fraction of sympathy, a strained consolation from a fellow victim. Then she turned, hailed a Checker Cab, and climbed inside. "Guthrie Nursing Home, Lincoln Square," she commanded to the driver, and slammed the door closed.

❦ 44 ❧

October 1945
Chicago, Illinois

"You knew all about this, didn't you?" Betty stood in the office doorway, arms layered, nails dug into her purse.

Julia looked up from her paperwork. "Betty, what are you doing here?"

"As if you didn't know."

Julia appeared at a loss. She spoke slowly. "Why don't you back up and tell me what happened?"

Betty studied her, unable to tell whether or not she was playing dumb. "A telegram came today. It was from a soldier named McClain, asking me to meet him at Union Station. That name ring a bell?"

Julia's face tightened. "You met up with Morgan?"

"I suppose that answers my first question."

"Does Liz know?"

"Why do you think I'm here?"

"Do you know how to find him? Is he still at the station?"

"I highly doubt it," Betty sneered. "And with the way he looked when I left, I'd be shocked if he had anything to say to either of you."

Behind her desk, Julia sank back into her armchair. "Oh no," she breathed.

"'Oh no' is right. What'd you two think, that he'd get a kick out of your practical joke?"

Julia's forehead crinkled as she met her gaze. "Gosh, no. It was nothing of the sort."

"Isn't that good to know."

"Betty," Julia said. "I admit I knew about the letters, but I had nothing to do with writing them. I give you my word." A deep sincerity filled her voice, attesting to her innocence.

"Fine. Then, where's Liz?"

Julia shook her head, gave a helpless shrug. "I have no idea. She said she was heading home to see *you*."

How's that for coincidence, Betty groaned to herself. "Well, if she turns up, tell her we need to talk." With a flip of her hat, she marched toward the entry.

"Wait," Julia called once, then again louder. "Wait, let me explain."

Betty wanted desperately to shut her out, but the words baited her curiosity—always that same maddening weakness. She turned to find Julia in the office doorway. "I'm listening," Betty huffed.

Julia gestured behind her. "Please," she said, "just come sit down." Her eyes shone with an appeal, strong as a magnet. Despite Betty's reluctance, they pulled her back to the room, where she dropped heavily into the visitor's chair.

Julia leaned against the edge of her desk to face her, and started. "A lot happened while you were away."

"Obviously," Betty lashed out, then remembered the news about Christian. Her own dilemma paled in comparison. She softened her reply. "Sorry. Go on."

Julia laced her fingers across her middle. "It's true, Liz kept writing Morgan under your name after you shipped out. But you and I were just as responsible.

"Me?"

"I believe you're the one who asked Liz to write him in the first place. Am I wrong?"

Betty cowered slightly in her chair. She'd forgotten about that. "I guess not."

"And," Julia added, "I'm the one who practically forced her to read the letter he wrote back."

Betty felt her humiliation over the debacle with Morgan draining away. But she straightened in her seat, salvaging her rightful indignation. "That still doesn't explain why she kept writing him after that."

"Because she started to care about him."

"But—what about Dalton?"

Julia hesitated. "You haven't heard?"

Hadn't heard what? Betty stared, waiting.

"It's really Liz's place to tell you," Julia said, "but I suppose you'll hear soon enough. She sighed before explaining. "They broke off their engagement last February."

"Engagement?" Betty suddenly felt like she'd been away for a decade rather than a year. Somehow in her mind, she had always envisioned her friends' lives going on as usual, even frozen in time. As if her own world was the only one that had flipped upside down. "So why did they break up?" she asked.

"Liz said they just realized how different they'd become. I guess the war has changed everyone, in one way or another. But then, I'm sure you know that better than anybody." Compassion flowed like a brook in Julia's tone, rounding and gentle.

Betty removed her hat and rested it atop the pocketbook on her lap. Still unsettled, she redirected to the issue at hand. "I don't understand, though. Why didn't Liz just tell Morgan the truth? If she cared for him, really cared for him, she should've told him."

"That's an easy one," Julia said with a light shrug. "Because she was scared of losing him. And I guess she loved him too much to risk it."

As Betty digested the logic of her friend's response, she saw her own statement for what it was: a vent not against Liz, but against Lieutenant Kelly.

Was it possible—could it be that Julia's reasoning applied to both?

Betty had spent months telling herself that everything with Leslie had been a farce, blame and anger padding her pain. Nonetheless, on occasion, the night she and Leslie shared behind the waterfall would surface in a dream, and she would see his eyes, a loving look in their depths, too ardent not to be real.

Perhaps her mother's scandalous affair hadn't been all that different. Being a fool in love, it seemed, didn't necessarily constitute a foolish person.

The thought linked Betty's focus back to Liz. She kneaded her hat, pressing down the guilt easing in from her earlier behavior. "I only wish I'd known. If I had, I could've helped. Or at least handled things better." She hated to think she'd prevented a dear friend's happy ending, even if Betty might never get her own. "You think there's a chance they'll work things out?"

Julia paused. "I don't know," she said. "I sure hope so."

"It'd be nice to think there's hope for the rest of us." Betty had tried for a light tone, but the phrase came out solemn, reflective.

Julia tilted her head, as if remembering. "So I take it you and the Australian pilot . . ." She stopped at that, inviting Betty to expound on the patient in her postcards. Oh, how things had changed since mailing those cards. Their tropical illustrations, like her writings, had too often represented how she wanted life to be, versus how it was.

She deliberated over where to begin, regarding her relationship with Leslie. She'd always been one to recount her romances, never shy about spicy details—but this particular story, she decided, was one she preferred to keep to herself, tucked in a warm place.

"Just wasn't meant to be," she replied simply.

Julia offered a rueful nod. "I'm sorry, Betty."

"Yeah," she said. "Me too." Fending off the moisture in her eyes, she pulled up a half-mast smile. "But hey, not to worry. If my love life doesn't pick up, I could eventually move in here. A rest home's a swell place for lonely old maids, right?"

Julia leaned forward and touched her hand. "Sweetheart, you of all people are *not* going to end up alone. I promise."

As Betty absorbed the assurance, needed so greatly her chest ached in response, a drop leaked down each of her cheeks. "Neither will you," she told Julia, whose eyes now glistened. Then, following Rosalyn's advice, Betty dashed away her tears and prepared to forge on.

"So," she said, "what should I do now? I'm open to suggestion."

Julia produced a handkerchief from her skirt pocket. She handed it over with a warm look. "I wish I could help you, hon. But really, you're the only person who should decide where your life goes from here."

Betty had intended her question to address how she could best remedy the Liz-Morgan situation, yet inadvertently, Julia had stumbled upon another of her troubling crossroads.

Where *did* Betty want her life to go? Where would she find her calling, her purpose?

"I don't know," she answered the thought aloud. "The only place I've ever actually felt useful was working in the hospital. But I can't exactly run out and become a nurse."

"Why not?" Julia asked, a gentle challenge. No hint of teasing. "You could do it now, couldn't you? Using the GI Bill?"

Betty hadn't given any of that much thought. "Well, yes . . . I guess I could but . . ."

"But what?"

Wasn't it obvious? Did she seriously have to say it? "School has never been my forte, you know that."

Julia sat back and raised an eyebrow at her. "Quite honestly, Betty? I believe you could accomplish anything you put your mind to."

At those words, Betty's memories skimmed through the past year, flashing on things that, until then, she'd have never thought herself capable: nursing duties in leaky tents; emergency care with limited supplies. Imagine what she could do in a nice, clean, civilized hospital. Plus, she couldn't deny the tinge of envy she still harbored for those fancy blue capes. "Maybe you're right," she said. "We'll see."

And that was the most certain answer she could give. For a powerful truth had come to her: Before she could spring into her future, she needed to smooth over the bumps of her past.

Betty dabbed at her cheeks, finally knowing what she had to do. She looked at Julia. "Any chance you'd be up for taking a trip with me, in the meantime?"

"Sure." She sounded intrigued. "Where to?"

"Kansas."

"Kansas?" Julia echoed. "Why there?"

"My mom and I—we've never been great about writing each other, as you probably know. I just figured a visit might be nice, now that I'm home."

After a thoughtful beat, Julia nodded. "I'm sure she'd like that," she replied. "But are you certain this shouldn't be just the two of you? I wouldn't want to intrude, if you'd prefer having family time."

"But you *are* family," Betty said, realizing that Julia and Liz both were. Their wartime stations may have differed, but they'd all still served together, and survived. "What's more, I'll need the support. New Guinea, I can handle; going to Wichita alone, I'm not so sure."

"Well, since you put it that way." Julia let out a giggle and collected her hankie. "Say, what are you doing tonight? Want to hit the town, a way to officially welcome you back?"

Betty started to accept, then remembered her other roommate. "I'd love to, but I think Liz and I have some catching up to do." Starting with a strategy of locating a specific GI.

"Actually," Julia said, "she has an awards thing tonight. Told me not to expect her until late."

Betty glanced at her watch, confirming that not much could be accomplished until morning, anyway.

"So, what do you think?" Julia asked. "Dinner at Parnell's?"

Parnell's. A beloved oldie featuring the three C's: chatting, chili, and cherry Cokes. And, best of all, a slice of normality.

"You're on," Betty said. "Although I should warn you. After living in a god-awful jungle, my table manners might need polishing." Over more than the remark, they exchanged smiles, reflective of the women they'd become, enduring and strong. And no matter where their journeys took them, those traits would only grow.

∽ 45 ∽

October 1945
Chicago Union Station

In the station's Great Hall, Morgan stooped while seated on a long wooden bench. A good hundred feet up, the curved atrium ceiling encased the waiting room like a fishbowl. Surrounded by towering Corinthian columns and an ocean of pink marble flooring, he could recall only one time in his life he'd ever felt so small, so lost: the day he stood at his mother's funeral, devastated in the wake of his father's lie.

Once again, someone he'd trusted had pulled the world out from under him. Another brutal swoop had left him sprawled on the floor, too despondent to pick himself up.

Already, he'd purchased a one-way voucher to reach Belknap. He felt like a fugitive outrunning the law, needing to flee as fast as possible. Given that he no longer had a place to call home, his uncle's farm was the only destination that made sense. Morgan knew how to harvest a crop, if nothing else. He just wished the thought of going there alone didn't seem so empty, a feeling underscored by the surrounding scene: servicemen holding their sweethearts, spouting tears and exclamations of bliss. At the sight, a dull ache cycled through his body, from his knee to his chest to his head, then back down again.

He glanced at his watch. The train couldn't get here soon enough.

"Candy bar, mister?" A young boy with plaid knickers and a woolen cap seemed to magically appear.

"Sorry. I didn't bring any home." He didn't know the D-ration treats were as sought after back in the States as they were overseas.

"No, sir, do *you* wanna buy a candy bar?" The youngster gestured to an oversized cardboard box toted by a shorter kid, presumably his little brother, who was dressed in a similar hand-me-down outfit. The pair projected such earnestness Morgan couldn't bring himself to say no.

"How much they going for these days?"

"Eight cents apiece," the first one replied.

"Eight cents?" Morgan acted indignant. "That's a bit steep, don't you think?"

"Hey, mister," said the smaller kid with a slight lisp, "a guy's gotta make a livin'." He flashed a grin enhanced by two missing front teeth.

Boy, did he sound familiar.

"Your name wouldn't be Charlie by any chance, would it?"

"Naw, it's Tommy. But fellas call me Lucky, 'cause I'm so popular with the dames."

Morgan smiled at the vision of the grade schooler chasing little shrieking girls around the playground, girls who would undoubtedly be chasing *him* in a few years. "Then I guess I'd better buy something, so you can take care of those pretty ladies of yours."

Lucky vigorously nodded his capped head.

"So how many would ya like?" the elder brother asked.

"Let's see . . . eight cents apiece, huh? How does three bars for twenty cents strike you?"

After a few seconds of silent calculating, the salesman sighed. "You drive a hard bargain, but you got yourself a deal."

Morgan scrounged his pant pocket for loose change, yet came up with only a dime. He'd stowed all his cash in the bottom of his cigar box—just about the last thing he wanted to rifle through. The enthusiasm brightening the youngsters' eyes, however, gave him no choice.

From his barracks bag, Morgan pulled out the container. He released the binding rope and flipped open the lid. His fingers naturally slid into the weathered cardboard grooves. He fumbled beneath the pile of keepsakes until he located a wrinkled greenback. When Lucky handed over the merchandise, Morgan presented him with the money.

"Oh, no, mister," the older one said, holding out his palm. "*I'm* in charge of the dough."

Smart kid.

"Well, then, here you go, John D. Rockefeller." The boy accepted the buck and reached into his jingling pocket to make change. "It's all right. Keep the difference."

"No foolin'?" he exclaimed as if the single dollar bill were a million.

"With all your brother's girlfriends, sounds like you're gonna need it."

"Thanks a lot!" they chimed, and trampled off, probably out of fear that he'd have second thoughts.

Morgan shook his head, imagining how similar the "rowdy McClain brothers" must have been at that age. He was about to close the carton when his gaze caught the corner of a snapshot amidst the letter stack. He knew what the image was before pulling it out: a photo Frank had given him during his visit in New York. The picture, taken on a Leica camera "liberated" from a German POW, featured Morgan and Charlie at a camp in a Belgian village. Side by side they stood, caught mid-laughter, layered with Army gear from head to toe.

No longer were they kids dressed in handmade costumes to play cops and robbers or cowboys and Indians. They had become real-life soldiers, men who were willing to sacrifice everything for the needs of strangers and fight for something greater than themselves.

His eyes settled on Charlie's face. "So now what do I do?" he whispered. Never in his life had he wished he could turn to his little brother for advice like he did at this moment. "Just tell me what to do."

As if receiving a reply, Morgan felt his attention pulled from the snapshot in his hand to his open box. There lay Betty's photo. He picked up the worn keepsake, placed it over his brother's, and for the umpteenth time, he studied her striking features. Here was the image of a woman whom he apparently didn't know the first thing about. Yet it was with her he'd envisioned spending his future, her face he'd melded with the very letters that had brought him comfort while shivering in sodden foxholes, praying he would survive until morning.

Recalling the note that had started it all, he flipped over her picture.

To Morgan,
Take care of yourself.
Betty Cordell

It was so obvious now. Even the handwriting should have been a dead giveaway. Not a single stroke in the scrawled message mirrored the eloquent script in the letters he'd been duped into believing were from her.

The letters.

Were there clues he'd missed all along? Hints that would have exposed the ruse had he just read between the lines?

Reluctantly, he picked up the top envelope. He unfolded the paper from inside, its feminine scent fading along with his dreams, and revisited the words he knew by heart. He was only a third down the page when his train rolled into the station.

❦ 46 ❧

October 1945
Evanston, Illinois

A cape of darkness fell over the room as day passed into night. Seated at the kitchen table, hand propping her head, Liz stared at the telegram. The lilting jazz tune playing on the radio did little to alleviate the throbbing behind her eyes.

She waited for the all-knowing skeptic inside her to proclaim *I told you so.* To chide her for naïvely thinking a glass slipper existed, and wasn't she sorry for giving up a secure and enviable future as Mrs. Dalton Harris.

Yet the reprimand didn't come. A truth had quieted the disparaging voice. And that truth was this: She didn't regret a single word, or moment, she had shared with Morgan. Even if the happy ending wasn't meant to be hers.

A sound turned her head. It was a knock on the front door. Her body bristled. The moment she'd been dreading since leaving the station was upon her. Morgan and Betty had arrived.

She took a breath. Forcefully, she prodded herself to rise, until a thought hit her. Betty wouldn't have bothered knocking. She'd be standing in the kitchen, demanding an explanation, with or without the soldier at her side.

So who could it be?

More knocks.

Liz remained still and waited for the caller to give up. But then the doorbell chimed, summoning the answer: Dot hadn't received the message not to pick her up for the awards gala. Now Liz would have to tell her friend in person that she was under the weather.

On second thought, no. Regardless of how white the lie, she was done with deceiving people she cared about.

She trudged her way to the entry, pausing to flip on a lamp in the hallway. The light flared in her eyes. Pupils recovering, she tucked her hair behind her ears and opened the door. It took her a few seconds to register the sight.

"Morgan." The word slipped out.

It was *him*. My God, it was actually him! She couldn't move, could hardly breathe.

The light from inside projected a warm glow over his face, his features almost exactly as she had remembered. His emerald eyes held the same vibrancy beneath his angled service hat, his build just as broad in his uniform.

But what was he doing here? Where was Betty?

Morgan blinked hard before he said, "Liz? Is that you?" Amazement, not sternness, filled his tone. His lips spread into a smile. "What are you doing here?"

He didn't know the story. *How could he not know yet?*

"Morgan," she said again. Feeling her vocal cords collapsing, she forced out the first phrase to come to mind. "I'm so sorry, for everything."

His forehead crinkled. Eyes dimming, his expression hardened in degrees, as if he were remembering what brought him here. "Wait. Are you telling me . . ."

"The last thing I wanted to do was deceive you." She spoke quickly, in case his reaction prevented her from saying much more.

"Hold on," he ordered. "*You're* Betty's roommate?"

Liz strained to recall the speech she had rehearsed in her head, the one she'd even delivered in her dreams while imagining this confrontation, always waking before he'd presented his judgment. Yet now, when she actually needed articulate pleas, her nerves had sent them into hiding.

"Are you the one who's been writing me?" he pressed.

She hesitated before replying with a nod. Then all was quiet save the sharp pulsing in her ears.

From a pocket he pulled out a wrinkled envelope. It was upside down from her view, but she recognized the return address and handwriting. For they were her own.

"Was this all some kind of joke?" he asked, even and cool.

A joke? She straightened. "No. That's not it. It was nothing like that."

"If it wasn't a gag, then why did you intentionally lie to me?"

"It wasn't intentional—well, not at first anyway. I didn't mean for it to happen—not like this." Her words tripped over themselves, struggling for footing. "I just didn't think you'd want to hear from me. But I didn't want you to stop writing either."

A crevice split his brow, from either confusion or disbelief. "Why'd you think I wouldn't want to hear from you?"

At a measured pace, pushing down her tears, she began her confession. "The night we met, I felt like there was something between us. But when I came back, you weren't there. And then I saw you and Betty dancing."

"*That's* why you left?"

"Well—yes," she stammered. She was about to explain her other reason—that she was already going steady at the time—yet she refrained. The fact was, had she not seen him carrying on with her roommate, Liz would have ultimately tossed out her moral compass. "Like I was saying," she returned to the point, "from how cozy you two were together, it was clear there was no reason for me to stay."

"What you saw," he said defensively, "isn't what you think. I was just helping her out of a bind. The fact is, I searched everywhere for you that night. But I didn't know your last name, or where you lived. And then"—his gaze dropped to the envelope in his hand—"well, then I started getting these."

A favor. According to his claim, that's why he'd danced with Betty. Had the same scenario involved any other girl, Liz would be inclined to rule the excuse a hokey one. But she knew much too well how challenging her roommate was to refuse.

Shaking her head, Liz cupped the front of her neck. How foolish she'd been to jump to such conclusions, to be less than up front since the moment they met. Although belated, he deserved the truth. All of it.

"Please, Morgan, at least let me tell you how it all started," she said. "You see, Betty asked me to help write you, but then she went away. I would've told you everything had things not been so complicated, with my father and—"

"Liz." His expression remained unchanged. "It doesn't matter anymore. I only came here to find out one thing." He raised the envelope between them. "Was there a shred of truth in these letters? That's all I want to know."

She considered his question carefully, the most critical exam of her life. The answer formed as solidly as any she had ever known. "Everything but the name I signed was real. Absolutely everything." Voice wavering, she peered into his eyes. "Morgan, believe me. I never meant to hurt you."

He stayed silent, unflinching, no reaction she could gauge. Finally, he wheeled around and descended the porch steps with the help of a cane she hadn't noticed until then. He was leaving. For good.

She wanted to call after him, to tell him she loved him, to ask for another chance. But after deceiving him for so long, she knew she had no right.

Morgan was halfway down the path when the ignition of a taxi started. Once he'd ducked into the cab, Liz turned away. She gripped the door frame with both hands to prevent her knees from buckling.

Keep it together, she told herself. *Just keep it together.*

She heard the car door slam and the engine rev. The diminishing sound of the motor let her know he was gone. Emotions poured out in a river down her cheeks.

Another minute and she attempted to steady herself. She took a step into the house.

"Liz?"

She froze at the voice. Praying to the Almighty that she hadn't imagined it, she slowly pivoted. Her eyes widened to see around her tears.

It was Morgan. Climbing the stairs.

He dropped his Army bag on the porch swing. His mouth eased into a smile that reached his eyes. "You didn't think I was leaving, did you?"

Her feelings sought a conduit, a channel to fully communicate the remorse echoing within. "If I could do it over again," she offered, "you have to believe I would." And he indeed had to believe her, to know how deeply she cared, and just how much she needed him.

Morgan nodded in assurance. Yet he had no desire for them to start over. They were right where they belonged, and he was done with regrets.

Against the house, he leaned his cane, a reminder of his own half-truths. A symbol of the medical scare he'd never shared for fear of losing her affection.

"Why don't we just pick up from where we left off?" He held out his palm, welcoming her touch. "I think you owe me a dance."

Shuddering a sigh, she returned his smile and placed her hand in his. Together, fingers interlocked, they swayed to the rich notes of a jazz horn drifting through the doorway. As their heartbeats joined in a single rhythm, Morgan shut his eyes. He savored the radiating warmth of her body, the silkiness of her hair on his cheek. He drank in the sweet lavender fragrance on her skin, a scent forever captured in his heart.

Nothing in this world felt more natural than holding her. As if she were a part of him that had always been missing until now, a part of him he might never have found without guidance from his brother. Charlie—the one who had led him back to the angel in his arms.

Morgan tossed a glance up toward the heavens, beyond the parting clouds and lucid white moon, and winked in gratitude.

"It's Stephens," Liz whispered.

"Sorry?" He drew his head back and looked into her amber eyes.

"My name," she said. "It's Elizabeth Stephens."

He smiled. With his thumb, he wiped away the last of her tears. "Nice to meet you, Miss Stephens."

Studying the graceful curves of her face only confirmed what he already knew: Standing before him, regardless of names, was the woman he'd never stopped waiting for, the woman he wanted to spend the rest of his life with.

He slid his fingers beneath her chin, and ever so slowly he pulled her close. Desire swelled as the heat of her breath reached his skin. When her eyelids lowered, he paused. Their mouths but an inch apart, he relished the sensations running through him, the thrill, the anticipation.

At last, he leaned in and kissed her tenderly. Her lips were petal soft, the movement so comfortable he could spend a lifetime doing exactly this. When she laid her head against his chest, he smoothed her chestnut hair. Eyes closed, he held her tight, and thanked God for bringing him home.

AUTHOR'S NOTE

It all started with a family Christmas gift. That was my sole intent, anyhow, when I self-published a cookbook several years ago featuring recipes my grandmother had collected and created over several decades. For the biographical chapter, I interviewed Grandma Jean about her life—which entailed walking a minimum of six miles a day to attend school, in addition to caring for her siblings and keeping up with chores on her dad's Iowa farm.

She then went on to recount familiar details of her courtship with my late grandfather during World War II, yet this time revealing an astounding fact: She had dated the U.S. Navy signalman during merely two of his leaves before they exchanged vows. To best explain why, Grandma retrieved from her closet a bound stack of wartime love letters written by "Papa," a collection no one in the family knew existed. I needed to read only a few pages of his script, as elegant as his words despite the "plow jockey's" youth, to understand the reason she so readily said, "I do."

Long after the cookbook was complete, I continued to ponder their era, one charged with romance, tragedy, uncertainty, and loss of innocence. A time of self-discovery, sacrifice, and female independence. Intrigued by this dramatic setting, and with Papa's correspondence lingering in my mind, I found myself wondering how different the couple's relationship would have been had their courtship been woven with fibers of deception. Therein bloomed the idea for my first novel.

The deeper I delved into research, the more compelled I became to honor what has aptly been dubbed the Greatest Generation. Of the many firsthand accounts and texts I found invaluable, these gems could not go unmentioned: *The Good Soldier* by Selene H. C. Weise, *They Called Them Angels* by Kathi Jackson, *Letters Home* by Sally Hitchcock Pullman, *Foot Soldier* by Roscoe C. Blunt Jr., *Roll Me Over* by Raymond Gantter, *Yorkie Doodle Dandy* by William A. Wynne, and *The Women's Army Corps* by Mattie E. Treadwell.

Although mine is a work of fiction, I strove to be as historically accurate as possible. The only significant poetic liberties I have taken involve: military personnel processing, wartime postal speed and forwarding, and the fictitious village Slevant, inspired by the battle of Stoumont, allowing for flexibility of weather and combat specifics.

Conversely, I enjoyed incorporating such authentic elements as Smoky, the legendary Yorkie who made hospital rounds with nurses on New Guinea, lifting spirits of wounded soldiers with her clever tricks. I was also moved by accounts from families who first learned of their soldiers' passing through a radio report or "letter from the grave." And the most fundamental to my story was a documented instance of twin brothers assigned to serve side by side in World War II, even after the Sullivan brothers' infamous naval tragedy. Authorities confirmed that legislation commonly known as the Sullivan Act or Law requiring the separation of siblings in the military was proposed but never enacted; and though the practice was thereafter frowned upon, there were exceptions to every rule— as always seems the case in love and war.

For more historical tidbits, actual excerpts from Papa's letters, and creative ideas for book clubs, visit www.KristinaMcMorris.com.

Book Club "Victory Recipes"

These deliciously unique 1940s recipes, coupled with the Reading Group Guide Discussion Questions, are sure to make your book club gathering nostalgic and unforgettable. Each *Letters from Home* recipe was adapted from Hugh and Judy Gowan's *Cooking on the Home Front* and *The Lily Wallace New American Cook Book* (a longtime favorite of Grandma Jean's). More available at www.KristinaMcMorris.com.

Sweet Carrot Pie

A memorable treat from Viola's first date at the carrot festival!
(If the recipe title has you cringing, rest assured it's akin
to pumpkin pie and just as yummy.)

2 cups chopped carrots	1 tablespoon flour
⅔ cup sugar	1 tablespoon butter, melted
1⅓ cups milk	1 teaspoon vanilla
3 eggs, well beaten	9" refrigerated piecrust

Boil chopped carrots in water until tender (approximately 10 min.). Drain and set aside. In a blender or food processor, mix all remaining ingredients (2–3 min.), then add carrots and blend again until smooth. Pour evenly into unbaked piecrust. Bake at 350°F for 50–60 minutes. Serve warm, topped with whipped cream.

Baconized Cornbread Muffins

Just the way Morgan's mother made them on their Iowa farm!

1 cup flour	1 teaspoon salt
1 cup cornmeal	1 egg
¼ cup sugar	1 cup buttermilk
1 tablespoon baking powder	2 tablespoons melted butter
½ teaspoon baking soda	4 uncooked bacon strips, diced

Sift flour, cornmeal, sugar, baking powder, baking soda, and salt together. Beat the egg with buttermilk, then combine with flour mixture. Add melted butter and mix well. Fill paper muffin cups ⅔ full. Sprinkle tops with uncooked diced bacon. Bake at 400°F for 15 minutes, then broil to crisp bacon. Serve warm with honey or honey butter. Yield: 12 muffins.

Herb's Jungle Juice

Without the "zip" of island-brewed alcohol, this is a much safer refreshment, according to Betty.

1 cup sugar	2 cups orange juice
2 cups boiling water	1 quart ginger ale
2 cups cranberry juice	Orange and lemon slices
⅓ cup lemon juice	Mint sprigs

Dissolve sugar in boiling water. Add all three juices. Chill. Just before serving, turn into punch bowl; add ginger ale and fruit slices. Serve decorated with mint sprigs. (The fresh mint truly makes this drink a swell one!) Serves 10.

Ham, Broccoli, Cheese Pie

*In times of rationing, Cora took pride in serving this
nutritious "one-pot meal" to her boys.*

10-oz. package frozen broccoli florets
9" refrigerated piecrust
1 cup cooked ham, thinly sliced
2 tablespoons chopped onion
1½ cups total shredded cheddar
and swiss cheese

1 cup milk
4 eggs, slightly beaten
½ teaspoon salt
¼ teaspoon pepper
¼ teaspoon dry mustard

Blanch broccoli. Drain well. Layer in unbaked piecrust as follows:
ham, broccoli, onion, and cheese (reserve some cheese for topping).
In a medium bowl, gradually blend milk and beaten eggs. Add salt,
pepper, and mustard, then pour liquid mixture over pie. Sprinkle
with remaining cheese. Bake at 350°F for 45 minutes or until center is
firm.

Fried Green Tomatoes

*Rosalyn says any respectable woman, Southern or not,
should have a good recipe for these!*

4 medium firm green tomatoes
1 tablespoon sugar
½ teaspoon pepper
1 teaspoon salt

1 egg, well beaten
½ cup Italian-style bread crumbs
Vegetable oil

Cut tomatoes into ½-inch slices. In a small bowl, add sugar,
pepper, and salt to the beaten egg. (Garlic powder and/or cayenne
pepper optional.) Fully dip each tomato slice in mixture, then coat
both sides in bread crumbs. Heat an oiled frying pan on medium-
high. Brown tomato slices on both sides.

Peach Basket Turnover

A tasty twist on pineapple upside-down cake, this was another of Liz's favorites made by Nana.

2 eggs (yolks and whites separated)	1 teaspoon baking powder
½ cup sugar	½ teaspoon salt, divided
2 15-oz. cans sliced peaches in light syrup	1 teaspoon vanilla
	1 cup brown sugar
1 cup flour	2 tablespoons butter

In a bowl, beat yolks with sugar until light. Drain syrup from canned peaches into a cup. Set peaches aside. Add ⅓ cup of the syrup to yolk mixture. Beat 5 minutes. Fold in egg whites. Sift together flour, baking powder, and ¼ teaspoon salt. Blend with mixture and add vanilla. In a separate medium bowl, cream together brown sugar and butter, then add peaches and rest of salt. Spread peach mixture evenly in greased 8" x 8" baking pan. Pour batter over top. Bake at 400°F for 40 minutes or until done. Turn out upside down. Serve hot with whipped cream.

Butterscotch-Coconut Marshmallows

These remind Julia of Christian's letters, which always read "sweet and smooth as butterscotch."

1 cup butterscotch chips (or milk chocolate)	1½ cups shredded dried coconut
16 large marshmallows	Wax paper

Slowly heat chips over low heat in a saucepan until melted. (If it starts to thicken, reduce or remove from heat and stir well.) Dip marshmallows in the sauce, immediately roll in coconut, and place on wax paper. Let solidify at room temperature before serving.

LETTERS FROM HOME

Kristina McMorris

ABOUT THIS GUIDE

The suggested questions are included to enhance
your group's reading of Kristina McMorris's
Letters from Home.

Discussion Questions

1. Life-changing letters are the common link among all three major female characters. Typically the messages are ones the sender would not have expressed in person. What is it about writing that allows for more freedom and/or courage? If you were to compose a single farewell letter, to whom would it be addressed and what would you say? Is there a reason you are waiting to tell the person?

2. In each of Liz's letters to Morgan, she reveals hints of the secret she is keeping from him. Can you pinpoint the clues? (Answers are available on author's Web site.) Do you think these are merely slips, or are they reflective of Liz's intention to come clean?

3. Of all the characters, which one surprised you the most with their secret? Is Morgan hypocritical regarding his firm stance on honesty? By withholding truths, did Frank and Julia benefit anyone other than themselves? Is opting for a burden of silence a sacrificial or selfish choice? Is it better to be honest about a wrongdoing, even if no one would ever find out?

4. By most standards of the era, Liz's view of societal roles for women is unconventional. When offered an internship, Julia struggles with this very issue. How are Liz's and Julia's dilemmas over a career and motherhood relevant to women today?

5. After Morgan's harrowing recon patrol, he wonders, "Were prayers of murderers, when fighting on the 'right side' of the war, ever heard—let alone answered?" And later, he watches a chaplain praying over a soldier. Do you believe any type of murder is wrong, or does it depend on the circumstance?

How would you feel as the chaplain? Did your attitude toward the "Kraut" Morgan confronted change upon the discovery of the man's photograph?

6. Through the course of the story, Liz and Betty realize they were unknowingly following the paths of their mothers. How do the results of these revelations contrast? Why do you think people often copy actions or behavior they disliked growing up?

7. While the contexts differ greatly, "cover me" is one of the first and last phrases Charlie and Morgan exchange in the story. Discuss the dynamics of their relationship as the duty of "covering" the other gradually shifts. In what ways do Liz and Julia reverse roles? Which character ultimately grows the most?

8. Discuss Leslie and Betty's relationship. How do you feel about his actions? Under what circumstances, if any, would they have been justified? What do you think his letter might have said? Would you have reacted differently if you were Betty?

9. In search of support, Liz turns to her beloved friend Viola. Were you surprised by the message in the elderly woman's anecdote? Did you agree with her? If you were Liz, would you have felt betrayed or grateful for Viola's advice?

10. As is often found in time-travel stories, characters in *Letters from Home* wind up causing an event as a direct result of trying to prevent it. Do you think major events in our lives are predestined and unavoidable, no matter which action we take? Is the coin Charlie finds in the abandoned village, just as a sniper opens fire, random or an element of fate? If Dalton hadn't canceled on Liz at the USO dance, where would her life have taken her?

11. Among the central themes of the novel is loss of innocence. A prime example is the little girl who drops her doll on the slushy road from the Belgian village. What is the irony of her devastation? Why doesn't anyone help her? Discuss the possible symbolism of the road, the girl, the travelers, and the soldiers in that scene.

12. What is the significance of Morgan's two bedside neighbors, "Jabber" and the airman in the French hospital? Which one of them would most likely feel like a hero upon returning home? Did the book change how you viewed veterans, both male and female, of World War II? If so, in what ways?

13. From the origin of "Jungle Juice" to the use of ski suits for camouflaging German soldiers, the story is sprinkled with historical tidbits from both the home front and front lines. What is the most interesting information you learned?

14. Describe how you envision the life of each major character five years after the story ends.

Read on for an exclusive interview with Kristina McMorris

LETTERS FROM HOME
Kristina McMorris

1. *If you were stranded on a desert island, which book would you take with you?*

   I would take the most comprehensive survivor's handbook ever created! A bonus chapter on boat building would also be helpful. If I were allowed one more book for pleasure reading, however, it would be *The Book Thief* by Markus Zusak.

2. *Where does your inspiration come from?*

   My inspiration definitely comes from a personal connection, as well as gems found in true accounts. History is rich with lessons that are too often overlooked; sharing pieces of those lessons through a fictionalized story has been extremely rewarding.

3. *Have you always wanted to become a writer?*

   I wish I could say yes, but the truth is, I was barely a fiction reader when I acted on the impulse to pen *Letters from Home.* Mind you, I'm so grateful I hadn't foreseen the challenging road ahead; otherwise, I might have reconsidered the decision, and missed out on an incredible journey.

4. *Where do you write? And what's your routine?*

   I wish I could be one of those ever-chic authors who enjoys writing in a bustling coffee shop. For me, I need a quiet space, preferably my home. As soon as the kids leave for school in the morning, I cozy up in my fuzzy socks (the uglier, the better), pour a cup of half-caffeinated coffee, and settle in with my keyboard. Then, I spend the next several hours writing and editing, all the while fighting my incessant urge to check emails and play on social media sites.

5. *What inspired you to write this novel?*
Given that I was pregnant with my second child at the time, I like to blame an overabundance of hormones. What else could have caused the flash of insanity that allowed me to believe tackling a novel set during World War II would be reasonably simple for a first project?

As for the origin of the book's premise, the idea stemmed from a collection of beautiful courtship letters sent from my late grandfather to my grandmother during the war. (To find out more details, please see my Author's Note.)

6. *What's the strangest job you've ever had?*
Perhaps considered more unusual than strange, I began working as a weekly television-show host at the age of nine. I spent every Tuesday memorizing my scripts, every Wednesday evening filming at the TV station (doing homework between edits), and many weekends shooting on-location reports. From this, I learned early on how to interact with adults, and I developed a strong work ethic that continues to serve me well.

7. *When you're not writing, what are your favourite things to do?*
I love to spend quality time with family and friends, especially over a delicious meal. I also enjoy watching movies, savoring wine and cheese, and chipping away at my teetering to-be-read pile.

8. *Have you ever had writer's block? If so, how did you cope with it?*
Fortunately, I haven't encountered that problem yet. (I hope I'm not jinxing myself here.) That's not to say that every chapter flows effortlessly from my fingers. Some days, a root canal sounds more appealing than creating another chapter from scratch. But, treating my profession

as a regular job, I force myself to sit in the chair and write regardless.

9. *Do you have any secret ambitions?*
I admit, I can't help but imagine the joy of seeing my novel turned into a film for the silver screen. For the red carpet stroll that would then ensue, my literary agent has already put dibs on Gucci, while I personally would have to go with Versace.

Now, if I had a better singing voice, playing the lead in "Miss Saigon" would have been at the top of my list.

10. *What can't you live without?*
That's an easy one: my husband and two children. Because of them, not a day goes by when I don't laugh, learn, and feel an overwhelming sense of love and unconditional acceptance.

11. *When you were a child, what did you want to be when you grew up?*
Due to their equally fascinating outfits, I recall being torn between two choices: a belly dancer and a nun. I believe my attraction to a habit was based solely on my love of "The Sound of Music." But then, what young girl didn't dream of singing like Julie Andrews and marrying Captain Von Trapp?

12. *Which five people, living or dead, would you invite to a dinner party?*
I would invite: Steven Spielberg for the deserved spotlight he's helped shine on World War II veterans; Sandra Bullock for her charm and humor; Dean Martin for his suave entertainment value; William Shakespeare for his poetic brilliance; and, of course, my grandfather "Papa," whose letters have touched my heart and forever changed my life.